A STANDARD DEVIATION

JAMIE SINGLETON

A
STANDARD
DEVIATION

Pillar Press New York

Pillar Press
910 Park Avenue
New York, New York 10075

ISBN 978-0-615-27400-3

Printed in the United States of America

To Cristina

PREFACE

Efficient Market Theory, a foundational tenant of capital markets and investment performance, is heavily debated by pragmatists and technical analysts and taught in most business schools and to candidates studying for post-graduate degrees in economics. The Theory claims that markets are efficient and cannot be gamed because market participants receive and act on all relevant information as soon as it becomes available to them. Proponents of this theory believe that there is perfect information in the stock market. That means that whatever information is available about a single stock is available to all investors, except of course in the case of insider information, the use of which is illegal. Students of Efficient Market Theory believe therefore that it is a random event when an individual investor can post better investment results than the overall market. Exhaustive research has been conducted over the years at think tanks inside academic economic powerhouses like The University of Chicago and MIT to prove the theoretical underpinning of the concept. Investors, however, want to believe that they can beat the market—Freud's concept of ego ensures that response. The evidence of such "market beaters" is infrequent though well publicized when it occurs. Efficient Market theorists do not discount an investor's ability to beat the market on occasion. Their theory seems to prove that it is nearly impossible to outperform the market consistently over time. That occurrence would certainly represent an outlier in the normal statistical pattern of investment returns—more than one standard deviation away from the mean expectation.

The modern capital markets are characterized by the enormous amount of economic and performance related information that is available to all investors. Every major country around the world publishes data that presents the condition of their economic health on a weekly and monthly basis. The calendar for the announcement of these measurements, as well as the daily disclosure of corporate earnings, drive an information network that has created financial newspapers, internet websites and cable channels to disseminate and interpret every morsel of economic news. Forty years ago, this massive amount of information was unavailable to the investor community as a whole. In those days, the detractors of Efficient Market Theory had a basis to challenge its validity. But in the modern era of instantaneous information, it is hard to argue that information that is available to one investor is not available to all investors. This is not to suggest that all investors must act similarly when confronted with the same information. That difference of opinion is what makes a market, bringing buyers of one security together with sellers of the same, at an instant in time.

A STANDARD DEVIATION

CHAPTER 1

Beaufort, South Carolina
November 28–29, 2006

Muddy Simmons leaned against the trunk of the limousine that the plantation used to pick up guests flying into the Beaufort County Airport. His large black hand flicked the filter of his smoked Chesterfield to the pavement where he crushed the butt under his shoe. The flattened filter joined three others that had kept him occupied while he waited to pick up the next VIP headed to the Ludlow shoot at DeSaussure Hall. Muddy had worked for the Eckhouse family for his entire life, just like his father did. He was a servant. Like many other black families in the Low Country, Muddy was tied to the region and to the family that provided for his family. He was born on DeSaussure Hall, a 10,000 acre plantation known as one of the grandest shooting plantations in South Carolina—a beautiful example of antebellum architecture and culture. The Eckhouse family amassed their wealth in the 1800's as trading merchants and later bought small regional banks across the South creating a financial services empire. They were one of the richest families in America.

Muddy checked his watch again. The charter carrying Alan

Solomon, the current Chairman of the Federal Reserve, was scheduled to arrive at 11:00 A.M. Muddy liked these days and the bustle surrounding the fall and winter shoots. The guests were mostly great men, rich or famous. They had an aura that Muddy had come to recognize. They enjoyed privilege in a world that favored the prosperous. Muddy saw it but mostly ignored it. He was black and they were white. His life day-in and day-out deviated very little. His privilege was to work at DeSaussure Hall.

Anne Eckhouse was the great granddaughter of Townsend Eckhouse, the patriarch of the family fortune. Her husband, Pennington Ludlow, was the current Secretary of the United States Treasury and a shooting enthusiast. An expert marksman, Ludlow hosted several shoots a year and typically invited a small group of industrial leaders and Washington insiders. He started this tradition when he was Chairman and CEO of Frontier Exploration Corp. Ludlow's special guest for this shoot was Muddy's pickup: Alan Solomon, the Fed Chairman and a lousy shot.

The government's Citation XLS+ flew over the airport to make its final approach into Beaufort. When it landed, it taxied over to the FBO where it joined five other aircraft whose owners had previously arrived. Muddy waved to a ground crew worker who opened the electric gate, allowing him to drive up near the plane's hatch. Alan Solomon climbed out of the plane, dressed like he came straight from the office with two satchels of documents. He didn't look like a hunter. Muddy reached for the bags and introduced himself but the din of the jet's engines all but drowned out his deep baritone drawl. Solomon got into the back seat while Muddy retrieved a suitcase from the co-pilot. When he closed his driver's side door, silence was restored and the unseasonable winter day tuned out.

Alan Solomon was not enthused to be in South Carolina. He had many other important things to do and his urban Jewish upbringing had not equipped him well for this type of sporting activity. His

singular experience with guns was not particularly pleasant and
it had of course involved Pennington Ludlow. Ludlow had asked
Solomon to join the Frontier Exploration Board many years earlier
and once arranged for an off-site Board meeting that involved a day
of duck hunting. Solomon, sitting in a wet and cold blind, nearly
killed one of the other hunter's prized Labrador retrievers when he
squeezed off several shots at decoys floating on the lake that he mis-
took for real birds. His partner in the blind, an experienced hunter,
knocked the gun out of his grip, cursing his stupidity. Solomon was
the butt of jokes that evening as the hunters recounted their kills
and drank their cocktails, but he always suspected that they were
really laughing at the only Jew in the room. Alone in the backseat
remembering that horrific embarrassment, Solomon silently cursed
South Carolina and his decision to accept Ludlow's invitation.

"Mister Solomon, sir, my name is Paul Simmons, but you can
call me Muddy. Please make yourself comfortable. Our ride should
take a little more than 30 minutes. I hope your flight was enjoyable.
This your first visit to DeSaussure Hall?" Muddy had a charm that
every visitor to the plantation enjoyed.

"Yes, fortunately," Solomon replied nasally. He could immediately
feel his allergies kicking in. He hated the South—too friendly, and
too much crap flying in the air.

"It's an excellent day for a shoot, sir. Plenty of doves and guns."

"Sounds like my kind of day," Solomon answered sarcastically,
staring out the window and avoiding eye contact with Muddy who
tried to engage him using his rear view mirror.

Muddy wasn't an educated man, but he was smart enough. He
figured there were two kinds of people in the world: the nice ones
and everybody else. His ride did not seem to fit into the first category. Muddy decided to do what he did best: drive the car. Alan
Solomon receded into his own world in the backseat and finished
reading a report on US productivity trends. Solomon had been a

lucky man to rule the Federal Reserve during a period of unprecedented economic growth. His stature had grown on Wall Street
and his admirers had lifted him to folk hero status. But Solomon
was fundamentally an uncomfortable person. What tortured him
most was the fact that he knew that he did not deserve any of the
recognition that had come his way.

Although his relationship with Pennington Ludlow spanned
many years, he was uneasy about these private outings that if publicized, would draw into question his independence as Fed Chairman.
Ludlow, of course, didn't care. He was the polar opposite of his longtime mentor: rich, engaging and self-deserving. Their collaboration
had led to many successes over the years and their role in supporting
President Chuck Lowery's "Economic Revolution" had been critical
to the country's economic turnaround. As the limousine pulled
through the gates of the secured plantation, Solomon wished he
had stayed in Washington with his wife Miriam.

Ludlow had asked Solomon to address the invited guests after
the dinner that evening and Solomon used his tight schedule as an
excuse to avoid the personal embarrassment of getting on a horse
and firing a gun in a futile attempt to kill a flying animal. It was a
safer decision for both men. As the hunting day ended and the sun
hung onto its low winter glow, the shooting party retired to their
rooms to prepare for the evening's dinner and camaraderie. The
Eckhouse servants in the main house lit the fireplaces in all the
public rooms and made their preparations for cocktail hour and
dinner as a bagpiper played traditional anthems in the mansion's
front courtyard.

The evening was a great success. The party was a stag event.
The men took their cocktails on a large veranda, overlooking a
great expanse of lawn that stretched down to a meandering river
that roamed through the marsh that dominated the horizon. After
dinner, they adjourned to the library for cigars and Armagnac and

Alan Solomon's talk. These hunters were some of the most powerful CEOs in the United States. President Lowery's "Economic Revolution" had propelled them to great wealth and success. Alan Solomon was an important man, but they were the straws stirring the economic drink. Solomon hit on a few opportunities and risks in the system, but generally offered an upbeat message about the next two years. When he finished, the men offered short but gracious applause and got back quickly to their backslapping revelry. Solomon felt like a rabbi at an Irish wake and wanted to escape to the solitude of his room. Ludlow slung his arm around Solomon's shoulder and walked him out of the library and into the long hallway that led to the mansion's main staircase.

"Good job, Alan. Well done. You're often dull but always right."

"I wish you'd stop asking me to these affairs. Most of those asses could care less what I said."

"They're all good Republicans and they've paid for the privilege of ignoring you if they want."

"That's sad and true and why I won't be back. I'm leaving tomorrow first thing to get back to the Capitol."

"That's fine. The shoot begins at 8:00 A.M.; let's meet for breakfast at 6:30 A.M. in the solarium. I want to review the calendar of announcements coming up and I need your view on consumer sentiment and the inflation outlook for the next several months."

"Good night, Pennington." Alan Solomon was caught in a six year dialogue with Pennington Ludlow that he wanted to end, but could not.

Three hours later, Pennington Ludlow bade good night to the last of his guests and climbed a private back staircase to his master suite. He opened the door and was greeted by the full embrace of his longtime mistress, Carmen Gomes, a stunning Mexican former model whom Ludlow had met ten years earlier during a Frontier Exploration Board meeting in Puerto Vallarta. Carmen was only eighteen at the time and Ludlow decided to keep her. At his command the sexual fireworks would begin, but he had one call to make first. Carmen's golden silk nightgown barely covered her full and brown breasts. She sat straddling a chair with her legs spread, tempting him to resist her. Ludlow had to call Harrison Teasedale to get a recap of the trading day. Teasedale oversaw his blind trust account at Morgan Greenville, where he was a senior Partner and head of the firm's proprietary trading desk. Teasedale also oversaw multiple other secret accounts that he maintained for Ludlow around the world.

As Treasury Secretary, Ludlow was prohibited from participating in the active management of his personal fortune, but such rules were virtually meaningless to him. Ludlow's actual fortune was a multi-billion dollar secret network of securities and assets. Public, regulatory filings estimated his net worth at between $150 and $250 million. His extraordinary wealth was not the result of keen investment acumen and analysis but merely the consequence of plain, old-fashioned insider trading with one clever, devastating twist for the rest of the market and the world. Ludlow's call did not last long since Carmen could not seem to keep her nightgown on or her hands off Pennington Ludlow, and he could not resist her sexual aggression.

When Ludlow made his way to the Solarium at 6:35 A.M., Alan Solomon had already finished his second cup of tea and read *The Financial Times* and *The Wall Street Journal* cover to cover. Despite his misgivings about being in South Carolina, he had slept well in his antebellum suite and was anxious to return to Washington. Ludlow, on the other hand, had not gotten much sleep at all since Carmen had tempted him into second and third sexual encores. Carmen made him feel years younger and the mere smell of her perfumed body overwhelmed his ability to think rationally.

"Well don't you look like hell this morning," Solomon observed as he placed the folded newspapers on the floor next to his chair and looked at Ludlow over his half glasses.

"What do you expect? Carmen is upstairs and I spent no time with her during the day yesterday."

"Poor man. Now I understand. Well, I hope you recover. Perhaps some B-12 is in order."

Alan Solomon's sarcasm belied his contempt for Ludlow's infidelity. Solomon's forty year marriage to his wife, Miriam, meant everything to him. Ludlow's marriage to Anne Eckhouse was about politics, money and perception. Solomon's idyllic union had only been jeopardized once. He, like Ludlow, had met Carmen Gomes ten years earlier at the same Frontier Exploration board meeting. She was invited entertainment along with five other beautiful Mexican girls whose job it was to make the board members feel special during the evenings' dinners. After a long day and too many drinks, Solomon allowed Carmen's playful flirtation to get to him—make him feel attractive and wanted. She led him back to his suite and they had awkward sex. Sixty at the time, Solomon was physically unappealing and sexually inexperienced. At eighteen, she was a goddess and a sexual tigress. The private resort had video surveillance in all the Board members' rooms and Ludlow quickly learned of Solomon's tryst. He held it over Solomon like a terminal sentence. Solomon could never release his guilt, and he lived in fear that Miriam would learn of his indiscretion and leave him. Ludlow did not know what guilt felt like.

"Thanks for your heartfelt concern. Listen, I need your insight. I'm very concerned about consumer leverage. Per capita credit balances are still growing. The non-core inflation numbers are showing signs of growth, as well. Your asshole colleagues in the

EU are going to attack inflation like they always do. I hope you
are not considering the same tactics."

President Chuck Lowery's "Economic Revolution" was a six year
phenomenon. When Lowery was elected, the nation was in a pre-
carious state—far more vulnerable than the average citizen or media
outlets realized. A massive wave of bankruptcies had reorganized
$1 trillion of assets in less than eighteen months—more than forty
times all the bankruptcies that had been filed in the prior ten years.
The stock market had crashed from its all time highs and America
had been attacked on its own soil. Lowery had committed to fight
two wars and revive an economy that was beginning to lose speed
to the dual emerging economic juggernauts of India and China.
Even Russia with its vast natural resources was clawing its way to
prominence and a seat at the economic grown-up table.

Lowery's "Economic Revolution" was in its simplest form a
massive stimulus package using interest rates and tax rates. Lowery
won legislative victories to lower the latter and used dramatic personal pressure to lower the former. Pennington Ludlow and Alan
Solomon both played prominent roles in achieving the program's
success. But the world economy was a vastly more complex organ-
ism during Lowery's Presidency than it had been at any time in the
past. Lowering tax and interest rates were the critical tools, but that
alone couldn't get the job done. America needed results—results
that the rest of the world could rely on. The American economy
was still the biggest consumer of goods and services. Every nation
and every market looked to the health of America as a barometer
of stability and growth. Chuck Lowery could not put America
at risk of losing its pre-eminent position as leader of the world's
economies. America would restore itself to its rightful place by
putting numbers on the board. President Lowery and his loyal
lieutenants would make sure that those results told a strong story.
There was no alternative.

"You see the same trends that I see. Pretty soon it's going to get very tough to hide the 800 pound gorilla in the room."

"Thanks for that insight, Alan. Why don't you leave the gorilla to me and keep on script. I'm getting a little bit nervous about the notes that are coming out of your meetings and the message that is being sent to the market. We can't afford a rate increase at this time. Non-core inflation is non-core. There are enough economists who believe in that crap to give us all the cover we need for the time being. We don't need consumers believing that gas prices are going to $4 a gallon and staying there."

"I don't know how long I can control the regional governors. They get their own inputs and they think inflation is rising above target levels. You've made them believe that the economy is chugging along. They think that the only way to deal with rising costs is to tighten."

"I don't think you're listening. I don't give a rat's ass whether they're right or wrong. It's fucking irrelevant. You are not going to touch interest rates. We're barely eking by at this point and inflation is not the President's concern. If you raise rates, you'll push the economy into recession, and there will be hell to pay. By the way, how is Miriam doing?"

Alan Solomon recoiled. He hated Pennington Ludlow at that moment, but he was caught. His love and guilt trumped his sense of honesty and duty. He actually hated himself more.

"Alright, I'll deal with the other governors, but you are not battling me. The rest of the world is getting the joke." Solomon pointed to the newspapers on the floor. "Even the idiots writing for these papers are finally raising doubts. It only took them three years to figure out that something was off. They're going to stumble over the truth sooner or later."

"Twelve months is all we need. Now be a good Fed Chairman and follow the game plan. It will all be over soon and you can retire to hundred thousand dollar speaking engagements and write your memoirs. You'll go down in history with all your great predecessors."

"I'm afraid it will be infamy."

Muddy waited for Alan Solomon on the steps of DeSaussure Hall's main house. The seven white columns that stretched up to the massive roof were at least six feet thick. Each column represented one of the original states of the Southern Confederacy that seceded before the Union's attack on Fort Sumter. Muddy always wondered how the men who built DeSaussure Hall had ever made those massive columns. He supposed that one or more of his relatives had probably been involved. Solomon walked out into cold morning air and nodded to Muddy. The drive to Beaufort was just as quiet as the drive in had been the day before. Alan Solomon hid his head behind *The New York Times* as Muddy hummed a spiritual tune in the front seat. Muddy was as straight and true as the tallest loblolly pine in the county, and Alan Solomon was a man contorted and pulled in directions that he could not manage. When Muddy bade Solomon a safe flight back home, he was quite certain that he would not see Alan Solomon back at DeSaussure Hall anytime soon.

CHAPTER 2

New York City
December 14–15, 2006

Kirby Haines was in a foul mood. He hated the wet sensation that was seeping through the bottoms of his handmade Tanino Crisci loafers. He was walking to the subway in the cold December rain because his assistant could not find him a radio car on a miserable night in the middle of the Christmas party season. All he could think about was his outrageously expensive wet shoes. While hundreds of others made their way through the puddled sidewalks to the subway entrance on Broadway and Wall, Haines felt particularly victimized. He was a Managing Director at Morgan Greenville, the most prominent investment banking firm in New York and the world at that moment. Richer than he could have imagined twelve years ago when he started his career, Haines could now afford virtually anything that he wanted within reason. But tonight he couldn't get a car and his feet were wet and he just wanted to get to The Post House as quickly as he could so that he could decompress with a drink.

The smell in the subway was a bad combination of wet wool, body odor and soggy newspaper. Haines' senses were familiar with the class bound nature of his surroundings. His years in investment banking did not represent the sum total of his life's experience. His past was more colorful than some of his other colleagues, like Peter Bolger, the Greenwich-born son of a banker whom he was meeting later for dinner. While Haines occupied a rarified place given his job and pay scale, he actually came from very little and somewhere that was very far away from the Upper East Side of Manhattan and the paneled conference rooms of Wall Street. On the rocking subway ride north, he allowed that acknowledgement to enter his mind briefly as he closed his eyes and senses to the others that sat or stood in silence around him. He got off at the 59th Street stop and walked four more blocks where he knew he would find some relief from the dreary evening. The bottoms of his socks were wet.

The long dark wood bar at The Post House was one of Kirby Haines' favorite places in New York. Despite the crowd that was waiting to be fed, he found a seat at the far end and ordered a Ketel One Gibson on the rocks. He still had about 30 minutes to relax before Peter Bolger would arrive. Kirby and Peter had met at Harvard Business School during their section orientation fourteen years ago. They were both recruited to Morgan Greenville, joined the firm, and had progressed in tandem up the ranks. Considered at the top of their class, both were up for Partner in a few months. They were buddies and confidants in a business environment that relished individual failure. Those who made it to the top fought many battles, engineered questionable alliances, and sacrificed personal ethics at times. Kirby and Peter's relationship had transcended all the obstacles that should have made them threatening combatants. Along the way, Peter had married Samantha and they had produced two cute kids. Kirby was still single. Tall, athletic and handsome enough, Kirby Haines was an independent operator. His relation-ship of the moment was with a lawyer who worked in Washington, D.C. named Hillary Thomas. Their separate professional pursuits made their involvement an on-again-off-again entanglement of frustration, lust, self-indulgence and pleasure. Haines bided the time talking with Joe Funghini, his favorite barkeep, about the sorry state of the Knicks, Joe's recent trip to Montreal, and the pair of Texas-twanging blonds at the middle of the bar. He really loved the world in that place.

"Hey Kirby, how'd you get up here so fast? Catch a ride with Teasedale? I bet your tongue was about two miles up his ass." Bolger had arrived. Peter slapped Kirby on his back, "Man, this weather sucks. I had to wait 45 minutes for a fricking Skyline."

"You did better than me. I gave up and went underground. I had no idea how much shit was growing down there."

"Kirby Haines took the subway? Wait, maybe someone from Page Six is here. Jerry, did you hear that?"

"Shut up, Peter and order a drink. I'm already two ahead of you." Establishing potable superiority was an alpha male tradition, and Kirby and Peter loved to spar.

"Good evening, Gerry. Could you pour me a Dewar's on the rocks with a splash? You're looking very Christmassy tonight in an Irish kind of way." Gerry, The Post House's other bartender, was from Dublin and had a reddish complexion that was the same in June, July and December.

"Cummin' up, Mr. Bolger and tanks for noticing."

One of the restaurant's hosts led the men to a quiet table just off the main floor where the decibel level was a bit lower. Tonight was a night to celebrate. Bonuses had just been announced and Kirby and Peter had received very good news. Morgan Greenville had had another amazing year and both were beneficiaries of the firm's success. Three million dollars would be deposited in each of their accounts sometime during the third week in January. They had reason to celebrate and both were on course to the most coveted title in a Wall Street firm: Partner. That's when the real payoff came.

While they ate their steaks, Kirby and Peter exchanged Morgan Greenville gossip. Kirby was on the verge of completing his first, sole-sourced private equity transaction. His target was a small-cap defense manufacturer called Comsdef Inc. that focused on sensory and optic technology and communication encryption. Peter, an M&A banker, had kept his eyes and ears open on the Street to protect Kirby from any threats to his proposed bid. Even though every investment bank established high Chinese Walls between their principal and agency businesses, Kirby and Peter had a more important agenda to follow than the protocols put in place to avoid conflicts. Peter was ready to watch Kirby's back and Kirby would do the same for Peter. They were going to reach the summit at the same time. That was their oath and they would plant their Partner's flag together. They may not have come from the same place in life, but they were going to become Partners together.

When dinner ended, their waiter offered the boys an after dinner drink on the house. After a couple of cocktails and two bottles of full mouthed Cabernet, they politely refused his kind offer and asked for the check.

"Let's go watch some Native American folk dancing buddy boy," Peter announced with a tone of conviction that made the decision a done deal.

"I thought the family would be calling you home this close to Christmas."

"Look, I'm sure you'll end up there without me anyway, so let's just hop in a cab and spend some more dough. We deserve a little entertainment on a fine night like tonight."

"Okay. I'm good to go but I've got Teasedale's final Investment Committee meeting in the morning. This isn't going to be a late one."

"Sure buddy. I've heard that before."

Closing a celebration at a strip club was standard fare for

Kirby and Peter. The circus atmosphere of loud music, naked entrepreneurs, watered-down drinks and hints of organized crime represented a world so opposite from their normal existence that they liked to succumb to its oddly unsatisfying appeal from time to time. Haines was a free man anyway. He was involved with Hillary Thomas but he was independent. For Bolger, a night out was a distraction from the responsibilities he kept at home. Living in a fantasy world for an hour or two certainly wasn't cheating—it was just expensive fun, and they could both afford it.

Kirby Haines made it in to work by 8:30 A.M. He hadn't gotten much sleep. His cultural excursion to the club featuring Native American folk dancing did not end until after 1:30 A.M., and he was trying to offset its effects with three Extra Strength Advil's and a tall cup of coffee. Haines had an uncanny ability to rebound from those long evenings. Now the adrenaline was kicking in as he waited his turn to address the Investment Committee on the merits of committing $200 million dollars of equity capital to the acquisition of Comsdef Inc. The good news was that he knew the company cold and had lobbied all the Committee members in advance, answering their questions and feeding them additional information as requested. Haines was well liked and as a top performer benefited from the good will he had built up over his twelve years at the firm.

Morgan Greenville's Investment Committee met at 9:30 A.M. sharp in a conference room on the 30th floor of its downtown headquarters. The Committee was chaired by Harrison Teasedale, a member of the firm's Management Committee who oversaw Morgan Greenville's global principal activities, including private equity and proprietary trading. He was a legend. If asked in confidence, most of his partners considered him an effete snob and obnoxious intellectual. Teasedale took pleasure in berating associates for the most insignificant transgressions. He read every memo with meticulous care and pointed out minor grammatical errors, even terrorizing newly minted Harvard MBAs when the margins of their committee memos were too wide. Harrison Teasedale was widely loathed and he seemed to take pleasure in that attention. In addition to his notoriety, Teasedale was extremely wealthy which contributed to his social standing among the philanthropically inclined do-gooders in the highest New York circles. Never married, there were rumors about his sexual orientation. His too thin physique, his fashion predisposition for tightly tailored Italian suits and his austere manner only added fuel to the "must-be-gay" rumors.

At 10:00 A.M., Haines and his team were called into the conference room to make their presentation. Forty minutes later, the Committee voted unanimously to approve the investment.

"Good job Kirby. Go get this done, and no fucking surprises. I don't want to hear about a last minute price renegotiation or balance sheet adjustment. We've agreed to a valuation and not a penny more." Teasedale always had the last word.

"Thanks everyone for your time. We'll let you know as we proceed." Haines and his team got up to leave. He could go back to his office and deal with his hangover. He suddenly felt tired now that the rush of the meeting was fading. He decided that December 15th was officially over. He looked at his watch. It was only 10:55 A.M. He would waste some time, make some calls, and get lunch. He had gotten his first solo deal approved. He figured becoming a Partner was his next stop.

CHAPTER 3

New York City
January 2, 2007

The passing of the New Year and a long holiday weekend had done nothing to change the condition of John Aichenhead's desk on the 10th floor of the FBI building at 26 Federal Plaza in lower Manhattan. It was a cluttered mess of black and white. File folders and their contents were stacked in piles of varying heights and their proximity to his chair was some indication, if not necessarily the primary indication, of their importance to him and maybe even the Agency. Aichenhead had signed up for the FBI after he returned from the first Gulf War where he served as a Marine. His commitment to his country had not resulted in any payoff when it came to his personal or professional pursuits. He had originally believed that his path as a Special Agent would lead to a management job atop one of the field offices or in Washington. He hadn't assumed that the Agency would possess the same bureaucratic qualities as the Corps. By the time he realized that he was stuck in a vector that was leading nowhere, he no longer cared very much.

Aichenhead lived alone in the Village in a one bedroom walk-up on Minetta Street. His marriage had ended six years earlier, and he had a hard time remembering many of the details of that three year episode. His marriage was part of his post-war distress syndrome. Actually he hadn't called it that, one of his bartender friends had. They had laughed together one night when they exchanged stories about love gone bad. Aichenhead's therapist had a degree in mixology. His apartment provided space for him, two cats and thousands of books that he had purchased over the years from street vendors or in flea markets. His shabby collection of material covered every topic imaginable from securities law to zoology to literary analysis. Aichenhead had read them all. His life was a precise routine, and he rarely deviated from it. The Marine Corps had embedded that discipline, but his compunction leaned toward obsession. He worked, drank and read—and not necessarily in that order, although he never mixed alcohol with work. That was another lesson he learned in the service. John Aichenhead knew something about everything, and nobody else cared. Other than his clique of bar stool buddies at Floyd's and The Spain, he had few other relationships. He liked the simplicity of that set-up since it created less friction if something different ever happened in his life.

Aichenhead's Field Manager in New York's Criminal Investigative Division dropped a black folder on top of the lowest pile of files on his desk.

"John, here's a simple little something that shouldn't take too long. I need you to interview the subject for National Security clearance. His name is Kirby Haines and he's an investment banker that works for Morgan Greenville about five blocks from here. Do you think you can fit it into your schedule?" Aichenhead's boss, Martha Torres, was a buttoned-down, professional who had gotten a lot further in the Agency than he ever would. She was tough, Hispanic and obviously a woman. He could not compete against two of her assets that the Agency seemed to value very highly these days.

"That's no problem. Any rush?"

"Only if you figure that the request came through Washington and I got called directly."

"You know, Martha, this world is just upside down. We're supposed to be hunting terrorists, fighting crime and I'm interviewing some rich investment banker?"

"Comes with the territory, John."

"What am I going to find out about this twit? Let's see. Went to Harvard, lives on the Upper East Side, drives a BMW, summers in the Hamptons, and belongs to some exclusive clubs. Oh yeah, probably smoked a little hooch in college. Maybe even inhaled."

Aichenhead didn't care for the privileged class. The way he saw it, he made less in a year than lots of those Wall Street assholes made in a week. They all wore patriot pins on their $3000 suits but none of them had served their country. Because of their extravagance, everything in New York was more expensive. They bid up the value of real estate because money meant nothing to them. They were living in a monopoly world and he was low on cash. They even had infiltrated his Village neighborhood. Luckily his favorite places were beneath their need for exclusivity.

"I know how you feel, John. At least it won't take long. Let me know when it's done."

Aichenhead opened the folder and scanned the two page summary and accompanying legal, tax, and credit reports. Kirby Haines looked like the standard investment banker. He laughed to himself. The profile he described to Martha Torres was a virtual match to the details he was reading. He resented wasting his time on this assignment, but his was not to question why. He'd figure out a way to make Kirby Haines share his pain.

CHAPTER 4

Bert Washington thought moving his family from their Anacostia neighborhood in Washington, D.C. to the suburbs of Prince George's County, Maryland was a smart move that would give his two young children access to better schools and a safer environment. He didn't consider his decision an example of "black flight," just a practical call given he and his wife's desire to live with a backyard. His daily commute from Bowie, Maryland to his office on Massachusetts Avenue was the downside of their decision. The twenty mile drive was supposed to take about thirty-five minutes but on that Wednesday, even at 6:15 A.M., Washington knew that he might have trouble getting to his desk by 8:00 A.M. It was after all the first official workday of the New Year and everyone seemed to have made the same resolution to start off early on the right foot.

Washington had worked at the Bureau of Labor Statistics within the Department of Labor for the last twelve years. He joined the BLS after returning from the first Gulf War and got his law degree on a full ride from American University going part time and at night. Washington had climbed up the government's bureaucratic

ladder slowly but surely until he was named Commissioner of the
BLS two years ago, its top job. Bert and his wife, Cathy, were life-
long Democrats, but his job was not political although he knew
his last promotion was either a concession by President Lowery's
Republican strategists or a gesture to the Congressional Black
Caucus. One way or the other, he didn't care—he had moved up
another notch. In the Marine Corps, he had served his country as
a desert rat, marching through the heat and sand storms on the
way to Baghdad. He had done more than most Americans do for
their country. Many of his Marine buddies had little to show for
the sacrifices they had made. Washington had something but not
a lot. He had worked hard for the status he had attained, but he
knew that the concessions and gestures had nothing to do with
him in particular. He had received a benefit because he was in the
right place at the right time. Most of his life did not include such
lucky deviations. He had grown up in East Orange, New Jersey in
a black ghetto that boiled over like many others in the summer of
1968. He was just a young boy, but he understood the indifference
and pain that being poor and black meant for all of the families
that constituted the world that was his neighborhood. Washington
vowed to raise himself out of that place and he succeeded. He moved
on and made his own life, but he knew that there were still limits
that held him back. Now older, married and secure, he had become
resigned to his better life. He hated his growing indifference to
his new status quo, but he wasn't a leader for anyone other than
himself and his family. And he was tired from his long journey out
of East Orange.

He considered his move to Bowie the end of that journey. His
wife Cathy was a Legal Aid lawyer in Upper Marlboro. Although
Prince George's County had become a predominantly middle-class
African American suburb of Washington, D.C., Bowie was still two-
thirds white. Bert and Cathy's combined salaries certainly supported

their decision to settle in a more affluent area of the county. As Washington waited in traffic, he knew they had come far but it still seemed like others were passing them by on the economic left lane. They were living through President Chuck Lowery's "Economic Revolution." Lower interest rates and reduced taxes combined with surging economic growth to create great wealth for many Americans and seemingly improved the lot of most. Unfortunately, Bert and Cathy were not one of those couples who had figured out how to buy a second home, travel out West or to Europe for annual vacations, or even buy a third car. Their net worth had not quadrupled over the last six years. They laughed that they were middle class poor, despite their two law degrees and combined incomes. Chuck Lowery's "revolution" certainly didn't reach the black community. At times, mostly at work or when he was stuck in traffic, Washington wondered whether the "revolution" was real at all.

As he pulled onto New York Avenue, his mind snapped back to his day's schedule and the meeting he would chair in about twenty minutes. The Bureau of Labor Statistics was a critical data collecting group operating inside the Department of Labor. The BLS published reams of economic information every month, but perhaps one of its most important reports was the monthly data on new job creation which helped the nation understand its unemployment rate and the underlying health of the US economy. On the first Wednesday of every month, Washington convened a meeting of his senior statisticians and economists to review the preliminary findings for the jobs report that would be released the following Friday morning before the markets opened. He pulled into his reserved parking space at the garage under his office and hurried to get upstairs. After grabbing a cup of coffee, Washington entered the meeting conference room at 8:03 A.M.

"Good morning everyone and Happy New Year! Sorry I'm a bit late but I got caught behind the parade again. Why don't we get started?" Washington's direct reports were happy campers. He treated his team with respect and they responded to his leadership. "Who's going to take us through December's numbers?"

Marcy Stanger, a senior statistician, indicated her role that morning and began to lay the numbers out for the team's review. December's numbers once again showed an expanding work force and shrinking unemployment. For the last twenty quarters, President Lowery's "Economic Revolution" had delivered an almost stair-step progression of increasingly better results. Steady job growth was the basis for economic expansion and prosperity. When Marcy completed her presentation thirty minutes later, Washington opened the meeting up for comments and questions. While there was some discussion about what appeared to be a numerical outlier in a sub category involving financial service sector job numbers in the San Francisco region, nothing else was particularly unusual or worthy of discussion. Their job done, Washington adjourned the meeting and thanked everyone for their participation.

Back in his office, Bert called Cathy at home to remind her that he had a dinner that night with a couple of Labor Department cronies.

"So you got to your meeting on time?"

"The traffic always kills me, but I slid in under the tag."

"And December's numbers?"

"You know that's privileged information that I am not permitted to tell you." Cathy laughed at his officious accent. She loved her husband's sense of humor.

"Isn't there something that I could do to entice you to tell me, Mr. Commissioner?"

"Keep talking baby." Bert could still get excited when Cathy played with him on the phone.

"I wish I had time for this now. I have to get to work too."

"Fine, I'll let you entice me this weekend. By the way, the numbers

still amaze me. In fact they're hard to believe. The price of everything is up: gas, food, commodities, healthcare; but nothing seems
to slow Lowery's 'Economic Revolution.' I just don't get it. Maybe
everything has changed. Maybe the economic models don't matter
anymore. You know: global economy, billions of Chinese suddenly
driving cars and eating chocolates. I don't know. I just don't believe
it. Everyone we know is cutting back but the national numbers just
keep chugging along."

"Bert, you're so negative. Lighten up, baby. The Republicans are
in charge and you can't believe that they're getting it right. Don't
you remember that we work for them? Always have. Nothing's
changed about that."

Bert loved his wife; she knew just how to get under his skin. "I'll
be home for the news. Now don't go telling your defendants about
how good the numbers are going to be on Friday. We don't want
the undeserving tied up in some insider trading scandal."

"Yes, dear. Please go back to work and think about me."

"Always do. That's how I keep productivity so low at the
Bureau."

Washington hung up as his assistant walked in with the final
draft of the December jobs report. He initialed it in the normal
spot, allowing it to move up the chain of command for review
and approval by his superiors. Besides the Secretaries of the
Department of Labor and Commerce, the draft report also got
ferried to the Department of the Treasury. At 8:30 A.M. on Friday
morning, Rick Santelli would read the numbers in the report off
the electronic newsreel from the floor of the Chicago Options
Exchange for CNBC viewers and the entire world to know. After
that, the market would march higher as the good news was greeted
by investors and the rest of the world marveled at the continuing
US economic expansion.

Washington's assistant placed the initial jobs report in a secure pouch and called down to the Bureau's messenger desk to arrange for delivery of the package to Pennington Ludlow's office at the Treasury Department. The walk to 1500 Pennsylvania Avenue from 2 Massachusetts Avenue would not take more than five minutes, assuming the courier didn't stop for a smoke or breakfast sandwich along the way. When burdened with certain high priority deliveries, the messengers usually took the direct route.

Waiting at the other end was Hillary Thomas, Pennington Ludlow's Chief of Staff at the Treasury Department. Thomas was Ludlow's newest senior staffer and had replaced his former deputy who died suddenly of a heart attack while jogging during lunch through Potomac Park six months earlier. She had accepted her post at Treasury after spending eight years at the Washington law firm of Frost, McIntire & Smelser LLC as the lead partner in their SEC practice. She was highly intelligent and particularly attractive—a potent combination in Washington. Though living in Georgetown, she was dating Kirby Haines, a Managing Director with Morgan Greenville in New York. They had met several years ago while working on a takeover deal and had struck up a romance. Like two driven, single professionals, they awkwardly tried to carry on a long distance relationship that was more about sex and expensive vacations than mutual support and love. Thomas was too busy for love anyway. She had left her practice at Frost, McIntire & Smelser for a shot at the political world. Her roots were driven deep in the Eastern Shore of Maryland and she considered a run for the House representing Easton to be one of her potential opportunities after her service to the Lowery administration concluded.

Secretary Ludlow had left Thomas in charge while he travelled that week to South America—with Carmen Gomes, of course—to promote a new trade agreement that President Lowery was trying hard to push through Congress. Although she was reasonably new in her job, Thomas had quickly grown comfortable with the protocols and mission critical elements of her role. That Wednesday, she knew that a package from the BLS containing the jobs report for the month of December would be hand delivered for Pennington Ludlow's review. Her responsibility upon receiving the package was to review the results, get Secretary Ludlow's sign off and communicate that sign off back to her counterpart at both The Department of Commerce and The Department of Labor. She would also send an acknowledgment to Bert Washington.

At 10:00 A.M., Thomas's assistant brought the package from BLS into her office and she opened and reviewed the summary data. She was pleased with the numbers; who wouldn't be. In the last six weeks, really starting in late November, the stock market had grown increasingly volatile as differing views about the underlying strength of the economy and the emerging threat of inflation crept into investors' psyches. The bullish jobs report that she just reviewed would send a positive signal and calm some of the uncertainty creating fears in the market. Steady growth and low inflation had been the tonic of President Lowery's "Economic Revolution" and had pushed the S&P 500 Index from 1100 to 2700 over the last five years. Fed Chairman Alan Solomon and Secretary Ludlow had garnered much of the credit for keeping the economy on a controlled and confident course. To Hillary Thomas, the administration—her team—was winning and it felt good to win. That after all was what politics was fundamentally about. Hillary attached a cover note to the BLS's data summary and had it encrypted and sent via email to Secretary Ludlow who was in Santiago, Chile according to his itinerary.

While she waited for Ludlow's reply, which would trigger her next set of actions, she decided to call Kirby Haines in New York. She knew he'd be in the office and probably done with any early morning meetings. Kirby and Hillary had just spent eight days together in Barbados over the Christmas and New Years stretch. They had had a great time together. Some of their prior trips included episodes and arguments that made her wonder about their long term possibilities. But this trip had been different. The sex, as usual, was athletic and satisfying with just the right tinge of kinkiness.

"Kirby Haines." In another surprise, Haines answered his own phone.

"Hey baby, it's me. How's your first day back? Where's Joanne? Do you type and sharpen pencils as well?"

"I'm a full service banker. What can I tell you."

"I like your service, but you probably know that."

"And I like to service you, in any position you like."

"Umm. It's getting a little hot in here. The NSA may be listening."

"If they are, they've probably heard it all before."

"Kirby, I already miss you, baby. When are you coming down to see me?"

"I am dying to see you but I'm going to be completely tied up with this Comsdef closing. Nothing is going to get done if I'm not around and we have a big push to comply with the contract's closing date. I really can't afford a weekend right now. But I wish I could. I want to jump on your bones so bad."

"Me too. I have this itch from our vacation and I need you to scratch it, but it doesn't sound like my tempting is going to change your mind. It's okay. Remind me, when is that big charity event that you told me about."

"It's Valentine's Day. I know you won't forget that. I can't believe it's five or six weeks from now."

"Yeah, it's way too long to be apart. I'm sure it will be over the top. You know I won't be able to keep my hands off you. Who are we sitting with?"

"Peter and Sam Bolger and some other couples from the firm. No client work that night; just fun."

"Excellent. I'll wear something sexy for you."

"I'm more interested in what you forget to wear."

"Oh, I see. I think I can probably accommodate you on that score." Hillary's other line rang and she knew it was probably Pennington Ludlow calling in from Chile with his reaction to her email.

"Honey, I got to go. I think Ludlow's calling in. I'll call you later. Love you."

Hillary picked up the blinking line where Ludlow was holding. "Thomas here."

"Good morning, Hillary. How are things back at the fort? And how was your vacation?"

"Just great, Mr. Secretary. Thanks for asking. Everything here is fine too and so are the December numbers. What did you think?"

"The numbers are good—very good. I think they will settle the market down. The naysayers just don't want to believe that we're doing a cracker-jack job. They'll lose their bets on Friday when the report is released and they'll deserve it. Maybe this will shut up the Speaker for a change. None of those Democrats like a winner and President Lowery is at the top of their list. Our economy just keeps chugging along. What a great engine—the world's envy."

"Is there anything you want me to do on my end before forwarding the report along?"

"No, Hillary. I liked your note and summary. Just have Helen retype it on my letterhead, initial it and send it along. By the way, you know the President is in Moscow at the G8 meeting so make sure Horace Grant gets the report and sends it on to him. I think he's heading for Rome on Thursday for a stop over."

"Will do, Mr. Secretary. How is your trip going?"

"Just terrific. I love the Latin culture. So alive and vibrant. They love the United States. Great people, just great." Ludlow could care less about the Chileans, but he was having an extravagant time with Carmen Gomes.

"I'm so glad to hear it. Well, have a safe flight back and I guess I will see you back in the office next week. Bye now."

"Bye Hillary. Be good."

Hillary Thomas hung up the phone, gave Helen her instructions and reviewed the emails one last time before they were sent. At 11:15 A.M., Secretary Ludlow's sign off was forwarded as instructed to the President's attention, as well as to the chief of staff at both the Department of Commerce and Department of Labor and to Bert Washington. Thomas had fulfilled her responsibility.

At the White House, Horace Grant, President Lowery's chief of staff received Thomas' message and packaged the BLS report with other daily briefing notes and sent them all on to the President's travelling secretary who would arrange to have it delivered to Lowery in Moscow where it was 7:30 P.M.

After hanging up with Hillary Thomas, Pennington Ludlow used his secure satellite phone to call Harrison Teasedale at Morgan Greenville. Ludlow followed established protocols when calling Teasedale that included the use of aliases and certain codes. Ludlow never sent email messages to Teasedale because of the internet's uncanny ability to never forget anything. Once connected, Ludlow passed along the important content of the jobs report that would be released on Friday. Teasedale decoded the message, reviewed the information and immediately began the process of putting capital to work to ensure a profitable trading outcome for Morgan Greenville, Pennington Ludlow, and of course for himself, over the next two days. Sometimes Teasedale maneuvered large amounts of capital into long or short positions in the Treasury market, using maturities that he thought represented the largest potential for gain given the pre-announcement data that he received. Other times he used stock market indexes or highly liquid individual bank stocks that would move in sympathy to the announced information. Harrison Teasedale was an expert trader but his legend both

within the firm and outside had not been built on the basis of his
enormous genius. His genius was built on the fact that he had
access to the most confidential economic information 24–48 hours
before any of his competitors. His rivals had to rely on their own
analysis and hunches, but no matter how smart they were, they
were no match for Harrison Teasedale and Morgan Greenville's
proprietary trading desk.

CHAPTER 5

Moscow, Russia
Sardinia, Italy
January 2–3, 2007

Hosting the Group of Eight meeting on Russian soil was an important coup for Russian leader Sergei Podrochov. President Chuck Lowery's diplomatic efforts to hold it elsewhere had not resulted in his preferred outcome, but when he sensed the G8's consensus opinion, he made sure his proposal was withdrawn quietly without suffering an international embarrassment. Lowery's wartime experience in Viet Nam had taught him the practical intelligence of when to fight and when to retreat. He knew that Podrochov would be under great pressure to make Russia look good and Lowery's mission would be to steal his limelight.

Chuck Lowery was a natural politician. He was eloquent and obtuse; commanding and sensitive; worldly and pedestrian—the consummate actor and orator. He was also a keen strategist and shameless patriot. If central casting had called for a Presidential character, Chuck Lowery would have fit the bill. He was a dashing former Navy pilot who had lost his wife to cancer after a brave fight. His perpetual tan and unnaturally white teeth complemented his light blue eyes. At age 61, President Lowery was also America's most eligible bachelor. Chuck Lowery was spotless. He was the most popular American President in modern times and he had led a resurgence in America's fortunes that was the envy of the world community. Despite his Republican Party affiliation, even the media liked him because he was open, accessible and quotable. His "Economic Revolution" was so successful that it was the model for candidates seeking electoral mandates across Western Europe. President Lowery was a rock star and he had just proven it again on Sergei Podrochov's home field.

After the Group's traditional photo op, which was staged in the Kremlin's Great Hall, Podrochov had pulled Lowery aside with a smile on his face and an acknowledgment of Lowery's deft handling of an anti-terrorism resolution championed by the United States that was the centerpiece of the G8's agenda that meeting. Podrochov had thought that his pre-meeting lobbying had determined a differ-ent outcome, but Lowery had out-flanked him and the resolution had passed without amendment. The men shook hands but Lowery could feel in Podrochov's grip that they would remain adversaries. He could not erase his home-grown hatred of the hammer and sickle communism that had driven the Cold War. Lowery attended a closing dinner on Wednesday evening and the next morning he boarded Air Force One to begin his trip home. But before return-ing to the Capitol, Lowery's official itinerary had him landing in Rome for a two day stop and brief break for some relaxation. His unofficial itinerary was actually taking him to Sardinia to visit his best friend and most significant supporter, Bob Fletcher.

Bob Fletcher and Chuck Lowery met on the campus of the University of North Carolina at Chapel Hill in the fall of 1964.

They both had applied for Air Force ROTC scholarships and went through the program together. Fletcher and Lowery were two of the most popular students on a campus full of popular people. Lowery came from modest means and Fletcher's father owned a company that he started after World War II called Marine Logistics, Inc., which transported fuel and industrial supplies across the southeastern portion of the United States. Fletcher knew that someday he would take over the family business and that knowledge opened his horizons to other adventures, like war and flying. Both men started on the Tar Heel football team, dated the college's prettiest co-eds and were inseparable. After graduation, Fletcher's father used his influence to get them commissions in the Navy as pilots because they wanted to go to Viet Nam and the Air Force route would take them too long. They survived their two tours of duty and returned home as civilians in 1973. But their lives were forever joined.

The two friends had shared every important adult experience together from the age of eighteen onward, including the life and death experience of flying missions to Hanoi. Lowery and Fletcher were as close as brothers but without the family jealousies that went with blood lines. After Viet Nam, Fletcher married his college sweetheart, and Lowery got his law degree from Georgetown University. Lowery met his late wife while clerking for a Federal Judge in Atlanta. The two couples were extremely close, but Fletcher and Lowery were each other's wingman. Over the years, Fletcher grew the business he inherited from his father into a multi-billion dollar international distributor through numerous acquisitions. He became rich and used his wealth to support his best friend's foray into politics. Lowery won successive races in the House of Representatives representing North Carolina and was eventually elected Governor. He rose to national prominence as a keynote speaker at the Republican National Convention in 1992. The TV screen loved Chuck Lowery. He was a new face attached to a tired party. He was the future for the Republicans who would suffer an embarrassing defeat that year. Eight years later, after the devastating loss of his wife, he was elected President of the United States.

Bob Fletcher was Chuck Lowery's biggest supporter and he underwrote many of Lowery's expenses through intricate and secretive machinations that were outside the laws regulating campaign finance. Lowery's election was too important for the country to let political bullshit get in the way. Using his invisible hand, Chuck Lowery in return made sure that Fletcher had every advantage in building his international business through the awarding of lucrative government contracts administered by agencies within agencies. Lowery and Fletcher were comrades and life partners. They had an agenda to restore America's greatness and if improving their own lot in life was an outcome of the deal, they had no qualms backing up their trucks to the US mint. They knew what was principally important. All the rest was just the spoils of war.

Bob Fletcher was looking forward to seeing his old friend again. His home in Sardinia was set on a craggy bluff above the azure sea. The compound itself was on a peninsula that offered security and privacy. Fletcher travelled extensively because of his international business dealings. Still married after thirty-two years, he maintained a bevy of women around the world that he shuttled between homes in Asia, Europe, the Middle East and in Sardinia. Fletcher liked to call these women his "cheese" and was apt to fly his cheese around the globe on his small fleet of private jets, often times keeping them steps ahead or just behind the steps of his wife. With his buddy flying over for some R and R, Fletcher had ordered some of his favorite varieties of cheese for his two day visit. He knew President Lowery would enjoy his selection.

Among the numerous roles that Bob Fletcher played for President Lowery, his role as private banker would have the most profound impact on his friend's life after he left the White House. Fletcher owned several foreign banks that he purchased over time in countries including Jordan, the Philippines and Ukraine where he had business interests. Those banks maintained secret and unregulated accounts for both Fletcher and Chuck Lowery. Although his name never appeared on any *Forbes* annual listing, Fletcher was one of the 50 richest men in the world thanks to his father and to Chuck Lowery's "Economic Revolution." Chuck Lowery, unbeknownst to the US voters, watchdogs and media outlets, had also become a very rich man through Fletcher's handling of his trading accounts. Both men were the beneficiaries of extraordinary investment returns generated through a six year series of bets made by Fletcher and his investment team based in Ireland in trading markets around the world. Their good fortune, like the fortune being accumulated by Treasury Secretary Pennington Ludlow, was not the result of keen analysis and execution, but rather from an insider's access to non-public economic information. When Lowery stepped down as President in two years, he would be free from the constraints of civil service and the scrutiny of oversight groups. With the media's focus on the next President, Lowery would gradually tap into his secret accounts to live the life of a king who continued to hold the respect of the entire world. Lowery and Fletcher's collaboration was a masterpiece of planning and execution. They were nearing the end of their Presidential journey together and their two strategies were succeeding. America was once again on top, and they were receiving the benefit of their noble work through a payoff that was unimaginable.

President Lowery's helicopter approached Fletcher's landing pad with seeming anonymity. The Secret Service had set up a decoy operation that was risky but demanded by the President so that he could enjoy a private 48 hours with his best friend. Lowery's helicopter looked like countless others that flew billionaires over to the island's Costa Esmeralda for a few days of extravagant fun. As it landed on his property, Fletcher ran over to greet his tired guest.

Over the noise of propeller's whops, Fletcher yelled out to his friend as he climbed out the chopper. "Hey Chuck! How the hell are you? Welcome to paradise again. It's great to see you, but you look like shit."

"I'm beat but it's great to be here," President Lowery yelled back.

"Looks like you kicked a little tail in Moscow. How's your new best friend Sergei?"

"Well, he was a little pissed when the meeting ended, but he tried to diddle with us and got caught. Next time he'll be smarter. He's some interesting little bastard. I bet he's sowed away a fortune. I'd love to see his balance sheet when he finally steps down."

"He's never going to leave office—that's a sure way to end up dead in his dacha. No, he'll be ruling Russia until they carry him out with his boots on. We'll be long gone and he'll still be looking over his shoulder. The Russians are vicious."

"You're probably right, but I'm done with that now. I want to wash up and get out of these clothes. How about a drink? I'm in need."

"Well luckily we can handle that and probably about anything else you may end up wanting. Marco, bring President Lowery a Tanqueray martini on the rocks and one for me as well. Come on. Let me walk you over and introduce you to some new cheese. I think you're going to like what I ordered."

With drinks on the way, Fletcher led Lowery through the garden and up a wide set of stone steps to the main villa. The large pool was set in front of seven magnificent arches, under which tables were arranged for al fresco dining or to provide shade from the strong midday sun during the summer. Five exquisite beauties were sun bathing on lounges next to each other. All them were deeply tanned and wore only their sunglasses and thongs. Although it was early January, they were enjoying an unseasonably warm day as the thermometer reached about seventy-five degrees.

"Ladies, my guest has finally arrived and I want you to say hello to Chuck." Four of the women had never met Chuck, but for one blonde Russian named Misha, this was something of a reunion. While the others propped themselves up on their elbows and offered sweet hellos in a mixture of accents, Misha bounced up to hug Lowery, draping her long slender arms around his neck as she lifted her left leg at the knee and kissed him. Lowery loved Fletcher—he always delivered the goods. Fletcher knew that Lowery had a weakness for tall Russian blondes and Lowery had had a particularly good time with Misha the first time they met.

"I've missed you, Chucky," Misha cooed in Lowery's ear. The smell of the tanning lotion on her skin was ambrosia. As they partly separated but still in embrace, Lowery stole a glance at her high, firm breasts and erect nipples. She leaned her thigh between his legs. He could feel the excitement of his two day stay beginning.

"I've got to change out of these clothes and shower, my dear. And then I can come back and join you by the pool."

"Why don't you let me help you change and draw you a bath? You look like you need a good massage and you know I'm an expert at making you relax."

"I remember that vividly."

"Good. I know which suite Bobby has put you in. Now follow me. I'm in charge."

Misha was a Russian through and through. She took Lowery's hand and led him away from the pool and toward one of the villa's large open doorways. Lowery was like a schoolboy following Misha except this teacher had legs that resembled perfectly crafted stilts

and wore a thong that rode high on her hips. Bob Fletcher was a
good friend indeed. They would have plenty of time later to review
all the procedures they had established to safeguard their global
trading venture. Their military training never deserted them. Every
time they met they reviewed chain of command procedures, communication protocols, and the fire walls that separated their trading
schemes from their sources of the critical information. For six years
they had treated their trading endeavors like their flying missions
over Hanoi. They were meticulous in checking and rechecking every
element of their architecture. They were secure, confident but ever
mindful that one slip could cost them everything.

Later that afternoon after President Lowery had been adequately
relaxed by Misha, he rejoined Fletcher by the pool and discussed
the employment report that would be issued on Friday morning
in Washington, D.C. The markets in New York and across Europe
would rally. Pleased with their prospects, they got up and walked
into the salon and dialed up a video link to Dublin where Monroe
Desmond was waiting for their call. Desmond was a former CIA
operative and quantum mathematician who oversaw the financial
side of Bob Fletcher's empire. Desmond had received the advanced
employment report from his normal Washington source and had
dispatched instructions to a group of traders who worked at inter-
secting desks that were crammed with computer monitors in their
Dublin office. Desmond had made his first bets in Asia. But he
had laid out additional positions in New York and Chicago as well.
Fletcher and Lowery operated under one simple rule: no one was
allowed to break the bank. Desmond understood this rule intuitively.
There was a lot of money to be made. They didn't have to make it
all at once. Their rule had worked quite well since they put it in
place almost six years ago. Month after month they made money.
Their performance beat every pro whose numbers were touted in
Barron's or on CNBC.

When they finished their call with Monroe Desmond, Lowery and Fletcher walked out to the edge of the property. From their position on top of the craggy cliff they looked west out into the sea. Although it was still early, the sun's angle in January was shallow and its reflection off the water was a bit blinding. Both men were happy to be in each other's company. The world was good and working according their plan. They pulled the strings and America was on top. Desmond traded their accounts and they became richer. Fletcher ordered the cheese and they were both satisfied. This was their reality, their doing and destiny. They had determined the outcome of the game, and they were winning playing by their own set of rules.

CHAPTER 6

New York City
February 11, 2007

John Aichenhead had been able to waste about a month, always
finding something better to do than schedule his interview with
Kirby Haines at Morgan Greenville. He had found the time to
read at least a dozen books in the five weeks since his boss Martha
Torres gave him his easy assignment. But he didn't want to deal
with the assignment because he found it a colossal waste of time,
and his frustration only grew the more he procrastinated. Once
again, Aichenhead was caught in his all too familiar dilemma. It
was the reason why he couldn't advance in the Agency and why he
didn't care. When he was given stupid things to work on, it made
him confront his personal frustration with himself and the world
that was changing around him, leaving him behind or at least alone
with his books and his bars.

On his way to work that Monday morning, he decided that
February 11th was a reasonable day to call Kirby Haines' and set up a
date for his National Security Clearance interview. Digging into one
of his black and white piles—the Comsdef pile had been pushed two

rows backward on the extreme right edge of his desk—Aichenhead found the personal data sheet with Kirby Haines' business phone number. He dialed the number. After two rings, Joanne Fruilli, Haines' assistant answered the phone.

"Morgan Greenville. Mr. Haines' office."

"Hello, this is Special Agent John Aichenhead speaking. I am calling from the FBI and would like to speak to Kirby Haines."

Joanne Fruilli started to laugh on the phone. "Okay, okay. Who is this? Is that you Peter? I know it's you. I know it. You are too much. What did you call yourself? John Aichenhead?" Joanne laughed out loud. "The FBI calling? April Fool's Day has come a little early hasn't it? John Aichenhead?" She started laughing again.

"I'm sorry, Miss, that you find this funny, but I am calling on official US government business."

Aichenhead was a little miffed at Joanne Fruilli's hysteria, but it was not the first time that his name had caused a minor ruckus. Ever since he could remember, people had reacted with a variety of responses to the sound of his family surname. The kids on his block growing up had tortured him and his adolescence had not been pleasant since every girl that he wanted to date had a hard time coming to grips with his odd handle. After all, Aichenhead was not exactly a common name.

"Oh my." Joanne started to calm down a little as she caught her breath from her laughing fit. "Okay, let's start again. And whoever you are, if this is one of Peter's stunts we will get him back." Joanne's threat was delivered with serious Sicilian intent but her accent was pure Staten Island.

"I'm sorry, Miss. I did not get your name."

"My name is Joanne Fruilli. I am Kirby Haines' assistant."

"Yes, good. Once again. I am Special Agent Aichenhead from the FBI."

Joanne lost it again. She couldn't help it. She had gotten the giggles and nothing short of electrocution could stop her now. Special Agent Aichenhead continued undeterred.

"I need to make an appointment to interview Kirby Haines for National Security Clearance. If you would like to check with him about this requirement, I am sure he will tell you that this is no laughing matter. He cannot assume his position on the Comsdef board of directors without my okay."

Joanne caught enough of his last sentence to begin to collect herself. Maybe this call was for real. She tried to calm down. If she said his name and lost it, he'd probably arrest her.

"I'm so sorry Special Agent. It's just been one of those days. Please let me know how I can be helpful."

"I need to schedule an appointment with Mr. Haines. I would like to get this done as soon as I can so I can get back to more important Agency matters." Aichenhead let his frustration show.

"Well, as luck would have it, Mr. Haines is in New York today and tomorrow but scheduled to be out of town travelling all of next week. By any chance, could we try to schedule something today?"

"Yes, Ms. Fruilli today would work. Could we do something at the end of the day?" Aichenhead typically folded up shop around 5–5:30 P.M. like most good government employees.

"Yes, Special Agent that works. Mr. Haines is free for forty-five minutes starting at 6:30 P.M. Could you be here then?"

Aichenhead couldn't believe it—6:30 P.M. to interview this investment banker jerk. Well, he had taken the step to make the call. Now he had no choice but to finish the project. His first beer of the evening would be delayed. He was adjusting his schedule as they talked.

"If that's the earliest he can make it that will have to work. I'll be at your offices at 6:30 P.M. Please arrange with your security for my arrival. I will be carrying my weapon and building security does better when they know a Federal Agent is coming."

"Oh, thanks for telling me. I will certainly let them know." Fruilli, still single, was a little more interested in this super cop packing a loaded weapon. Maybe she would stick around to see what this agent with a funny name looked like.

"Thank you, Ms. Fruilli. I will see Mr. Haines at 6:30 P.M. Please tell him to be on time."

"Thank you, Special Agent. Sorry about earlier."

"No reason to apologize. It's become pretty standard at this point."

At precisely 6:15 P.M., John Aichenhead walked through the doors of Morgan Greenville's headquarters at 275 Vesey Street. He identified himself to building security by presenting his FBI credentials, un-holstered his weapon for inspection and was led through the building's check point to the elevator bank that would take him to the 28th floor where Kirby Haines had his office. Morgan Greenville's building was thoroughly modern, unlike the FBI headquarters. No expense had been spared on the security and electronic monitoring systems that guarded all the high priced talent that temporarily occupied the building every day. Even the elevator had cable television that was broadcasting the news. Aichenhead wondered why anyone needed entertainment in an elevator that took about 20 seconds to ascend 28 floors. When the elevator doors opened, Aichenhead entered into a large, opulent reception area with leather sofas and chairs and an incredible view of the Lower Hudson River. Across the way he could see Ellis Island and the Statue of Liberty. To his right, Jersey City was illuminated with thousands of lights. He had a new appreciation for Jersey City at that moment. He always thought of it as a shit hole, but at night it almost looked beautiful. He identified himself to the receptionist and took a seat on one of the large leather sofas. Aichenhead figured that the sofa probably cost more than all the furniture in his apartment. He looked at his watch. It was 6:25 P.M. He was early as usual.

As he waited, a steady stream of Morgan Greenville's employees walked back and forth through the reception area. He was struck by the heavy traffic pattern. It was just about 6:30 P.M. and the place was buzzing like it was 9:00 A.M. And everyone looked kind of the same: the men in dark suit pants, white shirts with cuff links, polished shoes and bright, patterned ties—that must be their fashion statement given how black and white everything else seemed. The women were elegantly dressed but in understated suits, expensive mid-heeled shoes, and simple gold bracelets or necklaces. All of them were trim, handsome, young and serious. No they looked determined. There wasn't much chatter and no laughter. Morgan Greenville did not seem like a very pleasant place to work by the look on the faces of its employees. They didn't look unhappy, just determined and serious. Aichenhead thought they looked too serious for their age. The pursuit of money was obviously their obsession, and it was a thief stealing their souls. At that moment, Aichenhead felt sorry for them. His distaste for them would probably return momentarily.

Joanne Fruilli entered the reception area from the left corridor. She walked right up to the sofa where Aichenhead was seated and introduced herself. "Special Agent Aichenhead? I'm Joanne Fruilli, Mr. Haines' assistant." Joanne had a smile on her face. She was still amused by his unusual surname. "I'm sorry about this morning. I just got the giggles and couldn't stop."

Aichenhead took her in completely in a quick once over. She looked about 32 years old and was about five foot four. She was attractive with a Mediterranean look and dark straight hair. She had a terrific figure and was wearing a tight, above the knee skirt and form fitting white blouse that highlighted her breasts that were slightly too big for her slender frame. A small gold cross hung from a necklace and rested at the top of her cleavage that was just visible. Aichenhead could forgive her earlier rudeness now that he saw whom he was dealing with. She was clearly a member of the bridge and tunnel legion, but that separated her from the affluent snobs that she worked for. She had beautiful dark eyes and a dose of outer borough spunk.

"Thanks for arranging my meeting on short notice. And don't worry about this morning. My sister changed her last name years ago to Aichen just to end the agony that she had to deal with in high school. I guess I was the glutton for punishment. I figured God gave me this challenge to deal with for some reason, so why run away from it."

"We've all got something to carry, don't we? Why don't you follow me and I'll bring you back to Mr. Haines office." Joanne Fruilli was pleasantly surprised by Special Agent Aichenhead. She hadn't known what to expect.

Aichenhead got up and followed Joanne out of the reception area and down the corridor from which she had come. Aichenhead trailed her and couldn't help but notice her firm rump and athletically shaped legs. Joanne Fruilli was pretty hot. He didn't have any visual entertainment at FBI headquarters. He now realized that the investment bankers had a monopoly on everything including cute secretaries. He hated them more. Maybe it was better not to have the distraction.

Fruilli could feel Special Agent Aichenhead checking her out. She added a little swing to her gait as she led him into the interior of the banking division's offices. She liked all guys who worked as cops or firemen, but she had never met an FBI agent. Guys like that were tough and physical. She was attracted to anyone who carried a weapon. And Special Agent Aichenhead was good looking if unfashionable. She noticed he wasn't wearing a wedding ring.

"How long have you worked here, Ms. Fruilli?"

"Please call me Joanne, Special Agent. About five years now."

"I think it would be safer for you if you called me John. That might help with giggle issue."

"Thanks, if I'm not breaking any rules. I wouldn't want to be arrested, you know, although you don't look like the kind who'd bring me in without good reason."

"I wouldn't be too sure of that. Depending on how my interview goes with Mr. Haines, I may have to question you." Aichenhead's intonation indicated an attempt to flirt. He wasn't particularly good at it but Joanne took the bait.

"Well, you'll have to do what you have to do. Just no handcuffs, please." Joanne turned and smiled in a coquettish volley.

"When does your day end around here? Does anyone go home or do you all sleep here?"

"My schedule is pretty flexible since I'm single. I usually stay until Mr. Haines lets me know it's okay to leave."

Aichenhead appreciated Joanne's reference to her non-married status. "Well, I hope he doesn't send you home before I'm done, just in case I have a few questions for you."

"If he does, at least you know where to reach me." Joanne turned and posed outside the door of Kirby Haines' office. She cocked her head slightly and arched her back subtlety, straining the buttons on her white blouse. Aichenhead was intrigued. She could probably put a seriously dent in his reading regimen.

"Yes, I do. Thanks."

"Mr. Haines. This is Special Agent Aichenhead for your 6:30 P.M. meeting."

"Special Agent. Please come in and have a seat. Since I've never gone through this clearance process before, maybe you could give me an overview of what we need to do. Am I going to have to pee in a cup?" Kirby Haines attempt at casualness opened the door for Aichenhead's personal agenda.

"Mr. Haines. National Security Clearance is a very serious matter. There are no limits set on my investigation. I hold your directorship position in my hands and I will go as far as I need to go to make sure that you pose no potential threat to our country should you receive clearance certification."

"Special Agent, I'm just an investment banker, not a criminal." Haines was caught off guard by Aichenhead's no nonsense approach.

"Mr. Haines, some of the 20th century's most notable criminals were financial figures. Your access to information and your need to support an extravagant lifestyle make you a prime target for foreign interests who might be interested in Comsdef's sensitive technical assets. Other prurient interests of yours that might include prostitution, deviant sexual behavior, or drug use make you an easy target for extortion. Let me assure you that your status as an investment banker does not make you a criminal, Mr. Haines. But it does make you a criminal or foreign agent's best mark."

Kirby Haines had not expected this line of conversation. His winning personality endeared him to clients and higher-ups in his own organization. But Special Agent Aichenhead was going to prove impervious to his charm. Haines thought that maybe the Agent's last name had turned him into the hard ass that he appeared to be.

"Okay, Special Agent. I understand. Could we please get on with the process then?"

Aichenhead was satisfied. He was the visiting team on Morgan Greenville's home field but he had firmly established his superiority. He had satisfied his inner frustration. Now he could get the job done and secure Joanne's number on the way out. Over the next thirty minutes, Aichenhead covered Haines last twelve years at Morgan

Greenville, his romantic and sexual encounters over the last five years, his graduate school experience at Harvard and his college years at Yale. Aichenhead's questions were pointed. He had warned Haines that the truth was paramount and that any lies constituted perjury under Federal statutes. Haines answered all of Aichenhead's questions honestly and without attitude. As the interview stretched toward the forty-five minute limit, Aichenhead's impression of Kirby Haines began to change.

Haines was not a son of the privileged class—far from it. As irony would have it, both Aichenhead and Haines were roughly the same age and grew up in Union County, New Jersey. Haines was 39 years old and Aichenhead 40. They both came from working class families and were middle class poor products of their different towns. Haines had gone through the public school system and Aichenhead through the parochial counterpart. When it came to college, Haines got accepted to Yale which changed his life's direction and Aichenhead enrolled at Georgetown and through Washington, D.C. gained his exposure to public service. After college, their life paths diverged: Aichenhead entered the Marine Corps and Haines got recruited to work as an analyst on Wall Street. But they had a lot more in common than Aichenhead could have imagined when he first got his assignment from Torres.

As the interview ended, they shook hands and Aichenhead told Haines that he thought everything would go smoothly for his clearance certification. Aichenhead gave Haines his card, "It's not a bad thing to have a contact at the Agency."

"I appreciate that Special Agent. Let me return the favor. You never know when you may need help or information about some of the esoteric stuff we do these days. I'd be happy to help if you need any."

"Thanks for that. Good luck, Mr. Haines."

"Kirby, please."

"That's done. And please call me John. I'm sure you'll never forget my last name anyway."

That was a prediction that Aichenhead did not have to offer. Kirby Haines was not going to forget John Aichenhead although he had no reason to believe that he would ever meet him again.

"Joanne! Please show John out."

Joanne Fruilli popped out of her seat, just as pert as she was in John Aichenhead's short term memory. She walked Aichenhead back through the corridor that led back to the reception area.

"So now you're John to everyone? I guess everything went ok?"

"Joanne, that's classified information."

Aichenhead's official tone was playful and turned Joanne on. She hoped he'd ask her for her number directly. The cat and mouse game they were playing had a chance to lead somewhere.

"Oh, of course it is. I was just trying to do my job."

You're resourceful, aren't you? I think I'd like to interview you further. Do you mind if I call you to schedule something?"

"I'd mind it if you didn't."

Morgan Greenville was still a bee hive of activity. It was almost 7:30 P.M. and young bankers were hustling back and forth through the corridor where John and Joanne were walking. In the reception area two small groups were conferring with intensity. Aichenhead's interest in Morgan Greenville and its culture was changing. His disdain was giving way to curiosity. Kirby Haines was a deviation from Aichenhead's expectation and Joanne Fruilli was a special bonus. His procrastination had denied him an earlier encounter with the engaging Ms. Fruilli—he would try to internalize that as a lesson learned. The elevator doors opened and Aichenhead walked in and turned around. Joanne winked and gave him a little wave good-bye. As the doors closed, Aichenhead locked in the vision of her body, her eyes and her other notable features. He'd have something to talk about tonight at The Spain with his favorite psychologist behind the bar.

CHAPTER 7

Washington, D.C.
February 14, 2007

Bert Washington's staff at the Bureau of Labor Statistics was at the beginning of their cycle for accumulating and analyzing data for the next jobs report that would be released at the end of the first week in March. The January numbers that were reported the first Friday of the month had continued the steady progress that had been building unabated. The stock and bond markets had once again rallied as short sellers were forced to cover the bets they had made in anticipation of results that confirmed economic weakness. The big money felt that President Lowery's juggernaut was losing steam, but the economy kept proving them wrong, or at least premature. Bert Washington, if he had been a betting man, would certainly have placed a wager against the trend line. But he would have lost too. Still, everything that he knew and felt made him think the economy was slowing down. The Christmas retail season had not been particularly strong. Washington always felt that Christmas was the most resilient indicator of the economy's condition. Even in tough times, people bought presents and spent beyond their means, either slightly or grossly. But this past Christmas, retail sales were up only 2% despite solid GDP growth of over 3% and job creation of about 80,000 per month on average. He felt that something was off. He just couldn't put the pieces together.

Data gathering at the BLS was a hectic process. Regional information streamed into the Bureau's mainframes at 2 Massachusetts Avenue but processing was incredibly slow. Investment in information technology had dried up after the Y2K debacle seven years earlier. The Labor Department's annual budget was not a favorite child with the Office of Management and Budget and BLS suffered from capital starvation as a result. Those mainframes were fifteen years old and the Bureau's server farm was in need of significant upgrading. System crashes were as common as electrical failures on Caribbean islands. Bert Washington lit a candle every month that he would get through another critical final week without an IT disaster. Luckily his prayers had been working recently.

On Valentine's Day, Bert usually tried to arrange something special with Cathy—maybe a romantic lunch and an afternoon of pleasure at one of the swanky hotels near his office. This Valentine's Day that midday celebration had been trumped by his monthly lunch with Rosemary Guillson, his counterpart within the Department of Commerce. Guillson was the Under Secretary at the Economics and Statistics Administration. The ESA was responsible for generating a number of important economic reports including Gross Domestic Product, Personal Income, the Balance of Payments, Durable Goods Orders and Inventories. Washington and Guillson got together every month to share thoughts and best practices. Over the last two years, they had built an unusual but close friendship. Guillson was an Irish Catholic from the Back Bay area of Boston. Her rough and tumble neighborhood was not exactly diverse or tolerant, but every family voted Democratic.

Bert Washington was really the first African American that she had ever gotten to know well. The only thing they really had in common was their politics. Having dinner with their spouses or a weekend picnic with the kids was probably not in the cards. They enjoyed their friendly arguments over lunch about whose economic reports had the greatest sway on the markets. Washington always claimed that PPI, CPI and Employment were greater determinants of economic and consumer health and therefore market performance than Guillson's bag of data. Rosemary laughed at Bert's contention since the market had only moved in one direction over the last five years. Their argument was moot. No matter what they reported, the market marched higher. President Lowery's "Economic Revolution" was the critical catalyst. They may not like their Republican boss but his message seemed a whole lot more meaningful than their monthly reports.

Washington was a few minutes early and seated when Guillson was escorted to their table by the restaurant's hostess. Washington had chosen B. Smith's for lunch that month. It was his turn to buy. He enjoyed taking her to ethnic restaurants like B. Smith's whose combination of southern and Creole specialties were a challenge to her Boston tastes. Washington liked to avoid the traditional power lunch scenes at places like The Palm or The Washington Grill. He knew that she would have been much more comfortable there. It wasn't that she wanted to be seen. She wanted to see what was going on. She was a political voyeur. Just for those reasons, Washington always took her, when it was his turn to make the reservation, to a place where she wouldn't be distracted. The agenda he had set for today's lunch was too important. He needed her rapt attention. He wanted to propose a highly unusual exercise that would raise some eyebrows, and without Guillson's support he knew he would be targeted inside the Department of Labor as an alarmist.

"Rosemary, welcome. You're right on time."

"You're gracious as always but I'm ten minutes late as usual. What a lovely spot. I've never eaten here before." Bert detected a hint of apprehension in her voice.

"I kind of figured this might be a little off your beaten track. Today I thought we'd eat some down home soul food—although they offer some New Orleans specials if you want to try some Creole delicacies. I can attest for the jambalaya; best in the city."

"Why that sounds just delicious. We didn't eat much soul food growing up. Maybe I can rely on your knowledge when we order."

"I'm not sure you want to go there. I just might order something that will curl your toes."

"Please, Bert. I have a lot to do this afternoon. You wouldn't be that cruel, would you?"

"I can be bad, but I'll try to resist."

After they placed their orders, Bert and Rosemary got down to their usual discussion about general and specific economic conditions. Like Bert, Rosemary believed that the economy was beginning to slow down but the numbers in her bailiwick didn't seem to provide clear evidence to back up her gut feel. The BLS reports on PPI and CPI continued to show core inflation under control. Of course, the core inflation calculation didn't take into account consumer staples like food, energy or healthcare. Everyone in the country knew that the price of gas, milk, bread, eggs and a trip to the doctor or to the pharmacy was increasing a whole lot more than the modest numbers that his department reported. But every month when the BLS issued its reports, everything seemed manageable. At the same time, their European counterparts seemed to be generating different data and the European Central Bank was obsessed with the threat of inflation and had warned the markets that they would raise interest rates to prevent it from growing beyond their target guidelines.

"Rosemary, I just can't believe that the numbers we are generating can be right. It's really beginning to bother me. I'm even thinking about it at night when I'm trying to go to sleep."

"Have you tried a glass of warm milk or maybe a Scotch before you turn in?"

"I'm serious. Something is wrong with our models or the way we survey or collect data. Maybe it's the algorithms we use to factor in seasonal adjustments. Maybe they're outdated. I don't know, but I can feel it in my bones. I feel like I've got to do something to insure that the numbers I'm signing off on are right."

"Oh boy. You really want to open that can of worms? Can you imagine what the Secretaries are going to say? Maybe you forgot. You're a Democrat, Bert. The next election is less than two years away. You're going to stir up a hornet's nest just so you can sleep better?"

"Believe it or not, this is not about politics. I am legitimately worried. Come on. Deep down you can't believe the numbers either, can you?"

"Look, what we do is not an exact science. I know that's what the nightly news likes to think but look at the systems and the employee network we rely on. Of course the numbers aren't right. We all know that. But I don't think they could be that wrong either."

"I think you're ducking the issue. We owe it to the Departments to make sure that our calculations are correct. It's even in our mission statements. I'm not talking about going to the *Wall Street Journal* or the *Washington Post* with some half-baked theory. I just want to do some internal auditing to satisfy myself that the processes are working correctly. Nobody is going to object to that. It's just following best practices. Christ, every public company does more than we do to represent accuracy in their financial reporting."

"You know we can't do anything without reporting up the chain, even to Ludlow at Treasury. I'm not going on a wild goose chase where the result is my own termination."

"We're not going to get fired for doing the right thing. Would you agree to conduct a similar audit of your processes at ESA and BEA if you got proper sign-off from above?"

"Well, I guess so. But I don't want it to be my idea. We're talking about your insomnia; I sleep like a baby."

"Don't worry, if someone goes nuts, I'll make sure they shoot me. I don't mind the heat, speaking of which how do you like your blackened grouper? Hot enough for you?"

Washington and Guillson finished their lunch, ordered coffee and Bert paid the check. Before they left, they agreed how they would proceed with his idea for an internal audit. Washington would submit an informational memo to the Secretary of Labor, which he had already conveniently prepared, describing his proposed project to conduct an audit of the collection and analytical processes within the BLS. His memo would paint the proposed project as a best practices procedure that could be completed over a four week period. He would suggest that the Department of Commerce conduct a similar review and that he coordinate the project with Guillson to insure the integrity of the outcome. Washington figured that his boss would be less alarmed if the Commerce Department was doing the same thing. No bureaucrat liked to be hung out to dry alone. Washington thought that his boss would go along with his experiment if it didn't appear threatening or assumed a negative outcome. He would have to get Treasury's sign-off as well, although that sign-off was more of a courtesy than a hard prerequisite. When they got up to leave the restaurant, Bert Washington was satisfied that he had accomplished his goal. After lunch, Washington called Hillary Thomas, Treasury Secretary Ludlow's Chief of Staff to let her know he was sending a memo to her boss about the proposed audit process. Washington assumed that if someone was going to object to his idea that he would know about it within twenty-four hours.

Washington was hopeful that he could slip this one by his higher ups if he made the request look strictly procedural. Little did he know that his effort to cure his insomnia would set off a series actions and repercussions that would reach the furthest outposts of the global capital markets.

CHAPTER 8

New York City
February 14, 2007

Valentine's Day marked the official start of New York's spring social season. Every year the New York Society of the Arts had the distinct honor of hosting the kick-off event. The social seasons in New York were effectively spring and fall-based since everyone who could afford it and therefore deemed to be prominent left for Palm Beach in the dead of winter and for the Hamptons in the summer. The New York Society of the Arts was one of the oldest organizations in the city. It had no specific purpose and didn't raise that much money compared to organizations like The Robin Hood Foundation or Memorial Sloane-Kettering Cancer Center, but it was extraordinarily exclusive and attracted the true blue bloods in the city. Only the Frick, the Central Park Conservancy and the Public Library could compete with the crowd that was invited to the New York Society of the Arts gala. This year's dinner chairman and honoree was Harrison Teasedale, the enigmatic senior Partner at Morgan Greenville. Teasedale was chosen for his notoriety on Wall Street and in Washington, D.C. circles as well as for his philanthropic involvements. It didn't hurt that Teasedale and Morgan Greenville were willing to pony up $300,000 for the event and guarantee the purchase of ten premium tables for their clients and investment bankers. After all, charities were about money and Wall Street had a perennial urge to legitimize itself by giving money away in return for social recognition.

Harrison Teasedale was actually a perfect choice by the committee of the Society who chose the annual honoree. His power base on the Street would ensure that the leaders of all his competitors would attend as well as the major players in the private equity and hedge fund worlds. But more important to public relations managers, his connection to the Republican majority in Washington, D.C. would attract certain high level officials from out of town who would not otherwise be seen at a New York social event. In fact, Teasedale had convinced the Secretary of the Treasury, Pennington Ludlow and his wife Anne to fly up from Washington for the evening. Ludlow's appearance in turn would ensure that the Governor, Mayor, and at least one of New York's Senators would show up to be counted among the elite and get their picture in a slew of newspapers and social magazines.

Teasedale, of course, was heavily involved in the dinner's planning. He was a stickler for all details and any event as important as this required his full attention. He reviewed the guest list and seating arrangements to make sure that every consideration was discreetly handled. For instance, he knew that he couldn't seat Tom Flexnord near Stan DiVechio since they were both trying to buy BTS Communications in what was becoming a battle between two of the most powerful private equity titans. Similarly, Jim Flannery, the noted short seller and Greg Joseph, CEO of Computer Solutions would kill each other if seated on the same side of the room since Flannery was waging a public campaign impugning Joseph's accounting treatment for his many acquisitions. Everything had to be perfect and Harrison Teasedale was a perfectionist. Pennington Ludlow had informed Teasedale that he needed two additional tickets for Carmen Gomes and Kurt Denton, his personal security chief from DeSaussure Hall in South Carolina. Teasedale knew about Ludlow's affair with Gomes and thought Ludlow's decision to invite her was madness, but it was Valentine's Day and Ludlow was a considerable risk taker in all his endeavors. Teasedale wasn't a risk taker like Ludlow. He was more Machiavellian and devious. Teasedale would never have invited his lover, but he didn't have one. His sexual pursuits were his deepest secret and he protected them with all his considerable intelligence and resources.

The gala event was being held at Cipriani's on 42nd Street between Park and Lexington Avenues. The building was the site of a former bank and the room, which holds about 500 people, had ceilings that seemed at least eighty feet tall. The tables were magnificently set with an endless array of crystal. A single red rose adorned each place setting. The Valentine motif was everywhere but in an elegant and understated display. Kirby Haines was hosting a table and Hillary Thomas had arrived on the Shuttle earlier that afternoon to prepare for the evening. Peter and Sam Bolger and three other couples with Morgan Greenville credentials filled out Haines' table.

Upon their arrival, the guests were met by a phalanx of waiters who took each couple's outerwear with exquisite efficiency and then directed them to stations where organizers where handing out table assignments. Once registered, the guests were greeted by another wave of waiters offering champagne, Bellinis and cosmopolitans. The outside temperature was cold and the wind chill was numbing, but inside Cipriani's it was warm and energized. Despite the season, many of the women favored strapless or backless dresses. They were creating their own heat for the crowd. It was as if everyone had been waiting for this party since well before Thanksgiving and they were ready for a night of revelry.

When Pennington and Anne Ludlow arrived, one might have guessed that Madonna had entered the building. Flashes bounced off the dazzle that emanated from all the reflective surfaces in the room. People stopped and tried to observe what was happening. Ludlow was the country's chief economic leader and he was the star of the moment. Everything in the hall echoed opulence and he was one of the chief architects of all the value that had been created over the last five years for the benefit of the wealthy people in attendance. If President Lowery was the king of his "Economic Revolution" then Ludlow was his prince of prosperity. After greeting many of the guests who crowded around him and his wife upon their arrival, Ludlow headed toward the bar in the ante-room that was reserved for VIPs at this already ultra exclusive dinner. After retrieving a glass of champagne for his wife and a vodka martini for himself, Ludlow spied Harrison Teasdale who was surrounded by Morgan Greenville customers and trading partners. Teasedale caught Ludlow's eye almost at the same time.

"Mr. Secretary, how wonderful for you to make it to New York this evening. I hope all of your accommodations are in order. Anne looks simply beautiful."

"Harrison, great to see you. Congratulations on your recognition tonight. Long overdue. I rather enjoy a visit to New York every now and again, especially when I don't have to address the Bond Club or trek from one bank to another in rapid fire." Ludlow's attempt at casualness was greeted by a hearty laughs from those sycophants trying to make an impression. "Tonight is all about having a good time and it's Valentine's Day to boot. It's a great evening, don't you all agree?" The group of men surrounding Teasedale and Ludlow nodded like a herd of goats.

"Gentlemen, can you excuse tonight's honoree for a few moments. I need to speak with Harrison in private. I won't keep him from you but for a few moments."

Ludlow and Teasedale moved to the far corner of the ante-room so that they could have a moment to catch up alone. Earlier in the afternoon, Hillary Thomas had informed Ludlow about the memo he had received from Bert Washington, the Commissioner who ran the Bureau of Labor Statistics. Ludlow did not know Washington personally and had no reason to recognize the name except for the fact that he knew Washington was an African American whom the President had appointed to his current position. Ludlow kept a place in his brain for outliers.

Washington's memo had informed Ludlow as a matter of protocol that Washington had sought approval from his boss at the Labor Department to conduct an internal audit of the data collection and analyzing processes employed by his department. His memo also stated that the ESA and BEA within the Commerce Department would conduct a similar audit. Thomas told Ludlow that Washington was trying to employ best practices and that there was no evidence or reason to believe that anything was amiss. Ludlow clearly did not like the idea but realized that his objection to a best practices exercise would look suspicious or too hands on. Thomas had asked him if he was okay with Washington's exercise and he replied that he had no objection but didn't understand why someone would want to waste their time if everything appeared to be in order. Ludlow asked Thomas to stay involved and keep him informed of Washington's project. As was standard procedure, Ludlow had sent an encrypted message to Bob Fletcher informing him of this recent development after Thomas had informed him earlier that afternoon. Nothing ever went to President Lowery directly. It was Fletcher's responsibility to inform the President, when required.

"Listen Harrison, what I am about to tell you is sensitive—probably more sensitive in some ways than the information you usually receive. The Department of Labor and Commerce are going to be conducting an internal audit of their data collection and analyzing processes over the next four or five weeks. I have no reason to believe that this is anything more than a standard review, but I think you should know it and I want you to be extra cautious in your trading while the audit is being performed."

"I don't understand how this has any bearing on our trading. First, all of our protocols are air-tight and this type of audit has nothing to do with trading patterns. It all sounds internal to me. Frankly, I'm glad someone in Washington cares about the accuracy of the numbers announced every week. I just like to see them first." Teasedale was smiling but Ludlow was not.

"You're most likely right. Still, I want to you to be careful. That probably sounds funny coming from me, but you know how a worm crawling up the trunk of a tree can ruin a perfectly good apple. Let's just keep an eye on this worm."

Teasedale was flush with exuberance for the evening and his position of primary focus. Ludlow could have told him that his Maserati was on fire and Teasedale would have shrugged it off. Ludlow had no intention of telling Teasedale why he was concerned. Teasedale thought their game only involved getting advance information and trading profitably. He had no idea that the economic data that he was being fed was a fiction.

"Harrison, enjoy the evening. It seems like a grand event. I'm going to have some fun and catch up with some old friends. I'll see you again before we leave."

At promptly 7:45 P.M., the Cipriani staff began to push the elite to their tables. Evenings like this were designed to end promptly at 10:00 P.M. and there was truffle-filled ravioli and beef tenderloin to be served before dancing and Harrison Teasedale's brief speech. Kirby Haines and his dinner guests took their seats in a festive mood. A couple of cocktails before dinner had elevated them. Over their first course of cloud-like ravioli they sipped white wine and talked about the March ski trip to Vail that Kirby and Hillary were taking with the Bolger's. They had decided to rent two suites at the Sonnenalp Resort and had scheduled massages everyday at 5:30 P.M. after their après ski margaritas. They'd rent their equipment locally at Gorsuch and avoid the hassle of lugging out skis and boots. Sam had already made dinner reservations at the best new hot spots and old reliables. Everything was done and it would be first class. Kirby had even reserved his favorite ski instructor, Christian, an Austrian god on the slopes. Things were good.

Hillary Thomas was stunning that evening. She wore a floor length red dress with a tight bodice that held her round and medium sized breasts in place. The dress featured a slit up the right leg to allow for comfortable movement given its narrow design. Hillary had gorgeous legs that still maintained some of the Bajan tan that she had acquired during her stay in Barbados over New Years. She was always slightly uncomfortable around Kirby and his friends when they talked about money and the extravagances they could afford. They were all on top of the world and Morgan Greenville was the investment bank of the moment. Kirby and Peter had this swagger that nothing could stop them. Their fate was in their hands and only good was coming their way. With the talk of vacation planning over, the group moved on to politics, the economy and President Lowery's extraordinary track record over the last six years.

"Negativity always creeps into the market after three or four years of a good run."

"The shorts have to make money every once in a while. They figure now's as good a time as any to stir up the shit."

"Hillary, you sit at the seat of power. How long do you think the economy can keep chugging along at this pace?"

"Well, Peter, who really knows for sure."

"Sounds like a lawyer's answer; no, more like a candidate's answer to me."

"Look, I am optimistic of course but the market is knowledgeable and analyzes lots of information to come up with its view of value. In the last couple weeks, the market seems worried about the sustainability of Lowery's 'Economic Revolution.' I'm not worried myself, but my opinion doesn't really matter. Folks like Alan Solomon or Pennington Ludlow can move the market with their actions or signals, but ultimately the market takes in all the data available to it and makes its own call."

"Ah, spoken like a true Efficient Market theorist. Brava!"

"Please! I'm just a lawyer. It's prudent to realize that all good things can come to an end for a myriad of reasons, many of which are beyond our control."

Hillary always had to be the voice of reason when she got together with Kirby and Peter. They were the wide-eyed optimists who were making way too much money and enjoying every minute of it. They were intelligent enough to understand the nuances that affected economies, like interest rates, inflation or the cost of labor, but in big up markets they were as giddy as teenagers.

"Hillary, you're such a buzz kill. Just because things are great doesn't mean they have turn negative."

"I don't disagree. I'm just saying that the market ultimately dictates valuation through its confidence in the future. Look, just today a colleague of mine at the Department of Labor decided to review the underlying processes they use to calculate the jobs report. One of our responsibilities is to give the markets confidence that the information we release is accurate and reflects the real economic conditions across the nation."

"That's great Hillary, even noble. But the numbers are great, have been great and will be great as long as the Republicans control the agenda! The only thing I worry about is who is going to replace Chuck Lowery."

Thomas immediately regretted the words that had slipped out of her mouth. It wasn't like her to speak out of school, but a few glasses of wine had knocked down her guard. She never talked about internal Treasury Department work or anything that had to do with policy in front of Kirby, yet alone Peter Bolger. The good news was that everyone at the table had had more to drink than her. No one would probably remember her comments about the internal audit and the inference that the government itself was checking the validity of its own pronouncements. She had no reason to believe that it was anything other than best practices. She just thought the disclosure of such a review would be misinterpreted by political enemies who had an ax to grind. She was grateful when the waiters surrounded their table with large platters of beef tenderloin, French cut string beans, and heart shaped pipettes of potato puree. Kirby Haines motioned to one of the waiters stationed nearby, "Could I bother you for two more bottles of red?" Full table discussion was temporarily suspended as the carnivores fed.

Holding the gala on Valentine's Day brought out many of the City's most beautiful women, but one in particular stood out and she was imported. Carmen Gomes had caught the eye of every man at the party at one point or another during the evening. It wasn't her incredible good looks alone. She wore an outfit that made every woman mad. While everyone else was in a long gown, Carmen had chosen a short black dress that showed a lot of her perfect brown legs. The dress was completely backless and the back bottom barely covered the top of her firm, upward tilting buttocks. She obviously was not wearing a bra and her full round breasts pressed against the fitted top. She was beyond sexy. Her shoulder length brown hair bounced as she walked, and the rest of her bounced in perfect sequence. It was obvious that her acute sensuality was upsetting to some of the older society doyens who still found her irresistible to watch.

Carmen was a car crash waiting to happen. She loved New York and the energy of the event that evening. Her walker was

Kurt Denton, the muscular chief of security for Ludlow's South Carolina plantation. After three glasses of champagne, her Latina DNA kicked in and she asked Kurt to dance. As the waiters began to clear the main course, Carmen and Kurt walked to the middle of the open floor. Almost immediately, 500 pairs of eyes turned to notice. Carmen found it erotic to dance in front of so many men but she was really performing for Pennington Ludlow. Carmen was a natural and graceful dancer. The orchestra leader sensed the moment and changed his musical selection to a salsa. Carmen drew closer to Kurt, pressing her hips against his groin as they moved in unison to a faster beat. Everyone with any testosterone was fascinated.

Pennington Ludlow was watching too, but excused himself to his wife Anne and table guests to get up and stretch his legs. He walked out to the bar to get a fresh glass of wine and ran into the Mayor who was on a similar mission.

"Mr. Mayor. How's your golf game?"

"I actually played last weekend at Lyford Cay. Absolutely awful golf but beautiful weather."

"I always enjoy Lyford, but I'm more of a hunter, as you know."

When the band finished with the salsa, Carmen was hot and flushed from her performance. Ludlow had told her about a secure meeting room off the bar area that had been reserved for him in case of an emergency or need to communicate in private with someone at the party or by telephone with Washington, D.C. As Kurt Denton led her back to their table, she excused herself to freshen up and headed toward the VIP bar. As she passed through the nearly empty bar area, she caught Ludlow's eye who was still chatting with the Mayor. She put her fingers to her mouth and licked them as she grabbed the doorknob and walked through the entrance of the private room. Showing a modicum of discretion, Ludlow finished up his conversation, giving himself two or three minutes before pursuing his urge. When Ludlow entered the private room, Carmen was on him in seconds. She was decidedly horny as a result of the champagne, her exercise on the dance floor and the fact that hundreds of men wanted to fuck her at that moment. Ludlow grabbed her and drove his hands down the back of her dress. Carmen was biting his ear and groped him as he got hard. Even though Anne Ludlow was no more than 100 yards away at their table, Ludlow could not resist Carmen's body. Ludlow pulled off her dress leaving her naked except for her thong and high heels. Her nipples were large and hard. She deftly unhooked his belt and pulled down his pants. She was on her knees. Ludlow closed his eyes as he enjoyed her talent.

While Ludlow and Gomes mauled each other, Kirby Haines was getting physical with Hillary under their table. He rubbed her thigh slowly. Hillary had promised him to forget to wear something and Kirby was excited to discover that five weeks later she was a women of her word. His hand moved further up her thigh and he gently fingered her mound. Hillary spread her legs just slightly to give him more access. Kirby enjoyed the concept of getting away with sex in plain view, simply because no one would suspect it in such a public place. The group's conversation carried on as normal but beneath the table Kirby and Hillary were rubbing each other toward orgasm. Their lustful kinkiness was an important part of their relationship. Just after they first met, they consummated their sexual attraction in a private telephone room off the Partners' boardroom at Frost, McIntire & Smelser. Their desires led them to spontaneous sex in bathrooms at parties, on the beach, on the terrace of hotel rooms, and almost anywhere else. Hillary was turned on by his audacity, and she liked the sensation of her sexual power when she felt him aroused.

Ludlow's tryst with Gomes lasted about ten minutes. He had finished himself off as he bent her over the back of sofa. He quickly put himself back together, his heart pumping. Carmen lay on the sofa, completely naked except for her heels and Ludlow kissed her gently on her lips and told her he would see her again as soon as he returned to Washington, D.C. and Anne left town. Carmen nodded, her eyes half closed as she continued to feel the physical effects of her passion as she rubbed herself. As Ludlow closed the door of the private room, he signaled to Kurt Denton who had positioned himself nearby. Denton's job was to escort Carmen back to the hotel where he had made arrangements for her to stay. Denton entered the room and found her on the sofa. She motioned to him realizing that she was barely satisfied with Ludlow's performance. Carmen was like a distance runner and a ten minute sprint was not enough for her. She needed a second helping and seducing Kurt Denton was not a problem, nor was it their first session. Denton was a physical specimen, all muscle and leanness. Gomes dragged her nails down his hard chest. He lifted her up and carried her over and up against the wall. Carmen liked it rough and Kurt Denton could give her what Pennington Ludlow could not.

Harrison Teasedale's speech during the dessert course was short and gracious. He dutifully thanked the New York Society of the Arts and all of the evening's benefactors and honored guests, especially Secretary Ludlow, now seated once again with his wife. As Teasedale returned to his table, the orchestra played "New York, New York" and hands reached out to shake his and offer congratulations, but Teasedale was already thinking about tomorrow's trades and how Ludlow's message of caution was not going to affect his modus operandi. He had made a tidy profit for Ludlow, himself and Morgan Greenville using his advanced access to the January numbers. His long positions increased nicely in value as the shorts raced to cover their losing bets. His instinct told him the shorts would re-place their negative bets in February trusting that the economy would turn down sooner rather than later. Teasedale knew they were wrong. He looked around the room at the opulence in place. He had no reason to doubt the long lasting benefits of President Lowery's "Economic Revolution." The last five or six years had been good to every rich American. Apartment prices in Manhattan had more than tripled and homes in the Hamptons had skyrocketed. Contractors were so busy that you couldn't find a plumber if you needed one. Teasedale couldn't make sense of Ludlow's concern. There was nothing wrong with the numbers being broadcast by the government's agencies. He only cared that he continued to make easy money taking the bullish bet against a growing sentiment of negativism that was creeping into the market. Teasedale liked the naysayers. They made it easy for him to win big for himself, his firm and for Pennington Ludlow.

CHAPTER 9

Washington, D.C.
February 18, 2007

President Chuck Lowery's G8 triumph over Podrochov and his decadent stay in Sardinia were a distant memory although only five weeks had passed. On the morning of February 18th, Lowery was in a particularly sour mood. In public, the President carried himself with the swagger of a conquering hero but in private, at times like these, he showed his penchant for petulance. Things were supposed to go his way and he didn't like it when they didn't.

Lowery had risen before 5:00 A.M. for his regular, strenuous workout. On the treadmill, his mood darkened. The Asian markets had crashed overnight, dropping nearly 5% on fears of a slowing US economy. He placed a call to Bob Fletcher and told him to fly up that morning from Florida for a face-to-face. The European markets were taking Asia's lead, showing across-the-board declines in all the major country indices. The way Lowery saw it, the world was beginning to bet against him. Vast sums of speculative capital were predicting that GDP for the fourth quarter would be weaker than anticipated when released next week. He ran faster on the treadmill, pushing himself as his heart pounded harder.

When Lowery cooled off from his forty minute run, he realized that he just wasn't mad. He was worried. He could feel the footsteps of his enemies catching up to him. He had started his "Economic Revolution" six years ago with the goal of restoring America to its rightful position as the economic leader of the Free World. He was fighting a war that would determine the American way of life in the future. The way he saw it, the choices were stark: win the war and prosper for generations to come, or lose the war and watch America slowly decline to second class status. Chuck Lowery, like a good soldier, understood the potential outcomes, but there was only one choice and defeat was not it.

When Chuck Lowery was inaugurated in January 2001, the mood of the country was sinking. China was supplanting US manufacturers' market share with an endless supply of cheap labor and millions of US workers had lost their jobs. Our European allies no longer respected us. They argued with our policies and voted against us in the United Nations. Chuck Lowery entered office recognizing that the US was in an unconventional struggle for survival fought not on a battle field but in every major financial market around the world. Capital was fleeing the United States. He knew there was only one reason to fight a war. He had learned that lesson in Viet Nam. When he took possession of the Oval Office, he knew he would do whatever it took to win.

President Lowery launched his "Economic Revolution" 60 days after he took office. His revolution was all about cutting taxes; pumping money into the economy to spur investment and create jobs; and building up the morale of his troops—the US

consumer. He thought that if he could rally their allegiance, support, and participation, that he would raise the US economy back
to its rightful position as the beacon for capitalism. In the early
days after his inauguration, Lowery convened a meeting of his
three most trusted advisors who were both loyal and committed
to his mission. They devised a multi-faceted plan and the tactics
to press the President's revolution. Pennington Ludlow, the new
Secretary of the Treasury, would spearhead a legislative initiative
aimed at reducing the tax burden on every American—especially
those with capital to invest. Alan Solomon, the Chairman of the
Federal Reserve, would lead the stimulus initiative that required
the steady reduction of interest rates. As Fed Chairman, Solomon
was required to work independently of the Executive Branch, but
Pennington Ludlow's video of Solomon's tryst with Carmen Gomes
insured Solomon's cooperation with President Lowery's mission.
Solomon acquiesced to the threat and forcefully cut interest rates
over a three year period until capital was essentially free for anyone
who wanted it. Lowery's revolution required an enormous amount
of stimulus, and Ludlow and Solomon were the public catalysts of
that strategy.

President Lowery's first two initiatives to lower taxes and reduce
interest rates were fairly straightforward but not necessarily dunk
shots. His third initiative was far more difficult and dangerous. For
Pennington Ludlow and Alan Solomon to be successful, they needed
the ammunition to convince the Congress on the one hand, and
the Fed Governors on the other that the actions they were taking
were supported by the performance of the broader economy. The
only way the President could provide that proof was to supply the
evidence himself. Well not quite by himself. Luckily for Lowery,
the third member of his inner circle was Bob Fletcher. Fletcher
was the only man with the resources to pull off Chuck Lowery's
third initiative.

Bob Fletcher's private company, Marine Logistics Inc., was a secret society of former CIA operatives and Navy Seal veterans. His business dealings in rogue states and lawless regions required a pool of managers and employees who were highly trained, disciplined and loyal. Fletcher's business success relied on bribes, extortion and intimidation. A Harvard MBA was useless in places like Syria or Ukraine. To be successful at Marine Logistics you had to have brains, brawn and guts. Fletcher had built his team without a weak link. Fletcher and his small army were responsible for leading Lowery's third initiative that called for the infiltration of the Department of Labor and Commerce. Specifically, Fletcher's men would obtain positions at the Bureau of Labor Statistics and at the Bureau of Economic Analysis. Fletcher estimated that his mission would require approximately 30 professionals who would obtain jobs as senior analysts, IT specialists and regional managers. The team had to be in positions where data was being aggregated so that its manipulation would be easier to execute. Once the raw data was manipulated and passed up through the layers of bureaucratic over-sight, the senior officials responsible for final review and approval would have no basis for questioning the calculations. Their mission was a delicate one. They could not sledge-hammer their solution. The numbers had to be massaged and their work could not be discoverable. As the markets absorbed their refined data, President Lowery's "Economic Revolution" would become a self-fulfilling prophecy as the army of US consumers spent the country into economic growth and prosperity. President Lowery's plan worked like a dream. As Lowery's approval ratings soared, Fletcher's army made sure the drip of disinformation kept flowing into the arms of the US consumers and capital markets investors.

After showering, Chuck Lowery called his chief of staff, Horace Grant and told him to get Pennington Ludlow and Alan Solomon to his private residence by 9:00 A.M. Fletcher would have landed by then. As Lowery picked at his breakfast, he knew that his "Economic Revolution" was losing steam and perhaps more importantly, could be at risk of being exposed. The US consumers had done their patriotic part over the last six years. They had borrowed and spent in a pattern never seen before, believing that the economy would grow without pause. They had borrowed against the inflated value of their homes. They had borrowed using their credit cards, and when they reached their borrowing limits, they opened new credit card accounts. They borrowed to buy new cars. And they borrowed to make investments, believing that the market would reach new highs every month. They were obsessed with life style "reality" shows and hung on every word that came out of the talking heads on financial news channels like CNBC. But they had been completely bamboozled; led to the edge of the financial cliff and a mob was growing behind them, forcing the nearest ones over the edge.

By the time 9:00 A.M. rolled around, Chuck Lowery was fully pissed off. His team had successfully manipulated nearly every piece of economic information released into the market place over the last six years, and now he needed to know how to deal with the tsunami of hurt that seemed to be building on the United States' beach-front economy. His excellent plan and execution was threatening to unravel, and with it, his legacy as the greatest modern American President in the post World War II era. Ludlow, Solomon and Fletcher entered the President's private dining room.

"I wish I could say 'good morning' and mean it, but I can't. What the fuck is going on? The markets are suddenly getting crushed and the Today Show is starting to notice. Pundits are talking about bubbles and questioning our 'Economic Revolution.' I don't like it. I don't like it at all. And I want answers—fast."

Alan Solomon thought it best to level-set the meeting with an assessment of the current environment and he came to the meeting armed with a file folder full of information. As he talked, Solomon presented a comprehensive summary of US and world-wide economic performance over the last two years. He used the "real" numbers, not the manipulated data that had been fed for public consumption. It wasn't pretty.

"Mr. President, as you know the US economy is weak and weaker than the general market thinks. Real inflation is accelerating and the nation is severely over-leveraged. The Federal Government's deficit as a percentage of GDP is approaching its highest level at any time in the last 40 years. On top of that, the consumer has effectively tapped out its borrowing capacity and the net worth assumptions supporting their debt will decline if asset valuations drop, particularly the value of their homes."

"Goddammit Solomon, I don't need a fucking weather report to tell that it's raining outside. I want to know what we can do about it."

"Mr. President, if you let me continue, I believe there are three scenarios that we must consider as potential outcomes over the next 18–24 months given the factual basis characterizing the current environment. I want to emphasize that I do not believe we are facing a 90–120 day melt down. Once we understand those scenarios, we can consider our options. Scenario One is the most benign of the three but is not good. Our projections under that scenario predict a mild recession, beginning in six months that lasts two quarters and is followed by a slow recovery. As you leave office Mr. President, the first signs of recovery might be visible, but the political campaign would be over at that point and any positives going forward would be credited to the next President. Scenario Three is the most troubling model and has significant negative implications. We believe this worst case scenario is characterized by a deep six quarter recession, beginning in three to six months and followed by years of stagflation—very much like the Japanese post-boom period that lasted more than a decade. Such an outcome would include a record number of corporate bankruptcies and the failure of several major banking institutions and thousands of local and regional banks. We believe unemployment could approach 13%, but would go higher if the recession lasted longer than 18 months. The Second Scenario simply lies somewhere in the middle, not quite as bad as the worst case outcome but more painful than the first."

"Alan, you've painted a picture that seems inevitable. It's like we're sitting on a beach waiting for the tidal wave to roll us over. How much time do we have until the wave hits and what can we do to change its direction?"

"Mr. President, the timing is really a matter of conjecture. At this point, we continue to produce numbers that obfuscate the reality of our economic condition. If we continue with that strategy, we will build up a tremendous amount of pressure, like flood water building up behind a dam—I think it's a better metaphor. When the truth finally comes out, the markets will crack or perhaps implode like the dam would. The magnitude of the destruction would be immeasurable and a mere guess on my part. But the outcome would impugn your Presidency and put us at great personal risk. Such a sudden reversal of fortune would clearly lead to a focus by economists and reporters that would be unprecedented. People would demand answers."

"Okay. I understand that. What are our other choices?"

"The world markets are just beginning to speculate about the staying power of the current US economic boom. What occurred last night in Asia is a symptom of speculative excess. Those traders have no fundamental basis for their selling since we've given them none. We could begin to expose the weakness more gradually, producing numbers that are not quite accurate but directionally more revealing. The markets would drop but the extremis would be controlled. I frankly think that's our only choice."

The minds of Lowery, Ludlow and Fletcher were all racing. They had heard everything that Alan Solomon had said but they were focusing on the one bit of information that Alan Solomon did not possess: their individual trading schemes that had taken advantage of the disinformation fed into the market over the last six years. They had billions of dollars at risk in long positions that anticipated continued economic strength. Whatever decision they made in this meeting would have significant implications on their personal wealth and on the risks they would face in safe-guarding their ill-gotten gains. None of them had anticipated the threat that confronted them now. They had all hoped that President Lowery would finish his last two years, continuing to enjoy the economic vibrancy that had characterized his Presidency. They had not anticipated all of the consequences of his "Economic Revolution." Historical low tax rates and no-cost borrowing had created numerous bubbles throughout the economy. Up to now, most people hadn't noticed them because a bubble of naïve exuberance had taken everyone in. Now all of these bubbles posed significant risks. They had limited choices, if any.

"Ludlow, you've been completely silent. That's certainly not like you. What the hell do you think?"

"Well, Mr. President. I'm honestly not sure. Alan's proposition seems to make the most sense, but I'm not sure the risks are any less. His message is we don't have two years. If that's true—something we'll have to decide—then manipulating the data toward a more truthful representation is a reasonable course."

"Fletcher, what about you?"

"Look Chuck, we've fucked around with the numbers successfully for the last six years. We did it when things were worse than reality and we did it when things were fine. I'm not sure why we don't try to ride this out. You've only got two years left and the next campaign will be well underway in twelve months. We've got lots of guys to blame this on—the Chinese, Saudis, Al Qaeda. Why are we about to fall on our own sword? We've got to keep rates low and keep pumping air into the tire so that this leak doesn't turn into a blow-out."

Lowery knew Fletcher would never accept defeat. Alan Solomon shook his head in his professorial way.

"Bob, the systemic issues underlying this potential crisis are much, much bigger than China's currency policy or OPEC's desire to control the production of oil. If we continue to fictionalize the state of the US economy, we will only create a larger crisis of confidence in the US economy and in our governmental system itself. We all know that the cover-up is always worse than the crime. We have to begin to course correct or we risk ruining America and its standing in the world for generations to come."

"Okay gentleman. I've heard enough this morning, but I still don't like the alternatives. I want you to leave here and come up with some other solutions fast. I'm taking nothing off the table but I want some other choices. Pennington, that means you too."

CHAPTER 10

Washington, D.C.
February 18, 2007

Pennington Ludlow and Alan Solomon got up without a word and opened the door to a hallway that led from the President's private residence to an elevator that would take them downstairs to the White House rear exit. As they left, Bob Fletcher got up from his chair and kicked the door closed behind them. He and Lowery had some planning to do. They needed to figure out how to safeguard the trading fortunes they had accumulated and Fletcher was already pondering how they could take advantage of the impending up-heaval that would eventually turn every bull into a market bear.

"Let's get Desmond on the line. We need our own analysis. Alan Solomon is the grim reaper. We've got a group of high priced brains in Dublin so let's put them to work." Within minutes, Fletcher had established a secure video link to his trading operation in Dublin.

"How was your lunch Monroe?"

"Took it early, thanks. Lots of volatility, in every market. We hit a few rough patches but generally speaking we're doing okay. I've kept the hedges at a minimum given the outlook for the data you've been feeding us. I'm only 10% short so my longs got hammered last night in Asia. Same thing in Europe today. The futures market in your neck of the woods isn't too rosy either."

"Monroe, it's Lowery. Make it easy for me—are we making any fucking money today or not?"

"We're down a little bit, sir. But we're not worried. As long as the data you give us is consistent with what you announce, we should be fine."

"Listen Monroe, the President and I are getting a little concerned about the broader market sentiment. The speculative money is beginning to bet against us and the problem is they're right. We need you and your team to begin to drive some scenario analysis for us. We're considering giving the speculators what they want, maybe in small doses over time. The economy is weakening and prices are inflating, no matter what we report. The macro outcome we can't live with is some cataclysmic crash. We need to decide how we should best proceed. But we need you to tell us how much time you need to liquidate our long trades and whether you can set up a new strategy to take advantage of the weakening economy and the data we will dribble out that confirms that speculation. What do you say, Monroe? Can you do that for us? And how long do you need?"

"Well, I'll figure that out, right? The next big announcement is GDP next week. I take it that that number is not going to change at this point. Is that correct?"

"That's right. We're not going to fuck with anything right away. I want to aim before I fire. It usually works better that way."

"Got you, sir. Okay, let us work on some things here. I will assume that we have six to eight weeks to execute the reversal of our longest duration bets. Any new strategies to take advantage of a new direction in information can be made quickly once you determine when that operation will start. Does that sound right?"

"Yeah, that works. Let's start turning things to cash. Do we have capacity in the accounts you've established to accept the proceeds you'll generate?"

"Yes sir, we'll set up more secondary accounts as well. I've got feet on the street in Dubai setting up new options there as well."

"Okay, Monroe. That sounds fine. Get your guys cracking and give me an update in 72 hours. There is a lot of money at stake and we've got to be careful not to make any mistakes that draw attention to our trading patterns."

"I think we have enough time to ensure that we avoid that trap."

"Monroe, I don't want to know what you think. I want to know that it's done."

"Yes sir. It will be done. Out."

The video screen went black and Fletcher and Lowery were satisfied that Desmond and his band of quantitative experts were doing what they do best. Now they had to make some important decisions and needed time to reflect on their next move. The President was focused on his economic team that had left the meeting minutes earlier.

"I want you to start keeping a closer eye on Ludlow and Solomon."

"What's up?"

"I'm not sure. Ludlow seemed distracted. If things get tough, I want to make sure that he stays on the team."

"I can take care of that. What about Solomon?"

"Same thing but I'm less concerned. He's knee deep in this shit and doesn't have any alternatives."

As Ludlow and Solomon left President Lowery's private residence and walked down the hallway, they heard the door slam behind them. When they passed an open coat closet, Solomon grabbed Ludlow by the arm and pulled him inside.

"This has gone too far. You forced me into this scheme and now it's going to end badly. I'm not going down alone when this ship sinks. You're going down with me."

"Calm down Alan. You're losing it. Nothing has happened and nothing is going to happen. If you go off the reservation now, it will all fall around your neck. Do you have any intuition left in your old brain? Bob Fletcher is ruthless, and he will protect Chuck Lowery at all costs. If you open your mouth, bad things may happen. Don't be a fool. Get your shit together."

"I've given my life to this country and I've made you rich as well. It might as well be over for me. I sacrificed my principles to protect my marriage. You've used me. I really won't care what happens to you when this whole mess implodes."

"Listen to me. Nothing is going to happen. Nothing! We have plenty of time to get this right. Washington, D.C. is the capital of scapegoats and if this was to end badly and someone takes a fall it won't be you, me or Chuck Lowery. I give you my word on that."

"I don't know what to do. I'm upset. We didn't plan for this. It wasn't in our models. You told me it would be simple, but it's turned very complex. We've corrupted the economic system and for what?"

"We did it for our country, you ass. For our children and their children. Don't you remember what it was like six years ago? We've made America great again."

"We may just have done the opposite despite Lowery's best intentions."

"Let's let history be the judge, Alan. I suggest you calm down and go back to work. We have time to consider our options. Whatever we think is the right option today will undoubtedly seem wrong tomorrow after reflection."

"I'll give it time but I've got a bad feeling. We have to correct things. Following the path we've been on is a non-starter. Bob Fletcher may be rich but he knows nothing about the world's capital markets."

"You're probably right, but I wouldn't argue with a man like Fletcher. Even if you're right, you'll lose. Let's leave separately. I'll call you later after you've cooled down. Nothing's going to happen."

Letting Solomon leave before him, Ludlow called his administrative assistant and told her he was running late and to cancel his next two appointments. He would get back on schedule after lunch. His next call was to his driver to alert him that he would be down in three minutes. Ludlow had to get back to the office quickly and speak with Harrison Teasedale. Their conversation at the New York Society of the Arts dinner had put Teasedale on notice that he had to proceed cautiously while the idiotic internal audit moved ahead. Now he had to tell him more. He had to tell him that their plan was changing. He needed to raise cash fast and exit those trades that would turn decidedly down when more accurate financial data started to enter the general market. He knew he had time, but he had a lot to do over the short-term. On his way back to the office, Ludlow weighed the pluses and minuses of bringing Teasedale completely over the wall. Teasedale didn't realize that the information he was trading on was incorrect, just that he knew about it before anyone else. Ludlow quickly rejected the idea of telling Teasedale more. If he needed a scapegoat, he knew Harrison Teasedale would make a perfect choice. When he got to his office, Ludlow told his administrative assistant to hold his calls. He closed his door and dialed Teasedale on a secure line. After a brief moment, Teasedale got on the line, still gushing from his honor the prior week.

"Pennington, hello there. Thanks again for attending the gala. You and Anne were most gracious to come."

"It was our pleasure, but I'm calling about our business and it's important. I want you to start liquidating my long positions. My folks are telling me that we may be entering a rough patch and the upcoming jobs reports are likely to show some weakness."

"I'm happy to do what you want, but why don't we just use that data when it's available to make the right bets like we always do?"

"I'm more concerned with locking in the profits that we've made. I know you've done very well playing the long end of the curve and in the illiquid stuff we've accumulated. I would just feel better if we started to turn those gains into cash. We're seeing large flows of speculative capital taking the negative view. I just don't want to get caught on the wrong side of the tape."

"But what about the GDP number next week. Your information suggests it will be strong again. That is the number that's going to be released, correct?"

"Yes, that number is solid. But it's a fourth quarter number. I'm more concerned with what this year's numbers are going to show. If the trend begins to disappoint the market, we'll get a big sell-off and we'll regret not taking our profits now."

"Okay, Pennington. I've got it. I still plan on making money on the GDP announcement. The shorts are going to get killed again and I'm not going to miss it. I will separately begin to raise cash. But you know we have a mammoth amount of profits. It's going to take some time to move all that shit and I don't want to queer the markets."

Pennington Ludlow thought that an ironic use of the infinitive by Teasedale. He had to be careful not to go too much further in his reasoning with him. He knew that Teasedale had been using the information he obtained to not only make a fortune for himself but also for Morgan Greenville. If Morgan Greenville started raising cash, it would certainly be noticed by the markets.

"Harrison, you've got to be careful. We can't afford sloppy execution. I don't want questions raised. Do you understand?"

"Perfectly. I'll get things going and let me know about next month's jobs report as soon as you can. We can make money in any market."

Ludlow was sure of that. But he wasn't necessarily focused on making more money. He had already made billions. He was more concerned about making sure that that money was still there when he left office in two years.

"Okay, Harrison. Let's get going. I want to know how you're proceeding at every moment. This is a delicate operation so no sharp moves. Call me tomorrow."

After Ludlow hung up, Teasedale placed the phone back in its holder. He still couldn't understand Ludlow's high level of concern. A slowdown in GDP growth over the next four quarters was not going to kill their golden goose today. Liquidating the long and illiquid trades seemed pretty extreme. Teasedale wondered whether Ludlow was being completely honest or telling him less than he knew. Morgan Greenville had borrowed heavily to balloon its balance sheet. At Teasedale's insistence they had increased their daily trading loss tolerance and his risk trading had made every Partner at Morgan Greenville very rich. Teasedale decided that he couldn't guess Ludlow's motivation with certainty. He would discern that in time. He did know one thing. The fourth quarter GDP number was going to be better than expected and a lot of money was betting that it would disappoint. Teasedale loved that dynamic. Given his uncertainty regarding Ludlow's message, he would bet heavier than normal next week and score big. After that he would follow Ludlow's instructions. One thing that he knew about Pennington Ludlow was that he took care of himself first, without fail. If Ludlow wanted to sell his illiquid and long dated bets, then Morgan Greenville would do the same. Teasedale had gotten rich following Ludlow's lead. He was not about to bet against him.

CHAPTER 11

Washington, D.C.
February 18, 2007

While President Lowery was holding his war room session with Ludlow, Solomon and Fletcher, Bert Washington was holding his own meeting at 2 Massachusetts Avenue. Having gotten the okay from the Secretary of Labor and a less than convincing endorsement from Secretary Ludlow at Treasury, Washington had pushed Rosemary Guillson to get approval from her boss at the Commerce Department as well. Washington's applied logic to his superior was that the audit would be over sooner if they started earlier. It was hard to argue with his point. No one particularly liked the idea, but the arguments he articulated were not worth fighting over. He stressed they he didn't expect to find anything wrong in the system—a conjecture that he didn't really believe—and checking the box on process controls was something that would make the Department look good when Congress haggled over their budget next year. With their tacit approvals, Washington had called a high level organizational meeting at his office that morning. Hillary Thomas, at Secretary Ludlow's insistence, attended the meeting and stayed involved in the process and Washington didn't object. He figured the Republican administration was not going to let two Democratic civil servants handle something as sensitive as this without oversight.

At 9:15 A.M. with fresh cups of coffee, Bert Washington began his meeting with Rosemary Guillson and Hillary Thomas. Washington asked one of his Associate Commissioners, Beverly Bitner, to join the group as a project leader, and Guillson brought along Ken Shue in the same capacity. Bitner had been with the BLS longer than Bert Washington. She was an accountant by training and had worked in various functions at the Bureau, including as a leader of several field teams. Ken Shue was a former Navy Seal and got his business degree from The University of Chicago's Graduate School of Business. Shue had been working at the BEA for about six years but quickly moved up the ranks and was Guillson's most reliable senior staffer. Shue happened to be one of Monroe Desmond's most reliable senior staffers as well. After introducing themselves and providing a brief history of their experience in their current roles, the five principles got down to business. Washington got things going.

"Thanks again for making yourselves available on such short notice. I know you have a basic intuition of what we're trying to do with this exercise. In the simplest form, we want to confirm to ourselves that the methods we are using to collect and analyze data are functioning properly. We want to follow an ISO 9001 certification approach to our processes. We don't need to actually map every process, but we want to finish our internal audit with the same level of satisfaction that we have captured and examined every crucial handoff and critical step. We also want to look backward over the last twelve months and satisfy ourselves that the only patterns we observe are patterns that support our standard procedures. I think we should start at the BLS by looking at the Employment Report and jobs data. Rosemary and I have spoken and we think that a similar approach should be taken regarding the GDP calculation. Rosemary would you like to talk about the process we are proposing in more detail?"

"Yes, of course Bert. We want to keep this simple and we need to conduct this process with great discretion. We do not want any leaks or water cooler conversations about our work. There is nothing to speculate about here. We are not looking for a problem, but our actions could be misinterpreted by those who have a political ax to grind. To insure the confidentiality of this project and to limit the involvement of the working staffs at our bureaus we are going to retain a third-party audit firm to perform most of the review work. McFee, Manguson & Worth is a forensic auditing company that is highly specialized and works specifically on sensitive government projects. They have worked extensively with the Defense Department on procurement and contracting processes. We consider them to be experts who can get this work done quickly and quietly."

Hillary Thomas knew Bart McFee and Bill Manguson from her SEC practice days at McIntire, Frost & Smelser. She was impressed that Washington and Guillson had moved so quickly to organize and launch the process. In Washington, D.C. she was used to things moving at a snail's pace. As the joke went, Washington, D.C.'s favorite form of suicide was getting run over by a glacier.

"Bert and I have agreed that Beverly will oversee the GDP review process and Ken will do the same for the Employment Report. Each of you will therefore have no interaction with any of your regular staff colleagues and maintain a posture of independence. McFee, Manguson & Worth will set up separate teams that will obtain data through you and they will conduct their analysis remotely, avoiding any contact or interference with the working analysts and economists. Hillary, if you agree, we would like you to assume the position Audit Director. You are independent of both the Labor and Commerce Departments which frees Bert and me from any issues of conflict."

"Besides that, you're a card carrying Republican!"

"Very funny, Bert. I would be happy to serve as Audit Director. For full disclosure, you should know that I worked with two of the principals of McFee, Magnuson in my prior legal life."

"Did you hire them or were you responsible for their fee negotiation?"

"No."

"Then I don't think there should be any problem, but I appreciate you letting us know. Okay then, that's how Rosemary and I think we should proceed. My guess is that this should probably take about four weeks or so. When we have a preliminary report, we will sit down and see what we've found out, if anything. Anybody got any questions?"

Bitner, Shue and Thomas all responded 'no' and Washington adjourned the meeting. They had gotten everything done quickly and hadn't violated their lunch hour. On the way back to her office, Hillary sent Kirby Haines a text message to let him know that over the next four weeks or so she would probably get reasonably busy with her new project. They would have to plan appropriately. She also called Pennington Ludlow with the morning's update. Ludlow acted that he was upset to hear that she would play such a prominent role in the audit exercise. She had more important things to do and he didn't need her working for two other Cabinet Departments when her main job was with Treasury. He was, of course, happy that she would assume an oversight role since he would get her earliest analysis of their findings. She told Ludlow that the initial audit testing period would last four or five weeks at the most and the ad hoc committee would meet again to review the preliminary results.

Rosemary Guillson and Ken Shue walked back to their offices

together. When he was back at his desk, Ken Shue sent an encrypted message to Monroe Desmond in Dublin. Desmond then called Fletcher who had been notified by Ludlow about the BLS and BEA exercise two days earlier. Desmond and Fletcher felt comfortable that the audit procedure should not uncover their manipulations. They were concerned of course, but Desmond's people were good. With Ken Shue assuming the position of project leader, Desmond was confident that nothing would turn up.

After his update from Hillary Thomas, Ludlow called Fletcher to debrief him about the initial internal audit meeting. Fletcher confirmed Ludlow's information with Ken Shue's identical account. Ludlow had closed the loop and hung up. But the audit wasn't the issue gnawing at these expert manipulators. After their meeting that morning, Lowery, Fletcher and Desmond were more concerned about the US economy and how much life was left in it. The audit would take care of itself. They had much bigger fish to fry.

CHAPTER 12

New York City
February 27, 2007

The fourth quarter GDP number hit the tape precisely at 8:30 A.M. The consensus forecast predicted a 3.5% increase, but a lot of smart money had bet that the number would fall short of expectations. When the number was announced, the market uttered a collective gasp. The economy had actually grown at 4.2%. A furious rally started in the futures market as the short sellers acted swiftly to cover their positions. By the time the market opened, the futures were sky high. Harrison Teasedale sat in his office with an uncharacteristic smile pursed across his lips. He had willingly taken all the action that was betting against the consensus. Morgan Greenville had committed an unusually hefty amount of capital in the days leading up to the announcement. By noontime, his proprietary trading desk had racked up trading profits of over $300 million. It was a monumental score. Teasedale had also recorded an impressive result for himself and Pennington Ludlow in their offshore trading accounts. He knew that the information driving his success might change, and he could not resist one last trading conquest. His next task would be to unwind a significant number of long and illiquid positions for Morgan Greenville and Pennington Ludlow. While Teasedale never told Ludlow the full extent of Morgan Greenville's profitable reliance on the inside information he provided over the years, his actions over the next two months would reveal his massive dilemma.

It didn't take long for Kirby Haines and Peter Bolger to get wind of Morgan Greenville's trading success that day. Even though the investment bankers sat floors above the trading desks, news traveled quickly. A $300 million profit in a single day trading was enormous and it couldn't come at a better time. Kirby and Peter figured that the prospective Partner review process would be easier to navigate if the firm was making outsized profits. They would know their fate soon enough. The friends decided to duck out for lunch at a Japanese restaurant known for its high quality sushi. The year was starting off brilliantly. M&A volumes were continuing to build at a record pace. Morgan Greenville was riding a reputational crest that irritated their competition on the Street. The firm was even being hailed as the savviest trader in the global capital markets. While they waited for the arrival of their specially ordered *uni,* Kirby's Blackberry chirped. Hillary was sending him a message. Apparently, word of Morgan Greenville's killing had already made it to Washington, D.C.

Hillary Thomas sat in her office and looked at the screens in front of her. The stock market was staging a strong rally on the back of the better than expected GDP number. She had spoken to one of her contacts at the New York Federal Reserve Bank a bit earlier, and he had told her that the rumor circulating around Street was that Morgan Greenville had made a killing in the market. Hillary figured she would call Kirby to find out more if he knew anything. After she sent him a message, she walked into Pennington Ludlow's office since he happened to be in town that day.

"Mr. Secretary, I can't believe the GDP number today. It's just fantastic, isn't it?"

"Well Hillary, we had a sense the fourth quarter was going to be a good one. I'm not very surprised. I think many sectors performed well. Exports were solid too. But the consumer is still driving this ship. As long as the consumer hangs in, we'll be in good shape."

Ludlow knew that the number was a sham. The short sellers had been right again, but once more they had taken a beating. Fourth quarter GDP growth was probably closer to 2.5% than the 4.2% number released by Rosemary Guillson's crew. Frankly, in hindsight, he wished that Lowery and Fletcher had dialed the result back somewhat. He was afraid that the first quarter news, when announced in May, could be quite a shocker given the slowing economy. After the President's meeting a week earlier, the next GDP announcement would certainly be lower than 4.2%. They would have to begin to bring the perceived performance of the US economy more in line with its actual results.

"Mr. Secretary, I heard through one of my contacts at the New York Fed that Morgan Greenville is having a killer day today. Apparently, they were the only firm on the Street who actually bet that the GDP number would beat the consensus. I heard they've already made hundreds of millions—maybe a firm record."

Ludlow received that news with a considerable degree of shock and almost laughed at her comment, but he did not allow Hillary to detect his surprise. "That's what makes our markets so successful. The market brings together buyers and sellers who see the same picture but walk away with opposite opinions. Morgan Greenville saw something that no one else saw. It takes guts and even at times good luck to win like they must have. But it's what keeps our markets the most dynamic ones in the world. It's really a beautiful thing—capitalism working at its best."

Thomas left Ludlow's office. Sitting in silence thinking, Ludlow was trying to control himself. He was actually counting to ten in the hopes of defusing his temper that had the potential to erupt in minor acts of violence. Teasedale must be out of his mind. Why would he do anything to draw such attention to his trading? It's probably already on the financial news networks. Wall Street junkies love these types of stories and then they sit around theorizing how one firm could be so good. Somebody ultimately suggests that they can't be that good. Only someone with inside information can score that big. Ludlow's mind was racing. He kept counting. He had to call Teasedale. In five minutes, he closed his office door and dialed his number. When Teasedale picked up, Ludlow let him have it.

"Harrison, have you lost any semblance of sanity?"

"Pennington, what a great day today! We made a major score. No one else had the balls to be long. We absolutely killed it. Killed it."

"Shut up you fucking idiot and listen to me. You violated our agreement. You stepped over the line. For over five years, we've played it so that no one would notice us. Today you're making headlines. What are you doing?"

"Calm down. You're making more of this than there is. Yes, we had a very good trading day. But we've had other good days in the past. Our reputation's been growing. The market knows we're aggressive and intelligent. The fact that we won big today shouldn't come as a surprise to anyone."

"Well, apparently it does, because even the New York Fed is talking about it according to my Chief of Staff. I've made you rich on one condition Harrison: that you follow my orders. Your trading today violated our agreement. You bet way too much and made way too much money. That wasn't our deal. I am beyond furious!"

"Don't you want to know how we did today?"

"Dammit, Harrison, you just don't get it. Commerce and Labor are starting to conduct an internal audit of controls. I told you to lay low while they did their thing. I also told you that I wanted to start turning my performance into cash. I specifically didn't tell you to bet the ranch on the GDP number. Is that correct?"

"Well yes that is correct but I just thought this would be the last chance to score big given what you told me about our going forward strategy. The market was set up perfectly for us."

"I know, Harrison. It was set up too perfectly. This better not come back to haunt us."

"I'm sure it won't."

Ludlow hung up. He feared Teasedale's aggressive trading that day could be a problem. It wouldn't take longer than tomorrow's newspapers to see whether Teasedale slid back behind the curtain or was front page news. Ludlow was most afraid of Fletcher. He didn't think Fletcher was suspicious of him but he couldn't be too careful. Ludlow was upset and concerned. He could see the finish line, less than two short years ahead of him but a minefield was being laid while he watched. Harrison Teasedale may have just activated the field but Ludlow hoped not. Time would tell.

CHAPTER 13

Washington, D.C.
May 14, 2007

After nearly three months, Bert Washington had finally been able to schedule a meeting to review the preliminary results of the internal audit process. Although the working teams had estimated that they could have preliminary results to review in four or five weeks time, the scope of their work was more complicated than they had anticipated. Seated around the table in Bert Washington's conference room were Rosemary Guillson, Hillary Thomas, Beverly Bittner and Ken Shue. Bittner and Shue had spent a great deal of time working with McFee, Magnuson and Worth, the outside forensic auditors, to track the data aggregation methodology used by the BLS and BEA. The investigation timetable had required an additional six weeks because the original scope of the project was simply too large. The teams spun in circles until they decided to narrow their focus. Instead of looking at country-wide data, they retooled their process to focus on just two of the Federal Bank reporting regions over four reporting periods: November 2006 — February 2007. The regions they selected for review comprised San Francisco, which included California's large and diverse economy, and Philadelphia, which included most of Pennsylvania and the large metropolitan areas surrounding Philadelphia as well as New Jersey. As project leader, Hillary Thomas began the meeting using a power point presentation.

"At long, long last, we have something to look at. I thought I would begin by presenting a schematic of the data generation process for the Employment Report produced by the BLS. For both Ken and Beverly's projects, we used similar methodologies, but I thought we could focus on Ken's work to begin with."

Thomas' opening remarks lasted about fifteen minutes and laid the groundwork for the process overview and mapped the steps each team took as they moved from local data collection up through the hierarchy of analysis and final sign-off by each bureau's team of senior economists. She then handed the discussion over to Bitner and Shue who separately took the group through their specific findings. Bitner walked through the GDP audit and concluded that all the processes seemed sound and nothing unusual was found that could constitute a material weakness in the Commerce Department's work. As Under Secretary of the ESA and BEA, Guillson uttered a sigh of relief when Bitner finished her report. Ken Shue's discussion of the Employment Report followed a similar pattern. He took the group through the step by step pattern used by the field analysts who gathered their hiring and firing data from local sources. That raw data was then fed and aggregated by state counties, and finally merged into regional baskets. Working with McFee, Magnuson and Worth, Shue had reviewed four months of data in fine detail and reported that they had found no irregularities. The two presentations of summary results each took about thirty minutes. When Ken Shue finished his presentation, he sat down and Washington and Guillson began to ask their questions.

"I'm interested to know whether you were able to review departmental personnel statistics including employee turnover, training and assessment." Bert Washington was not entirely happy with Beverly and Ken's conclusions. He just had a hard time believing the numbers were precisely right. If there was a gremlin in his system at the BLS given its size and scope, that gremlin would probably be human.

Shue answered, "We did actually look at a number of different areas that could impact performance and accuracy. Employee turnover has been extremely low at the BLS. In fact, in the two territories that we focused on in the audit process, there has been no turnover in the last five years. The average length of employment in those two regions is slightly more than six years. As far as training goes, both the BLS and BEA require the fulfillment of ongoing educational requirements and all employees are in compliance with those standards. Regarding assessment and review, every employee is interviewed on a semi-annual basis by their direct managers. In these areas, everything was in order and the records well maintained."

Bert Washington was impressed but incredulous nonetheless.

"Ken and Beverly, it's obvious that you've done a thorough and solid job. And Hillary, thank you for your oversight. I trust your findings and believe your sample size was large enough to satisfy our desire to test our systems. There's just something fascinating about our economy that I still don't understand. See whether you can follow me, or at least indulge me. In the last three months while you've been conducting your audit, the micro-economic news has been mixed at best. Corporate earnings in the March 31 quarter were generally weaker than Wall Street analysts had estimated. During the same quarter, auto manufacturers reported higher inventories of unsold vehicles and credit card companies reported a drop in transaction volume. It wouldn't be unreasonable to conclude that the consumer was beginning to trim back on discretionary spending. Even the home builders, who have been putting up houses as fast as they could over the last four or five years reported that they were holding a larger inventory of unsold homes than at any time since Chuck Lowery was elected President. In spite of those sample anecdotes, our macro-economic indicators continue to show relative strength and a steadily growing economy. Am I missing something?"

The group was silent, not sure where Bert was headed. Hillary, sensing the need to speak up given Washington's political innuendo, offered an answer.

"Bert, I'm not sure exactly where you are headed. We've conducted an audit process that you thought was necessary. Our report shows no material weaknesses. The scope of our review was well defined and we completed it without uncovering any problems. That's all we know for sure. I'm not sure it's our job to figure out why everything may not make precise sense to any one of us."

Thomas had to be somewhat discreet and she was walking the line. Washington and Guillson held higher positions than she did within their respective agencies. She was a political appointee and they were career civil servants.

"Maybe you're right Hillary. It just seems a bit strange to me. I'm a hole poker and I want to make sure that we didn't miss anything. If all our processes check out, is it possible that the very data itself could be wrong?"

Even Rosemary let out an uncomfortable laugh at that. "My god, Bert. You're beginning to sound like Oliver Stone. You realize that the probability of that being the case would have to be infinitesimal since such a conspiracy would require a serious amount of manipulation and purposeful fraud to have any significant impact."

"Rosemary, I like Oliver Stone. JFK was one of my favorite movies. Okay, never mind. I can see that you all have appointments and don't want to explore my theories. I want to think about what if

anything we need to do next. This meeting was billed as a preliminary review of your initial findings. Maybe Rosemary and Hillary,
you can stay for a few minutes? Beverly and Ken, great job. We may
be done with our internal audit, but Rosemary and I will let you
know after we reach our conclusions."

Ken Shue and Beverly Bittner collected their folders and left
the conference room. Shue would have an interesting report to
deliver to Monroe Desmond. He was slightly alarmed and annoyed
at Washington's intuition.

When Ken Shue closed the conference room door, Washington
got back on his soap box.

"Look, I don't mean to be so pig headed. Here's my problem in a
nutshell. Our gang went to work three months ago and meticulously
examined all the data gathering and aggregating processes in our
systems. And you know what they came up with? Absolutely nothing! That's astounding. They didn't find one itty bitty mistake, not
one. What are the odds of that Rosemary? Come on, they should
have found something wrong somewhere. We're talking about
hundreds of civil servants handling millions of pieces of data and
they did everything right? I'm sorry. This isn't about politics Hillary,
even if I wanted it to be."

"Bert, are you suggesting that the audit process was somehow
corrupted?"

"Hillary, I'm not sure exactly what I'm saying. It just seems
absolutely absurd that we could study a process that is decidedly
pseudo-scientific and come up with perfection. Come on guys, you
have to admit that it strains credibility."

Thomas and Guillson found themselves nodding in agreement.
They didn't want to believe Washington's assertion, but on reflection it was a bit strange that the three month audit did not come
up with a single discrepancy. Guillson thought about the fact that
her own administrative assistant didn't seem capable of routing

simple emails to the right people—and she had worked for the bureau for twelve years.

"Okay Bert. Let's assume you're right for the sake of argument. What do you want to do? We have to report our results to the Secretaries and the results are the results."

"Let's hold off on reporting anything right now, Rosemary. I have an idea but I don't want you both to react immediately. I simply ask you to consider it. Is that a deal?"

"If there's fine print I think you should probably give it to us in its entirety."

"Look, I promised you when we began this thing that I would not hang you out to dry. Okay, here's what I'm thinking. We should extend the audit for another two reporting cycles and selectively feed erroneous, negative data into the network at the local and county levels and see whether it is caught and manipulated. Before the report gets approved, we will know whether the system worked with integrity or not. If the system works, we correct the inputs immediately and release the corrected results. If the numbers are changed to reflect a more positive outcome, we know we've found a rat. At that point, we call in the FBI. The numbers we use will be impactful at the margin but won't move the needle more than 30,000 on the jobs report or more than two-tenths of one percent on the Employment Report. What do you say?"

Guillson and Thomas sat back in their chairs and stared back at Washington. He was way off the reservation. If they agreed to his plan, they could put themselves in a serious jam.

"Bert, if we agree to this, we have to get the okay from the higher-ups. This is just too risky for us to do on our own."

"Rosemary, the more people we tell the greater the chance that we'll never catch the rat, if there is one."

"Listen Bert, I may be the new kid on the block, but this seems like a career limiting decision. I'm actually intrigued by your trap, but I can only go along with it if Secretary Ludlow knows about it. Maybe we can get away with avoiding disclosure to Labor and Commerce since those Departments are responsible for the bureaus, but someone needs to know. Having Ludlow at Treasury on the inside can certainly provide a lot of protection."

"I understand your concern. Maybe that's a good compromise. Frankly, I'm more concerned that if something's wrong, it's probably located in our own neighborhood. Treasury is far enough removed to be safe. That works for me. What about you Rosemary?"

"My Irish mother had a name for people like you Bert."

"I hope it isn't something that requires a trip to Confession."

"You're incorrigible, Bert. You're stirring it up again and dragging me along for the sting. I guess I'm okay if Treasury signs off and is kept informed."

"Great. You guys are terrific. I'm taking you both to that new three star Ethiopian restaurant that just opened across from the Mayflower. Promise. It's on me; I owe you both."

"Bert, we accept. Dinner's on you, but we'll pick the restaurant."

"Okay, it's a deal."

"I'm just going to hold my nose until this whole thing is over."

CHAPTER 14

New York City
Dublin, Ireland
May 14, 2007

Peter Bolger sat in Kirby Haines' office, his feet pushing back several black books that were stacked on Haines' coffee table. Outside the office young investment bankers were buzzing back and forth, getting their projects done or conferring with senior colleagues about next steps and action items. Haines' office was an oasis of inactivity. Joanne Fruilli sat outside at her station, sipping her coffee and looking at the Intermix web site where she thought she might find some fashion inspiration for a Memorial Day date she hoped might materialize with Special Agent John Aichenhead. Their first two dates were mediocre on her hotness scale, but she figured he was older, shy and not particularly in tip-top dating shape. The third chance might be the charm. She was willing to give him a go. She had a hard time finding guys who weren't just looking for a good roll in the sack and someone to make the bed afterward. She needed something more liberating. She'd been dreaming of getting out of Staten Island to start a new life for the last ten years, but every guy she dated was pretty much the same.

Bolger and Haines weren't going to do anything productive because today was the day when Morgan Greenville would announce its new slate of Partners. The firm only elevated Managing Directors to the Partner level every two years. For those who hoped to make it but didn't, it was devastating. Some of those passed over took the negative outcome as an omen and began to look for positions at other firms. It was crazy to think that they had worked loyally for twelve years only to come to the conclusion that they could no longer prosper at the firm that had invested so much in them and who had received so much of their hard work and personal sacrifice in return. Bolger and Haines had no such thoughts. They were confident they were getting the title and believed that the odds of not being elevated were extremely remote.

"Hey Kirby, can you believe how much the guys on the prop desk are going to be paid this year? It's going to be obscene."

"Why are you trying to ruin my day? They've got the golden touch. We know that. Remember ancient history when there used to be an M&A premium? That was our heyday buddy."

"Well, you can kiss that M&A premium good bye. In fact, when they announce bonuses this year they should invite us of down to the trading floor so we can individually kiss all of their asses to thank them for paying us."

"I'll bring the video, Peter. You can bring the ChapStick."

"Very funny. Even you private equity guys get a shot at the turbo pay. Little ole me just has to live on the scraps falling off the table."

"I'm going to cue the violins momentarily."

"What do you think is taking them so long? I hate this waiting. It makes me feel like I did when I was looking for the mailman on college decision day. I'm going nuts."

"Peter, you go nuts waiting for a light to turn green. Relax, they're going to get this all done before noon and then we've got some serious celebrating to do."

"I'll drink to that."

The nervous energy that they felt was being driven by the proximity of the net worth boost they were about to receive. "Boost" doesn't really do justice to the reality of becoming a Morgan Greenville Partner. The fact was that their lives were about to change forever. Everything that they worked for was about to pay off. Within a few years, they would both have nine figure net worths. Their personal fortunes would rank them in the top one-tenth of one percent of the entire US population. There would be nothing standard about their lives going forward.

At precisely 10:00 A.M., Kirby Haines' phone rang and Joanne Fruilli answered it. She had been waiting for this day to come as well. When she hung up, she bounced out of her chair and rushed into Kirby's office, an uncontrollable smile stuck on her face.

"Kirby, it was Teasedale's assistant. She said he wants to see you—now!" Joanne almost cheered as she passed on the brief command. Trying to act nonchalant, Haines got out of his chair and straightened his tie by looking into a framed memento hanging on his wall that served as a mirror at times like this. Peter Bolger slapped him on his back and let out a low yelp.

"Whoeee Haines. Go follow that yellow brick road. And don't fall asleep in the poppy field before you get to Teasedale's Emerald City!"

"Don't worry Peter. They're working in reverse alphabetical order. You'll be next, friend."

Harrison Teasedale had two offices at Morgan Greenville. One was just off the trading floor where he could keep an eye on things. The other was much larger and on the same investment banking floor where Haines and Bolger sat. It took Haines about 30 seconds to walk over to Teasedale's office. He waited outside until Teasedale hung up the phone and unceremoniously motioned him in and pointed at a chair that sat opposite Teasedale's massive antique desk. Teasedale had a large sitting area with comfortable chairs and a sofa. Haines had thought maybe they'd sit there leisurely to discuss the joyous event, but Teasedale wanted to communicate the news in a more Spartan-like manner. Teasedale was all business and it didn't look like there would be any warm fuzzies or man hugs after the good news was delivered.

"Kirby, you've been a valued employee of the firm. We have invested a tremendous amount of money in you and you have lived up to our high expectations."

Haines was spacing out a little since Teasedale's prologue sounded more like a eulogy than a Super Bowl speech. Plus, Teasedale had an annoying voice.

"We have spent the last several months painstakingly reviewing a slate of candidates for admission to our Partnership. After an exhaustive process, we are pleased to extend you that honor."

As Teasedale was speaking, Haines' adult life was racing before his eyes. He was remembering his shitty New Jersey neighborhood; the break he got at Yale; the jobs he worked during the summer for pocket change; the death of his parents; the sacrifices he had made at Morgan Greenville; those eighteen hour days; all-nighters; seven day work weeks; endless flights around the globe; and the loss of much of his personal freedom. His father and mother would have been very proud of him if they had lived to see the day. Maybe he wouldn't have found his ambition if they were still alive. His heart played a measure of irregular beats. That happened sometimes, but not very often. But then he thought of the rewards: the ridiculous money and all the other benefits that his Partner position at Morgan Greenville would bring him. He snapped back into the moment when Teasedale mentioned something about "new responsibilities."

"Kirby, I want you to leave your position in the Merchant Banking Group. I know this will undoubtedly come as a surprise and I don't want you to do anything but hear me out at this point. I'm creating a new investment strategy group on the trading floor. I want you to come on board and be my second-in-command. I realize that you've never worked on a trading floor, but I think you have a keen sense for principal investing. I think a move like this could be very good for your career. The Management Committee is one hundred percent behind this initiative and will remain intimately involved with our work. Your position in the group will give you a spotlight. If you succeed, you're on a path to the Management Committee. If you fail, well you know what I do with failures."

Haines could not believe what he was hearing. This was beyond anything that he could have imagined. Teasedale had not only offered him the Partnership mantel; he had asked him to become his prince. And with Teasedale as the king, Haines knew his path to prosperity and prominence was there for the taking. He liked being in control of his own destiny. Some guys wanted the ball with the game tied and seconds left. Kirby Haines was one of those guys. Peter Bolger was right when he alluded to Teasedale's yellow brick road. Kirby Haines was on his way to the Emerald City for sure.

When Haines got back to his office with a wide smile on his face, Joanne Fruilli let out a Staten Island scream. It sounded like a combination of Jewish, Italian and Grand Ole Opry intonations. And everyone heard it if they weren't in a sound proof room. Bolger and Haines hugged while Joanne opened a bottle of champagne that she had in a plastic bucket under her desk next to her walking sneakers. Bolger's secretary waved at him and ran across to Haines' office after navigating through the bullpen of associate cubicles. Bolger had received his call. He was next. He tried to get serious, slapping himself on his face a couple of times to get back into the proper mood, and off he strode to Teasedale's office.

When Bolger left, Kirby hit the speed dial button for Hillary's cell phone. Now that he had attained the goal that he had set for his professional career, maybe marriage was his next challenge. They were really good together. Maybe she was the one. When Hillary heard the news she almost cried with happiness. She wished she could have been there to celebrate the precise moment but knew that was impossible. Kirby made her agree to fly up at the end of the day so they could celebrate that evening in style. He would make a reservation at Cru, one of their favorite restaurants in New York with a fabulous wine cellar. At Cru, fine wine and food was the objective and price was not. What did Kirby care? He could afford anything that he wanted—his future was his reality.

Hillary knew how much this promotion meant to Kirby. It was his way of measuring how far he had come from his middle class neighborhood in Maplewood, New Jersey. He had escaped the two-family home that had trapped his sister and younger brother. After his parents died, they never moved. They couldn't break away from all that bound them to that place. Kirby had to leave. He would have died if he had returned to the place where he was born. Hillary understood Kirby. She loved him because she knew how hard it was for him to love her back. Kirby stayed in the moment. Whatever was happening was where his spirit focused. Of course he planned and dreamed of goals, but his goals were like points of interest on a map. He was driven to get there, but there wasn't a lot of emotional content once he arrived. All the celebration was about the trip—then there was something else. She thought he would make an odd choice as a marriage partner, but they had so much in common. Hillary wanted to be loved, but she didn't want to be held back if that were the cost of love. Their sexual relationship was first class. That was the best way for her to measure their intimacy. They could talk to each other in the rawest terms. It was basic and instinctual—the way men and women were attracted to each other before culture ruined everything.

"Of course I'm coming up tonight to celebrate with you. Are you kidding? I can probably make the 5:30 P.M. shuttle if I get everything done fast. I have to finish writing a summary for Ludlow of a meeting I had this morning with Bert Washington. After that, I can leave. I can't wait to hug you."

"I'm going to do a lot more than hug you."

"I was hoping you would say that."

Thomas hung up and got to work. In her summary memo for Pennington Ludlow, she described Washington's plan to test the integrity of the reporting systems by feeding negative information into the field to see whether it passed through the various stages of review untouched. If the data was not manipulated, the system was working without defect. If the data was altered, they had a big problem that would have to be addressed. Thomas stressed the "need to know" basis of this next phase of the audit and the fact only the Secretary of the Treasury would be aware of this test. Neither the Secretary of Labor nor of Commerce would know anything about Washington's work unless an offense was discovered. When she had finished the memo, she reread it to make sure that she hadn't omitted anything and had captured all the nuances of Washington's plan. Satisfied that the memo accurately reflected the morning's meeting and subsequent discussion, she encrypted the memo text and forwarded it with "Secret" status to Pennington Ludlow who was in Dublin, Ireland on government business. Given the late hour in Dublin, she was not sure whether Ludlow would see her message tonight or tomorrow morning. With Kirby's emergency invitation to New York, Hillary was grateful that Ludlow was out of the country so that she could leave the office a little earlier and run back to her apartment to put a few things in an overnight bag and dash to the airport. She wasn't sure how Ludlow would react to Washington's plan of entrapment. It was no doubt imaginative, but well outside the lines of standard procedure. Thomas hoped that Ludlow wouldn't blow a gasket when he read her report.

Pennington Ludlow had had a long day in Dublin, conferring with Ireland's Prime Minister and Finance chief over EU matters. He had also been feted by the President at a ceremonial luncheon held at her official residence. Ludlow's day ended with a private dinner at the Eden Restaurant in the Temple Bar section of Dublin. His hosts were the three richest men in the Republic. They were all hunters, golfers and billionaires—just like him. They had a lot of laughs and Ludlow made a mental note to get them all down to DeSaussure Hall for the first fall shoot. Ludlow was looking forward to getting into the backseat of his chauffeured Mercedes sedan that would whisk him back to the K Club in Kildaire where he was staying during his visit. When Ludlow climbed into the car, he was pleasantly surprised to see that Carmen Gomes had come to pick him up. Ludlow took Gomes on as many overseas trips as he could because he craved their lust sessions and his wife hated to go. Carmen loved to travel. She truly enjoyed all the foreign places that they visited. People outside America were different. They were more passionate about all the little things that most Americans missed. She particularly liked the Irish and their extraordinary generosity and friendship. When Ludlow settled into the car, he kissed Carmen on the cheek and asked the driver how much traffic he thought they might encounter on their way back to Kildaire. The driver figured traffic would be light and it would take them twenty to twenty-five minutes. Carmen was wearing a trench coat to ward off the damp weather that evening. When the chauffeur put the car into gear, she unbuckled the belt around the coat's waist and the raincoat opened to reveal that she was completely naked underneath.

"Aren't you happy that I decided to come into town to surprise you, Penny?"

The driver quickly looked up to glance in his rear view mirror and spied Carmen's naked brown breasts. At ease with her sexual being, she didn't really care. When men looked at her, they always imagined her naked. This guy just got to see the real thing. Anyway, she liked it when someone was watching her and couldn't do anything about it.

"I am extremely happy, baby. You are always full of surprises, aren't you?'

Carmen was pinching her nipples to make them harder and more inviting for Ludlow's kisses. He indulged her immediately. She loved to be licked and kissed on the neck. Ludlow knew all her preferences by now, and he followed them step by step. Carmen reached down and began to massage the outside of Ludlow's trousers and his response was involuntary. By the time the car reached the highway, Carmen was facing Ludlow, on top of his lap. She was grinding him rhythmically and he was kissing her breasts with passion.

The twenty minute ride went by in a numbing moment. The driver's subtle announcement of their proximity allowed Carmen the chance to roll back onto her seat and close her trench coat. They both hurried out of the car as it stopped in front of the main entrance and Ludlow grabbed his key from the lonely night receptionist. Inside the elevator, Carmen kissed him while reopening her trench coat. She wanted some consummation and wanted it soon. Ludlow unlocked the door to their suite and threw his coat on a day bed. He reactivated his computer as Carmen turned on the stereo in the room. She liked to make love to music. Ludlow immediately saw a message marked "Secret" from Hillary Thomas. It was encrypted and Ludlow would have to access a special software application to decode the memo. He was tempted to take the time to do just that but when he looked up Carmen had stripped off everything and slipped into a sexy nightshirt that hugged her breasts but exposed the rest of her hairless body. She was dancing and approaching him with a look that commanded his attention. She had work for him to do and she wanted no distractions.

CHAPTER 15

Dublin, Ireland
May 14, 2007

Monroe Desmond and his crew at Custom House Quay had tracked Pennington Ludlow's movements since he arrived in Dublin. By tapping their local network and stimulating it with cash, they had been able to watch Ludlow closely, whether at dinner, in his car, or in his suite at the K Club. Bob Fletcher and Chuck Lowery decided after the February meeting with Ludlow and Alan Solomon that they needed to watch their co-conspirators more closely as their "Economic Revolution" began to lose pace. They had no reason to suspect that either man would flip or turn their fear into a reason to betray their common mission. Watergate only became a household word because of "Deep Throat." Lowery and Fletcher knew that they only had two potential weak links to worry about.

In their assessment, Lowery and Fletcher thought that Alan Solomon was an extremely low risk to go off the reservation. They knew that Ludlow possessed the compromising evidence of Solomon's regrettable dalliance with Carmen Gomes. Solomon would never risk his marriage or the embarrassment to his public image from the exposure of a sex video with Carmen Gomes.

Pennington Ludlow was a different story. Ludlow was a wealthy man due in large part to his wife's family fortune. Ludlow was a risk taker as evidenced by his continuing affair with Carmen Gomes, and Fletcher and Lowery were unsure how he would react if he found himself trapped or threatened with exposure and personal scandal. He might be the first one to turn on the President to save his own hide. They figured that Ludlow would protect himself at all costs since he had the resources to survive if all hell broke loose. Of course, Ludlow did not realize that Carmen Gomes was Fletcher and Lowery's sleeper cell. As long as she was fucking him on his command, he was effectively blind to everything else.

Fletcher had instructed Desmond to monitor Ludlow while he was in Ireland and intercept all his calls, messages and emails, both incoming and outgoing. Lowery, using his Presidential power, had others in unnamed organizations within the US government doing the same thing. Fletcher knew that Carmen Gomes would watch for anything else that eavesdropping could not capture: his mood, changes in schedule, or any actions or reactions that might seem strange.

At around 8:00 P.M. in Dublin, Desmond's team intercepted Hillary Thomas's encrypted "secret" memorandum to Secretary Ludlow that described Bert Washington's plan to test the integrity of his bureau's data collection and analysis system. Since Ludlow would know from Thomas' memo that Ken Shue had been excluded from the portion of the meeting that described Washington's plan, he would be compelled to report this development to Fletcher or Lowery immediately given its grave potential to undermine and expose their conspiracy. If Ludlow failed to communicate this critical development, it would be a dramatic sign of his disloyalty. Desmond knew Ludlow's every step that night. Thomas' encrypted memo arrived while Ludlow was having dinner. After Ludlow's driver, who was also on Desmond's payroll, deposited Ludlow and the nearly naked Carmen at the entrance of the K Club Hotel, Desmond waited to see if Ludlow would dial Fletcher or try to reach the President. By that time it was almost midnight. Ludlow made no calls that night. Given Carmen's performance in the car, Desmond decided not to draw any conclusions that evening. He would be prepared to take action tomorrow morning if Ludlow remained silent.

CHAPTER 16

Dublin, Ireland
May 15, 2007

As was his custom, Ludlow rose early before the sun came up, leaving Gomes' brown body partially covered by the bed sheets on the king size canopy bed in the suite's master bedroom. She was an exquisite creative. Ludlow was pleased with himself and with his life. He called room service to order two large pots of coffee and a basket of pastry to kick start his day. He figured he could get some needed work done while Carmen slept. When she woke in two more hours she would be ready for another session of intimacy before they headed off to the airport to board the chartered flight that would take them back to Washington, D.C. After he showered, shaved and had his first cup of coffee, he remembered the unusual email from Hillary Thomas that he had considered opening last night before Carmen demanded his attention. Ludlow reactivated his hibernating laptop and accessed Thomas' memorandum. Remembering that it was encrypted, Ludlow applied the software tool which he downloaded from a CIA website available only to Cabinet-level Secretaries.

Ludlow poured himself a second cup of coffee as the program translated Thomas' report. As he read her account of Bert Washington's meeting, his early morning enthusiasm turned decidedly downbeat. He couldn't believe Washington's audacity. Ludlow knew that with Fletcher's men in critical positions throughout the BLS and BEA, the internal audit process would go smoothly. With Ken Shue as a team leader, Ludlow was even more confident. And everything went according to plan: no irregularities; disciplined consistency of process; and thorough investigative testing. How could Bert Washington reject the results of a clean report? Ludlow really knew very little about Bert Washington but he was becoming quite concerned with his resilient skepticism. Washington's plan was problematic: to prove the integrity of the data collection and analytical systems, the introduction of erroneous data would have to pass through their processes cleanly to mask the infiltration of the bureaus. The aggregated results would not be able to be manipulated. As a result, the BLS and BEA would produce economic indicators in the months ahead that demonstrated a different economic picture than the picture that Lowery, Fletcher, Solomon and he have been painting for the last six years. Monroe Desmond's small army of infiltrators would have to stand down while this testing phase was conducted. The resulting economic reports would shock the market, creating massive volatility as world-wide investors tried to figure out what the random pattern of past and present data really represented.

Ludlow sat back in his chair and drew a long and slow deep breath. The threat to President Lowery's "Economic Revolution" had changed as a result of Washington's plan. The broad understanding of the slowing US economy could now be just around the corner. Alan Solomon's suggestion to gradually introduce the flagging economy over the next three to twelve months to help insure the President's legacy had seemed reasonable. With Washington's plan, the systemic cracks would be revealed much more quickly. The ominous truth about the fragile condition of the US economy would become a reality in three to seven weeks. Bert Washington's plan was the market killer. Luckily, only two other high ranking officials knew about it: Rosemary Guillson and Hillary Thomas. But Ludlow was about to increase that universe by fifty percent. He left the sitting room where he was taking coffee and walked into the suite's small library and closed the door. He had to raise Harrison Teasedale.

When Teasedale's bedroom phone rang, it was 2:15 A.M. in the morning in New York. Teasedale was alone in his town house except for three staff servants who were asleep in their basement apartments. Teasedale, who slept in total darkness with black eye shades, awoke with a start. He groped for a light switch on the wall next to his night table and pulled the night shade from his eyes. The light was blinding and Teasedale's small eyes squinted to the narrowest of slits as he searched for the cordless phone that he had left somewhere on top of his bedspread. He remembered his mother saying that no good news came from a call in the middle of the night.

One of Monroe Desmond's men signaled to Desmond that Ludlow had just made an outgoing call from his suite at the K Club to a number in New York. Desmond instructed his man to trace the number since there were no bugs in Ludlow's suite. There hadn't been a need to tap that phone since Carmen was always with Ludlow when they were in the room. Fletcher had wanted Ludlow monitored and Desmond's concern grew now that Ludlow had made his first call of the day to someone other than Bob Fletcher or the President of the United States.

Teasedale found the phone and pressed the talk button, "Okay, okay. Who's calling?"

"Harrison, it's Pennington Ludlow."

"It's 2:15 A.M. in the morning. What's going on?"

"I've got something very important to tell you and I want you to listen carefully. Do you understand me?"

"I always listen carefully. Can you just get on with it?"

"This is different. What I am about to tell you is highly sensitive and known only to the President's inner circle. Once you hear it, you cannot tell another soul. If you do, it will be known and your life will change."

"Look Pennington, if something is that important, why bring me over the wall?"

"Because it's too late and there's too much at risk."

Over the next thirty minutes, Pennington Ludlow described what made President Lowery's "Economic Revolution" so successful. Ludlow avoided naming names since he knew that he was already taking a big risk telling Teasedale anything at all. But Ludlow had crossed that bridge years ago when he decided to make Teasedale his trading partner. Teasedale thought he was the lone conspirator in a fail-safe insider trading scheme. Now he realized he was involved in something entirely more complicated. As Ludlow got ready to sign-off with Teasedale, he told him to stay calm and think. If the US economy was going to tank they would have to move even more quickly to liquidate their massive trading positions.

"Listen Harrison, we are where we are. We can't retrace our steps. I warned you three months ago that I was concerned about this audit and we should lay low and begin to turn our profits into cash. Now the situation is acute. We don't have months or even a year. We have weeks. We both have a lot at stake and I don't want to end up poor and carry the legacy of the Treasury Secretary who served while the economy fell off a cliff. I'll take the reputational hit but I want my money."

Teasedale pressed the off button on his phone and thought to himself that he wanted his money too.

When Ludlow finished his conversation with Harrison Teasedale, he placed a call to President Lowery's special line which was always answered by Horace Grant, Lowery's Chief of Staff. It was now about 3:00 A.M. in Washington, D.C., but Horace Grant answered the phone promptly after the first ring. In Horace Grant's job, he didn't need a watch.

"Horace, it's Pennington Ludlow calling from Dublin. I need to speak with the President."

"Secretary Ludlow, it's 3:00 A.M. in the morning sir. The President is sleeping and is not scheduled to wake until 5:00 A.M., as usual."

"I understand all that. I wouldn't ask to speak with him if it wasn't a matter of national security. Please wake the President. It's extremely urgent."

In a matter of minutes, Chuck Lowery got on the line. "Pennington, what the fuck is so important that you decided to wake me up at 3:00 A.M.? "

Lowery already knew about Hillary Thomas' memo since it had been intercepted the prior evening by Fletcher's men who were monitoring Ludlow. Lowery was alarmed by Washington's plan, but Fletcher and Desmond's team were already considering strategies.

"Sir, the Commissioner of the BLS, Bert Washington, is about to turn our efforts over the last six years upside down."

Ludlow was careful on the phone not to discuss any actions that he, Fletcher or the President might take to deal with Bert Washington and his plan. That discussion could come later in person. While he had the President on the phone, he carefully took him through Hillary Thomas' report and Bert Washington's plan. He noted that other than himself only Guillson, Thomas, and Washington were aware of the audit's next phase. The circle was obviously small which would make their alternatives easier to enumerate. When Ludlow finished his reporting, he hung up and went to the bathroom to relieve himself of the three cups of coffee he'd been holding. President Lowery was now fully awake too. He got up and called Fletcher to relay his conversation with Ludlow, satisfied that Ludlow was still on the reservation but happy that he was being watched carefully. Fletcher had some sobering news for Lowery: Pennington Ludlow made one call before he called the President. Monroe Desmond had just informed Fletcher that Ludlow's call had been made to Harrison Teasedale, a senior Partner at Morgan Greenville and one of Wall Street's most renowned traders.

After his conversation with Ludlow, Harrison Teasedale was shaken and could not go back to sleep. His mind was racing. In his most fantastic thinking, he never imagined that he was doing anything more than front running the market using information that was going to be available to every other investor 24 to 48 hours later. As he sat on the edge of his bed, he realized that he was a participant in a massive scheme orchestrated by senior members of the President's inner circle. Teasedale appreciated the brilliance of the plan on one level. Rebuilding the US economy's strength had attracted a flow of global capital that had driven the cost of servicing the country's enormous debt to a low and manageable level. The plan had also driven the stock market to record highs, creating wealth for millions of Americans and their retirement accounts. President Lowery's concocted "Economic Revolution" had also made Morgan Greenville the most profitable and successful investment bank on Wall Street, and Teasedale its most successful Partner. But the game was about to end. According to Ludlow, the real US economy was about to break out of the secret vault where it had been kept for the majority of President Lowery's two terms. Teasedale's massive trading positions were placed around the world, all based on a bullish view of the long term prospects of the US economy.

Teasedale began to think about the complex series of bets he had in place based on his premise of the US economy's strength. Given what Ludlow just told him, every one of those positions would have to be sold or the opposite side of the trade bought. Teasedale had made a bundle trading in front of the fourth quarter GDP report in February. Ludlow had castigated him for his high profile and had instructed Teasedale to begin to liquidate their profitable long and illiquid positions, but Teasedale had moved very slowly. In fact, Teasedale had placed additional long bets on the assumption of a strong GDP number for the first quarter that would be released in two weeks. All his presumptions were wrong; everything would have to be changed. Apart from the considerable bets he had placed on Morgan Greenville's behalf, Teasedale was using $4 billion of his and Ludlow's equity capital to support $20 billion dollars of leverage he had borrowed to magnify their potential returns. A mere 17% decline in the value of his investments would virtually wipe out the entire fortune they had built over the last five years. Teasedale's hands were shaking as if he realized he was standing on the edge of a great cliff. It was a long way down.

Teasedale walked out of his bedroom and to the kitchen. He turned on his massive, imported Italian espresso machine. Teasedale drank two quick doubles. Now his heart was pounding and he could feel his pulse beating like a metronome in his neck. He had little time and a mountain of trades to clear. If he was successful, he would preserve his wealth. If he failed, he was through. He only had one choice. But he had to reverse Morgan Greenville's book as well. While everyone else had grown cautious, Morgan Greenville was a charging bull. If he didn't change course fast, Morgan Greenville would quickly move from being the most revered firm on Wall Street to becoming the biggest loser since the government put Drexel Burnham out of business in 1990.

CHAPTER 17

New York City
May 15, 2007

Kirby and Hillary's celebration the night before at Cru was simply fantastic. They sat at a private table where they went on a culinary journey of incredible tastes and sublime bouquets. Their tasting menu was paired with the rarest of wines, each one a masterpiece. Three hours later, the couple was in a state of bliss. When Michele, the sommelier, brought Kirby a half bottle of Chateau D'Yquem, Haines gave him his Platinum Card, told him to tack on 20% and send him the receipt later. As they got up to leave, Kirby and Hillary thanked the staff as curious other dinners watched them. They got into a waiting car and travelled north to Kirby's apartment to end the perfect evening with their usual romp.

The phone in Kirby's apartment rang at 5:00 A.M. Kirby woke up with a shock and fumbled to find the receiver. As he mumbled out a tired greeting, he realized Harrison Teasedale was on the line.

"Kirby, I need to see you as soon as you get to the office. It's important. When can I expect you?"

Kirby was in a bit of a stupor but did notice that Teasedale had not even offered a "Good Morning." "I'm sorry. Harrison, is that you? I was not expecting to hear from you so...so early."

"Kirby, it's not early. Traders have been executing orders all night in Asia. Europe is getting ready to break for lunch. There is no time of day in the capital markets. You better get used to that. When are you getting here?"

Kirby picked up on the "here" in Teasedale's question. Harrison was already at work and Kirby was sleeping off a memorable evening. Obviously Harrison Teasedale didn't remember what it was like to celebrate crossing over into Partner territory. A shot of reality kicked in: if this was what it was going to be like to become extremely rich, he would have to deal with it.

"I can be there in 45 minutes."

"Come directly to my office." Teasedale hung up as abruptly as he had started their conversation. Hillary was lying on her stomach, a simple sheet covering the lower half of her body. She offered a bit of a groan and rolled onto her left side trying to continue her sleep. She was in no hurry that morning. She had planned to wake up leisurely and get back to Washington, D.C. around noon time. Haines quickly showered, shaved and threw on a suit. He kissed Hillary goodbye as he checked his watch. He had twenty minutes to get downtown. He picked up his newspapers that were lying on his landing and signaled for a taxi by pressing the alert button in the elevator. The building's morning staff did not reach full force until 7:00 A.M. The night doorman had flagged down a yellow cab and held it waiting as Haines pushed through the building's front door.

"I'm going to 275 Vesey Street and if you can get me there in fifteen minutes, there's a $20 tip in it for you."

The cab shot off like a scud missile. Haines, as promised, delivered the extra $20 when the cab pulled up in front of Morgan Greenville's headquarters less than fifteen minutes later. It was 5:40 A.M. Haines would be in Teasedale's office on time as promised. He knew Teasedale would be looking at his watch and counting the seconds.

Teasedale's office looked like a storm cell had passed through it. Haines could surmise that Teasedale had either been there for hours or possibly had never left at all. The morning's newspapers, at least the six that Teasedale read, were sitting in an untidy pile next to his leather trash can and two empty cups of Starbuck's coffee stood guard on the edge of his desk; their lids blotting brown stains on the memos they had been dropped on. Teasedale was on the phone yelling at someone in London, browbeating him about his inability to move a $50 million block of stock at the limit price he was given by Teasedale two hours ago. Teasedale motioned to Haines to take a seat with a scowl on his face. Haines did as he was directed. When Teasedale hung up, he launched into a discourse on Morgan Greenville's trading strategies and where the company has made its money over the last several years. Kirby was still attempting to get his bearings.

"Kirby, you are going to get the world's quickest tutorial in the next hour and then you are going to get to work. And you are going to work your butt off. Listen to me and no questions until I'm done. Over the last four years or so, Morgan Greenville has become the largest trader of debt and equity securities in the world. You may think we are in the investment banking business, but your merchant banking group and investment banking combined for less than 10% of our revenue last year. You think your hedge fund friends are kings; well we are the world's biggest hedge fund. During the last four years we have consistently raised our daily risk tolerance. At the same time our balance sheet has grown to over $1 trillion.

Here's how we got there. The Fed became our best friend and cut interest rates dramatically over the last five years. We borrowed all the money the system would give us and invested that capital in an enormous number of higher yielding, longer duration securities of all kinds. We then hedged a portion of those "carry trades" taking advantage of small swings in the price of the underlying insurance we were either buying or selling. This is the simple shit Kirby. Are you with me?"

Kirby Haines was a sponge absorbing every word that was coming out of Teasedale's mouth. "Yes, I'm with you."

Teasedale continued his discourse describing in more detail a variety of strategies he had implemented to make Morgan Greenville extremely profitable. Haines' opinion of Teasedale grew as he continued. Teasedale was a trading wizard. His hands were in every pie, moving gigantic notional amounts of capital in and out of markets, and almost always getting it right. Harrison Teasedale was the living proof that Efficient Market Theory was an economic fallacy. Morgan Greenville was the leading trader of coffee in Brazil, platinum in South Africa and oil in Djibouti. Haines was stunned to learn that the firm was the dominant player in emerging equity markets like China, India, the Philippines, Indonesia, Argentina, Chile and Mexico. Morgan Greenville bet on currencies, interest rates and stocks and bonds in all of those markets. The firm bet even bigger in all the European markets and especially in Eastern Europe. Even if a market was small and illiquid, Morgan Greenville embraced the opportunity to put its risk capital at work there. Haines sat in amazement. How did the firm even keep all of this straight? He didn't realize that the firm had the research capability to drive expert knowledge in so many different geographies, particularly in places where the Company had no offices or significant local nominees. When he asked Teasedale that question, he was told that no such capability actually existed. Haines' intuition was kicking in at the same time the caffeine from his second cup was hitting his central nervous system.

"Harrison, I think I can appreciate the breadth and depth of the trading operation. It's staggering and complex. But fundamentally, it seems like we've been long everything that we can buy. Is that a fair conclusion? We are the biggest bulls in the biggest bull market ever."

"Yes, that's a simple and succinct conclusion, but I'm not giving you the Nobel Prize in Economics for getting that right. Everyone has made money in this market thanks to the Fed and fiscal policy. We've succeeded by taking risks that others weren't prepared to take, and we were paid outsized gains for doing it."

"I can see that. The firm must own some things that make my investment in Comsdef look downright liquid."

"You're absolutely right, Kirby, and that's why I asked you to join the new trading strategies group. We own a lot of deeply illiquid positions. Interests in companies or projects where there is no actively traded market. One of your jobs is going to be to organize and oversee that portfolio."

"That should be interesting. How much capital has been invested in those types of opportunities?"

"That's going to be another one of your jobs. You have to figure out precisely our exposure. My best guess is that worldwide our exposure is somewhere between $30 and $40 billion."

Haines' jaw slackened. His merchant banking group's portfolio was only $8 billion and 95% of that was third party capital. He couldn't believe it. Morgan Greenville had more than $30 billion invested directly on its balance sheet in security interests with no active markets to support them.

"Kirby, here's the critical point. Our view of the world is chang-ing. We have been the biggest bull for the last five years. But the world is changing fast. Very fast. And we need to be ahead of that curve, which will not be easy because, because our balance sheet is so much bigger than all our rivals."

"You just lost me for a second."

"Well listen carefully, because your life is going to be turned upside down for the next several weeks. I believe a dramatic market correction is just around the corner. Right now, you can assume that we are on the wrong side of every trade that we are holding for our own account. Do you get that?"

Haines was nodding but he was still lost.

"Over the next few weeks, but as quickly as possible, we are going to raise as much cash as we can. That is going to be your job. That and figuring out exits for our deeply illiquid crap. We've been playing a massive, global "carry trade" and we have to close that trade now. As we generate cash, we'll shrink the balance sheet and delever. I want the balance sheet to be less than $800 billion when we're done."

Kirby was extremely curious why Teasedale was calling for this major market correction now, but knew that Teasedale would cut him off at the knees if he interrupted his chain of thought again.

"While you and your team are raising cash, I will lead a team that will build positions that should let us profit from the worsening domestic economic conditions that I believe are on the horizon. But my group cannot aggressively move forward until we see that you are making progress with your liquidations. That means you have to move quickly and decisively."

Haines had only spent six months on the trading floor during the standard associate rotation he was put through as a new employee of the firm. He wasn't a trader. He had heard everything that Teasedale had said but he was trying to figure out how he was going to get it done.

"Harrison, my only real question is why me? You have a legion of traders who got Morgan Greenville here, why not just have them reverse their trades?"

"A logical question. Your intuition is one of the reasons why I chose you. The traders believe that every one of the trades they made is golden. They've already been paid for the profits we've booked and they've moved on. Your background is analysis and relative valuation. To address the deeply illiquid positions on our balance sheet, you are the best candidate. On all the long trades, you just have to be decisive and persevere. It's going to be like shoveling a long driveway while it's still snowing. You are just going to have to keep going and then go back to the beginning and start again. This is not going to be easy. You will have to be very tough and not give up. That's why I chose you. I know you won't stop, you have too much at risk."

Haines realized that Teasedale was also a master of psychology. Teasedale knew Haines very well. He understood how Kirby thought and what mattered to him. And Teasedale knew that the only thing that frightened him was failure. Haines had built a life from nothing or at least from a modest heap of nothing. It was a motivator that worked. Teasedale knew that Haines had the intellectual capacity and fear to succeed. It wasn't the standard motivation, but it was a powerful one.

"What about price sensitivity? I'm not going to be able to move any of this stuff, liquid or illiquid, without taking a haircut. Who is going to make those decisions?"

"Let me be clear, Kirby. I want to get this stuff sold. Any reasonable discount is acceptable but you can't give it away. You are going to have to make the call. You can't sit on my lap all day. If something is large and you are concerned, then consult. Anything within a 20% discount is acceptable. We will make most of that back, and maybe even a profit from the new bets my team will make."

Haines was stunned. Teasedale was giving him free reign to dispose of billions of dollars of investments at discounts of up to 20%. The whole meeting and discussion was surreal. Yes, there was volatility in the market. That typically happened along the way in bull markets. Corrections were normal and some could be severe. There was nothing that Haines could see, read or glean from any source that suggested that the US economy was headed straight for the crapper. Every economic indicator suggested moderate growth, solid productivity gains, and an expanding global economy. Kirby couldn't see what Harrison Teasedale saw, but that really didn't matter.

Teasedale walked Haines out of his office off the trading floor and showed Haines his new second office. There was no wood paneling, or comfortable sofa or even an Oriental rug or mahogany desk. Haines' new digs was a glass cubicle off the trading floor right next to Harrison Teasedale's—only smaller. From his perch, everyone and anyone could catch a glimpse of Harrison Teasedale's new prince. With the trading floor humming and the temperature rising from the ambient heat of thousands of computer terminals, Kirby Haines wondered if he had bitten off more than he could chew.

As soon as Haines left his office, Harrison Teasedale picked up his phone to call Pennington Ludlow. His mind had been racing since Ludlow's call to him five hours ago. Ludlow's executive assistant answered the phone.

"Secretary Ludlow is in transit on his way back to the Capitol. I will relay your message to him when he lands."

"That won't do. Patch me through to him on his plane."

After some back and forth, Ludlow's assistant agreed to patch Teasedale through to the plane. Ludlow picked up the phone when it rang. Carmen was seated across the aisle facing him. She was reading a magazine and pumping her crossed legs slowly.

"Pennington Ludlow here."

"Pennington, this is Harrison. Listen to me. I've been upset for the last five hours. I don't understand why you've put me in this position. I am totally fucked because you hatched this plan and brought me in as your accomplice. Now the world is about to end and I've got to get rid of $200–300 billion worth of paper. I don't think I can get it done."

"Calm down Harrison. The fact that you made Morgan Green-ville our trading partner is your problem. That was never part of our deal, although I knew you would do what was in your own best interest. I want my account liquidated fast and the proceeds deposited in the various money-market accounts that have been set up outside the country. Get rid of everything but I don't want to get screwed on excessive discounts. And don't fuck this up Teasedale because the consequences will not be pretty for you."

"That's fine. But I want to know what my exposure is. You and the President and whoever else concocted this entire 'Economic Revolution' and now I'm right in the middle of it. What's going to happen to me if this charade gets exposed?"

Ludlow was silenced by Teasedale's question and inference. Teasedale had been a cooperative partner when it was just about front running the market. Could this pompous Wall Street twit turn on him?

"Listen to me Harrison. No one, including the President, knows about your involvement or our trading arrangement. Is that completely clear? No one knows about you and no one knows about us. And I intend to keep it that way. And if you open your mouth, you will regret it. I hope you understand what I'm saying."

Harrison Teasedale did not need to respond to Ludlow's rhetorical question and clear threat. Carmen Gomes listened and did her best to remember everything that Ludlow was saying to Teasedale. He was angry and anxious in a way the Carmen had never seen before.

"Harrison, you have a lot of work to do. I suggest you get off the phone and start protecting our balances. I will check in with you daily to track your progress. Get this done, but do it without causing significant carnage. I don't want your greed and fear to leave a trail that leads us both off the edge of a cliff." After an awkward moment of silence, Teasedale responded, "I understand."

Ludlow placed the satellite phone back in its holder and sat in silence thinking about his situation. He had kept Teasedale a secret to create his own fortune and could use him as a scapegoat should the need arise. He knew that Teasedale had always been a risk, but Ludlow had evaluated that risk in the context of the opportunity. Frankly, he rationalized that keeping his trading a secret from the President was an intelligent decision because it established another wall that protected the Presidency if something went wrong—which of course couldn't happen; he thought.

Ludlow hadn't taken something that he wasn't entitled to. He had signed on to Lowery's mission to restore the United States on top of the world's pecking order. In return, he devised his own payoff with Harrison Teasedale's assistance. If Harrison Teasedale faltered or weakened under the pressure, Kurt Denton would eliminate him from the equation. The beauty of having one accomplice was the opportunity to eliminate that link if it proved to be weak. Harrison Teasedale wasn't a weak person per se, but he was weakening. Ludlow could do nothing about him now. Teasedale had to liquidate his trading accounts. When that was done and the capital was safely on deposit in accounts around the world, Ludlow would decide Harrison Teasedale's fate.

CHAPTER 18

Dublin, Ireland
May 15, 2007

Carmen Gomes got up from her seat to use the lavatory at the rear of the Gulfstream. When she came back she stopped to rub Pennington Ludlow's shoulders. He was tense and in thought. After a few minutes of kneading his neck muscles she came around and sat on his lap.

"Baby, do you want me to relax you some more?" Her right hand moved under her hips and she started to rub him.

"Maybe later, Carmen. I'm just tired and need to think. I'm sorry. You always know how to turn me on, but we'll have time before we land."

As Carmen sat, she recited to herself the particulars of Ludlow's conversation with Harrison Teasedale. Fletcher always told her to take in everything around her—conversations, people's faces, etc. She never wanted to disappoint her boss. He was demanding but generous. And sleeping with him was like reaching the top of the pyramid. He checked in regularly. She was sure she would hear from him soon.

In Dublin Monroe Desmond and his staff of analysts had worked quickly to prepare a number of trading strategies for Bob Fletcher's review. Their work had taken into account the likely disclosure of new, deteriorating economic data in the weeks ahead. Desmond connected with Fletcher via their video conference network.

"Look Monroe, our game is over. We should play out our next steps with that clear understanding. Do you agree?"

"Yes, sir. Completely. Once the BLS and BEA complete Washington's data tests and the unadulterated data is passed through, our men will not be able to resurrect their mission. It will simply be too risky."

"You're right. Those results are going shake things up. People will do a lot of analysis to try to figure out what happened so suddenly. Subsequent reports will confirm the economic downturn. Ludlow and Solomon will talk about China and the emerging markets, the threat of inflation, and early over-reaction. We can probably deal with that outcome. Market sentiment will take over and wash away our tracks."

"I'll keep my men in their positions and we can slowly let them attrite during President Lowery's remaining two years. They're totally loyal and no one will make any sudden moves."

"It's hard to believe that one middle level civil servant can threaten President Lowery's legacy. It's a development we didn't anticipate. If this plays out according to our current scenario, the President will be hurt but not fatally, and we will protect our trading accounts if we can move fast enough."

Fletcher had a soldier's understanding of victory and defeat. He was faced with a potentially overwhelming force—the cold, economic facts—and he knew that it was better to retreat now with honor and resources intact. There would be other battles to fight in the future. President Lowery's legacy might take a hit, but none of them were going to be tried for high crimes.

"Monroe, do you have a clear plan for accelerating the liquidation of the trading accounts?"

"Yes, we've been working out of our positions slowly since the beginning of March. It's going to be rough from here because our time frame's been compressed significantly. We have some pretty illiquid stuff outside the US and the EU and that could be tricky. We got that head start so I think we should be okay. We're going to have to take quick discounts on the liquid stuff but can probably get that done fast if no one steps on us."

"How are you going to wash the stuff after you trade out of your positions?"

"We're going to use the banks you own and certain others in Italy and Spain. Those corporate accounts will then make investments in real estate and other businesses that we can flip out of over 12 to 24 months. Once that's done, the accounts should be completely clean. Look, we've got a big elephant to hide after five years; it wouldn't surprise me if it took a couple years to round trip everything and I would consider that pretty good execution."

"Okay, I'm fine with that. I know you won't sit on your hands. I'll talk to President Lowery after we're through. I'm going to suggest a face to face in Florida over Memorial Day Weekend to see where we are. Ludlow is still a concern. I hope he doesn't become a bigger one. We're going to have to figure out what exactly he has going on with Harrison Teasedale and Morgan Greenville. I don't have a good feeling. He could present a major complication or opportunity depending on what we find out. We should be prepared for both potentials."

When Fletcher and Desmond disconnected, Fletcher immediately dialed the President's secure line. When Lowery was patched through, Fletcher described the approach that he and Desmond had agreed to and discussed his continuing concern with Ludlow. Fletcher suggested that Lowery join him at his estate on Jupiter

Island in Florida over Memorial Day. Fletcher would fly Desmond over from Ireland and they could use the time together to review their progress to date and perform a complete situation analysis and plan additional contingency tactics. Lowery was scheduled to be in Florida that Friday anyway to meet with the young Republican Governor who was one of the President's biggest supporters. At Fletcher's estate, they could have complete privacy. As always, Fletcher would arrange for diversions as well.

CHAPTER 19

Washington, D.C.
Dublin, Ireland
May 16—24, 2007

Pennington Ludlow's hands were tied. He had no real basis for disallowing Bert Washington's phase two testing in his internal audit process. Washington had insured that the network of informed participants would be extremely small and that no false information would be fed into the market for global consumption. If Ludlow had objected strenuously to the plan, it could have raised eyebrows since Guillson and Washington were both supporting this next step. Ludlow had settled on his own strategy and Harrison Teasedale was executing it. President Lowery and Bob Fletcher were weighing their options since Lowery's legacy and his "Economic Revolution" had to be salvaged. Everything was moving fast. Ludlow knew that Lowery and Fletcher would consider every option. Ludlow had taken out his former chief of staff when things got difficult. He had no doubt that Lowery and Fletcher would consider Bert Washington expendable, as well as every other member of the senior audit team. Ludlow was a hunter. The killing alternative was not something that shocked him. But it wasn't going to be his decision. He needed to keep his own activities with Harrison Teasedale private. There were enough potential targets in Bob Fletcher's crosshairs. He did not want to find himself there too.

With Pennington Ludlow's reluctant approval, Bert Washington and Rosemary Guillson began the process of feeding false information into the data collection process. They had decided to use the Fed's San Francisco and Philadelphia regions which were the focus of their first audit phase. Their tactic was to create higher jobless claims in certain high population areas and wait to see if the false data was captured and altered by someone within or outside of their organizations. Because of the complexities involved and the need to keep the circle of informed participants small, their process might take weeks. Hillary Thomas, at Ludlow's direction, was to follow and map every single step that Washington and Guillson took to insure the integrity of the process. Ludlow had Thomas voice his concern that no political agenda play a part in this experiment. Washington and Guillson brought Beverly Bittner and Ken Shue over the wall to assist in their planning and implementation process. Shue already had his instructions from Desmond. Washington concluded that they could disseminate their fictitious data immediately once they established credible entities in region to report their jobless claims. They would also need to intercept hiring data from certain major employers in those regions to impact the net jobs creation or loss figure.

It didn't take Monroe Desmond's communications team very long to pull up and study Pennington Ludlow's telephone records over the last year. They had started with the last three month period since the meeting in Washington, D.C. among Lowery, Solomon,

Ludlow and Fletcher. While nothing unusual popped up, Ludlow did maintain a regular dialogue with Harrison Teasedale, the partner at Morgan Greenville who received Ludlow's call early on the morning on May 15th. When the team stretched their phone record search over the prior year, Teasedale's office and home numbers were regularly and frequently dialed. One of Desmond's other men confirmed that Ludlow's blind trust was maintained by Morgan Greenville. Teasedale himself was a staunch Republican who was a generous supporter of the RNC and served briefly in the Treasury Department when he was quite a bit younger. Over the last five years, Morgan Greenville had grown considerably in stature and was recognized as the most profitable and savvy trading firm on Wall Street.

When Desmond processed the information that his teams had assembled on Pennington Ludlow's phone records and Harrison Teasedale's background, he called Bob Fletcher with an update.

"From what you're telling me Monroe, it looks like Secretary Ludlow may be a bit more involved in the management of his blind trust than what the Congress might be comfortable with."

"I think that's a fair conclusion. I'm still concerned with the frequency of the calls. Ludlow is a bit of a wild one. I never considered him obsessive or compulsive. He calls Harrison Teasedale almost as much as you call me. That seems a little out of character."

"I think you're right Monroe. There's something else going on."

"Do you think that Ludlow could be feeding information to Teasedale and getting a kick-back from Morgan Greenville in a separate account?"

"I don't know. That's a bit risky. The funds flows would be discoverable. No, I wonder whether Pennington Ludlow is playing the same game we've been playing. That son-of-a-bitch might just be building his own personal retirement account. Harrison Teasedale could be his trading desk and making enormous profits for Morgan Greenville to cover their steps. What do you think of that?"

"Well, it's plausible I guess, but that's a pretty damning theory based on a series of phone calls."

"You're right. From now on we'll need to listen to Ludlow's calls when we can. You can get to someone from the NSA today, right? Let's just focus on his cell phone for now. In the meantime, maybe my favorite piece of cheese can tell us a little more about Ludlow and Teasedale's phone conversations. I think I'll fly her in to Jupiter Island for the Memorial Day Weekend event. I'm sure she won't be spending it with Ludlow. Holidays are for the wife. I think I might have some fun tuning up her motor. It's always a good time for two or three days. She just can't stop."

"Alright boss, I'll get things set up with the NSA. Do you want us to go to Florida as well?"

"Yeah, bring your direct reports. President Lowery is flying in that Friday. It will be three days of work and pleasure. I'll expect your team to give us a complete progress report on your trading and liquidation activities. I also want to understand how we can take advantage of the down trend we're about to enter. We'll need more details on Ludlow and Teasedale. We may have to make some tough decisions if my theory turns out to be correct."

"You think we'll have to take them out?"

"Monroe, we're dealing with the President of the United States and a mission to keep America on top of world's list of leading powers. If Ludlow's been up to anything, every option is on the table."

CHAPTER 20

Memorial Day Weekend
Friday, May 24, 2007

Hillary Thomas was anxious to begin the long holiday weekend. She hadn't seen Kirby since their celebration at Cru two weeks earlier. His new trading duties at Morgan Greenville had him completely underwater and she was busy dealing with Pennington Ludlow who was suddenly in Washington, D.C. every day with no travel plans in sight. She missed Kirby, an unexpected and somewhat scary feeling, and the weekend could not begin too soon. She hoped their time apart would not create a gap in the progress she felt they were making in their relationship. She actually was confused. The best thing about their relationship was the freedom they both enjoyed from each other. But things had started to change. Hillary was beginning to worry that she was feeling more deeply about Kirby. She didn't know whether she wanted to be in no-man's land anymore. Kirby could be distant. She didn't want to commit her heart unless Kirby committed his. Most of all, she didn't want to be in a standoff. Maybe her time with him during the summer would provide the clarity she was looking for. Or maybe she didn't want to find out.

She had to take care of a few details before she could head out
to Dulles to catch a Southwest Air flight directly to Islip, Long
Island. A little longer ride at the beginning of her trip was worth it
to avoid LaGuardia and Queens' traffic on the long holiday weekend.
She knew that Secretary Ludlow would be leaving after lunch. He
and his wife were jetting out to East Hampton to spend the long
weekend with her sister. It was their annual pilgrimage. Hillary's
most important meeting of the day was with Bert Washington and
Rosemary Guillson. Washington had asked the women to meet at
his office first thing that morning so that he could give them an
initial read on the controversial phase of the internal audit they had
started two weeks earlier. Washington's meeting would also obligate
Thomas to create a record and meeting summary for Secretary
Ludlow that she would have to complete before she headed off for
Long Island.

Bert Washington had won another battle with the traffic that
morning and arrived at work before 7:30 A.M. so he could study
the data sheets that had been prepared for his morning meeting
with Guillson and Thomas. He had come to work in an upbeat
mood, thinking about three days off, picnics and downtime with
his wife. By 8:30 A.M. he had read and reread the preliminary jobs
report for May. The numbers were still subject to change since
Friday was the last workday of the month. He also had a separate report for the San Francisco and Philadelphia Fed reporting
regions where false data had been fed into the system in an attempt to entrap a bad actor, if such a person or group existed. Bert
Washington was confused and put his Bureau coffee mug down.
As he waited for Guillson and Thomas to show up, his thoughts
about the long weekend faded away. He tried to concentrate so
that he would be ready to summarize the reports for the women.
The words weren't coming to him. Washington picked up the reports again and looked at the line items he had highlighted. Holy

motherfucker. Those were the only two words he could come up with. Holy motherfucker.

Washington's assistant knocked on his open door and let him know that the women had arrived. "I'm going to put them in north conference room. That okay with you? Water or another cup of coffee?"

"How about one more cup of coffee, thanks."

Washington gathered up the papers in front of him. He was feeling like he was having an out-of-body experience as he walked down the hallway to the north conference room where Guillson and Thomas were sitting and talking about their weekend plans.

"So Rosemary, are you going back to Boston to see your family for the holiday?"

"Yes, we do it every year. Never fails. There's a local parade that the kids love. It's been the same for the last 50 years. Same little floats, veterans groups, flags waving. It's old fashioned but true blue American. How about you?"

"I'm flying up to Eastern Long Island to spend the weekend with my boy friend. He's rented a house for the summer. This is the big weekend when all the renters show up so it ought to be a scene."

"Hello there, Bert. We were just talking about our weekend plans. Are you and Cathy and the kids heading off somewhere?"

"Good morning, good morning. No we're staying close to home. Cathy's done the planning and I've already forgotten it all. The only thing I know I won't be doing is watching the Indy 500."

"Well, I didn't really picture you as a race car fan. So is this going to be a quickie meeting so Hillary and I can get home and pack?"

"I guess that depends on how you feel after we're done." Bert Washington's response to Rosemary's question took both women by surprise. He didn't intend his usual sarcasm. He looked and sounded serious.

"Bert, it sounds like you've got some news back and you're not too pleased."

"I'm not sure how I feel exactly. I guess the news is mixed. I have some good news and some bad news. What do you want to hear first?"

"Bert, why don't you just tell us what you found out!" Rosemary was interested in getting to the point and getting out of Dodge.

"Okay then. Let me tell you what I know so far. We fed about 15,000 job losses into the system and the good news is that they passed through the process and were not manipulated."

"That's excellent. Oliver Stone is dead. Long live Bert Washington. I knew it was just too complicated and big a process to manipulate."

"I bow to your intuition Rosemary, but you didn't let me finish. The false data passed through the system untouched so we know that the preliminary numbers we've compiled are overstated by 15,000. Here's the bad news. It looks like the overall employment numbers for May are way off. Not a little off. Way off. Based on what I looked at this morning and I've got copies here for you as well, it looks like the economy lost about 60,000 jobs in May. I think the consensus forecast predicted 90,000 new jobs added."

Hillary dropped her pen and Rosemary let out a burst.

"What! Bert, say that again. That can't be right. 60,000 jobs lost can't possibly be right."

It was Bert Washington's original instinct that had driven him to the opinion that the economy that he saw day-in and day-out was out of whack with the numbers that the government and his own Bureau was publishing. He and Cathy griped about it over dinner. Folks in the cafeteria complained about how everything was more expensive. Even the casual conversation with a security guard or next door neighbor usually got down to their shrinking paychecks. But even with all that, Bert had doubts about his opinion. He was used to be proven wrong. Most of his life he was wrong even when he knew he was right. That aspect of his black heritage in a white culture was always lingering—that little self doubt or the expectation that someone would stand up and prove him wrong. Now he was right and he had his proof, but he wished he was wrong. The numbers in the report he was holding were devastating and the markets would shudder violently when they were released the following week if they proved to be accurate. At that moment, he didn't feel particularly Democratic. He didn't like President Lowery's swagger or his party affiliation, but even he didn't want to see the impact of the reversal of Lowery's "Economic Revolution." Bert remembered what the economy was like six years ago and nobody wanted to go back there. Bert remembered something else.

"Oh, there's another thing. In the course of looking at May's numbers, the team did the normal recalculation and adjustment for April. If you remember, in April we reported that the economy added about 85,000 jobs. That number was wrong. We are going to report that the economy actually lost about 30,000 jobs in April. We are rechecking everything of course, but if these numbers are correct and are announced at the end of next week, you can just imagine the shit that is going to hit the fan. Excuse my French, ladies."

"Bert, I'm sorry. Something is wrong. Those numbers can't be right. Someone must have blown something. Maybe when the numbers were fed into the two regions somebody pushed the wrong button and screwed up the tabulation. Look, if the jobs number is wrong, how can my GDP calculation be right?"

Bert didn't know how to answer Rosemary's question, so he treated it like it was rhetorical. "Look guys, I don't have any answers either. I just got these reports this morning. I looked at them. I had another cup of coffee. I looked at them again and they didn't change. I don't know what to say. If you look at the fourteen reporting regions, the pattern is generally the same. Every one of the regions shows a net loss of jobs, whether it's small or large."

"But Bert, in the last 60 months we have had positive job

growth every month…every month. All of a sudden we're going to report two successive months of job losses? How could that be? If I remember Econ 101, two successive months of job losses is an early indicator of recession, isn't it?"

"Hillary, I think you're right, but I'm a little more concerned that our announcement next week is going to go off like a nuclear bomb. No one is going to see this coming. The speculators who have been creating volatility over the last several months don't know about this. They're playing with rumors, not facts. This is going to bring the bears out of their dens. When this hits the tape all hell is going to break loose. You could have a market reaction like 1987."

"Bert, what are you going to do? You obviously have to go back and recheck everything."

"Of course, Hillary. I've already emailed Beverly and Ken to get them working together to do just that. Rosemary, I hope you don't mind that I took the liberty of contacting Ken directly?"

"Use him and whoever else you want. This is unbefucking-lievable."

"Rosemary, I don't think that I've ever heard you use that term before."

"That's because I haven't since my mother washed my mouth out with soap when I was twelve."

"Guys, don't you agree that while your direct reports recheck everything, we do everything that we can to safeguard these initial findings? We cannot afford to let this leak out. We still have a week before the official announcement."

"You're absolutely right Hillary. We have to keep this completely under wraps. The numbers are the numbers. We have to make sure that what we announce is accurate."

"Bert, I think we have to inform our Secretaries, even though the numbers are preliminary. They can't be blindsided. We'd be killed if we didn't."

"I agree with you, but I don't want to discuss our test with them—just the results. We'll tell them to give us the week to sort through everything one or two more times."

"Okay, it sounds like we've got a consensus on that. I'm going to summarize our meeting for Secretary Ludlow. You guys will deal with Labor and Commerce on your own. I assume you will schedule something next week, Bert, before you announce anything."

"That's for sure. I can just imagine the crisis that's going to erupt at the White House when they read your summary. We may enjoy part of our Memorial Day Weekend, but my guess is the President is going to get into serious spin mode in preparation for the next week."

"Bert, you're not concerned about the political fallout, are you?"

"Let's not go there. This isn't good for anyone. Period."

"Well let's hope that we all have jobs when this is done. Bert, you are always full of surprises but I think this meeting sets a new high water mark."

"Rosemary, I wish it wasn't so. I'm afraid we may all be in for a world of hurt."

The meeting ended and Thomas headed back to Treasury. Her report to Ludlow was now her paramount assignment. She couldn't believe what she just heard. Everything that she observed or looked at within Treasury suggested an economy that was still moving forward. Her view and Washington's initial findings were in stark contrast. It was black and white, but they needed seven more days to figure out which one was correct. She knew that Pennington Ludlow would be horrified and incredulous. Ludlow liked good news. He was an optimist and an apostle of the President's "Economic Revolution." She knew that he wouldn't believe the numbers and she would tell him that everything was preliminary. The April adjustment would be the icing on the cake. Thomas hoped that Bert Washington would find a mistake in his rechecking, or she knew there would be market madness. She also realized that for the next three days she would have to keep her mouth shut in front of Kirby. She was in possession of the type of inside information that could make someone hundreds of millions of dollars or lose it for that matter. That wasn't going to be easy.

Anne Eckhouse's driver swung the limousine by the Treasury Building to pick Ludlow up and take them both to the airport. Ludlow had scheduled an early lunch so they could be wheels up by 3:00 P.M. They were flying a Hawker 800 over to East Hampton and the short flight wouldn't take more than 40 minutes. Every Memorial Day, they were invited to spend the weekend with Anne's sister and her husband who owned a magnificent ocean fronting estate on Further Lane, next to The Maidstone Club. Ludlow actually enjoyed this trip to visit Anne's sister, Claire, and her husband Percy, because of the unique combination of privacy and social altitude found in that slice of East Hampton. For the most part, East Hampton was a swarm of new money, crass wannabes, but Maidstone was an oasis of class, privilege and old wasp wealth. In that setting, Ludlow was respected for his lineage, particularly his wife's, and his political power but never fawned over. As the pilots went through their final preparations, Ludlow's cell phone rang. It was Hillary Thomas. She had tried to call Ludlow shortly after her morning meeting, but his early lunch and departure for the airport had kept him from returning any calls. Thomas thought she should speak to him directly before she sent along her meeting summary.

"Mr. Secretary. It's Hillary, sir. Sorry to bother you. I know you must be ready to head off to East Hampton."

"Actually Hillary, we're sitting on the plane and we'll probably be off in another five minutes or so. What's up?"

Thomas explained her meeting with Washington and Guillson that morning. She was shocked by his preliminary findings but there was absolutely no evidence of any foul play.

"Well Goddammit. I knew there wasn't anything wrong with our system, but now I think there is. Is Bert Washington some kind of fucking idiot? Someone must have screwed up. Those numbers just aren't possible or reasonable. What are you guys doing about this?"

"Sir, I've prepared a summary memorandum that takes you through everything in detail including the rechecks that will be performed over the next seven days. The results are preliminary but I'm worried if they prove to be right. I thought you should know about this as soon as possible."

"Well, I appreciate that Hillary. You were right to treat this with urgency. You have to stay on top of this and keep me apprised of every development. I will personally alert the President. I assume this information is battened down—airtight?"

"Yes sir, absolutely. I am going to be in Southampton over the weekend if you need me."

"Thanks for letting me know. Everyone out there has ears and I know how discrete you are."

"There is nothing to worry about on that score, sir."

"Good Hillary. If I need you, I'll call you."

Ludlow hung up and cursed to himself but loudly enough that Anne looked up from her Town & Country magazine. "Everything alright dear?"

"Just the normal bullshit. Nobody can leave me alone. Everything's a crisis."

The Hawker taxied quickly to the active runway and was airborne in a matter of minutes. Ludlow pushed the recliner button on his seat and closed his eyes in thought. The May numbers were actually worse than he had anticipated and April's revision was a complete surprise. Even though he had stopped caring about the exact numbers that were fed into the system, he didn't think they were manipulated to the extent that Washington's report suggested. He thought the economy was treading water. Washington's jobs report showed an economy that was actually sinking. This was much worse than he imagined. He had counted on more time to liquidate the trades that were sitting in the accounts that Teasedale was managing for him. Now he knew he had seven days before things would get very, very ugly.

He had two quick calls to make. He picked up the plane's phone and dialed Harrison Teasedale's number. He needed to know where Teasedale's liquidation stood and that he only had seven days left. When he finished with Teasedale who cursed and hung up quickly, he called Bob Fletcher to give him the bad news from Washington's meeting. Fletcher, of course, had already gotten wind of the numbers from Ken Shue who alerted Desmond after he saw the preliminary results. Fletcher listened and said little. He told Ludlow to stay in touch and hung up. Ludlow sat back and stretched. He should have called Fletcher first, but it was too late. Desmond's communications chief picked up the call pattern and sent an alert to Fletcher. He was working on getting a complete transcript of the call.

As his security escort approached Percy Waters' house in East Hampton, Ludlow looked forward to a walk on the beach that evening. He felt at peace watching the waves and the setting sun. But Ludlow's peace would be short-lived.

CHAPTER 21

New York City
Jupiter Island, Florida
Friday, May 24, 2007

Even though the Friday afternoon before the start of the Memorial
Day Weekend was notoriously slow on Wall Street, you couldn't
convince Kirby Haines of that fact. For two weeks, Haines had
traded non-stop, logging sixteen hour days as a matter of course.
Morgan Greenville had been trading on a massive scale and in a
pattern that had not gone unnoticed to other sophisticated investors
in the market. Harrison Teasedale had been efficient and ruthless,
barking out orders and screaming at traders whose indecisiveness
delayed trades and cost the firm execution in markets with limited
liquidity. For Haines, it was baptism by fire. Teasedale did not care
about his lack of familiarity with many of the products, underlying credits, or issuers whose paper he was selling. Teasedale only
cared about closing the trades and confirming the settlement dates.
In some markets, their execution was clumsy and disruptive, but
Teasedale's orders were clear. He wanted everything that could be
sold to be sold. In the process, Morgan Greenville was reducing the

leverage on its balance sheet but its trading patterns had created wind shear in the prices of many securities.

Morgan Greenville's trading partners whispered about Teasedale's intentions. It would have been impossible to imagine that the most sophisticated investors would not notice the firm's actions. Even Teasedale's titular boss, Tom Lynch, had been contacted by his counterparts to discuss rumors that were circulating about the company's trading activities. Teasedale and Morgan Greenville maintained silence in regard to their strategies and intentions. But in every market around the world, they were making quite a commotion. To those that were watching, Teasedale the trading wizard was willing to take quick markdowns on securities with reasonable liquidity. The most interested observers of Morgan Greenville's unusual fire sale trading weren't the hedge funds or its trading counterparties. The group most focused was Monroe Desmond's financial staff in Dublin that was keeping Bob Fletcher informed around the clock. Morgan Greenville was doing exactly what Monroe Desmond was trying to do, and Bob Fletcher was not happy. The problem was that Morgan Greenville's tactics were screwing up Desmond's trading execution. Morgan Greenville was acting like an elephant in a circus parade, dumping shit everywhere and in very large amounts. As a result, Desmond's traders were often delayed or forced to accept prices that were substantially lower than where their positions were marked on their books.

By the time the equity market closed on Friday, Kirby Haines was physically exhausted. He thanked God that all the markets around the world would be shut for at least two days, giving him a break from his round-the-clock frenzy. He could hardly wait to lie in the hammock that hung on the front porch of his house on First Neck Lane, feel the sunshine on his face and smell the fresh cut grass and clean air. When he threw in a few days of sex with Hillary and maybe a round of golf with a one of his friends at Sebonac, he felt like he was a kid dreaming. Unfortunately, he knew that Teasedale would also be in Southampton over the weekend and his mansion was less than a half a mile away from Haines' expensive rental. He was fully prepared to have his short holiday interrupted several times by Teasedale who would probably call to review positions still in inventory and grouse about his trades and second-rate executions now that they were done. Second-guessing was one of Wall Street's favorite pastimes. The only upside to Teasedale's proximity in Southampton came in the form of an invitation to fly out to the Hamptons on Teasedale's helicopter. Once they left their office downtown, it would take them ten minutes to reach the heliport and a quick thirty minutes later they would touch down at the far end of Meadow Lane in Southampton. Haines would have a vodka tonic in his hand within an hour of leaving the building.

"Haines. Let's get moving. I'm walking out the door, now!"

Teasedale bellowed at Haines one last time. Haines scrambled to throw some homework into his satchel and ran to catch up with Teasedale who was already out of sight and headed to the elevator bank. Haines knew that Teasedale wouldn't wait for him if he didn't catch up. Teasedale wouldn't wait for his mother. Kirby was so tired, he wasn't making judgments. He just wanted to get a seat on that helicopter.

Jupiter Island is a narrow piece of land that lies directly north of Palm Beach. It is famously exclusive and boasts a long roster of wealthy homeowners. Bob Fletcher's father bought a ten acre compound on the island after the Second World War and many of his childhood memories were made there. After his father died, Fletcher renovated the property extensively and spared no expense.

Like his home in Sardinia, Fletcher's estate on Jupiter Island was remote, extremely private and absolutely beautiful. Located at the far end of the seventeen mile long island, Fletcher never worried about neighbors. It was another idyllic paradise in his long list of possessions. This Memorial Day Weekend, Fletcher's house guest was the President of the United States—a rare privilege for any American, but Bob Fletcher wasn't just any American. Fletcher was President Lowery's wingman. Fletcher also invited Monroe Desmond, several of Desmond's critical lieutenants in Dublin, Carmen Gomes, and a half dozen assortment of the finest imported cheese from France, Italy and Russia. Fletcher loved beautiful scenery—especially the kind that moved. Fletcher's house staff was fiercely loyal, well paid and cognizant of the price they would pay if they decided to misplace their loyalty. Fletcher's Jupiter Island residence was the perfect place to convene the most important meeting in President Lowery's two terms as President. Fletcher made certain that every element was in place to insure that the meeting would be constructive, fun and diverting. It was the only way he operated.

When Fletcher's helicopter landed on the property's lawn Friday afternoon, he was met by a golf cart driven by his property manager and head of security, Franz Curtiss. Curtiss was a former Stasi agent that Fletcher met on one his first business trips to East Germany. Franz was a master of detail and efficient in that traditional German manner.

"Welcome home, Mr. Fletcher. Mr. Desmond has arrived with his colleagues from Dublin. They are holding a meeting in your trading room on Level B. Ms. Gomes has also arrived and is taking sun by the pool. The rest of the female guests are either on the beach, at the gym or in the spa. Everything is in order sir and we've been in contact with President Lowery's security detail. He should be arriving in ninety minutes."

"That's great. I assume you've planned dinner and coordinated

with the additional security presence that will be around the property this weekend."

"Everything is done, sir. Nothing to worry about. Just enjoy yourself while you are home."

Fletcher had a dozen men like Curtiss. They were all efficient,
purposeful and completely responsible. Fletcher didn't need to know
any more details. Curtiss had planned everything and therefore
everything had been taken care of.

"Franz, why don't you take me over to the pool first so I can say
hello to Ms. Gomes."

"Of course, sir."

Carmen was lying on a lounge by the pool, taking in the late
afternoon sun. She was wearing the smallest of string bikinis that
barely covered the objects of its purpose. When she saw Fletcher
coming, she got up to meet him, her breasts swaying as she bounced
toward him.

'Oh Bob, it's so great to see you. I've missed you, you know. You
are never around you bad boy."

"Carmen, you are as beautiful as always. When I don't see you,
I still carry a picture of you in my mind."

"Give me a big kiss. You make me feel so good."

The two embraced and Fletcher could smell the mixture of tanning oil and incense-infused perfume that bathed her smooth and
brown body. Carmen pressed herself against Fletcher and rubbed
her hands up and down his back. He could feel her firm breasts
against his chest and momentarily felt his passion begin to rise.

Fletcher whispered in Carmen's ear, "Baby, I could fuck you
right now."

"Then do it, Bobby. And why not right here, where everyone
can see?"

Her hand reached down between them and she felt him. Fletcher
thought about turning her around, ripping her thong off and having

her there on the patio. Carmen even had that effect on him. But
Fletcher had to resist. Lowery would be arriving soon and Fletcher
had three days to enjoy Carmen as many times as he wanted, wher-
ever and whenever he desired. Bob Fletcher was not a patient man
but he decided that a bit of self-discipline was probably appropriate
at the moment.

"Baby, I want you to keep that thought because I am going to
tire you out this weekend. You're going to need a few days off when
I'm done with you."

"I was hoping you'd say that. It can't start too soon Bobby. I want
to feel it inside of me." She was touching herself and breathing out
loud.

"I do too but business comes first and the President is going
to arrive shortly. Sit down a minute. I want you to tell me about
Ludlow and Harrison Teasedale—particularly in the last couple
of weeks."

Carmen sat down and reclined against the back of the lounge
chair, her legs spread open in case Fletcher changed his mind.
"Well, Pennington has been in Washington, D.C. since we came
back from Dublin but he hasn't had much time for me since his
wife has been around. I did see him for a ride around the city one
afternoon when he needed me, but we didn't exactly talk about
Teasedale. In fact, given what he wanted, I wasn't able to really say
much and all he did was moan. Do you want more details Bobby?"
Carmen pulled one of the triangles of her bikini top aside and
massaged her nipple.

"I want to hear everything but let's stick to Teasedale for the
time being. Tell me about their recent conversations and what you
can remember."

Carmen told Fletcher everything that she remembered about
Ludlow's call with Teasedale as they flew back from Dublin. She
did a good job recalling certain phrases: "Morgan Greenville our

trading partner;" "liquidate my account fast;" "no one including the President knows about your involvement;" and "don't leave a trail that leads us off the edge of a cliff." Fletcher had heard enough. His suspicions were confirmed. Carmen added some details about the frequency of Ludlow's calls to Teasedale and how he seemed to call Teasedale first before anyone else, including Fletcher. The men always seemed to be talking about trading and Ludlow had become increasingly tense and impatient in the last two or three conversations she had overhead.

"You've done an excellent job Carmen. You are just as smart as you are beautiful."

Fletcher got up off the lounger where he was sitting across from Carmen and stood in front of her. She reached up and stroked his zipper, fingering the tab to pull it down. "Why don't you let me show you just how perfect I am?"

Fletcher knew she would have no problem pleasuring him right then and there, but he had to resist. He had to confer with Desmond before the President arrived. "Baby, you deserve a reward but I can't give it to you now. If you can wait until later, I'll give it to you more than once."

"That's a deal Bobby and if you forget, don't worry, I'll remind you."

Bob Fletcher left Carmen by the pool and entered the house through one of the series of French doors that opened up onto the terrace by the pool. Franz Curtiss had told Fletcher that Monroe Desmond and some of his men were meeting on Level B which was where his trading floor had been built when he renovated the home. The trading room was on a basement level and therefore windowless to insure that the beautiful surroundings would not become a distraction to the traders in residence. Fletcher took the elevator down to the lower level. The markets had just closed and the volume was typically light because most financial players liked to escape early for the long weekend. No one quit early in Bob Fletcher's operations.

"Welcome to Florida, Monroe. A bit warmer here, eh?"

"A wee bit but we've been down here working away so we haven't spent a lot of time in the Florida sun so far."

"So how'd we do today?"

"Well sir, we were able to move a series of blocks of some of the positions we've been holding for a long time. Given the day, there was a considerable volume in certain names like Citi, JP Morgan, Bank of America, and AIG. We thought we'd be able to size the blocks larger, but most of the action was on the sell side. I think a lot of buyers left early for the weekend. We've got a lot more to do in that sector."

"What about pricing?"

"It's been mixed. On the very liquid issues, the price discounts aren't that large but they're bigger than what we'd expect for the size blocks we're trying to move. Unfortunately, the discounts in some of the other markets where we're moving positions like Canada, Mexico, Italy and even Germany are much bigger. It's obvious that buying interest is being limited by another seller or group of sellers. It's hard for us to see every trade but we're getting indications about competitive activity. We were trying to unload a big equity block in Deutche Telecom and definitely ran into Morgan Greenville. One of my guys in Frankfurt had a lot to say about it. We were trying to move $50 million slowly and Morgan Greenville came in looking for a buyer of a single block of $100 million. They were like a bull in a china shop. They didn't use a beard, they just dropped the load in front of everyone and nothing happened. Then they preemptively dropped price by 10% and waited. Finally, apparently ABP bid down 15% and Morgan Greenville hit it. Talk about fucking clumsy. Now we have to wait for things to stabilize in that issue before we can proceed forward. Hopefully we won't see them again in that name."

"That's interesting, obviously, given our suspicions. What else concrete are your guys seeing?"

"I've had two guys just trying to follow Morgan Greenville around. They've definitely been a major seller over the last week or ten days. Most of that's coming from other trading partners so it's anecdotal. We'll probably pin more specifics to it as trades settle and guys talk. I'll tell you one thing. It seems like a fire sale when we can identify them. They're not wasting a lot of time and frankly not much brain power either. They may have this vaulted reputation as one of the savviest traders in the market, but some of the prices they seem to be taking make them look like rank amateurs."

"That's disturbing Monroe, given our mission. How are you dealing with it?"

"We're basically trying to identify and trade in markets where we're not seeing excessive volatility. So far we're doing okay, but it's adding time to our execution. I'd like to be 80% done at this point but I feel we've done less than 60%. The guys are working hard. I'm trying to stay disciplined but in some places I'm probably going to have to cave on price."

"I think you're right about that. Time is our enemy. We probably only have a week. Keep at it. We've got a lot riding on this."

"Of course. I'll catch up with you at cocktails."

"Right."

Bob Fletcher had enough information to confirm his hypothesis about Pennington Ludlow, Harrison Teasedale and Morgan Greenville. Morgan Greenville, the savviest trader on the Street, had used insider information to build its formidable position. Fletcher laughed to himself. What a fucking joke. Ludlow was probably receiving some kind of kickback from Teasedale. Ludlow was a greedy little shit but he had done something even worse. He had taken a dangerous step that could threaten Chuck Lowery's Presidency. Ludlow wasn't just cheating his partners. He had introduced a third-party to their conspiracy and that reckless decision may have already increased the risk that Lowery's "Economic Revolution" might be exposed for what it really was: a scam of untold proportion. Chuck Lowery was not going to like what Bob Fletcher was going to tell him when he landed later.

Around 6:00 P.M., the President's helicopter and its escort of military helicopters approached Fletcher's Jupiter Island estate. Fletcher had asked Franz Curtiss to plan a comfortable evening for his guests: cocktails on the terrace, an elegant dinner, and music and dancing afterward. When the Presidential helicopter powered down, Fletcher walked out to greet his friend.

"Hey Chuck welcome. How was your day with the governor?"

"Not bad. He's a smart young guy. But he's got a mess of problems. The housing market here is collapsing and the state hurricane fund is a real disaster. Other than that he's a great guy, loyal Republican and willing to help. He might turn into one of the permanent faces if he can survive two terms. Hey, am I on vacation now? Where are the drinks, Bob?"

"Just follow me. I've got some fun things planned for us after we take care of a little business. Let's get a drink in the library and spend a few moments."

When the men reached the house, they went directly to the library where Fletcher's head barman, Howard Sloane delivered two perfectly mixed vodka Southsides in silver cups as they sat in chairs that gave them an unobstructed view of the setting sun. Sloane had been in Fletcher's employ for twenty years and had memorized every guest's preferred drink after their first visit. President Lowery's favorite cocktail was a vodka Southside—the way Howard Sloane made it.

"Well Chuck, now I know we have a problem and I have some idea of its magnitude and scope." Lowery listened as Fletcher described his theory about Ludlow and Teasedale's relationship and Morgan Greenville's trading activity over the last two weeks. He also described Carmen Gomes' recollections of Teasedale and Ludlow's conversations. Lowery's face began to flush with anger but he almost laughed when Fletcher finished talking.

"That fucking snake. He's probably been trading for his own account for years. What a greedy little shit. If he'd been smart, he would have come to us with the plan. Why would he involve an outsider? That's just plain stupid."

"Look Chuck. A couple of other things. First, we know what Ludlow's been up to but he obviously doesn't know about Desmond and our operation. Second, if he's been doing this since you launched your 'Economic Revolution' six years ago he has made a lot of money and so has Harrison Teasedale. I mean a lot of money! Now they're running for the exit just like us since Ludlow found out about Bert Washington's goddamned audit. They know the bubble is about to burst and they're doing everything in their power to protect their profits before Washington stumbles on the truth. We've got some choices to make and even if they're a little bit messy, I think we'll have to make some decisions quickly."

Howard Sloane entered the library carrying two more chilled silver cups with ice cold vodka Southsides as if Fletcher or Lowery had sent him a telepathic message that they were ready for another round. Lowery liked Sloane. "Howard, when are you going to give me the recipe for this drink? My man at the White House ought to be able to make me these when I'm in residence."

"Mr. President, I would like to oblige you sir, but this recipe has been handed down from generation to generation among a select group of barman who have sworn not to divulge the recipe. It would be an act of dishonor if I broke my oath."

Lowery was impressed with Sloane's allegiance to duty. There weren't many people left in the world who couldn't be bought. Howard Sloane may have only been a barman, but he was a man of his word. All of Fletcher's men possessed that sense of loyalty. With his second drink in hand, Fletcher laughed this time.

"I even gave Ludlow my favorite cheese! Look Chuck, we've got some planning to do but let's enjoy the evening. We all could use a break for a few hours. We've got beautiful women, a beautiful night—the best of everything. We'll get the party started at 8:00 P.M."

A little before 8:00 P.M., a small band began to play Caribbean music on the outdoor terrace. Oil torches were lit and the property's outdoor lighting highlighted the exotic vegetation surrounding the expansive grass lawn in the back of the house. Slowly, Fletcher's guests, including Monroe Desmond, his crew from Dublin, and even Ken Shue who flew down from Washington, D.C. made their way from their rooms to the outdoor area. They were greeted by waiters who took drink orders and passed hors d'oeuvres and also by the seven female guests that Fletcher had arranged for their entertainment. The women were an exotic mix. Each was beautiful, classy and deliciously dressed to stimulate the men's interest in them. Their international backgrounds added a flavor of sophistication to the eroticism that would eventually take over the night. When dinner was called, President Lowery, who was partial to blondes, sat at the head of the table between a French and Russian variety. Fletcher had Carmen on his left and Lowery's Russian blonde to his right. The meal was wonderful and the atmosphere was carefree with an overtone of anticipated sexual energy. The night built on itself in a crescendo. The evening air was warm and heavy with humidity; the smell of burning torches carried on the light breeze. The stimulations surrounded everyone: rhythmic music, classic Bordeaux, close dancing, the glimpse of a breast, fine linens, long tanned legs, cigar wafts, soft lips, expensive perfume, slender necks, laughter, finger touches, and warm skin. Fletcher and Lowery were back in their element. For a common man there was nothing standard about any of it, but for Fletcher and Lowery, this was their world.

CHAPTER 22

Washington, D.C.
Jupiter Island, Florida
New York City
Southampton, New York
Saturday, May 25, 2007

On Saturday morning, Bert Washington woke up in his Bowie, Maryland home still hung over from the grim set of economic results that his audit test had produced. Perhaps the bottle and a half of pinot noir that he and Cathy shared as they sat on their deck the night before had also contributed to the cob webs he woke up with. When Bert walked into the kitchen to pour his first cup of coffee, Cathy was already up and the kids were watching the Cartoon Network. Luckily, they had planned a low key holiday weekend: the usual cookout with friends, Memorial Day parade and neighborhood activities.

"Good morning, sleeping beauty. How did it feel to steal an extra hour of sleep?"

"I wish I could tell you. Right now I feel like I'm in the middle of a maze. Maybe I'll find my way out after another cup or two."

"Well get ready for action. The kids are raring to go to the parade and it looks like it's going to be a beautiful day."

"Sweetie, don't worry. I'll be armed and ready. When's the parade start?"

"You're hopeless—10:00 A.M. And they don't want to be late!"

"Okay. Okay."

Washington grabbed the morning paper that one of the kids had retrieved from the driveway. As he leafed through the business section, he was struck by the upbeat headlines topping every column. The stock market had once again posted solid results for the week. But Washington was pre-occupied with the preliminary results for the May jobs report and the April revision that the news media knew nothing about. Even though the mechanics that produced the results appeared to be working perfectly, he couldn't understand the sharp downturn in the employment figures. Something had to be wrong inside the BLS; he just couldn't figure out what it was. When he thought the numbers were too good, he conducted the first test and the results showed that the systems were functioning properly. When he introduced false data, the data passed through the system un-manipulated but the overall results deteriorated significantly. Bert always trusted his instincts. If something were amiss at the Bureau, he wasn't sure who could be responsible and what purpose was being served. The country had been living through a long cycle of economic resurgence, clawing itself back to its pre-eminent position on top the world's ladder of wealth and power. Maybe the numbers for April and May simply reflected a pause or aberration that could be typical of such a long growth cycle. But the April restatement was the number that really bothered him. Downing his second cup of coffee, he couldn't help but wonder whether the restatement would have surfaced if his audit experiment had not been implemented.

While the kids tried to catch lightening bugs the night before,

Washington had confided in Cathy as they drank their wine. She told
Bert to follow his nose. She had no reason to trust the system and
nothing would surprise her. If Bert really thought that something
could be wrong, he should contact someone at the FBI and get
some advice. He knew that voicing his concern to his boss would
get him nowhere. The Secretary of Labor had grudgingly agreed to
Washington's initial internal audit process and everything appeared
to work properly. But Washington didn't like the result. His boss
would ride him out of town on a rail based on suspicion alone, but
his boss didn't know about the false data test. No, it was better to
go quietly to someone inside the FBI who could offer advice and
direction. If Bert used his leadership position at the BLS to speak to
someone with a senior leadership position at the Agency about his
theory, they would clearly think him insane. When Cathy pushed him
on agents he knew, he came up with one name: John Aichenhead.

"John Aichenhead. What kind of name is that? I know one thing
for sure: he's not a brother with a name like that."

"Very funny. I probably only remember him because of his name.
Aichenhead was a Marine and served with me in the Gulf. I know
he entered the FBI after the war and ended up in the New York
office working for the Criminal Investigative Division. I saw him
a couple years ago at a Marine event in DC. I remember that he
deals with white collar crime and national security issues in the
New York region."

"Well, why don't you reach out to him? He sounds like someone
you might be able to confide in. Send him an email in the morning.
You might as well try to get answers for yourself. If you don't, you'll
probably drive us both crazy."

His two cups of coffee brought back the details of his conversation with Cathy about John Aichenhead. Bert climbed back upstairs
and started the shower. He switched on his computer as he waited
for the water to warm up. After dressing he sat back down in front

of his laptop. He searched his Outlook trying to find Aichenhead's contact information. He found it in a file he had set up for old Marine correspondence. Aichenhead's email address was not an Agency address as luck would have it. Washington composed a quick message asking Aichenhead if he would be free for a brief phone call on an important matter later on Saturday. Washington clicked the send button and ran down the stairs where his two kids were waiting impatiently to leave for the local parade. Bert hoped Aichenhead would respond. He didn't even know if the email would reach him.

Despite their late night of debauchery, Bob Fletcher and Chuck Lowery were up early on Saturday, just like their days as Navy pilots. Monroe Desmond joined them as well and they sat down for breakfast on the east terrace as the sun began to rise.

"Monroe, why don't you take the President through the evidence that your team has put together over the last few weeks regarding Pennington Ludlow and Harrison Teasedale's relationship."

"Of course, Bob. We really only began to focus on their relationship after we intercepted Ludlow's call to Teasedale a couple of weeks ago. We've compiled a history of their phone calls going back four years, which I've included in this file for your review, as well as recent conversations we have been able to transcribe. They have clearly been careful with their communication. There are absolutely no email messages anywhere. They were smart enough to avoid any stupid mistakes. Their calling patterns demonstrate regular contact in the days leading up to any of the economic announcements we affected. Ludlow wasn't even permitted to talk to Teasedale about his blind trust. But these guys talked more than two old men playing checkers."

"Tell me more about Harrison Teasedale."

"Teasedale is a prominent Wall Street trader and probably the highest paid Partner at Morgan Greenville. He is a Republican and generous supporter of the RNC. Teasedale is not well liked by his competitors or frankly by his partners either. He uses Jack Rosenweig and his PR machine to make sure that his name does not appear in the newspapers, unless it's associated with some major charitable event. He's deeply in the closet and keeps his sexual preference to himself. He is very careful when in residence in New York. He never frequents any of the normal or exclusive gay clubs and he doesn't appear to have a companion in the city. His townhouse on East 70th Street is one of the largest private residences in New York but he never throws parties there and few people have ever been inside it. One of my guys went back to look at his overseas travel and picked up reliable leads of his apparent preference for hooking up with young Asian men. That seems to be his weakness but he only indulges himself when he travels outside the country."

"He sounds even worse than what I imagined."

"Mr. President, he's not someone anyone's going to shed many tears for when he exits the planet."

"Okay then. Let's review our situation and our options. Desmond, go on."

"At this point in our trading and liquidation process we are roughly 60% done toward our objective. Given the fact that we only have a week to go, it's a fair assumption that we will have to assume larger trading losses on the remainder of the unsold portfolio in order to move the rest of it. Regarding Teasedale and Ludlow and the risk they represent, Teasedale should be eliminated since he is the only outsider with knowledge of the entire operation now that Ludlow has apparently explained the mechanics of the 'Economic Revolution.' Neither man knows about our trading operation but there is a chance that a thorough investigation by any panel charged with looking at their dealings could possibly stumble across us as well. It is certainly not a sure thing, but it is a risk. Teasedale's elimination could scare Ludlow enough to shut him up. Or we could eliminate Ludlow as well."

"What about Morgan Greenville? If we take out Teasedale, could we take them down too to as a diversionary tactic?"

"That's interesting, Bob. Some collateral damage might help our cause but let's keep focused on Ludlow. I think we've made our decision about Teasedale."

"Listen Chuck, Ludlow went off the reservation and jeopardized our entire operation. My vote would be to kill him too. It's the cleanest solution. We implicate him carefully. The prospect of an investigation surfaces. He conveniently ends his own life and our potential whistle-blower is eliminated."

"Bob, I don't disagree that that may be the best course of action, but it's not without risk. A single slip up could bring down my Presidency. Are you sure we can't simply accomplish what we want by frightening him to death? Teasedale is expendable and the demise of a Wall Street powerhouse via a massive insider trading scandal would create an extraordinary misdirection and keep the White House out of the witness box. When Ludlow sees what happens to Teasedale, he'll never open his mouth."

"Okay Chuck. Let's work on that scenario. How do you want to set up Teasedale without implicating Ludlow? Where did Teasedale get his information?"

"It's got to be someone close to Ludlow. Maybe your roommate last night could be the leaker."

"God, I'd hate to waste a perfectly good piece of cheese. The convenient elements however are helpful. Other than her formidable sexual talents, Carmen has no past, present, or future to complicate things. Through her involvement, Ludlow would be forced to admit his extramarital affair and step down as Secretary of the

Treasury, but he would surely exchange that outcome for his life. We'll make him disgorge all his trading profits to us as soon as possible to insure that he stands as the unknowing leaker of economic information that Teasedale and Morgan Greenville obtained. His wife is rich enough. He'll still have millions to live on if she decides to keep him.

"Boss, I'm following your thought process but there are a lot of details that will need to be worked out."

"You're right, Monroe, and we don't have much time. Let's keep going. You and your team will have to plan each detail. We'll construct a relationship between Teasedale and Carmen Gomes through telephonic and cellular records. Other evidence will have to be planted to demonstrate their long relationship. I don't think we need to implicate them sexually since anyone who scratches the surface will find out about Teasedale's sexual preference. No, their relationship was about money. She fed Teasedale information and he paid her for it. She was a poor Mexican girl so we won't need to part with tons of money to make it all believable. Over five or six years, he would have paid her less than a million. You guys can create a quarterly deposit record over the last 60 months, and do it with one of the Mexican banks that we're friendly with. Gomes will disappear, unfortunately permanently. That should provide all the evidence that's necessary. Teasedale's personal trading accounts and Morgan Greenville's own trading records will seal their fate. The only wild card remains Ludlow, but the embarrassment of his own extramarital affair will always give us the cover to get rid of him if his resolve weakens or we change our mind."

"Alright guys. That sounds like a plan. We have precious little time to rewrite six years worth of history. Are we agreed on this course of action?"

"Yes. It's our best choice. We should be in position to get it all done in the next week. Waiting longer will only create additional risk. And Monroe, your guys are going to have to sprint to get our trading accounts liquidated."

"I understand. A little more than $3 billion has been deposited in three of our banks in jurisdictions beyond US oversight. No one could ever link them to President Lowery, or any of us without a treasure map. I've also spread about a billion of proceeds around a number of legitimate corporate accounts in standard banking institutions in New York, London and Hong Kong."

President Lowery stood up and looked out the window where the sun had risen over the blue Atlantic. "My entire Presidency is riding on the outcome of this operation. We've sacrificed a lot for America. This is a mission that has to succeed."

John Aichenhead's Memorial Day Weekend began like most of his other weekends. He spent Friday night on a bar stool in the Village drinking beer and eating tapas while he watched a ball game and commiserated with the bartender. At about 1:30 A.M., he wandered home, and collapsed unto his unmade bed. On Saturday morning he awoke early, just like any other work day. He pulled on a pair of old shorts and a tee shirt and stepped into his flip flops and walked out onto the deserted streets of the West Village. He didn't have to think about his morning ritual. He walked to his nearby bodega and picked up a large coffee and a breakfast sand-wich. On the way back to his apartment, he picked up the *Times*, *Daily News* and *Post*. He'd rip through them before starting his seri-ous reading for the day—a book about the birth of the Israeli State. The early morning sun and the sidewalk's dull heat promoted the dazed feeling that hung over his head from the prior evening's drinking. The Village would remain asleep until about lunch time. Around 10:00 A.M., Aichenhead turned on his computer to check his messages. He had a date that night with Joanne Fruilli. It was date number three. Date number three was the make-it or break-it date. He was thinking about that. It was too early to make any decisions about their potential relationship, although he knew that some sexual activity couldn't hurt and would stop the guys at the bar from needling him constantly. When Aichenhead scanned his inbox he saw a message from Bert Washington. That was odd. It took him a minute or two to remember Washington. But then it came back to him—the Marines and the Gulf War. Washington asked him to give him a call. He'd call Washington as he requested after lunch. Aichenhead sat back down in his reading chair and got lost in his Israeli and Palestinian history lesson.

Pennington Ludlow's Saturday morning called for a 9:00 A.M. tee time at The Maidstone Club. His brother-in-law, Percy, was a member and had arranged for a four ball with Tom Lynch, the CEO of Morgan Greenville, and Tom Flexnord, the founding partner of Flexnord et Fils, a large hedge fund and private equity firm based in New York. Flexnord was known as a fierce competitor and well-known golf cheat. As Ludlow prepared to head over to the club, his Blackberry buzzed with a coded message to call Harrison Teasedale. He quickly dialed Teasedale who wanted to alert him about some of the stories circulating on the Street about Morgan Greenville's recent trading activity and to give him some background information on Tom Lynch. When Ludlow finished with Teasedale, he got into the back seat of a Mercedes that would drive him the short distance to Maidstone's clubhouse and his Blackberry buzzed again. Bob Fletcher needed to reach him. Finished with his breakfast meeting with the President and Monroe Desmond, Bob Fletcher was ready to begin to ensnare Ludlow. Ludlow decided to ignore

Fletcher's message since he was already in the Maidstone parking lot and the use of cell phones was strictly prohibited on the Club's grounds. Ludlow who laughed in the face of every rule decided to let this convenience play to his advantage. When he returned Fletcher's call later, he would tell him that he left his phone in the car because of the Club's regulations. In Florida, Fletcher waited impatiently for Ludlow's return call. But it didn't come. After thirty minutes, Bob Fletcher was angry. He decided that the time frame for scaring Pennington Ludlow to death had just been accelerated. Fletcher reached his pilots who were stationed at the West Palm Beach airport and told them to get his Citation X ready. He would be flying up to East Hampton, New York as soon as they could file a flight plan. Fletcher went back to his room to tell Carmen to pack quickly. He was bringing her and two of her friends up to East Hampton. He was going to launch his plan immediately and needed every prop with him. Fletcher hadn't thought out many details but he would have several hours on the plane as they flew up. That should be enough time.

Kirby Haines and Hillary Thomas woke up on Saturday morning and headed out to the Golden Pear, Southampton's popular coffee and specialty food shop. They picked up the papers and two croissants and headed back to their house to relax on their large front porch and plan the rest of their day. They had dinner out the night before in Sag Harbor and walked around window shopping before heading home. They needed to break-in the rental house so they had sex in the living room and then in the dining room before going upstairs and collapsing in the master bedroom. The sun woke them up early but they were happy to be together. Hillary had been careful to keep her audit work at the BLS and BEA a non-topic in their conversations. Kirby's trading responsibilities with Morgan Greenville had made Hillary even more sensitive. On the other hand, Kirby couldn't stop talking about his work with Harrison Teasedale and their intricate trading schemes.

"Harrison is so intense. The pressure he puts on me is incredible. I mean I've been on the case for just about two weeks and he expects me to know everything that he's done for six years. When I make a trade he screams at me that I sold too cheap. When I tell him that I can't get a bid he goes nuts because I'm holding out for too much. Thank god for you. At least when I make you come you tell me how good it feels."

"You can include me in your permanent fan club, baby. But what I don't understand is why Teasedale is in so big a hurry. What's the big rush?"

"I can't completely explain it, but when Teasedale brought me on board he told me that his view of the macro environment was changing. He had put Morgan Greenville in a massive long position across markets and geographies and now he felt like he wanted to take the bets off the table. I think he believes that growth is about to grind to a halt and he doesn't want to lose everything that he's made. I don't know. I think the guy is a genius. He has such conviction about everything. I'm sitting there with my thumb up my ass trying to figure out the basics. He seems to know what the future holds. He's either going to make the cover of *Forbes* and *Fortune* as a result of this call or he is going to be crushed by the tape if the economy continues to hum along like it's been doing. I'm telling you, I don't know how the guy does it but he is amazing even if he is the biggest asshole on the face of the earth."

"Teasedale is obviously a man with strong convictions. You're lucky he's brought you inside his tent so you can see how he does it."

Hillary thought Teasedale must really be a genius since his view of the US economy would shortly be proven correct when the May data was released in about a week's time and the April numbers were adjusted. The stock market was going to tank and Teasedale's timing would be perfect. If he had moved Morgan Greenville into Treasuries, they were going to rally as investors sought safe havens. Morgan Greenville would make a killing. Hillary couldn't say anything but she was happy that Kirby was working for Teasedale. When everyone suffered a tremendous setback, Morgan Greenville would once again prove itself as the savviest trading firm on the Street.

John Aichenhead polished off his morning reading in about three hours. He knew more about Golda Meier and the fledgling Israeli republic than he ever wanted to and he stored all the details somewhere in his brain for a comment in a conversation sometime in the future. He picked up his phone at about 1:00 P.M. and dialed the number that Bert Washington had given him in his email message. Bert Washington's home phone rang three times.

"Hello." Washington answered the phone.

"Hi Bert? It's John Aichenhead calling. How are you doing? It's been a while."

"Hi John. You're great to call me back. I'm sorry to ask you to do this over Memorial Day."

"That's okay. I'm just at home relaxing and don't have anything planned until later today. I figured if a fellow Marine called it must be something important, especially on a holiday weekend. So what's up Bert? What can I do for you?"

"Well it's a bit complicated. Can I start at the beginning?"

"I've got plenty of time. The beginning is usually a good place to start."

Washington took Aichenhead through everything. He started by describing his job at the BLS. He told Aichenhead about his nagging doubts regarding the economy and his concern that the numbers the Bureau produced didn't seem to jive with his common sense observations. He explained his effort to use an audit to test the gathering and analytical processes within the BLS and ESA and how the results indicated no material weaknesses. He emphasized his doubt about whether any civil servant process could be error free. Both men laughed at that notion; they knew better. They had worked inside the government for too long When Washington described the extreme step of feeding false data into the collection system, Aichenhead more finely tuned into Bert's story. Washington just couldn't understand how the numbers had turned so negative and he couldn't justify the coincidence of those results with his own efforts to game the system.

"Look, John, I have no proof of anything. Just a Marine's instinct that something isn't right. If this were an FBI matter, what would you do with this fact pattern?"

"I'm used to dealing with facts. But I think you've given me mostly theory and some deductive reasoning. You really haven't given me many facts. Luckily, I know something about the protocol surrounding economic announcements and maybe even a little bit about how calculations like CPI and PPI are determined."

"Well that may even separate you from a majority of the people working in my bureau."

"Don't be too impressed. I spend all my time reading about stuff that nobody really cares about. I do know that those announcements can have a dramatic impact on the stock and bond markets. Why don't you retrace your steps for me one more time and let me see if something pops out."

Washington took him through everything one more time. He recounted every meeting and the principals involved in the audit process. When he was finished, he waited for Aichenhead's response.

"I don't know, Bert. You may just be seeing ghosts. Let's assume you're right for a minute. If a crime has been committed, who has benefited from the misinformation? Where is the evidence of wrongdoing if your own internal audit hasn't come up with any process deficiencies?"

"I wanted to talk to you because I've got more questions than I have answers. It's just my gut. I know that something isn't right. I've felt it in my bones that this economy has been slowing for the last six months. I can give you twenty anecdotal examples of the weakening economy, but they're all buried inside the corporate performance of the S&P 500. If I could aggregate all that evidence, it would paint a much different picture than the one presented by the steady growth numbers issued by the government. Then all of a sudden, I decide to fuck with the system, and the numbers hit the proverbial wall. I launch a secret audit of our field data procurement processes and what we end up with is the biggest surprise in sixty months. It's just too coincidental."

"Bert, you're not convincing me. There could be a hundred reasons why the numbers turned south and one of them could be the result of some nefarious intent. You see the unfortunate souls who haven't benefited from the President's 'Economic Revolution' and believe that some conspiracy is the culprit. Look man. Shit happens. I see it all the time. Your gut doesn't equate to evidence. You are entitled to your opinion but it doesn't give rise to a criminal investigation. Not here, not now."

"John, please. You're being absolutely rational and that's why I need your advice. Just follow me for a minute more. Chuck Lowery started his 'Economic Revolution' six years ago. For five years it has been a world beater. He's now the most popular President in modern history and has overseen the longest period of economic expansion in the last one hundred years. But what if the economy has not been as strong as reported? What if the administration has pushed the numbers to champion Lowery's legacy? My audit was the only tool that could have exposed a manipulation like this and all of a sudden the numbers hit the wall once we throw the monkey wrench into the machine. Something is going on."

"Bert, you've got an Oliver Stone complex."

"Someone else told me that, but Oliver Stone wasn't wrong with all of his theories. Let's switch gears then. Help me understand your methods of investigation when you are pursuing a potential case with only circumstantial evidence. If you did agree with my theory of potential manipulation, how would you proceed?"

Aichenhead liked this avenue of discussion much better than arguing with Bert Washington whether a crime had occurred or not.

"Well, there are a lot of nets that can be cast to attempt to uncover corroborating evidence. The first place I would start would be with your employee population. I would conduct a thorough background check on everyone in your bureau. I would be looking for correlations in previous work experience, dates of employment, family relationships—really anything that might connect one employee involved in a conspiracy of a large number of parties. If something came up as a result of that investigation, I would dig deeper. Although you mentioned motive in the context of preserving the President's legacy, I would probably look for a less noble motive—like personal financial gain. Given that potential motivation, I would contact my buddies at the SEC, NYSE and other financial markets and look for unusual trading patterns, particularly in the days leading up to the release of key economic reports. If that process turned up discernible patterns, I would use my friends at the NSA to obtain phone and email records, as well as other personal data on the individuals responsible for making trading decisions at those companies that showed evidence of unusual trading activity. That would be a start."

Washington had been scribbling notes as Aichenhead outlined

his investigative procedures. "John, that's excellent. I really need your help."

Aichenhead laughed, "I don't think you heard what I said before the part that you just liked."

"John, please. The economic reports I am sitting on are going to be released in about a week. They are going to sink the market and folks are going to lose billions and billions of dollars. We have to find out what, if anything, is behind this sudden economic reversal."

"Bert, those professors at the University of Chicago say that markets are efficient. Some folks will win and some will lose. I just can't see your conspiracy theory. It's just too big and complex to believe."

"Please. Just give me something. A little help on anything. You know I can't go to my superiors. Nobody is going to help me. I'd just be branded a political partisan or black man gone wild. Couldn't you just run background checks on my professional staff at the BLS? That would be a massive help. If nothing turns up, I go away quietly and leave you alone. How about this favor for a Corps brother?"

Aichenhead remained silent on the other end of the phone. Washington was asking him to do something that could get him in a lot of trouble. Aichenhead just couldn't go off and perform background checks on government employees without their consent or the sign off of his superiors. Such an invasion of privacy was itself a criminal offense. Washington waited on the other end of the phone in silence as well.

After an eternity, John Aichenhead spoke up. "Okay. I'll do it Bert."

"Excellent. How long will it take?"

"That depends on how quickly you can give me names, addresses and social security numbers for the employees you want checked."

"I can send you an email file in the next couple of hours."

"Don't do that Bert. I want a fighting chance to keep my job.

Just make a copy of that file and fax it to me at home. We can't leave any footprints that lead to my front door. I may not like my job, but I need the paycheck. I'll be back in contact once I've made some progress."

Aichenhead gave Washington his home fax number and the men hung up. Aichenhead wondered why he had just accepted this dangerous assignment. He barely knew Bert Washington. He wasn't being paid. He couldn't give a shit about the stock market or about President Lowery and his legacy for that matter. Maybe he just wanted to take a risk—that was something that he hadn't done for a very long time.

Bob Fletcher's Citation X sped up the East Coast headed toward the eastern end of Long Island. His cargo included Carmen Gomes and two of her girl friends. They were tempting him to have some fun after the pilots closed their cockpit door to give them some privacy. Bob might get to some of that fun, but first he had to reach Pennington Ludlow. He tried his cell phone once more and got no answer. Frustrated he placed a call and got the number for Hillary Thomas, Ludlow's Chief of Staff. He dialed Thomas and reached her immediately.

"Hello, Hillary Thomas? This is Bob Fletcher. We haven't met but I am calling on behalf of the President and I need to reach Secretary Ludlow. He has not answered his cell phone and I need a landline number for him if you have one."

Hillary had heard of Bob Fletcher before but never expected to speak to him. He was the insiders' insider—a man of supposed extraordinary influence and power who only dealt with a select few people in Washington, D.C.

"Certainly, Mr. Fletcher. Secretary Ludlow is staying at his sister-in-law's home in East Hampton. I know he was scheduled to play golf this morning which is why you might have had a hard time reaching him. I understand that the club where he is playing is extremely restrictive and probably prohibits cell phone use." Hillary gave Fletcher the Waters' home number and hung up.

"Who was that?" Kirby had finished the first four newspapers and was now scanning the Southampton Press.

"It was Bob Fletcher. Have you heard of him? He is one of President Lowery's best friends. He was looking for Secretary Ludlow and couldn't reach him."

With Percy Waters' home number, Fletcher dialed quickly while being slightly distracted by Carmen's antics with her friends. They were trying on sun dresses that they had quickly packed on short notice. Their mostly naked bodies were hard to ignore in the plane's small quarters. After two rings, the Waters' house manager answered the phone, "Waters' residence. Harold Cummings speaking. How can I help you?"

"This is Bob Fletcher calling on behalf of the President of the United States. I am trying to reach Secretary Ludlow and it's important."

"Yes, sir. Mr. Ludlow is presently still on the golf course where he is playing with Mr. Waters and two other men. I imagine that they will be done by 1:00 P.M."

Fletcher looked at his watch. It was just after 11:00 A.M. "Isn't there any way that I can reach him?"

"No, sir. Cell phone use is strictly prohibited. And since Mr. Ludlow is familiar with Maidstone's etiquette, I am sure he left his phone in the car."

Fletcher laughed out loud. "You're serious, aren't you?"

"Oh yes, sir. Those rules are strictly enforced."

Fletcher thought that Maidstone must be the only place in the world where communications actually stopped. And it stopped for golf of all things. Fletcher could think of a dozen activities more worthy of that distinction than golf. A half an hour with Carmen Gomes went to the top of that list.

"I'm sorry, Harold is it?"

"Yes, sir."

"Harold, please leave a message for Secretary Ludlow. Tell him that Bob Fletcher is flying up to East Hampton. I should be landing in about two hours and will be coming by Mr. Waters' house to see him privately. President Lowery asked me to do this personally. Do you have that?"

"Of course, sir. I will relay the message to Mr. Ludlow as soon as he returns."

Bob Fletcher hung up the phone amused. Pennington Ludlow was not going to see this coming. With the call done, Carmen and her friends directed their attention to Bob Fletcher. They had conspired to turn him on and their fashion show was doing the trick. Carmen draped herself across Fletcher's lap, her wrap dress untied. One of the other girls bent over and started to kiss Carmen's neck. The party had begun. Fletcher didn't have to do much for the next hour except enjoy himself. The girls were busy doing all the work.

CHAPTER 23

East Hampton, New York
Saturday, May 25, 2007

Pennington Ludlow was a better hunter than he was a golfer. To describe his game as mediocre would be a fair description, but like in all things, Ludlow was a fierce competitor, even at games where others had more skill. Carmen Gomes had done her best to keep his hips in flexible condition but their love making had done nothing to improve his chipping and putting. The only member of the four-some that morning who was lower on the skill ladder than Ludlow was his brother-in-law, Percy. Even though Percy was a Maidstone member and played the course regularly, the caddies had to turn their heads when he addressed the ball to avoid breaking out in laughter. Percy was as stiff as a board and when he prepared to swing, he stuck his flat Protestant ass out as far as he could just like they told him to do on the Golf Channel instructional videos. But Percy was about as athletic and fluid as a robot. When properly executed, the golf swing is a beautiful rotation of flexible strength, speed and agility. Percy's swing was more like a lift, shift, dip, chop and stumble motion. Breaking 115 would probably be Percy's greatest athletic achievement, if he could ever do that. The two other players in the foursome, Tom Lynch and Tom Flexnord, were the real deal. Both were single digit handicappers and very competitive guys.

The eighth hole at Maidstone is a rather famous par 3 that only measures about 150 yards from the members' tees. The tee shot must carry over tall sand dunes that protect a hidden green that abuts the beach and the Atlantic Ocean. When the wind howls, the petite 150 yard hole can play more like 200 yards which is one reason why the hole is so famous out East. In their match that morning, Ludlow and Lynch were battling against Flexnord and Waters. They were playing a $50 nassau with automatic presses and lots of junk. Heading to the eighth tee, Flexnord and Waters were two down with two holes left to play on the front side bet. With a press starting for the last two holes, the men hit their tee shots at the elusive target over the grass-topped dunes. Waters hit first and chunked one short of the green, but the other players hit respectable shots that looked like they probably made the putting surface. Part of the fun of the eighth hole was the anticipation of seeing where the balls actually ended up since the green was not visible to the players from the tee. When the men reached the green, only two balls were resting on the putting surface and each lay about 30 feet from the cup. Tom Flexnord's ball was nowhere in sight and he cursed as he began to look for it over the back of the green. His partner was inept. He couldn't find his ball. He was about to drop a hundred bucks on the front side bet. He was furious and he hated to lose. While the other golfers spread out to help look for his ball, Flexnord carefully reached into his pocket and cupped the spare ball he carried in his pants. He bent over to sweep his hand through the thick grass and skillfully dropped his spare ball and announced to the others that he had found his tee shot.

The other players went back to play their next shots, satisfied that the brief search had not turned into a lengthy delay. After Percy played his second shot, Flexnord was the next to hit. He chipped his ball expertly onto the green and it rolled up within two feet of the cup. Lynch and Ludlow conceded Flexnord's putt and Lynch's caddy walked toward the cup to kick Flexnord's ball back towards him. When the caddy reached to remove the pin from the cup, he saw a golf ball lying at the bottom. He announced his discovery with a laugh, suggesting that the foursome in front of them had probably left the ball behind as a joke. But when Tom Lynch bent over to pick the ball out of the cup, staring him right in the face was a corporate logo stamped on the face of the ball: Flexnord et Fils. Tom Flexnord, Wall Street's most suspected golf cheat had been caught red-handed and in the presence of a Cabinet member and the CEO of Wall Street's biggest power house. Flexnord's need to win at any cost had negated what would have been a spectacular hole-in-one. Flexnord said absolutely nothing. He reached out and took his ball from Lynch's grasp and walked off the green, turning his back on the others. Flummoxed and embarrassed that such a transgression could be committed on the hallowed ground of Maidstone, Percy Waters declared that his round was over and that he and Flexnord were leaving the course. Lynch and Ludlow were shocked. They stood on the edge of the eighth green trying to decide what to do. Should they finish their round or walk in too? After a minute or two of confusion, they walked to the ninth tee having made their decision. It was a beautiful late spring day and cheating, while certainly bad, was not going to ruin their round.

As they played their last nine holes, Ludlow and Lynch discussed the markets and the economy. While Lynch had no idea that Morgan Greenville's trading success was principally the result of Ludlow and Teasedale's conspiracy to make their own fortunes, Pennington Ludlow knew all the relevant facts.

"Tom, of late I've heard some rumors circulating about Morgan Greenville's trading strategies. It sounds like you've been very aggressive sellers recently. Some are saying that the firm's trading has disrupted certain markets and the pricing of certain securities and commodities around the world."

"Well, some of the rumors are probably true. Harrison Teasedale believes that the economy and inflation are starting to move in negative directions. He's launched a major trading initiative to reposition the firm's balance sheet for that likelihood."

"Tom, your firm has a major impact on our financial system as well as on the perception of the health of the economy through your trading decisions. We've had enough volatility over the last several months from all the hedge funds who have been fucking with the market. I don't think that it's asking too much for you to keep your country's interest in front of your own when you plan your strategies. President Lowery has done a spectacular job of leading this country back from the edge of the abyss. Your firm and all your competitors were dying on the vine when he was elected. His vision and leadership made you all rich. I hope you're not going to turn your back on the President now."

Lynch was all too familiar with the political gamesmanship that Ludlow was playing.

"Pennington, I am one of Chuck Lowery's biggest supporters and I think you know how much money I have given and raised for the RNC over the last twenty years. I love this country and will do everything within my power to keep it on top. As you well know, Morgan Greenville is only one firm. The market trades on information and sentiment. I can tell you as an example that even we have had trouble executing some trades in certain markets over the last few weeks. There are obviously other smart folks who see the same thing that we see. We're not leading the market with our view point. We are acting in our shareholders' best interests."

Ludlow had articulated any Treasury Secretary's concern. Both men understood the kabuki dance they were performing. But

Ludlow's regard for Lynch and his attitude was not high. He wished he could make Lynch understand that all of the considerable wealth that Lynch had made through his partnership interest in Morgan Greenville was the direct result of a Flexnord-like ball drop that no one had discovered. Lynch was like every other Wall Streeter—convinced that they deserved the outrageous wealth that fell into their laps. He thought that their insufferable egos deserved to be deflated. Unfortunately, Ludlow's own fortune was too closely connected to the fate of Morgan Greenville. That day of reckoning would just have to wait.

When Lynch and Ludlow finished their round, they walked into the men's locker room to change their shoes. Flexnord's transgression on the eighth hole was being whispered about everywhere and the echoes were thundering across the exclusive grounds. The sanctuary had been defiled. A cheater had been found out. The Club would never live the story down. What an indignity to such a noble club—and brought about by a guest, no small thanks. Percy Waters would certainly receive a letter from the Club President about that incident. The Club's real concern was that the story not end up on the front page of The Observer. The mood in clubhouse felt like someone had just died. Ludlow was somewhat amused by the entire debacle as he considered the vast number of cheaters who were actually dues paying members of that holy place. Golf infractions were chump change in the cheating universe of those titans. Pennington knew that everyone cheated at something. Even Jesus was a sinner, right? He laughed at the absurdity of it all.

After Ludlow freshened up, he walked to the Maidstone parking lot and climbed in the back of the Mercedes for the three minute drive back to the Waters' mansion. It was about 1:15 P.M. and Ludlow picked up his Blackberry to look through his email messages. Two items marked "urgent" caught his attention. The first message was from Hillary Thomas: Bob Fletcher had called her trying to get the

Waters' home phone number. The second message was from Harold Cummings, Waters' house manager: Bob Fletcher had called trying to reach him. Ludlow then remembered ignoring Fletcher's call that morning. According to Cummings' message, Fletcher was on his way up to East Hampton. Something serious must be up. A tinge of acidity began to curdle in the pit of Ludlow's empty gut. When he walked in the house, he could hear his brother-in-law lamenting about the Flexnord incident on the eighth hole to someone on the phone. Harold Cummings greeted Ludlow and informed him that Mr. Fletcher was in route to East Hampton airport and should be on the ground shortly if his plane remained on schedule.

Ludlow climbed the stairs and went to his bedroom where he closed the door and quickly called Harrison Teasedale who was at his Southampton waterfront mansion overseeing the preparations for his annual Memorial Day weekend cocktail party that evening. Teasedale's fastidiousness was even stitched tightly into his weekend persona. Ludlow was not going to tell Teasedale of Bob Fletcher's imminent surprise visit to the Hamptons.

"Hello Harrison. It's Pennington. Just thought I would check in to see if everything was peaceful on your end."

"Well, if you think I could find peace while getting ready for 400 hundred guests to arrive you have too high an opinion of me. How was your golf with Lynch? He's a bit of an idiot, but that's why he's the CEO."

"Everything went fine with Lynch. I played my role and he played his. By the way, remind me to tell you a good story about Tom Flexnord tonight. He really pulled one at Maidstone today. I doubt he'll ever play golf out here again."

"I will see you and Anne at 7:00 P.M. Good bye."

Satisfied that nothing was amiss with Teasedale, Ludlow speed-dialed Hillary Thomas in Southampton. Hillary and Kirby were lounging by the pool with Peter and Sam Bolger, while the Bolger youngsters were running in the yard under the watchful eye of their Ecuadorian nanny. They planned to have a late lunch and two bottles of rosé were chilling in an ice bucket.

"Hello Hillary. It's Pennington Ludlow. Sorry to bother you on Saturday but I got your message. I thought I would follow up. Did Bob Fletcher mention anything specifically that I should know about?"

"Hi Mr. Secretary. No, Mr. Fletcher didn't say much. Just that he was looking for you and couldn't reach you on your cell phone. He thought that I might have the Waters' phone number so I gave it to him; he thanked me and hung up. That was about it. He did seem like he was in a bit of a hurry and had something important to talk about, but I've never met him and didn't know whether that is just his style."

"Good. That's fine. Well, I'll be speaking with him shortly in any event."

"Sir, is there anything else I can do for you this afternoon."

"No, nothing. I take it that nothing else has come up since we spoke yesterday about the Bert Washington exercise?"

"No sir. Nothing new there but I expect to talk to Bert on Tuesday when we're all back at the Capitol. By the way, I assume I will see you tonight at Harrison Teasedale's cocktail party. My friend Kirby Haines is Teasedale's partner on Morgan Greenville's proprietary trading desk."

"We will be there and I look forward to seeing you and meeting Kirby again. Enjoy the sunshine."

Ludlow hung up. He had learned nothing that could give him any clue why Bob Fletcher was flying up to meet him. Still he had a bad feeling. He really didn't like Fletcher very much. He was a bit too mercenary for Ludlow's taste. For all the money he had, Fletcher was very rough around the edges. Bob Fletcher and Maidstone would not be a natural fit.

CHAPTER 24

East Hampton, New York
Saturday, May 26, 2007

Bob Fletcher's Citation X touched down on East Hampton's busy weekend air strip and quickly taxied to a stop near the small terminal building. East Hampton Airport had no gates but on summer weekends it seemed as busy as any metropolitan airport. Two black Chevy Suburbans waited outside the perimeter fence until the plane's engines were shut down. After 9/11, passenger cars had been prohibited from driving out on the tarmac at most non-commercial airports as a matter of security. Bob Fletcher's detail followed its own security guidelines. As the black cars passed through the gate and approached the plane, the other weekend travelers at the airport stopped to observe the unusual protocol. They waited to catch a glimpse of the party that was afforded such special treatment. Maybe it was Jay Z, or P Diddy, or Ron Perelman or some hedge fund billionaire. It had to be someone big since they couldn't get their cars to meet their planes no matter how insistently they argued with the airport manager.

No one watching could possibly know who Bob Fletcher was

or have any understanding of the wealth, power or influence he possessed. He liked it that way. But looking out the window before deplaning, Bob Fletcher knew who they were: they were the multi-millionaire trailer trash of the Hamptons. When Lowery and Fletcher set out to fix the economy, they couldn't pick and choose who would benefit from their plan. The curious onlookers could not fathom how different his life was than theirs. They were hoping for a Page Six moment: something that they could talk about with their vapid friends over cocktails that evening. Fletcher wouldn't disappoint them with his arrival. When the plane door opened, Fletcher climbed out quickly and was followed by the three stunning women who looked like they just got off a pornographic movie set. It was quite a scene. Nobody left disappointed.

Fletcher's brief motorcade made its way to East Hampton, slowly in the weekend traffic, and followed the road to Further Lane where the Waters' mansion stood stoically against the dunes. When the SUVs pulled up to the house, Fletcher got out of the first vehicle still dressed like he had been in Florida: black slacks and shoes and a Hawaiian style shirt hanging off his broad shoulders. He was physically imposing. His hands were large and rough; his forearms thick and muscular. Fletcher was permanently tanned since he only seemed to travel to destinations where it was summer. His straight sandy hair moved as the wind blew it gently. Bob Fletcher looked the part of a handsome war hero in his fifties with a lot of fight left in him.

Harold Cummings opened the large screen door and met Fletcher on the home's enormous front porch. "Good afternoon Mr. Fletcher. I am Harold Cummings, the Waters' house manager. We spoke earlier."

"Yes we did. Is Mr. Ludlow back from his golf game yet?"

"Yes sir. He's sitting on the back patio by the pool. If you would follow me."

Cummings led Fletcher through the mansion's public rooms and out to the back patio area that bordered a wide expanse of lawn that narrowed to a winding path, leading to the beach. The patio itself was very large with enormous white umbrellas covering four separate seating configurations. Pennington and Anne Eckhouse were relaxing beneath one of the umbrellas with Percy Waters. The staff had brought them light sandwiches since the golf ran late and they were sipping ice teas from tall smoked glasses. Percy, an always self-conscious host, bounded up to introduce himself to the guest walking toward him who looked a little more ready for South Beach than East Hampton's Main Beach.

"Hello there and welcome. I'm Percy Waters. Can I offer you something to drink?"

"Hello Percy. Bob Fletcher. It's a pleasure to meet you. Please excuse my intrusion. Hello Anne. How are you? What a beautiful house and setting. Pennington, nice to see you as well."

Fletcher was always polite if the situation demanded it. He knew he had arrived without proper notice or invitation. "Pennington, the President asked me to fly up to speak to you about some urgent business. Percy and Anne, would you excuse us for a few moments. I have to relay some sensitive matters. I will be out of your way before you know it. Again, my apologies for the intrusion."

Percy was now suitably impressed with this oddly dressed guest who obviously was there to discuss important government business with his brother-in-law. Anne and Percy got up, leaving Fletcher and Ludlow alone.

Fletcher and Ludlow had not seen each other in person since President Lowery's meeting in mid-February when they were summoned to discuss the country's deteriorating economic prospects. When Lowery had dispatched the men to come up with answers to help save his "Economic Revolution," Ludlow had left the meeting intent on saving his fortune. Ludlow had no idea that Bob Fletcher and Chuck Lowery had done the same thing. He also had no idea that his self-dealing had been discovered by Fletcher. His day of reckoning was upon him.

Sitting alone on the patio, Fletcher launched his surprise attack with a direct hit. "So Pennington, why don't you tell me have much money you and Teasedale have made for yourselves while putting the Presidency at risk."

Ludlow was startled by Fletcher's accusation and caught off guard. "Bob, I have no idea what you're talking about."

"Oh, you know exactly what I'm talking about."

As Fletcher spoke his large hand reached across and grabbed Ludlow's leg above the knee, squeezing it hard. Ludlow began to speak again but Fletcher interrupted. "Shut up Pennington. Let's take a walk on the beach."

Fletcher stood up quickly and pulled Ludlow out of his seat, clasping his arm above Ludlow's elbow. Ludlow had no choice but to comply and Fletcher escorted him across the lawn and to the path that led to the beach. Ludlow's mind was racing. What did Fletcher know? How could he know? Had Teasedale flipped on him? Why exactly had he come? Fletcher was capable of anything, even violence. But Ludlow dismissed that thought as quickly as it had entered his mind. He would have to be insane. As they reached the beach, the ambient noise level rose considerably as the waves broke against the sand and the wind whistled louder.

"Pennington, I've got all of the details that I need to prove your treason. We've been following you for months and uncovered the history of your dealings with Teasedale. The only decision we have to make is how we dispose of the evidence and preserve the Presidency and the Nation."

Ludlow surmised that Teasedale had not flipped on him. But he also realized that his life did not mean anything to Bob Fletcher. Maybe he was insane enough to kill him.

"You were weak and careless. Your actions have put President Lowery in grave danger. It would have been bad enough if you had free-wheeled your way to make some dough on the side, but you exposed our mission to an outsider. How could you do that? Harrison Teasedale could bring down the government with one phone call to *The Wall Street Journal* or *Washington Post*. You allowed him to turn Morgan Greenville into a financial powerhouse and now they are fucking up the global equity markets and every hedge fund asshole is riding their trades. Pennington, you are a greedy mother-fucking traitor and you are going to pay for it with your life."

Ludlow's knees buckled suddenly when Fletcher sentenced him, but Fletcher's grip on his arm kept him upright. Ludlow felt like he needed to piss as his nerves lost control of his muscles. "You are out of your mind, Fletcher. You can't kill a sitting Cabinet member."

"I can kill anyone I want. You won't be the first and probably not the last. I want everything you have on Teasedale. He is a dead man as well."

Ludlow captured the implication of Fletcher's remark. Teasedale was the outsider. He had to disappear sooner rather than later and certainly before Ludlow. Ludlow wondered how much time he actually had. He decided to tell Fletcher as much as he could. Perhaps he could slowly begin to change Fletcher's thinking if he could isolate Teasedale and make his elimination the end point of Fletcher's mission.

"I identified Teasedale from the outset as the most discreet but powerful partner I could find for my trading. As you may know, Teasedale is a recluse except for his charitable endeavors. He lives alone; has no friends; has never been married and has no living family; and he is a closeted queer who chooses not to have a partner since it could expose him in the financial world that wouldn't tolerate his homosexual lifestyle. Teasedale is an extreme deviation from anyone that you or I know. I chose him because I knew that he would serve as the perfect scapegoat if there was ever a need—if something ever threatened to go wrong or my trading was exposed."

"How do you know that this fucking faggot hasn't kept a record of everything that you've done together and he's ready to take you down if something begins to go wrong?"

"We had our rules, Bob, but he is more frightened of having his sexual orientation exposed than anything else. You'd have to know the man like I do to understand that. He would commit suicide before facing the ridicule of the society bigwigs whom he panders to for acceptance. This guy picks up young Asian kids for sadomasochistic sex whenever he leaves the country. Don't worry. I've got proof of that just like I got Alan Solomon fucking Carmen Gomes."

"You may be right but you may be wrong. Teasedale's involvement threatens all of us."

"Fletcher, let me deal with him then."

"Give me one reason."

"Remember my former Chief of Staff, Matthew Perry?"

"No."

"Well Perry died about a year ago of a sudden heart attack while he was jogging during lunch along the Potomac River. Perry didn't have a heart attack. I had him killed when he began to ask too many questions about my dealings with Teasedale. Kurt Denton, my security chief, poisoned Perry's water container using a tincture of aconite—it's never picked up in toxicology screens. We have a lot of that growing down at DeSaussure Hall. I eliminated Perry; I can eliminate Teasedale as well."

Fletcher was at once impressed with Ludlow's admission but alarmed that Ludlow's carelessness had nearly exposed his and Teasedale's dealings to another outsider within the same year.

"Ludlow, your game is over. You've taken too many chances. You flaunted your affair and flew Carmen around on government charters. You traded in markets around the world with thin cover. You brought a faggot on board as your trading partner. You murdered your own Chief of Staff. And you betrayed the very President who lifted you up into a circle of historical exclusivity. You are finished for sure."

Ludlow realized that his life was on the line. He shook free of Fletcher's grip and faced him shaking. "You can't kill me, Fletcher. Just tell me what you want. We can make some kind of arrangement."

Fletcher knew that his conversation would ultimately lead to a desperate plea by Ludlow for his life. Now Ludlow was offering him his ill-gotten fortune. It was the only piece of the puzzle that Monroe Desmond and his men had not been able to put together. Just how much money had Teasedale and Ludlow made? Fletcher was about to find out. Perhaps he and Lowery could double their fortune in a single trade: not bad.

Fletcher brushed Ludlow's hands away from his shirt. "Have you stopped trading?"

"Not completely. I figured we had a week more before all hell broke loose."

"How much more do you have to do?"

"We're about 70% done."

"I want everything Ludlow. Your account information. Trading history. Everything is going to disappear, Pennington. Every last fucking dollar."

"You're insane, Bob. You're talking about billions of dollars!"

Fletcher stared at him coldly. It was a lifelessness stare. Empty. Brutal. "I don't give a fuck about your life, your money or your reputation. You're already finished, whether you live or die."

Pennington realized that Fletcher was right. His only prayer was that he still might be alive when Fletcher's work was done and that wasn't going to be answered now.

"We're going to walk back to the house now, Pennington. And you are going to pull your sorry ass together and act like the self-important snob that you've always been. We are monitoring you, if you haven't guessed by now, so watch what you say or you'll stop talking sooner. I'm calling the shots now, every one of them. Keep on your schedule this weekend. I want the account information and trading history within 24 hours and wiring instructions as well. You will follow my directions."

"Harrison Teasedale is having a big cocktail party this evening in Southampton. Should I go?"

"Yes, you go. I'm going too, now that you've invited me. I don't want any fucking funny business, Ludlow. No tip-offs; nothing. I'll be watching. By the way, where have you hidden Carmen?"

Ludlow obviously had no idea that Carmen was sitting in the back of the second black Suburban parked in front of the Waters' house.

"I didn't invite her up. I'm spending the weekend with Anne and her sister—isn't that obvious?"

"Of course, I forgot. Well I invited her, Pennington. She's sitting right outside in the car. She's going to be my date this evening and I'm going to bang her over and over again tonight. She is one horny Mexican slut, isn't she? Make sure you let Teasedale know that he's going to have four more guests this evening."

The sun that Ludlow got on the golf course made it appear that not all of the blood had just been drained from his face. As they walked across the lawn, the large patio was still deserted, just as they had left it. The scenery surrounding the two men was breathtaking. The sky was a deep blue interrupted by wispy patterns of super white cirrus clouds. The grass they walked on was regally green. The scrub trees and brush that protected the dunes were twisted and contorted into shapes uniquely natural, like perfect Rodin's. The ocean and sandy beach behind them was like a postcard, frozen in perfection.

Fletcher walked away from Ludlow without saying another word, leaving him standing in the middle of his once perfect world. The last fifteen minutes had changed everything forever. Fletcher strode through the dark cool house and out onto the front porch. He motioned to his security staff and the SUVs fired up. Fletcher got into the second Suburban with Carmen and the other girls and the cars rolled out of the driveway on their way to Water Mill. Fletcher rented an enormous house there every August when he typically visited Long Island. His men had quickly informed the owner that he needed the house for the weekend. Since price didn't matter, the owner had quickly packed up and headed for the airport.

Fletcher had delivered his message to Pennington Ludlow. The mission had started. Fletcher would get what he wanted and more. There were still some details that he needed to work out in his mind. Every plan had twists and turns. It was like an aerial dogfight. Fletcher did not know how everything would unfold, but he knew he would win and his enemies would lose. In the end, that was all that mattered.

CHAPTER 25

East Hampton, New York
Saturday, May 26, 2007

Harrison Teasedale's Memorial Day weekend cocktail party was one of the most sought after invitations in the Hamptons. Teasedale owned a massive house on a five acre piece of property in between the ocean and Lake Agawam. Teasedale had been preoccupied with only two things in the last several weeks: trading like a gladiator and personally overseeing every last detail for his grand party. He had erected a massive tent in his yard with heaters just in case the temperature dropped too low. The floral arrangement on every table and throughout the house were designed and approved by Teasedale himself. The catering menu was painstakingly constructed to follow the party's theme which Harrison devised each year. This year Teasedale decided that the evening would be "an African safari." Choosing a menu to fit that theme could prove difficult for most organizers, but Teasedale relished every challenge. His parties were also known for the appearance of a special musical guest. Guests and gossipers loved to speculate on the entertainment. The prior year, everyone thought the Rolling Stones were going to perform, but Bon Jovi showed up and did not disappoint a soul. This year the early buzz was about Bruce Springsteen. But Teasedale had decided to surprise the crowd with the United States re-introduction of George Michael. Hopefully done with his public bathroom dalliances, Michael would rock the crowd with 30 minutes of Wham's greatest hits. Teasedale actually liked George Michael's music.

Teasedale's cell phone rang as he was going over final details about security and parking.

"Hello Harrison? It's Pennington again."

"Hello Pennington. I'm a bit busy right now with some people going over security for tonight. I thought we got everything straight an hour ago."

Ludlow was now on guard since he knew that Fletcher or one of his operatives was probably listening. He quickly tried to remember exactly what he had said to Teasedale an hour earlier. It didn't matter at this point. "We did, but something just came up. One of President Lowery's closest aides and confidantes is in the Hamptons this weekend and I ran into him after we spoke. It's Bob Fletcher. I told him that he should feel welcome to come by your party tonight. I wanted to make sure that you put him on your guest list. He's coming with three others."

"I know I've heard of Fletcher but don't believe that we've ever met."

"He's a very powerful guy. I'll introduce you when he arrives. You should get to know him if you can." Ludlow couldn't tell Teasedale anything more. He could have told Teasedale that he was a dead man, but Teasedale's elimination might be Ludlow's only hope of survival. Still he wasn't convinced that the odds of his living were any different at this point than they were when Fletcher left him minutes ago.

"That's fine Pennington. I will put Fletcher and three guests on the master list. I've really got to run and finish things up. I will see you and Anne later. Good bye."

Teasedale dropped the call and went back to the migraine-inducing detail. Ludlow sat on a lounge chair and cursed Fletcher as he thought about Carmen going down on him. Ludlow needed to try to work every angle he could. He wasn't coming up with a lot of ideas.

The guests started arriving at Teasedale's Agawam estate promptly at 7:00 P.M. that evening. Twenty-five parking valets had been hired to whisk the guests' cars away from the property's impressive front gate upon their arrival. The display of servants hired for Teasedale's party was staggering. It seemed like there must be one waiter, valet or bartender for every couple there. The staff was all dressed in black shirts and pants. Teasedale didn't want them to stand out against the tapestry of his guests' costumes. Teasedale had invited 200 VIPs plus their spouses, dates or escorts. There were a few last minute additions like Bob Fletcher, but for every invited guest there were a dozen social climbers who tried everything to score an invitation. They were all disappointed. As usual, Harrison Teasedale was date-less. He liked it that way: clean, tight, controlled with no distraction. For him, the party was like any other mechanic in his life. It was a means to an end, and it had to be executed perfectly.

Pennington and Anne Ludlow and the Waters' were driven over to Southampton by a discreet Secret Service detail that had been on duty since the Secretary landed in East Hampton Friday afternoon. As they pulled up to Teasedale's entrance on First Neck Lane, the Secret Service agents waved off the parking attendants. His SUVs would remain on the street just up from the property's

iron gates. Since the driveway was over 500 yards long, arriving
guests were being shuttled to the main house by eight-passenger
golf carts that had been decorated like safari Land Rovers, complete
with jungle camouflage. Teasedale had thought of everything. The
Ludlow's and Waters' got into their own Land Rover and headed
up the driveway.

Bob Fletcher's small caravan from Water Mill pulled up to the
Teasedale estate shortly after Ludlow's arrival. Fletcher's personal
security, while civilian, was well known to the Secret Service. All
of them were decorated veterans with Special Ops credentials.
Fletcher's SUVs parked right behind Ludlow's on the street. When
the car doors opened, Fletcher got out followed by Carmen Gomes
and her two other spectacularly gorgeous colleagues. The parking
valets stopped what they were doing, almost as if commanded.
Southampton had no shortage of pretty females during the summer
months, but these women were in a class by themselves. They were
dressed or barely dressed in exotic summer dresses that looked like
animal skins: one was a zebra, another was a leopard, and the third
was a peacock. All at once it seemed like the breathable oxygen has
been sucked out of the air. Fletcher walked with them over to the
next waiting Land Rover and they climbed in for their brief ride to
the main party. As they departed up the driveway, the tableau that
occurred upon their grand entrance sprang back to life. A buzz was
in the air. This party would be talked about for weeks on end.

By the time Fletcher and the women alighted from their trans-
port, the Ludlow's and Waters' had already waded through the
crowd toward the tent in the back yard where Teasedale was
greeting his guests. Fletcher and the girls were met by waiters
proffering trays loaded with glasses of champagne, cosmopolitans
and a special cocktail created for the party's theme called "Jane's
Revenge"—another Teasedale touch. Jane's Revenge was basically
a Mojito and the ladies each took one.

Bob Fletcher eased his way through the sea of blue-blazered gentlemen and floral printed woman. He felt like he'd traveled back to the 1960s. Half of the men were wearing ties with their jackets and their graying hair was Brylcreemed in place, a straight part separating the right from the left. Even though Fletcher was pushing 59 years of age, his attitude and lifestyle placed him squarely in his mid-thirties. He would have preferred to have been anywhere else in the world at that moment than in Southampton. Teasedale's party was pompous and self-important. As he looked at people, they quickly judged him and glanced away having calculated in their own minds his net worth or level of social importance. He could buy and sell everyone at that party. There was nothing real about the evening, the place or the people reveling in their safari-themed stupor. The only real thing was his mission and Harrison Teasedale's predicament. Although Teasedale had no inkling what lay in store for him, his life was about to begin its last chapter momentarily.

As Ludlow was being greeted by many of the guests, he spied Fletcher and his harem when they arrived. He could see Carmen but she didn't see him. The women seemed to make quite a commotion with their outfits. Pennington told Anne and Percy that he spotted Bob Fletcher and had to introduce him to Harrison Teasedale since he had traveled so far on Presidential business. Ludlow walked back through the crowd and Fletcher saw him coming.

"Hello Pennington. Thanks for arranging our invitations on such short notice. What an affair? This is really the Hamptons at its best. Can I introduce you to my friends?"

Ludlow was enraged that Fletcher would demean him with such a question. Carmen had been his mistress for almost ten years. Ludlow naively thought that he was the only man that enjoyed her pleasures; he certainly didn't realize that Carmen belonged to Fletcher. "Hello everyone. You all look gorgeous tonight."

Ludlow caught Carmen's eyes but she looked away quickly after giving him a sympathetic glance. Ludlow was devastated but he couldn't show it. He was somebody. He still had to save his own skin. "Bob, why don't I introduce you to Harrison Teasedale? He's just over there and I told him that you'd like to meet him and say hello."

"Pennington, by all means. Let's meet the evening's host."

As they moved in Teasedale's direction, Ludlow kept looking at Carmen. Her leopard wrap dress was barely closed by her waist belt. He could see the silhouette of her breast—the curved upslope that led to her erect nipple. Ludlow wanted to grab her and escape to pursue the passion that he was feeling, but he was not in control anymore. She was not at his sexual command. He wondered how she felt; whether she loved him, or pitied him, or might help him. Ludlow was confused and trying to get his bearings.

"Pennington, that's a beautiful blazer you're wearing and what a sporting tie!" Fletcher was mocking him and Ludlow could do nothing about it. Others receiving that complement would be consciously proud. Ludlow knew he was carrying his own cross across Teasedale's lawn. And then they were standing in front of Teasedale.

Harrison Teasedale was busy chatting away with two of the doyens on the Meadow Club's board. They were discussing some very important issues at the club like whether dinner should be extended for an hour now that people were eating so late, or whether children should be allowed to play on more of the grass courts during the week before noon time. Ludlow had absolutely no problem interrupting Teasedale's conversation.

"Harrison, excuse me. I want to introduce you to Bob Fletcher, President Lowery's real right hand man."

The two old dames took one look at Fletcher and stopped talking. He was an unlikely looking man with such access. He wasn't at all what they might have expected. Fletcher stuck out his large hand to shake Teasedale's and it enveloped Teasedale's diminutive alternative. Fletcher looked his prey in the eye. He would play with him for a while to assess the proper ending.

"Thanks for including us at the last minute. This is quite an event. I like your theme very much. Have you ever hunted big game, Mr. Teasedale?"

"It is my pleasure to meet you Mr. Fletcher. This has been a long standing tradition for me. It serves as a new beginning to each summer. I wanted to have a theme this year that was different but I must confess that I've never been on a safari or hunted big game myself."

"Oh, that's a pity. I find it a great thrill to track a beast for days; observe its patterns and preferences. It doesn't take long to establish an odd relationship with your prey. And when the opportunity presents itself, the relationship ends with death. There is an edge that's hard to describe when you pursue something that you ultimately kill. Sometimes it's a surprise for both the hunter and the hunted. But most of the time, the beast never sees it coming."

"That's quite fascinating, really. Perhaps I'll have to go to Africa one day for such a hunt."

"I wouldn't wait too long, Mr. Teasedale. Africa is changing very quickly."

"Mr. Fletcher, I'm wondering if we've met before. Perhaps in Washington—maybe at the last inauguration?"

"I don't think so. I try to avoid Washington as much as I can."

"Pennington told me that you and President Lowery are quite close and even grew up together. He said your involvement with the Republican Party has been invaluable."

"President Lowery and I went to Chapel Hill together and then flew in Viet Nam. I just try to keep under the radar screen really. I'm the President's wingman. I consider it my duty to protect him and the Presidency to my fullest ability."

"That is exceedingly noble. How do you keep yourself busy when you're not protecting the Presidency?" Teasedale asked the question with a tinge of sarcasm, now imagining Fletcher more as an inside confidante than a string puller.

Sensing his opening once Teasedale revealed his presumptive naiveté, Fletcher replied, "I eradicate threats and eliminate risks, Mr. Teasedale. Let's hope you don't ever represent either one of those alternatives."

Fletcher turned and walked away, leaving Teasedale and Ludlow alone and stunned. Ludlow grasped the full intent of Fletcher's message. Teasedale only thought the man rude and brusque—didn't he know anything about standard social behavior at a party such as this?

As Fletcher walked away he took Carmen by the arm, escorting her toward the dance floor where the DJ was warming up the guests for the evening's surprise entertainment. He was playing some Spanish-infused rock with a heavy beat. Carmen began to move her hips to the rhythm. Fletcher placed his large right hand on her firm backside and they danced closely to the music. As Ludlow watched them, Teasedale pulled him away to find out who the hell Bob Fletcher really was and what was he doing in Southampton.

"What the fuck was that about, Pennington?"

Ludlow looked Teasedale directly in his beady eyes. "President Lowery knows about our trading scheme and he sent Fletcher up here to deal with it."

Teasedale almost lost his footing and nearly slipped but shouldered up against a stone wall that separated his rose garden from the lawn. "What . . . what exactly does that mean?"

"I really don't know, Harrison." But Ludlow actually had a very good idea. He just wasn't willing to jeopardize any of his own alternatives at that point. "He came to Percy's house this afternoon and told me that they had you, Morgan Greenville and me under suspicion and surveillance for some time. Fletcher is not one of us. He and Lowery were fighter pilots in the same Navy squadron during Viet Nam. They know that I was passing information on to you and that you were using it to trade extensively for our benefit as well as your firm's. I don't know how far he will take it, but you know he is around to protect the Presidency and no one is big enough to stand in his way. We are in trouble, Harrison. There is no doubt about it. I suggest you enjoy this party tonight. It might be the last one you have for a long time. Lowery and Fletcher were on a patriotic mission. We were the profiteers of their work."

"Pennington, this is all preposterous."

"Harrison, didn't you ever think at some point along the way that it was too good to be true? Are you such a pompous ass that you thought you were riding the perfect wave? Lowery wanted America to become the dominant world economic leader again. That was noble. You and I were getting rich. They probably won't consider us possible nominees for the Medal of Honor."

"Pennington, I still can't believe that all the numbers were fiction. Look around you. Are you telling me that this all an illusion? Is the wealth that's been created over the last five years a figment of everyone's imagination? It can't be. Look at the people here. The house next door just sold for $58 million. This is all a sham? The country is experiencing a period of prosperity that will go down in history. What is the real story Pennington?"

"Harrison, you can choose to ignore what I told you but it won't change a thing. We told the markets lies for years. Some were bigger than others, but none of the numbers were true. We magnified the real growth and softened the corrections. We created stability in an economy that was still reeling from the tech bubble implosion. But along the way we created our own bubbles. Do you really think that real estate can appreciate 300% in five years? That oil prices can triple or Impressionist Art quadruple? At what point along the way did you lose your common sense, Harrison?"

Teasedale was quiet. Ludlow's points were sinking in. He realized that he was a central figure in the biggest economic fraud in history. "I can't believe this, Pennington. You're playing with me, aren't you? What do you want from me? I don't like this game. What you and the President did for the good of the country did not include me. I couldn't give a shit about that. I just wanted to make money."

"Listen to me Harrison. Fletcher knows everything. He has demanded our account and trading information. He has records of all our conversations and has been monitoring us closely since February. There is nothing you can do for me or for yourself at this point. We may be dead men; we may be spared. It's in Fletcher's hands and any false move on our part will force his decision. All we can do is wait until he decides his next steps. He is going to protect President Lowery at any cost."

"I'm not waiting for anything, Pennington. This is bull shit. You brought me into this. You used me and Morgan Greenville for five years and told me for the first time two weeks ago that the data you were feeding me was phony. You think I'm going to wait around to see whether this brute from god-knows-where is going to let me live? No fucking way. I'm going to Steve Croft at *60 Minutes* and drop this bombshell on his lap. In fact, I saw him at the bar just before you showed up."

"Harrison, doing something stupid like that will guarantee you a death sentence. We'll have to be a lot smarter than that. We have to figure out how to help Fletcher craft a solution for Lowery. The Presidency is what matters here. If the government starts disclosing the actual state of the economy, the President will take it on the chin. We have to come up with something."

Ludlow needed to slow Teasedale down until he could come up with the solution to save his own skin. If Teasedale continued to consider going to the press as his salvation, he would be dead long before he knew it. Ludlow could reveal Teasedale's intent to Fletcher as a demonstration of his will to survive.

"I don't know what I'm going to do, Pennington."

"We'll talk about it tomorrow. Now pull yourself together and get something strong to drink. You're the host and you better act like it again. We have time to figure this out. Nobody wants a scandal. We have to come up with a plan to cover this all up. There are only five of us who know anything about the underpinning of President Lowery's 'Economic Revolution.' Maybe we can convince them to keep it that way."

"I hope you're right, Pennington. I hope you're right."

Ludlow left Teasedale standing by the stone wall and returned toward to dance floor and the swaying crowd. The party was ascending with full force. The guests were loud and animated. Ludlow felt like he was in the middle of an out-of-body experience. He could observe everything from a distance and the noise from the music was muffled. Carmen was now dancing on the floor with her two girl friends. His wife and the Waters were laughing with another couple near one of the bars. Everyone was living it up. But Ludlow was contemplating his own mortality. He didn't know if he would be alive in 48 hours. Bob Fletcher was playing with him and enjoying it. That was the part that Ludlow hated and could not understand. Fletcher had a plan but Ludlow was not precisely sure what it meant for him and when it would unfold. When he looked back at Teasedale, he saw a dead man. Fletcher would never let him live. He was the outsider—the unwelcome third wheel that Ludlow had introduced without permission. Teasedale was also everything that Fletcher was not. Ludlow knew that Teasedale would be dead before the markets opened again.

CHAPTER 26

Southampton, New York
Sunday, May 27, 2007

Teasedale's Safari Party lasted until the early hours of the morning. The estate was so large that the neighbors barely heard the dance music that played on long after the George Michael concert ended. It helped of course that Teasedale had hired every Southampton policeman who wasn't on duty that night to act as security. They made sure everyone got home safely and complaints about noise disturbance were dealt with and forgotten. When Kirby and Hillary got home they opened a bottle of wine and collapsed on the sofa on their front porch.

"Was that over the top or what?"

"It was pretty wild. What a cast of characters."

"Did you see those three women dressed in animal prints? They must have been pros or strippers or something."

"I knew you wouldn't miss them. They were basically naked."

"If I had, you'd think I'd gone brain dead between my legs."

"That's the last thing that will go dead on your body."

"I'll take that as a compliment."

The two kissed and got up to head for their bedroom.

"You know, it was strange seeing Ludlow and Teasedale together in that party setting. They certainly seemed to be a lot closer than I would have guessed."

"Your boss is a strange dude but seems to know everybody."

"Did you see them when they were alone, talking together in the garden?"

"Yeah, it looked pretty intense. Maybe Ludlow was asking about Morgan Greenville's trading activity. It's not like people aren't buzzing about it. Come to think of it I'm actually talking to the horse's mouth."

"Yeah, yeah. But I seem to remember that you and I agreed not to talk shop given all the top secrets that we both have to deal with."

"Okay. Forget it. Ludlow didn't really seem his normal self. Maybe it was just a long day."

"Teasedale was somewhere else too. He seemed completely distracted when I said hello. When he and Ludlow were talking, it almost seemed like they were arguing."

"Who knows. I want to get up and run tomorrow but I still need at least six hours sleep."

"Sounds like I've got about forty-five minutes before I lose you."

"A little exercise before turning in always makes me sleep better."

Kirby and Hillary eventually went to sleep and didn't wake up until 8:30 A.M. They couldn't remember the last time they opened their eyes and saw that number on a digital clock. Sunday they relaxed and had absolutely nothing planned until a small cookout that evening at home with three other couples. The same was not true for either Harrison Teasedale or Pennington Ludlow.

All Sunday morning crews of workers roamed Teasedale's property deconstructing the prior night's party. The tent was taken down
after the tables and chairs and portable bars were stowed in waiting
trucks. Other men picked up stray cups and cigarette butts that had
been pounded into the grass, flower beds and driveway. Teasedale
sat at his breakfast table alone for most of the morning, reading the
newspapers and responding to emails. It was his normal weekend
routine, but he was not in control. He had surges of nervousness
that hit him like the nearby ocean waves. He wasn't use to feeling
that way and it disturbed him. Teasedale was use to order—the
order that he imposed on everyone and everything around him.
Now he couldn't control a thing. He was at once angry, frightened
and self-pitying. The only person he could rely on was Pennington
Ludlow since they were both in the same boat together.

Teasedale had the Darwinian sense to understand that the
strongest would survive. Ludlow was strong and probably stronger
than him. That meant that Teasedale was in trouble. As he thought,
he concluded that his only way to survive was to regain control. He
couldn't afford to wait for Ludlow. He didn't have the time that
Ludlow suggested last night. Everything was moving very fast and
Fletcher and Ludlow had both frightened him. If Teasedale was
going to survive, he'd have to tell his whole story to someone—
someone who could be trusted. Fletcher said he eradicated threats
and eliminated risks. Teasedale recognized himself as a legitimate
risk to President Lowery's future. If someone had the whole story,
he could be protected. Teasedale stood up and got another cup of
coffee. For the last five years, he had purposely destroyed all records
and evidence of his involvement with Pennington Ludlow. Now
he was going to have to recall as much of it as he could. He had
to write it all down. He had to create a history, complete with the
proof that would save him from the President, Fletcher and maybe
even Ludlow. He also had to figure out who he could trust with

his story. There was a lot to do and not much time. It was going to take him the rest of Sunday and probably all of Monday; he really didn't know. He had to start at the beginning and try to remember everything in chronological order. History might be the only thing that could save him.

Pennington Ludlow got up long before anyone else in the Waters' house was stirring. The sun rose about 5:30 A.M. on Sunday and Ludlow was wandering around the kitchen trying to figure out how to make himself a cup of coffee. When he finally succeeded, he sat in the library with a sheet of paper as if he was preparing to write a speech. But Ludlow was depressed and uninspired. He had to create a survival plan. He wrote four names across the top of the page: Chuck Lowery; Bob Fletcher; Harrison Teasedale; and Alan Solomon. Those individuals were the only people in the world who knew the details of how Lowery's "Economic Revolution" was planned, launched and sustained. He made his list to figure out who could win and who would lose. Who could live and who would die. Who could help and who would hinder. He needed to use all his intellectual capacity to plan a way out from his grim dilemma. The only people on his paper that he had spoken to since the weekend began were Bob Fletcher and Harrison Teasedale. The President and Solomon were sources of help or harm that he needed to bring into his plan or leave out. His mind was dull and not sharp enough to focus on the life and death challenge in front of him. He got up and walked out toward the beach. Maybe the morning air would help him crystallize his thinking. He didn't think that he had a lot of options but he needed to see if he could identify one strategy that might save his life. He also needed to assess his threats. They came in two forms: Bob Fletcher and Harrison Teasedale—both could cause his death.

John Aichenhead received Bert Washington's fax that included the personal employee information of everyone who worked at the BLS at about 5:00 P.M. Saturday night—all 2175 names. Aichenhead's fax machine ran out paper three times. Aichenhead had wanted to take a risk. Now he realized how much work he had to do and how little time he had to do it. On Sunday morning he woke up and followed his usual routine: get the newspapers, coffee and a breakfast sandwich. As he sat down at his small kitchen table, he looked at the 60 pages of names that represented the population of BLS employees. He was never going to be able to do this himself. He needed a helper. There were several junior staffers who had joined the New York office less than a month ago. They were greenhorns and knew that they'd be doing grunt work for a while until they earned their stripes. They couldn't distinguish one shit job from another and didn't have time to care. They knew that senior agents like Aichenhead were there to make their lives difficult for four or five months. Aichenhead decided to call Nick Bowa, one of the agents-in-waiting. He was going to ruin the rest of Bowa's weekend. It was the only way that Aichenhead was ever going to get the information that he promised Washington. Since Bowa would work around the clock to show his mettle, Aichenhead would probably have what he needed by the time he got to work on Tuesday. Bowa promptly returned Aichenhead's email message. They met at the office on Sunday at 10:00 A.M. where Aichenhead explained the assignment and gave Bowa the long list of names.

Bob Fletcher woke up Sunday morning with two naked women in his bed. After George Michael's performance, Fletcher and the harem had decided to leave and hit one of the hot spots before heading home to Water Mill. At the Pink Elephant, Fletcher threw down ten thousand dollars and the crowd parted like the Red Sea as he was led to a prime table in the corner of the club. When they got back to their estate, everyone striped and got into the Jacuzzi together. It didn't take long for the orgy to ensue. Fletcher had a good time but he always had a good time. In the morning, he got up from bed, put on a terry cloth robe and wandered into the kitchen where the housekeeper had already prepared coffee, fresh cut fruit, and pastries. Fletcher filled a large mug with coffee, grabbed his Blackberry and another cell phone and went outside to review the morning newspapers that were lying on a low glass table near the outdoor dining area. He had to call Chuck Lowery and Monroe Desmond and make a decision about Teasedale and Ludlow. He dialed Desmond first to check on his progress.

"Monroe, good morning. How goes it?"

"The plan's in motion. We've taken care of the Mexican bank and account history for Carmen. That took a little bit of work but the guys stayed on top of it and will recheck everything once we obtain the paperwork from the bank. We should get that tomorrow at the latest. After you left yesterday morning, I decided that the best way to create the evidence was to merely replace Ludlow's number with Carmen's number for all the phone records. The dates and call times already exist; we'll just have Ludlow's calls originate from Carmen's cell phone. We are looking at some other opportunities for evidence like coincident trips or meetings when Ludlow had Carmen in tow and Teasedale was in the same locale. Anyway we're getting there."

"That sounds good. I've decided I'm going to act on Teasedale sooner rather than later. I figure if he's eliminated in the next day or two, we can kill two birds with one stone. First we eliminate the weakest link. Second we get Morgan Greenville out of the market since Teasedale won't be around to sell anything and no one will be there to fill his void. With Morgan Greenville sidelined, we'll be able to get out of our positions with better execution and pricing. I'm also going to need a little more muscle up here. I'm sending the plane back down and I need you to pick two or three of your guys to come up here. I've settled on how to eliminate Teasedale and create a media event at the same time. He's going to die in a murder suicide after an evening of gay, masochistic sex with an unlucky stranger. What do you think?"

"Sounds perfect for that piece of shit. And it will certainly scare Ludlow to death."

"That's what I think too. It will also get him to transfer his accounts to us a little faster. While the papers and TV obsess over Teasedale's death and delve into his life, we can begin to drop the evidence of the insider trading scandal. As that unfolds, all hell will break lose. Morgan Greenville will be in a world of trouble and that should throw the market into turmoil. When the payroll number is released on Friday we'll get a big downdraft and our Treasury positions should rally like hell. We are going to make a lot of fucking money by killing Teasedale and bringing down Morgan Greenville. I can hardly wait to see those assholes groveling."

"Sounds like you've nailed this down. Other than the men, what else do you need?"

"We're going to need to find a young gay Asian prostitute. Either where you are or in New York. Can your guys handle that?"

"That should be no problem at all. My guys can find anything."

"Make sure the victim is presentable. I don't want some fucking heroin addict. I want it to look like someone that Teasedale might have had a relationship with. Fuck, I don't even care if he's gay or not. He's going to be dead too. Just make sure that he has no relationships, family, etc. That's the only thing that could come back to haunt us. Got it?"

"Yes sir. The guys will be up there before 5:00 P.M. Is tonight the night?"

"I don't think so. I think Monday night is the night. Teasedale will probably helicopter back to New York on Tuesday morning. He's going to miss that ride."

"Okay. That gives the guys a little more time to get things ready. Sounds like they'll need a few hours in the house to deal with security cameras, create the scene and make sure everything is clean before they leave. What about his staff?"

"I'm not positive but I saw two other buildings on the property so I assume the staff lives in one of them and the other is a guest house. The men will have to check that out beforehand. One way or the other, I know someone else is going to be on the property. We'll have to deal with it."

"Okay. I'll have everything ready on my end when the plane arrives. Sounds like I've got three or four hours?"

"That's right. We'll talk later, but that's the way I see it going down at this point."

Fletcher hung up and lay back onto the soft pillows of the outdoor sofa. The sun was filtering through a line of trees that constituted the border of the property. Everything was still except for the birds enjoying the cool of the morning. Sunday would be Fletcher's day of rest. Monday would be his day of retribution. He called Chuck Lowery next and gave him all the details. Lowery approved the plan but he wanted to hold back on eliminating Ludlow. He decided that they might be able to accomplish all they want by bringing down Teasedale and Morgan Greenville. Lowery thought that murdering the Secretary of the Treasury was too big a risk. Lowery needed to keep Fed Chairman Solomon in the right place. He most likely knew nothing about Teasedale, Morgan Greenville or Ludlow's trading activity. But if Ludlow turned up dead, Solomon could go over the edge. Lowery and Fletcher always recognized that Solomon

was an unwilling participant in the "Economic Revolution." If he
was given an excuse like a Congressional investigation, Solomon
could easily flip. Fletcher reluctantly agreed with Lowery's point.
Ludlow would live, at least for the time being. He was sitting on a
lot of money, and Fletcher was waiting for the account numbers
and wire instructions.

CHAPTER 27

Southampton, New York
Sunday afternoon, May 27, 2007
Monday morning, May 28, 2007

Pennington Ludlow spent the better part of Sunday morning trying to decide if he had any alternatives to save his skin. His gut told him to try to meet with President Lowery and effectively ask for mercy. He knew that Lowery was an uncanny politician who must be working feverously behind the scenes to try to protect his legacy. Fletcher was an executioner but Lowery was still the President. It was after all his "Economic Revolution" and reputation that were on the line. Lowery had to perform a delicate surgery. He needed to find a way to cut out the cancer threatening the Presidency without destroying himself. Ludlow was a high ranking member of his Cabinet—perhaps the most important Cabinet member over the last six years. Killing him would be Lowery's last resort. The left side of Ludlow's brain told him that the logical thing to do was to meet with Chuck Lowery. The right side of his brain was telling him something else.

Ludlow was scared of Bob Fletcher. Fletcher was powerful and arrogant. He operated outside the logical world. The combination of Lowery and Fletcher was a perfect complement. But Ludlow couldn't completely count on Lowery's intelligence to win out. Fletcher would probably be arguing to erase all the evidence that might link them to Ludlow and Teasedale's trading scheme which in turn could expose the infiltration of the BLS and BEA. The right side of Ludlow's brain was telling him to go to Alan Solomon. He had something to trade for Solomon's help—the video of Solomon's sexual tryst with Carmen Gomes. If Solomon agreed to help him, Ludlow would give him the video and eliminate the evidence of his extramarital failing. With Solomon standing with him, Ludlow could create a stalemate with Lowery and Fletcher. There was no way that Lowery and Fletcher would kill the Fed Chairman and the Treasury Secretary. Ludlow believed that Solomon would do almost anything to get his hands on the video that had been held over his head for so long. The right side of Ludlow's brain won the argument. Ludlow used Percy Waters' Blackberry to send a message to Alan Solomon before lunch telling him that they needed to talk as soon as possible. He wasn't sure where Solomon was staying that weekend, but he remembered that Alan and Miriam liked to go to their small cabin in New Hampshire on Lake Sunapee when he wanted to get away from everything. Solomon returned Ludlow's email. He told him that he could call him around 4:00 P.M. that afternoon.

At 4:00 P.M. Sunday afternoon, Pennington Ludlow walked over to the Maidstone Club to call Alan Solomon from a private telephone room on the main floor. He knew Fletcher would be monitoring the landlines and cell phones at Ludlow's disposure. The golf course was crowded and the streak of perfect weather had continued. The beaches were filled with visitors who were spend-

ing another day immersed in the beautiful colors of Eastern Long Island. The reality of returning to their black and white world was still a day away.

"Good afternoon, Alan. Thanks for agreeing to talk to me."

"Well, your message was marked 'urgent' so I figured you must have something important to discuss."

"Where are you, this weekend?"

"Miriam and I are up in New Hampshire relaxing. It's very quiet and peaceful. And you?"

"We're out in the Hamptons. And it's anything but quiet and relaxing."

"Pennington, you said there was something urgent to discuss. We can talk about our Memorial Day weekends some other time, right?"

"Well of course. Bob Fletcher flew out to East Hampton to pay me a visit yesterday."

Solomon's ears perked up when Ludlow mentioned Fletcher's name. As much as Solomon had despised his relationship with Ludlow, he disliked Fletcher even more. Their last meeting in February had made Solomon very uncomfortable. Fletcher was a man who would do or say almost anything to suit his purpose. His moral compass was permanently broken. "Why did Fletcher fly all the way out there to see you?"

"He flew out to tell me that he and Lowery knew all about the fortune I have made front-running the markets using the economic reports that we've been fabricating for the last six years."

There was silence on the other end of the line. Solomon had literally dropped the phone.

"Alan, are you still there? Did you hear me?"

"I'm here but I don't think I could have heard you correctly. You said he knows about trading you've done using the economic reports?"

"That's correct."

"Pennington, are you insane?" Solomon's question was asked in a tone that Ludlow had never heard before. "Why are you telling me this? It sounds like you're going to jail and confessing your sins to me wouldn't strike me as a great strategy."

"I'm not going anywhere Alan—at least not if you agree to help me."

"Help you? Your arrogance is astounding. You have abused me for the last ten years and now you expect me to help you. I hope you rot in hell's worst prison. Nothing would make me happier."

"Alan, that's especially cruel of you. If you calm down for a second, let me at least make an offer for you to consider."

"I don't want your money. I've lived within my means all my life and I'm old enough not to care anymore."

"I'm not going to offer you money. You wouldn't know how to enjoy it anyway. I'm actually going to give you the only copy of the video that captured your fuck session with Carmen Gomes. How would you like to have that weight lifted off your scrawny little shoulders?"

"You're a pig, Pennington. Why should I trust you at this point?"

"Because I'm afraid that Bob Fletcher is going to kill me. Any evidence of my trading will focus the media and investigators and certainly Congress on the information that was used. I've been doing this for more than five years, Alan, and I've made a very serious amount of money. I also engaged Morgan Greenville through their chief of proprietary trading to carry out my plan. Fletcher wants all the money I made. Once he gets it, I'm convinced he will eliminate me and my partner in short order. But if Fletcher knows that you know all about this, it will create a standoff. They will never move against both you and me."

Solomon could not believe what he was hearing. His mind was

working quickly. As one of the original conspirators to Lowery's "Economic Revolution," he was already guilty of defrauding millions of investors around the world. If the scheme ever reached the light of day, he would spend the rest of his life in jail. If Fletcher and Lowery moved to eliminate Ludlow, what would prevent them for eliminating him as well? They could arrange for an accident to happen—perhaps a hit-and-run or something else tragic that strikes regular citizens every day. Solomon could feel the anger welling up inside his small frame. Once again, Ludlow was dictating his life. If Ludlow hadn't cheated for himself, he wouldn't be calling Solomon for help. Now Solomon had to take a calculated risk. Since Ludlow's trading could have already put his life at risk, should he help Ludlow and get possession of the lurid tape in return? He believed that Ludlow was probably right—Lowery would never order the murder of the Fed Chairman and Treasury Secretary. That could never work. If he helped Ludlow, it would be he and Ludlow against Lowery and Fletcher forever. Mutual Nuclear Deterrence was effective during the Cold War. Perhaps the same concept could work between them. Solomon wanted that tape so he could burn it and destroy the memory forever. He could suffer with the weight of the standoff with Lowery and Fletcher if he could live without the fear that Miriam would leave him to live alone.

"How do I know that you haven't made copies of the tape?"

"You don't but I haven't. The single copy of the tape is locked in my vault down at DeSaussure Hall. I sealed it in an envelope years ago and wax stamped it with a date. I will have Kurt Denton deliver it to you Tuesday morning in Washington, D.C. and you will see for yourself. I'm very serious about this Alan. I believe my life is in danger and I believe your life is in danger too. We can survive this if we stand together. I'm willing to give you the one thing that I have that you want. That should be a pretty clear indication of just how serious I am."

"Alright, Pennington. Let me be clear. I want the tape delivered to my office first thing on Tuesday. If it shows up and it has been opened or there isn't a wax stamp with a date embossed on it, you can go straight to hell. If the tape is a phony, the deal is off. Once I decide that I got what I wanted, I will call you and give you my decision. That is how I want this to work. Is that clear?"

"That's clear Alan, but I want you to remember one thing: you're going to have to cooperate if you want to live to enjoy the rest of your life with Miriam. I'm giving you what you want to demonstrate my commitment to you. But you really don't have any choice."

Solomon knew that Ludlow was probably right. "Get me the tape on Tuesday Pennington, and then we can talk. It sounds like you anticipate having a meeting with President Lowery that day as well. Is that your plan?"

"Yes, but I have no idea what his schedule is like. It's imperative that we see him before the end of the day."

"I'll be waiting for the package, Pennington. Good-bye."

The men hung up and Solomon walked in his bathroom and popped two Zantac. Ludlow had churned up the acid in his stomach. He walked out onto his deck that overlooked the lake. Miriam was reading the classified ads in the local newspaper. Solomon took her coffee cup and went back into the kitchen to refill it.

"Well thank you dear. That was extra kind of you. Who were you talking to on the phone?"

"Just Pennington Ludlow. He never leaves me alone. I really hate that man."

"Oh Alan. That's not true. You've worked with him so long. How many years now, fifteen or twenty? You made a lot of money from the Frontier Exploration board."

"He always ate first Miriam. I'm going to have a stressful week coming up. I can hardly wait for my term to expire. Maybe I'll talk to Lowery about an earlier retirement. I'm sure he has someone he'd love to pay back with my position. I'm tired Miriam. Maybe it's time for you and me to spend a lot more time up here. We love it here. What do you think?"

"Alan, whatever you want dear. I'll do whatever makes you happy."

After Ludlow hung up with Alan Solomon, he called Kurt Denton and told him what he wanted done. Denton confirmed he would take care of it and the package would be delivered to the Fed Chairman's office on Tuesday morning before 10:00 A.M. Ludlow didn't like the trade he had just made but he knew that he was up against a wall. He had been able to keep Alan Solomon under his thumb for the last ten years. Now he was setting him free. But Alan Solomon was one of the few people that he knew would hold up his end of the bargain, and not just because he thought his life might be in jeopardy. Alan Solomon actually had principles. He lived in a world that was black and white; right and wrong. He would deliver his side of the trade because to fail to do so would lump him in the same flawed character group as Ludlow. No, Ludlow could count on Solomon.

Now Ludlow had to try his best to stall Fletcher until he could see the President with Alan Solomon. Ludlow's other priority was figuring out whether his new plan could salvage the wealth he had accumulated with Teasedale. Ludlow liked win-win situations, particularly when he was playing both sides. He was thinking that maybe he could outsmart Bob Fletcher. Getting even would feel good. Ludlow was still smarting from Carmen's defection to Fletcher's bed. He missed her smell and the feel of her lips on his body. But that was over. The next 48 hours would be critical. If his plan worked, he could find another Carmen Gomes. He'd have enough money to buy half of Mexico. Ludlow walked back to Percy's house from Maidstone. The sky was a perfect shade of blue.

Harrison Teasedale spent all day Sunday working to reconstruct the history of his trading with Pennington Ludlow. He created hard copies of all the accounts and account numbers that he had used during their trading history. The list was pages long, since their plan involved using individual accounts for no more than eleven months before opening new ones. From there, he began to write a narrative of their history—when he was first approached; how they exchanged information; the codes they used; the protocols they established. By the time Teasedale went to bed Sunday night, he realized he had never left the house and he hadn't eaten.

Teasedale got up Monday morning and continued his work. He decided that when he was done, he would seal the document in an envelope and deliver it by Federal Express to Kirby Haines. He chose Haines because he was loyal. The sealed envelope would come with a set of instructions: Haines could not open it without Teasedale's personal okay; the envelope had to be stored in a safe deposit box to keep it secure; and in the event that something happened to Teasedale, Haines would deliver the envelope to the FBI. With his job done, Teasedale would schedule a meeting on Tuesday with Ludlow to tell him what he had done. He would then have Ludlow call Fletcher so the three of them could meet. Teasedale believed that he was purchasing his own life insurance policy. Nobody was going to kill him if they knew the evidence would go straight to the FBI upon his death.

Teasedale worked nervously. He took plenty of risks every day of his life but those risks never actually involved his life. Teasedale was not a brave man. He was a cheater, just like Pennington Ludlow. He wasn't going to let Ludlow or Fletcher take him down. He kept writing as fast as he could. He wanted to mail the Fed Ex package that night in Southampton. He remembered that there was a drop box near town and when he was ready, he could deposit the package there. He had given the staff Monday afternoon and evening off since they had worked around the clock preparing for his cocktail party and cleaning up afterwards. His helicopter ride was scheduled to depart for New York at 7:00 A.M. Tuesday morning. He was flying back with Tom Lynch and two other Morgan Greenville partners. He had a lot to do and he was running out of time. He kept writing as fast as he could. He knew his life depended on it.

CHAPTER 28

Southampton, New York
Monday Evening, May 28, 2007

Desmond's muscle from Florida had arrived in the Hamptons on Sunday night. Together with two other men from Fletcher's security detail, they staked out Teasedale's First Neck Lane estate starting early Monday morning. They posed as Verizon telecom technicians working on a project that had torn up a portion of the street just down from Teasedale's estate for the greater part of the spring. Shortly after lunch, a station wagon carrying three staff workers from Teasedale's home left from the service entrance and did not return. Teasedale had eliminated one problem for Fletcher's men that they were concerned about: he had apparently given his staff the rest of the day off. Teasedale was alone in the house.

At about 7:00 P.M., Teasedale finished writing the narrative he had been working on non-stop since Sunday morning. He put the document in an envelope and composed a hand-written letter to Kirby Haines that included the instructions he wanted him to follow. He then sealed that envelope in a larger one addressed to Haines that included the inscription "To be opened by addressee only." He placed that envelope inside a small Federal Express box and tucked the mailing label in the clear plastic pouch on the front. Teasedale realized he was hungry. He couldn't remember if he had anything to eat after his staff had made him coffee and left him croissants and jams that morning. In completely non-Teasedale fashion he decided that he wanted a pizza, and he called up La Parmigiana in Southampton and placed his order. He would drop off the Federal Express package on his way to pick up the pizza and return home to eat, watch a little TV and go to bed early. It had been an exhausting weekend.

When Teasedale left the house and got into his Maserati, Desmond's men were not prepared for his exit. Two men were in the Verizon truck up the street, facing south and the other two men had moved to the far side of the property and had hidden themselves near the guest house which was about seventy-five yards from the main house. They had wanted to confirm that all of Teasedale's help had left for the day. Everyone was gone. Teasedale drove his Maserati down the long driveway and turned right out of his gate. The telecom truck was parked one hundred yards up the street facing the wrong way. Teasedale sped down the deserted street in the other direction.

Fletcher's men realized it was fruitless to try to follow Teasedale. They had lost him and Fletcher would not be pleased. They had confirmed his plan to fly back to New York in the morning. They had no choice but to wait for him to return. The two men in the truck called Fletcher to let him know about Teasedale's unplanned excursion. Fletcher was still in Water Mill and his men were holding an eighteen year old Philippine prostitute whom they had abducted outside a gay bar in Newark, New Jersey the night before. The young man had been given a cocktail of Oxycotin and vodka. He was heavily drugged and almost comatose, but one of Fletcher's men slapped him in the face whenever he got close to passing out.

The men in the telecom truck asked Fletcher what he wanted them to do. Fletcher told one man to enter Teasedale's house and position himself in the kitchen. The other man was told to hide inside Teasedale's garage. Fletcher would bring Teasedale's companion for the evening over to Southampton when Teasedale returned and the men had him in their possession.

Teasedale drove through Southampton toward County Road 39. He knew that there was a Federal Express drop box by the Suffolk Lighting Store. The long line of cars moving west was creeping slowly. Teasedale was going against the traffic. He pulled into the empty parking lot and got out with the package. Teasedale removed the receipt copy from the mailing slip, sealed the clear plastic enclosure, and dropped the small box into the metal container. He had done it. He would call Ludlow tomorrow and endure his anger and threats. Teasedale was intent on living and he was counting on the threat of exposing the entire scandal as his life line. He got back into the Maserati and headed to the Italian restaurant. He felt like he could breathe again, at least for one evening. He knew tomorrow would be a very stressful day. His pizza was waiting for him on top of the large oven used to make the pies. Teasedale had never stepped foot in La Parmigiana before. It was filled with young kids and families enjoying their last night of a glorious weekend. Teasedale looked at them but didn't feel anything. The noise, chaos and happiness around him were not things he could reconcile with his own life. He paid for his pizza and left. Teasedale was back home in three minutes. He turned off the car, opened his door, reached for his pizza and stepped out onto the driveway. One of Fletcher's men in a black camouflage suit appeared out of nowhere and stuck a Glock between his eyebrows.

"Mr. Teasedale, I suggest you come with me quietly into your house. My colleague will take care of your pizza."

Teasedale lost his breath. His heart began to race. Who were these men? Even though he had spent the last two days compiling a document to save his life, he couldn't immediately comprehend that the men he was talking to were somehow connected to the fear that had driven him for the last thirty-six hours.

"Who are you?"

The men did not answer. "Inside the house Teasedale, now."

Teasedale walked into the kitchen and was immediately surrounded by four hooded men. One of the men hit Teasedale with a knotted rope in his lower stomach. Teasedale cried out in pain.

"Mr. Teasedale, you will do exactly what we tell you to do. Is that clear, or do you need further convincing?"

"I'll do whatever you say."

"Good. Let's go down to the gym."

Fletcher's four men wore outfits and shoe coverings that left no residue or textile markers. For any investigator combing a murder scene, this small army would be invisible. When they reached the gym in the lower level, two of the men searched Teasedale thoroughly, removing his wallet, car keys and cell phone from his pockets. They pushed Teasedale in the room and closed the door behind him. Fletcher was called to alert him that Teasedale was in their possession.

Sitting on the floor in the gym, Teasedale was shaking. He tried to avoid the thought that he was about to die, but he couldn't subordinate the obvious. The men in his house were professionals; they were not criminals. They barely spoke to him and asked him for nothing except for his cooperation after they showed him the penalty for non-compliance. As much as Teasedale was used to being alone, he was terrified as he sat in the gym.

Bob Fletcher's SUV drove by Teasedale's First Neck Lane driveway and kept going. He was not going to leave the last set of tire tracks in Teasedale's driveway. That honor would go to Teasedale's Maserati. Fletcher's driver passed the Verizon truck and pulled into the next driveway, about one hundred yards further south and turned off the engine. Besides his driver, Fletcher had two other men and the Philippine prostitute with him. The boy was awake but didn't know where he was. Two pieces of duck tape sealed his mouth in case he tried to scream. Fletcher told his men to take the boy and enter Teasedale's property from the Lake Agawam side of the estate. Properties in the estate section were not separated by hard fences. Some of the properties even had neighborly gates between them. The boy was brought to Teasedale's house via a path where he could not be seen. Fletcher and his driver walked down the street and entered Teasedale's property from the next closest neighbor's lot. The small stake out group had earlier disabled the surveillance equipment and alarm systems on Teasedale's property. It was just Teasedale, Fletcher, a drugged male prostitute and seven of Fletcher's men alone on the estate. The odds were not in Teasedale's favor.

"Where did you put Teasedale?"

"He's in the gym in the basement."

"Alright, let's get this thing done."

The men went down to the lower level and opened the door to the gym. Teasedale was startled and backed up against the mirror on the far wall. Bob Fletcher walked in behind the hooded men.

"Well Harrison. We meet again so soon. I didn't get to see this part of the house during the party. I didn't picture you as a physical fitness nut."

"What do you want with me Fletcher?"

"I thought I told you that I eliminate risks and eradicate threats against President Lowery. Did you forget that part? No, I didn't think so. Well you and Pennington Ludlow have been caught committing high crimes against the United States of America. You didn't serve in the military did you Teasedale? My guess is that you've never faced death before."

"I've committed no crimes, Fletcher. Ludlow is the man who is responsible for all of this. I was merely trading. He was the one betraying you and the President."

"You know, you're probably right Teasedale. You're so logical. I bet you were a Baker Scholar at Harvard. Well, here's a clue asshole — I don't give a fuck about your logic. You're going to die and Pennington Ludlow is going to save himself by giving me all the money you've made for him. And you know what else; Morgan Greenville is going collapse in the biggest insider trading scandal in the country's history. Come to think of it, it's probably better that you're going to die now. As much as you would like to spend the next fifty years in jail being some black man's bitch, you'll probably be happier dead. It will be faster and you'll miss the scandal that will cast you as the notorious gay villain who brought down Wall Street's greatest firm."

"Go ahead and kill me if you're that insane. I've already sent my story to someone. If anything happens to me, the evidence will go directly to the FBI."

"Teasedale, you don't have any friends and I've heard that story before. Don't you remember? We are the government. We control the FBI, the CIA, the NSA and every other spook establishment that you've never heard of. Your story, if you even wrote one, is never going to see the light of day."

Fletcher was hiding his fury. He had four men watching Teasedale all day and no one had said a word about any communication or actions he had taken. Teasedale's phones lines and cable modem had been compromised to intercept any outgoing communication. Teasedale had seen no one. If Teasedale had given his story to someone, when had he done it and who had received it?

"Teasedale, you're about to go on a long strange trip. You should consider me a kind executioner since you're not going to remember anything in another ten minutes."

Fletcher motioned to one of his men who was holding a syringe filled with chemically pure LSD. Three of his colleagues grabbed Teasedale and held him against the wall. The man with the syringe plunged it into Teasedale's arm and pushed a full load of the drug into his system. Teasedale didn't feel a thing for the first three or four minutes, and then the drug took its effect. Fletcher had prescribed a non-lethal dose. Teasedale was going to play a starring role in the murder of his Philippine prostitute during a night of drug-induced sexual perversion. Fletcher wondered if the LSD would coax Teasedale out of the closet. Maybe he was going to enjoy his death. Fletcher told the men to bring in the young man. In the course of the next two hours, Fletcher's men carefully directed a video that documented in shocking fashion Teasedale's sadistic murder of the prostitute and his own suicide.

Teasedale and the boy were stripped of their clothes and redressed in spandex and leather. They put a leather mask on Teasedale. He was hallucinating and completely incapable of resisting their actions. At times he broke into hysterically fits of laughter and then he would sob uncontrollably. The Philippine boy was clothed in a leather vest and nothing else. Fletcher's men set up a video camera as if Teasedale typically filmed his perverted encounters in the basement gym. The tape would remain in the camera for the authorities to find once the gruesome scene was discovered. At one point, the boy was tied to a chair with his legs spread and one of Fletcher's men from beyond the camera's range took a whip and struck him numerous times on his thighs and genital area. He then put the whip in Teasedale's hand and told him to do the same. The camera captured Teasedale's torturing in full frame. After that, the men tied Teasedale up and hung him from a high bar apparatus in his gym. Again, they staged the filming of his masochistic torture and ultimately positioned the Philippine boy in the shot. Both men were too drugged to get sexually aroused but Fletcher's men professionally staged the scene to capture the oral sex that the boy performed on Teasedale as he hung from the bar.

The LSD had taken over Teasedale. He was someone else. Fletcher's men could make him do almost anything that they wanted. After almost two hours of extreme perversion, they gave Teasedale a Smith & Wesson 1911 pistol and told him to shoot the Philippine boy between the eyes. On command, Teasedale took the gun and walked straight up to the boy. He squeezed the trigger and blew a hole out of the back of the boy's head. Teasedale erupted in laughter as the discharge from the gun mixed with the steely smell of the victim's blood. Fletcher's men grabbed Teasedale as he rocked out the camera's field of focus from the shock of the gun blast and pulled off his spandex pants, exposing him in full nakedness. Then they pushed him back in the camera's range where he stood in front of the bloody scenery with a bizarre smile on his face. The men told him to stick the gun in his mouth and suck it. Teasedale did exactly as he was told. And when they told him to pull the trigger for some extra fun, he blew off the top of his head. And then it was over. It was almost 11:00 P.M.

Fletcher and his men carefully surveyed the murder scene. The microphone on the video camera had been disabled to insure that the video would be a silent feature. One of the men carefully removed the camera from the tripod and left the gym to review the footage to make sure that nothing incriminating had been captured inadvertently, like a reflection in a mirror or a shadow on the floor. Fletcher's men were experts and they were going to leave nothing to chance. Once the video was reviewed, the camera would be replaced on the tripod and started again so that it would run out of tape or battery life while filming the motionless death scene. Fletcher and the other men then moved back upstairs. Teasedale had mentioned detailing his history with Ludlow, and Fletcher ordered the group to check everywhere in the house to search for clues to corroborate

Teasedale's claim. They didn't have to look far. When they got to the breakfast room, the table was cluttered with papers. Fletcher told his guys not to touch anything. Maybe Teasedale had left enough incriminating evidence to justify his suicide. Fletcher looked at lists of account numbers scribbled out in pencil with dates next to each one. Another sheet had a tally of account totals and the sum was staggering: over $9 billion. Fletcher concluded that Teasedale had spent most of Sunday and probably Monday putting together his history. But where was it? Who had he sent it to? Fletcher checked all the papers and removed anything that implicated Lowery, Ludlow or himself. He had one of his men record all the account information that Teasedale left behind. When he was done, Fletcher summoned his men into the living room.

"Okay, let's review the entire operation."

The group reviewed every detail and retraced all their steps three times in succession. Fletcher was not about to make any mistakes. When he was satisfied that they were ready to exit the house, he focused on the topic of Teasedale's claim of creating a history of his conspiracy with Ludlow. Four of the men had watched Teasedale's house all day. What had they seen? The only departures were the staff station wagon and Teasedale's exit to pick up the pizza. Both excursions had to be tracked down. Two teams would separately follow both loose ends. Fletcher needed to know an answer to this mystery before Teasedale's body was found sometime the next day. The teams did not have much time and Fletcher was afraid that their failure could bring down the Presidency.

CHAPTER 29

New York City
Washington, D.C.
Tuesday Morning, May 29, 2008

The Bell 430 helicopter left its pad at the end of Meadow Lane without Harrison Teasedale at precisely 7:00 A.M. Several other helicopters were staged above the beach, waiting for their turn to pick up their Wall Street passengers, and Tom Lynch could not delay his pilots any longer. It was unusual for Teasedale to be late or to fail to communicate a change in his plans. It really didn't matter. Lynch couldn't wait for Teasedale any longer. He had tried Teasedale's cell phone and Southampton home. Maybe he had headed back to New York Monday night and would be in the office before Lynch and the other partners showed up.

Kirby Haines and Hillary Thomas had returned to his apartment around 7:00 P.M. on Monday night. They decided to finish the perfect weekend by ordering in Chinese food, opening a bottle of wine and watching some TV. They both woke up at 5:00 A.M. so that Hillary could get to the airport and catch the first shuttle back to Washington, D.C. Over the weekend Kirby had gotten the mental break he needed from the frenetic trading that had consumed him. He wasn't looking forward to returning to the grind. They left his Park Avenue building together and Kirby put Hillary in the first cab.

"I'll give you a call later. I loved the house and the weekend and everything. I'm going to miss you in about 30 seconds."

"Me too, Hil. But we've got ten more weekends to enjoy. Have a safe flight and let me know what plane you think you're going to take next Friday. Love you."

"Love you too."

Haines jumped into the next cab speeding down Park Avenue. It was still very early for anyone to be going to work. Most people on the street were jogging to Central Park or returning from it. By 6:15 A.M. he was sitting in his glass cubicle off the trading floor. A few traders were settling into their desks. Haines remembered that Teasedale was scheduled to fly back from Southampton that morning. He should be in the office by 8:00 A.M. Kirby still had more than an hour and one half before the chaos would begin. He decided to enjoy the temporary peace and picked up the newspapers he had purchased in downstairs shopping arcade and popped off the lid on his paper coffee cup.

A garbage truck helped John Aichenhead roll out of bed on Tuesday morning. His alarm sounded at 6:15 A.M. but he hit the snooze button and drifted back off. Fifteen minutes later, a NY City Sanitation version of a wake-up call lumbered down his narrow street off Sixth Avenue. Twice a week he really didn't need to set his alarm. He was groggy and headed to his small kitchen to make a cup of coffee. He didn't remember what was on his schedule for the week, but he expected Nick Bowa to have made some progress on the project for Bert Washington. He had never worked with Bowa before so he had no basis for any expectation. At least Bowa had not bothered him Sunday afternoon or Monday with a litany of clarifying questions. Aichenhead hated to waste his time telling people the obvious. After he showered and dressed, Special Agent Aichenhead locked his apartment door and headed down to FBI Headquarters. He figured he would get there by 8:30 A.M.

Pennington and Anne Ludlow had flown back to Washington, D.C. on Monday afternoon. They decided to leave a little earlier to beat the plane traffic out of East Hampton Airport. Ludlow and Fletcher had spoken before he left. Ludlow had provided Fletcher with a list of trading accounts at about a dozen foreign banks but told him that he would need Tuesday to gather the rest of the information from a safe in his home in Chevy Chase. He would also need time to get wiring instructions. Ludlow after all was not an administrator and most of the information had been coordinated by Teasedale. But Ludlow was also buying time. He expected to speak with Alan Solomon sometime before lunch and solidify their alliance. With Solomon on board, he would go directly to President Lowery and try to negotiate a truce. Ludlow was looking forward to getting even with Fletcher.

Bob Fletcher and his men had worked into early Tuesday morning at Harrison Teasedale's estate. When they were finished, they essentially scattered. The surveillance team took the Verizon truck they had borrowed and returned it. Those four men then drove back to Manhattan and found their way to hotel rooms that had been booked using aliases. Fletcher and his security detail headed back to Water Mill and incinerated the outfits they had worn during the evening. Fletcher had sent Carmen and her two friends back to Florida on his plane earlier in the afternoon. He still wasn't sure what he was going to do with her but he wanted her out of the way and under his control. After cleaning up, Fletcher opened a bottle of Irish whiskey and the four men drank it before crashing. When Fletcher woke up Tuesday morning, he called Chuck Lowery on his secure private line.

"Hi Chuck. How was your workout?"

"More importantly, how was yours?"

"Everything was taken care of according to plan. My guess is that someone will come looking by noon when he doesn't show up for work. When the newspapers get hold of this, no one is going to pay much attention to the jobs report on Friday. We got almost everything on video. He also left us enough evidence to lead the FBI directly to Morgan Greenville. I didn't imagine he was going to be so cooperative. There is one loose end. He told us that he wrote a history and sent it to someone. We're not sure if he was lying to trying to save his skin or whether he actually did it. We discovered papers and notes that lead me to think that he could have created a tell-all. Assuming he wrote something, I doubt he sent it to the FBI but I can't be sure. My gut tells me that he would have sent it to someone to hold for him. That greedy shit didn't want to part with his billions. He probably wanted to cut a deal. We didn't think negotiating with him would change anything. My guys are checking the post office and Federal Express to see if a package was actually sent. The problem is none of my guys saw him send anything and he did not use his cell or email to contact anyone."

"That could be a problem, Bob. When do you think we'll know?"

"I'm hoping in the next few hours. If it was sent yesterday, it will be delivered before noon. We should know the recipient by the time he receives the package."

"What about Ludlow? Has he given you all the information that you need so that Desmond can begin our collection process?"

"He's passed along some information but needed today to get the rest of it together. Unfortunately, Harrison Teasedale is not going to be able to help him with any of the details. When we get the rest of the information from Ludlow, we will compare it with the account data that we found at Teasedale's house. I'm sure that Ludlow will try to short us on some accounts. I plan on calling him in a little bit to let him know what happened to his partner. That should make him comply a little faster."

"All right, keep me posted. This should be an interesting news day."

Alan and Miriam Solomon had driven back from Lake Sunapee, New Hampshire after a hearty breakfast early Monday morning. They didn't mind the nine hour drive. They actually enjoyed their time together in the car. Alan would drive the first and last three hours and Miriam would handle the middle part. They left at 6:00 A.M. because they wanted to beat the traffic that would build during the course of the day. Their plan worked out just fine. They pulled into their garage in Georgetown just after 4:00 p.m. They had made two thirty minute stops along the way to stretch their legs and break the driving monotony. Solomon thought about the deal that Ludlow had presented to him during the long drive. He wanted the tape of his infidelity but he didn't want to help Pennington

Ludlow. He really wanted revenge. He thought about just going to President Lowery on his own and betraying Ludlow. That would be fitting justice. On the other hand, Solomon was worried that Ludlow's insight about Fletcher's propensity to eliminate threats was more true than not.

Solomon was worried and torn. The only person he trusted was Miriam, but he could not ask her for her opinion. Once he got his hands on the tape he would destroy it. But he knew he would have to watch it first. Ludlow had only given him a sneak preview when he first told him of its existence. Solomon had vomited in his office's private bathroom after Ludlow left with the film. Ten years later, he wasn't sure he could handle watching the entire tape, but he knew he had no choice.

On Tuesday morning, Alan Solomon rose at his regular time; had his breakfast tea with Miriam; read his five or six newspapers; and then was driven to his office by his chauffeur at precisely 8:15 A.M. Although Ludlow's package was not coming via Federal Express, Solomon imagined that he would have something on his desk no later than 10:00 A.M.

At 8:00 A.M., Kirby Haines walked out of his office and over to Harrison Teasedale's administrative assistant on the trading floor. "Hi Becky, good morning. Where's the boss? I figured he'd be here by now. Wasn't he flying back with Lynch?"

"That's what he told me. He must have changed his plans. I tried to call him on the helicopter but was told that he wasn't on board. I tried his house in Southampton and New York and got no one.

Perhaps the perfect man ran into the unexpected perfect storm. His cell phone probably lost its charge. Or maybe his alarm clock misfired and he missed the chopper. He's probably driving back now and cursing up a storm."

"Well, maybe you're right, but it's certainly out of character. We have a lot to do today and I figured he would start off the morning meeting with his usual call to action."

"It doesn't look like he's going to make it and someone has to chair the meeting. If he's not here by the time it begins, it looks like you'll have the honor."

"I suppose you're right. Would you let me know when you hear from him?"

"No problem Kirby. I'll let you know as soon as he calls. But you know he wouldn't know how to use a public telephone." Becky laughed because she knew that was true.

At 10:00 A.M., it was Becky's turn to worry. She still had not heard a thing. Teasedale's staff had showed up at his New York townhouse and told her that Teasedale had not been home. There was no answer at his estate in Southampton and no word from him. Becky was listening to the radio to see if there had been any traffic accidents on the Long Island Expressway or Northern State Parkway. Nothing. She walked into Haines' office.

"Kirby, I'm worried. I'm not a worrier, but this is just not like Harrison. I should have heard from him by now. I spoke to Tom Lynch's assistant and she said that Tom had tried to reach Harrison just before they took off and he couldn't get him on either his cell phone or home number. If he were driving back, he would have been here by now. I'm really worried."

"Okay Becky. I'll go talk to Lynch and see what he thinks."

Haines took the elevator upstairs and walked over to Tom Lynch's corner office. He had three assistants stationed outside who shuttled inbound and outbound calls to him all day long. Kirby poked his head into Lynch's office; he was talking to someone important on his speaker phone. Haines put his thumb and forefinger together to indicate that he needed a second of Lynch's time. Lynch waved him in and finished his conversation in two or three more minutes.

"What's up Kirby?"

"Teasedale has still not showed up and Becky is very worried that something may be wrong. Maybe he had an accident or fell in the house. Who knows? We have no idea but we can't find him and we want to do something about it."

"I understand. So what are you thinking?"

"I think I should go out to Southampton and check his house. Driving will take too long and I have a lot to do here, particularly in his absence."

"Okay, that makes sense. Mary! Call over to the South Street heliport and tell them to get the helicopter ready for Mr. Haines. He needs to fly out to Southampton."

"Right away sir."

"I hope you're wrong Kirby. Maybe Harrison just wanted to escape for a little while."

"I hope I'm wrong too."

When John Aichenhead sat down at his desk after three days off, it seemed as if the black and white piles of files had grown in his absence. He knew it couldn't be true but their height and volume depressed him almost immediately. He had nothing important to do but he had enough work to last him well into next year. The message light on Aichenhead's phone was flashing. Aichenhead picked up the phone and dialed his voice mail. Nick Bowa had left him a message. He had finished the first full screen of the BLS data and found a few interesting bits of information. He was around all morning if Aichenhead wanted him to swing by. Aichenhead was impressed. Bowa was a fast worker. Maybe he had the same dreams of succeeding in the Agency that Aichenhead had when he first signed up. Unfortunately, it would take a couple years of frustration to find out that advancement in the FBI was in large part random. Aichenhead phoned Bowa and told him to come by. They could meet in Conference Room C which was the closest private space to Aichenhead's desk. Bowa came by Aichenhead's station and they grabbed a cup of coffee from the kitchen on their way to the meeting room.

"So Nick, it sounds like you got a lot done on Sunday and Monday. What did you find out?"

"I think some interesting stuff. I used the computer system to look for correlations among the BLS employee list based on family name, place of birth, employment history, sibling relationships and employment, and military service. I also looked at their dates of employment and home addresses as a second screen if the first screen showed any matches."

"That sounds pretty logical. So were there any matches?"

"Actually there were. As a statistical matter, I assumed I would discover some matches in the ordinary course. I actually performed a regression analysis on another set of unrelated employment data to see what I might expect normally."

"That was pretty enterprising. What did you use?"

"I used the Agency's New York area employees."

"You're kidding me, right?" Aichenhead thought that if his boss found that out, she would have his head. This little project was supposed to be conducted under the radar screen, but Teasedale had not told Bowa that.

"No, I'm not kidding. From my training, I knew I had to have a comparison set so that I could at least have some intuition about the statistical significance of my data findings."

"Okay, okay. That makes sense. So what did you find out?"

"I found fifteen matches. In the first screen, all of them hit on prior military service, but even their service history was oddly correlated. Every one of those employees either served in Special Ops or was a Navy Seal. I wouldn't even know how to estimate the odds of that occurring—no regular Army or Navy and no Air Force or Marines. And all of them had at least eight years of service under their belts before leaving."

"That is interesting. Where did they work after they left the service?"

"Looked like a few different places but I didn't have time to check out that piece of the story completely."

"So that's what popped out of your first screen. What about the second screen on those fifteen folks? What did that tell you?"

"Every one of them was hired between February 2000 and March 2001. And all of them are obviously still employed there."

"Can you tell whether that is an unusual pattern or not? Obviously a new Administration came to town. Was this just a changing of the guard?"

"I don't really know at this point. I didn't have time to research that either."

"What about their jobs? What are they doing for the BLS?"

"They are all senior folks. Probably half are senior analysts working in Washington, D.C. They deal with the IT infrastructure that aggregates and calculates the data. Three of the subjects actually head regional offices. The others are senior economists and two of them are assistants to Associate Commissioners. They are all pretty high ranking folks."

Aichenhead was trying to make some sense of Bowa's findings. He didn't know if the screening results were a coincidence or something else. "Can you give me a list of those fifteen employees?"

"Of course, I made a copy for you."

"Good work, Bowa. Why don't you keep bird-dogging this to see what else you can come up with? I'll do a little checking on these folks and we can get back together tomorrow and exchange notes."

"Thanks, John. I'll see what else I can find."

When Nick Bowa left the conference room, Aichenhead closed the door and dialed Bert Washington's number. Washington's assistant answered the phone and told Aichenhead to hold while she checked to see if Washington was available—she didn't know John Aichenhead and always checked with her boss before routing calls through to him. When Washington heard that Aichenhead was on the line, he quickly picked up.

"Good morning John. How is our little project going? Are you enjoying your risk taking?"

"When my fax ran out of paper three times on Saturday night, I knew there was nothing little about your request. I enlisted the help of analyst here who went through some preliminary screening over the weekend."

"So what did you guys find out? Is there anything interesting?"

"Could be. A couple of things turned up. The BLS hired fifteen former Navy Seals or Special Ops officers during a one year period starting in February 2000. All of those folks still work for you and they are all senior employees in your shop."

"Really. That's interesting. They were hired before I was put in charge. Are you going to send me the list?"

"Yes. I'll fax it to you when we are done. We are going to do a lot more work here to look into their prior work experience before the BLS but we think the coincidence is more than what the statistical odds would predict. Why don't you look at the list and tell me where they fit into the organization from the perspective of your theory."

"That will be easy. So that's pretty interesting, yes?"

"Well, it's a start. Sometimes when you flip a coin five times, you come up with five heads even though the statistics wouldn't predict that. We've got a lot more spade work to do, and you can give us some insight as well. Why don't we talk again in the next 24 hours and see what else there is."

"Okay. Thanks John, really. I think there's something funny here and maybe this is going to lead us somewhere."

"Who knows, Bert. We'll talk later."

CHAPTER 30

Southampton, New York
Tuesday, May 29, 2007

Kirby Haines had a bad feeling as he flew out on Morgan Greenville's corporate helicopter. He was alone with the two pilots and they made fast time flying over Nassau and Suffolk counties. Kirby thought that as a precaution he should call the Southampton police department since he didn't have a key for Teasedale's home and he wanted to have company in case he found Teasedale there and he was injured or ill. After 30 minutes, the helicopter approached the helipad that was free from competing traffic. Haines could see a police cruiser in the parking lot. When the helicopter shut down its engines, Haines instructed the pilots to wait for him and he got out and introduced himself to the two police officers who were standing beside their car.

"Thank you for meeting me, officers. I'm Kirby Haines and Mr. Teasedale's partner at Morgan Greenville. We are concerned since Mr. Teasedale missed his helicopter this morning and has not shown up for work. We tried his residences and cell phone and couldn't reach him."

"We understand. I'm Officer Sullivan and this is Officer McNamara. We are familiar with Mr. Teasedale and worked security for his party on Saturday night. Why don't you get into the back seat and we'll go over to his house."

On the short ride over to Teasedale's estate the officers suggested that sometimes guys like Teasedale go AWOL for a day or two when they get lucky or just want to go on a bender. Haines explained that Teasedale didn't really fit that profile. The officers nodded but obviously believed that their experience was more relevant than some investment banker's opinion. As they drove up Teasedale's long driveway, everything seemed in order. It was so green and peaceful. It was hard to imagine that just a couple days ago four hundred people attended an African safari and had partied there most of the night. The cruiser pulled up in front of the main entrance. The three men got out and one of the officers went over to check the front door. It was locked. They asked Haines to remain on the porch while they inspected the perimeter of the house, looking for open windows or doors. Sullivan and McNamara headed in opposite directions and met at the back door. All the windows were locked as was the back door and the French doors that opened onto the patio surrounding the pool. There was no evidence of foul play. The officers then went over to the guest house and pool house and checked those structures. Again they found everything to be in order. They walked back to the main house's front porch and confirmed the findings of their search to Kirby.

"Everything is locked and looks normal. It really doesn't look like anyone is home. Teasedale's Maserati is parked in his garage so unless he has another car out here it doesn't look like he drove back to New York—at least alone. Maybe he got a ride from someone or shacked up with some babe that he met."

"Harrison Teasedale is not the shacking up kind of guy, officers. If he was injured or fell down, he could still be inside the house.

I'm sure he locks up everything at night before he goes to sleep. He could have had a heart attack or something. Please officers, we have to get into the house."

"Okay, Mr. Haines. We understand but we don't typically break into people's houses. I hope you have a key. That would make our lives a lot easier."

"Officers, I just flew out from New York because I'm worried that something has happened to my partner. Mr. Teasedale is not married and his staff is obviously not at home and not working today. I don't have a key because I don't live here and I'm not a member of his family. He could be dying in there or unconscious. We've got to break in. Please, we're wasting time. What do you do in situations like this?"

"We usually don't do anything since it won't get us into trouble with the owner. Folks don't like us to break down their doors or shatter their windows unless they give us permission. Since you're not family, you can't give us permission to destroy his property."

"Oh my god. You're kidding me, right?"

"We're not kidders, Mr. Haines."

"Okay. Then I'll do it."

Kirby looked around on the driveway for the biggest rock he could find. He found one large enough in a flower bed and he walked around to the back of the house while the policeman waited on the front porch. Kirby used the rock to break a window pane in the backdoor—no alarm sounded. He then unlocked the door and walked through the house to the front entrance which he unlocked for the policemen.

"Now if there's any issue with Mr. Teasedale, you won't have to take the blame. I'm going to look upstairs."

Kirby bounded up the central staircase and looked in all the rooms. Teasedale was nowhere to be found. The master bedroom looked like no one had slept in it and Teasedale's overnight bag was sitting on a chair by the window. If Teasedale went back to New York, why would he have left his bag in the bedroom? Haines went back downstairs to the main floor where the policemen were looking around. He called out to tell them that he had found Teasedale's bag and found them standing in the breakfast room where the table was cluttered with papers filled with numbers and financial information.

"There's a lot of stuff here, Mr. Haines. Wouldn't Mr. Teasedale carry this type of information back with him to the office? It looks like he was working on something yesterday. Does any of this look familiar?"

Kirby looked at all the papers and recognized dollar figures and account numbers. They didn't correspond to anything at Morgan Greenville. All Morgan Greenville accounts started with the letters MG and had twelve number sequences. These accounts were completely different and none of them were exactly alike. "I don't know what any of this is officers, but I found his overnight bag upstairs. I don't think he left for New York. And his bed has not been slept in."

"Seems like maybe our hunch was right, Mr. Haines. Maybe Mr. Teasedale found some action and didn't come home."

"Then why would his Maserati be parked in the garage?"

"Maybe a friend picked him up."

"Teasedale doesn't have any friends."

"Then what would you suggest we do?"

"Can we please just check the rest of the house? I know he has a large finished basement. We haven't looked down there yet."

"Okay, let's go. If you're really worried, you can file a missing person's report when we're done."

Kirby paid no attention to the officer's suggestion and started down the main stairs to the basement. He opened a closed door and as he proceeded down the long hallway he smelled something very odd. It almost smelled like someone had forgotten to take out the garbage. As he continued in front of the officers, the smell got decidedly worse.

"What the fuck is that smell?"

Kirby could hear Officer Sullivan calling in for assistance on his two way radio pager. And then he stood in front of the entrance to Teasedale's gym. He turned around and vomited on the carpet. Haines stumbled back toward the officers who pushed him aside as they moved toward the door and entered the gym.

"Holy shit."

"Oh my god."

"Tim, don't touch anything. We've got to get out of here. They're both dead."

Officers Sullivan and McNamara were smart enough to resist compromising the crime scene. Sullivan got back on his radio and called for additional help. There had been a murder. They needed a crime scene unit, the coroner and additional backup. Haines was down the hallway, pushed up against the wall. He had looked in the gym for maybe two seconds but the scene in there was seared in his mind. There was blood splattered against the walls and mirrors. The two bodies were grotesque and lying near each other, their legs folded underneath them. Haines couldn't understand what the dead men were wearing but it looked oddly perverted. And he saw a tripod and a video camera aimed at the wall behind the bodies. Haines had to get outside and get some air or he was going to wretch again. As he rushed onto the porch, he heard the screaming sirens in the distance. A moment later, the driveway was full of vehicles. He sat on the porch steps as the officers ran by him and he wondered what had just happened and what it meant. He was dazed. Officer McNamara found him on the steps and told him that he needed to get a statement from him. He led Haines away from the front steps and back to his vehicle where he leaned against the trunk.

"Mr. Haines. I know this is not going to seem like the right time, but I need to collect some critical information about the victim, your relationship to him, and your weekend activities. This is all standard procedure. We have to begin to piece the puzzle together and you are our only starting point right now. I'm going to record our conversation so it can be transcribed later. You are not a suspect at this time. Do you agree to proceed as I have described?"

Kirby didn't care. "Of course, officer."

McNamara started with all the basic facts about Haines and his background and then his relationship with Teasedale. The officer asked him to recount his activities over the weekend which Haines did in some detail. The officer had worked security at Teasedale's cocktail party but asked Haines about the invitees and whether any of them were enemies or whether he had witnessed any disagreements at the party that involved Teasedale. He told him what he could remember but he couldn't recall anything unusual. After seeing Teasedale Saturday night, he hadn't seen or spoken to him on either Sunday or Monday.

"Was that unusual? I would have thought that given your close working relationship you would be in daily contact with the victim."

Haines thought about that. "You know. I thought it was too good to be true. It was so terrific to have some down time that I just thought he was doing something else more important."

"Maybe he was. From the look of the breakfast room he was working on something. Are you sure you didn't recognize anything on that table?"

Haines had forgotten about the mess of papers on the breakfast table. Teasedale must have been working on something, but Haines didn't see anything familiar when he and the officers looked quickly at the notes that Teasedale had written down. "I only looked at it quickly before we went downstairs, but it didn't look familiar. The information did not conform to the account coding that we use at our firm."

"Well it must have meant something and it might tell us why he left you alone for 48 hours. Frankly other than the crime scene evidence it's the only other thing in the house that we have to go on."

"Officer, I have to call Tom Lynch. He's the CEO of our firm. He sent me out here and I have to tell him what happened. Is that okay?"

"Yeah, go ahead. We don't know exactly what happened in that gym yet. You can tell him that we found the victim dead and have begun a full investigation. By the way, was Mr. Lynch at the party of Saturday?"

"Yes he was."

"I'll also need his office phone number and other contact information."

Haines gave him everything and asked if he could leave.

"Yeah, I'll have Officer Randolph drive you back to the helipad."

Officer Randolph was summoned and led Haines to his vehicle. They rode back to the helipad in silence. Kirby couldn't keep his thoughts straight. When he got to the helicopter he dialed Tom Lynch told him that Teasedale was dead and had probably been murdered. Lynch was floored. He wanted to know everything but Haines told him that the police were just beginning their investigation and would probably be calling him directly. Lynch couldn't understand why anyone would murder Harrison Teasedale.

"Kirby, was it a robbery? Did someone break in?"

"No Tom."

"Was it random? What do the cops think?"

"Someone else was murdered with Teasedale. They were both dead in his gym."

"What? Someone else was there? Who was it?"

"I have no idea. I couldn't even recognize Teasedale. The cops are trying to sort everything out. I just don't get it. His bag was packed in his room but he hadn't slept in his bed. The breakfast room table was full of notes with lists of accounts and trading information, but I didn't recognize any of it. And then I saw the two of them lying in the gym. And the smell was something I can't describe."

"It's okay Kirby. Thank god you went out there. You did the right thing."

"I don't think it really matters. Teasedale is dead. What are we going to do?"

"Right now, nothing. Just get back here and go home. I don't want you coming back into the office. Do you have a friend in New York or someone who will stay with you? I don't want you to be alone at this point."

"No, my girl friend flew back to Washington, D.C. this morning. Nobody else is around."

"Kirby, go home and have a drink and stay put. You need some time. I'll have my driver meet you and take you to your apartment."

"Thanks, Tom. I'll call you later."

Kirby Haines hung up. He had one more call to make. He dialed Hillary's number and reached her assistant. She was in a meeting so he asked to leave a message on her voice mail.

"Hillary, it's me. Harrison Teasedale was murdered last night. I discovered his body when I flew out to Southampton around 11:00 A.M. It was awful. I know this doesn't make any sense. Call me later. Lynch told me to go home. I love you."

With that done, Haines tried to close his eyes but all he could see was the chaos in the gym. Who would want to kill Harrison Teasedale? Kirby didn't have that answer.

After his call with Kirby Haines, Tom Lynch quickly convened an emergency meeting of Morgan Greenville's Management Com-

mittee. It was a few minutes after noon. Lynch informed them of
Teasedale's death. The men were shocked. They wanted details but
Lynch didn't have many—just what Kirby Haines had told him.
Another man was murdered with Teasedale and the police were
investigating everything. The Management Committee had to release the news to the employees and to the market as well. They
didn't want the news to leak out from other sources. Teasedale
was their most prominent partner. They couldn't hide his death
for long without risking their own reputation. Lynch prepared a
memorandum addressed to all of Morgan Greenville's employees
that described the tragic and sudden death of Harrison Teasedale.
Lynch listed his numerous accomplishments and lavished high
praise on the man who had led Morgan Greenville's ascent to the
top position among Wall Street's elite. The memo was short on
the details surrounding Teasedale's death. He didn't even specifically indicate that Teasedale was murdered. He simply said that the
police were investigating the circumstances surrounding his death
and everyone would be told more once the police determined what
had actually occurred.

Tally Warner was an intrepid reporter from The Southampton Press and had heard the initial rush of sirens responding to
Teasedale's estate. He decided to find out where they were going and
followed the noise. Tally parked near Teasedale's driveway but was
kept off the property by the police. By noon he had coaxed enough
information out of a policeman guarding the entrance to know that
Harrison Teasedale had been murdered along with another uniden-
tified man. That policeman stationed at the driveway's entrance was
replaced by one working closer to the crime scene who happened
to be an old high school classmate of Warner's. His friend provided

him with a few more details that turned an unusual murder into a potential blockbuster. The two men seemed to have been engaged in a sadomasochistic sexual encounter and it appeared that drugs were involved. The police were beginning to believe that what they actually had on their hands was a murder/suicide and they had the murder weapon. Tally walked back to his car and scribbled down everything that the two cops had told him. He called up his editor to let him know that Thursday's paper was going to have a new front page story with a banner headline. The Southampton Press was published once a week. Tally Warner was sitting on top of a story that could be front page news on every New York City newspaper the next day. Maybe this was his opportunity to move a hundred miles west to a bigger job. He drove straight to the carriage house he was renting and placed a blind call to the *New York Post*. He asked to speak to the Business Page editor. In ten minutes, Tally Warner was speaking to the managing editor of the entire newspaper and two feature reporters. They quickly cut a deal that would list Tally as the lead contributor on the article and then they got down to business. This had the making of the biggest Wall Street scandal in a long time.

Large Federal Express trucks delivered packages to Morgan Greenville's headquarters several times a day. All the packages were delivered to the mail room in the basement and then sorted for delivery to the recipients. Around 11:00 A.M., a mail room clerk dropped off a small Fed Ex box at Joanne Fruilli's desk. She placed it with Kirbs other mail on top of his inbox on his desk. Kirby had phoned Joanne from the helicopter to tell her that Lynch had sent him home for the day. There wasn't any reason to messenger his mail to him at home. He could catch up with everything the next morning. By 1:00 P.M., the news of Teasedale's death was leaking around the Street as people relayed the shocking information by email.

CHAPTER 31

Washington, D.C.
Tuesday, May 29, 2007

Bob Fletcher waited until 10:00 A.M. to place a call to Pennington Ludlow's office. He knew that Ludlow would not be rushing into work that morning. He'd drag his feet as long as he could. Fletcher also knew that Ludlow had tried Harrison Teasedale's various numbers several times, probably hoping to hatch a last minute scheme to try to hide some of their trading profits. Fletcher imagined that Ludlow was more than a little frustrated by Teasedale's unresponsiveness. Fletcher was about to tell Ludlow just how unresponsive Teasedale was. He dialed Ludlow's office and reached his assistant.

"Good morning. This is Bob Fletcher calling for Pennington Ludlow. I need to speak to him immediately."

"Yes sir. Let me see if he's available."

In about thirty seconds, Ludlow picked up the line. "I am trying to get you the rest of the information. I need to get a few details from Teasedale first, but I haven't been able to reach him."

"Ludlow, you're going to need a psychic to speak to Harrison

Teasedale. Your partner died last night. Haven't you heard? Oh my god it was awful. Maybe the news hasn't been released just yet. But he's certainly dead. He was very cooperative though. I hear he actually even pulled the trigger himself. Now I want what you owe me. And if I don't have it before the markets close today, maybe you'll be seeing Teasedale sooner than you expect. Is that clear?"

Ludlow was speechless on the other end of the phone. He knew Fletcher was cold-blooded but he hadn't expected him to move against Teasedale so quickly. Ludlow had no doubt that he would meet the same fate as Teasedale once he delivered all the account information and wiring instructions to Fletcher. Ludlow's only chance was Alan Solomon.

"Fletcher, you're a butcher."

"I asked you if my request and timetable were clear. You didn't answer me. Do you want me to ask you again?"

"No, I don't. I will get back to you when the markets close."

"Don't play with me, Pennington. I'm a hunter just like you, and you know that one trophy is never enough once you go after big game."

Ludlow knew exactly what Fletcher meant. He was in Bob Fletcher's crosshairs.

Alan Solomon got to his office and was reviewing the last set of Fed meeting minutes. At about 9:30 A.M. one of his assistants brought a package into his office that had been hand delivered by a Treasury Department courier. The package was a brown manila envelope that had a bubble wrap interior to protect its contents. The front of the envelope had Alan Solomon's name on it and the simple labeling "Highly confidential. To be opened by addressee only." When Solomon's assistant left his office, he waited a few moments before he got up and walked over to close the door. When he sat back down at his desk, he opened up the envelope and took out a smaller package with a wax stamp on it. Solomon opened the smaller package and removed a cassette. The tape had been made ten years earlier, before the introduction of DVD's. So far Solomon was satisfied that Ludlow was holding up his end of the bargain. The cassette itself had tape around it which Solomon removed. He had brought an old video camera from home and placed the cassette in it and pushed the play button. In the small fold out screen he could see the image of the bedroom where he had his encounter with Carmen Gomes. After a minute or two of play time, two images entered the room. He was embarrassed to see himself, obviously drunk and acting like an adolescent. Carmen Gomes was beautiful and young. He felt odd but wanted to see how his adultery actually occurred. He had only felt guilt for years. He found himself staring at Carmen Gomes flawless body. He couldn't look at himself. She was an incredible actress, moaning and emoting as she brought him to orgasm. He knew he did nothing for her and she left the room as soon as they finished the abbreviated scene.

When Solomon finished watching the tape he removed it from the camera and tore the tape from its plastic holder. He rolled the tape into a ball and cut it in pieces with a scissors. He diced it like it was an onion—finer and finer until it was just a thousand small pieces of celluloid. He took the scraps and put them in an envelope. Burning the shreds would create a smell. He decided he would walk over to the Potomac River at some point during the day and dump the contents of the envelope into the river as he walked along its bank.

Solomon's phone rang as he finished filling the envelope with the scraps, and his assistant knocked on his closed door. Solomon placed the video camera on the floor under his desk and told her to come in.

·

"Sorry to interrupt, sir, but Secretary Ludlow is on the phone."

"Alright, put him through." Solomon knew that Ludlow wouldn't wait for his call. He was desperate and running out of time.

"Harrison Teasedale is dead."

"What did you say?"

"Bob Fletcher just called to tell me that Harrison Teasedale is dead. They murdered him. I told you what they were capable of on Sunday."

Solomon was stunned. He didn't know Teasedale except by reputation. Now he was frightened that Ludlow's warning about Fletcher was true.

"You got the tape just as I promised, didn't you? I hope you are satisfied that I am a man of my word."

"I wouldn't go that far, Pennington."

"I promised you the tape and I delivered it to you. I'm sure by now you've probably destroyed it."

"You're right about that."

"That threat is over Alan. No one can hold that over your head anymore. But Bob Fletcher is going to kill me and probably you. There is nothing stopping him now. Every President needs a clean-up guy and Bob Fletcher is Lowery's janitor. Alan, we have to see the President today."

"I can't believe that it's come to this. You've used me from the first day we met. I can't believe that I'm going to help you."

"Save your bull shit, Alan. You're not helping me. You're saving Miriam from a lonely life without you."

Miriam was the only reason he was talking to Ludlow. She had been the only reason that he had kept talking to Ludlow over the last ten years. Now he had the chance to end the dialogue that he hated so much, but Bob Fletcher was preventing that from happening.

"Alright, I'll go with you. How are you going to set this up?"

"I think you should make the call Alan. If you set up the appointment, Lowery won't suspect anything in particular. There is no reason why you would know anything about me and Teasedale. If I call, who knows what will happen. I know they've bugged my calls and are monitoring me."

"How do you know that they are not monitoring this call?"

"I've taken precautions, Alan. They can't tap every phone in Washington. Listen to me. You have to believe that Chuck Lowery knows that Harrison Teasedale is dead. He probably okayed it before Fletcher made his move. We can surprise Lowery if you set up the appointment."

Ludlow's logic made some sense to Solomon. When they hung up, Solomon asked his assistant to call the President's secretary who handled his appointment schedule and request a fifteen minute meeting anytime that afternoon. Luckily, President Lowery had no official responsibilities until a State dinner that evening for the Prime Minister of Italy. The appointment was confirmed for 3:45 P.M.

Fletcher's men had not had any luck tracking down Teasedale's claim that he had passed on enough incriminating evidence to bring down Lowery's "Economic Revolution." They met with Teasedale's Southampton staff that had left the property in a station wagon Monday afternoon. Posing as Federal Agents, they interviewed the three women who knew nothing about any package or mailing that Teasedale was preparing. He hadn't given them anything. If he had prepared a package for sending, he must have taken it with him when he left the property Monday night to pick up his dinner. Unless he left it with a personal courier, his only other option would have been to send it using Federal Express.

Fletcher's men found the only drop box in Southampton but it was not proximate to the restaurant where Teasdale bought his pizza. They used their connections at Federal Express' Memphis head-quarters to discover that seven packages had been picked up from that location on Monday evening at 8:00 P.M. Without tracking numbers, they could not identify who the senders or the recipients were. But they were able to confirm that two of the packages were sent to Morgan Greenville's headquarters. That by itself didn't prove anything. Without the tracking numbers it would take 24–36 hours to retrieve the details they needed to establish the identities of the parties who sent and received the parcels.

After getting that news, Fletcher was called and told everything. They were still facing a dead end but Fletcher's gut told him that Teasedale hadn't lied. He wasn't sophisticated enough to come up with such a ploy facing death for the first time. Fletcher had a few hunches about possible recipients of Teasedale's information. One possibility was Tom Lynch, Morgan Greenville's CEO. Another pos-sibility was Teasedale's personal attorney—someone that Monroe Desmond and his group were trying to identify. A third possibility was someone close to Teasedale at the firm—perhaps his admin-istrative assistant. He told Desmond to follow every possibility. But Fletcher was worried himself. If Teasedale had sent a package, someone was receiving it that day. He had an extensive network of eyes and ears working every angle at the FBI and within the NY Police Department. He hoped that if a phone call came in with information about the murder that his network would intercept the information and lead him to the source. Fletcher was used to dealing with the unknown but he usually had the controls in his hands. This time he had to wait to respond. He was playing defense and he didn't like it.

The investigation at the crime scene in Southampton continued throughout the day in painstaking fashion. The Southampton police were exceedingly careful not to make any mistakes that would cause a major embarrassment. They were handling a very high profile murder and did not want to screw up. The Southampton police chief phoned Martha Torres, the FBI's office chief in Manhattan in the early afternoon after reviewing the circumstances and evidence at the Teasedale estate. What concerned him most was the lack of motive. Harrison Teasedale had not been murdered. He had committed suicide—a review of the video tape in the camera in the basement gym confirmed that. Teasedale was an extremely wealthy man who had just thrown an enormous cocktail party over the weekend that was a major social event. Other than the video tape, the only other evidence in the house was the collection of papers on Teasedale's breakfast table that seemed to contain a litany of account information and balances, as well as dates and wiring instructions. The Southampton police knew they needed assistance. The FBI would be able to help them sort out the evidence that they could not understand. When Martha Torres hung up with the police chief, she called John Aichenhead.

"Hello John. I seem to remember that you did some security clearance work on an individual at Morgan Greenville. Is my memory correct?"

"Yeah, your mind is a steel trap. Why do you ask?"

"There's been a murder/suicide in Southampton that involves one of Morgan Greenville's senior partners. The police out there need some help and don't want to screw things up. Apparently, there's a video tape of the crime—the victims were involved in some perverted sadomasochistic sex games—so they know what happened. They need our help to figure out why. The suicide victim's name is Harrison Teasedale and he is some big mucky-muck at Morgan Greenville. The police chief said they found something that he was working on before his death that could be a clue to his motive, and they can't decipher it but it looks like coded financial accounts. I want you to take this on. It's going to be very high profile as it breaks because of the sex and money angle. I think you'll have to move on it quickly."

Aichenhead was cursing his good luck. Normally, working on a plum case like this would go to some other agent and not to him. Torres must have decided to do him this favor because he'd been inside Morgan Greenville's offices before. Now he regretted taking on his surreptitious assignment for Bert Washington. The Teasedale case was real meat on the bone; the BLS conspiracy exercise was still just smoke. He knew Nick Bowa was digging deeper into the fifteen employees' prior work experience that turned up as matches in his screens. He'd figure out how to keep that project going, but now he had some real investigative work to do.

CHAPTER 32

Washington, D.C.
New York City
Tuesday, May 29, 2007

The news of Teasedale's death was first announced on CNBC about an hour before the market closed when one of its investigative reporters got wind of the murder from an employee at Morgan Greenville. The reporter took what he was told and followed up by calling the Southampton police station and asking for the desk detective on duty. Since everyone with any seniority was at the crime scene, the call was funneled to one of the department's newer officers. Without much effort, the reporter quickly learned a lot more than what he had been told by his Morgan Greenville contact. The incident was a murder/suicide involving an unknown party and Harrison Teasedale. There was solid evidence that led them to understand that Teasedale had killed himself after murdering the other party. When the reporter asked about motive, the young officer replied that there was some kind of kinky sex going on in the basement. That was all that the reporter needed. At about 3:00 P.M. in the afternoon, CNBC shocked its television audience with what it had found out about Teasedale's death from a "credible" source.

Kirby Haines was sitting at home watching the TV. His world was imploding. He was supposed to become Teasedale's prince. Now the king was dead, but Haines had no lines of lineage to assume the throne. That could have happened years from now, but not now. Seeing the story on TV was surreal. A flashback of the scene in the gym rushed into Haines' mind—murder/suicide. He couldn't put it together. Why would Teasedale kill himself? CNBC had held back on the sexual angle to the story because they didn't want to get sued straight away. Morgan Greenville was still the biggest, most powerful investment bank on Wall Street. Some things were more important than the news.

Alan Solomon and Pennington Ludlow drove over to the White House together in Solomon's limousine. Ludlow would be a surprise guest for the 3:45 P.M. meeting with the President, but given his Cabinet position, his attendance would not seem odd to the White House staff. On the short ride over, the news of Teasedale's death dominated their conversation.

"Fletcher's men are extraordinary. CNBC is saying that it was a murder/suicide and the police have solid evidence. I've even heard rumors circulating that Teasedale was involved in some type of sadomasochistic sex with the other victim. Alan, don't forget who we are dealing with here. Fletcher is a cold-blooded killer and he is Lowery's right hand. Whatever we hoped to achieve six years ago with this 'Economic Revolution' has spun completely out of control. Teasedale and I did the wrong thing but look how they're settling it. Believe me, they're not finished yet. We have one chance to save our lives. We can do this together."

"Tell me Pennington, just how much money did you and Teasedale make in your insider trading scheme?"

"We made a lot."

"Actually I was asking for an exact figure. If you expect me to stand beside you when we see Lowery, I suggest that you answer my question. How much did you two make?"

"About $9 billion."

"$9 billion?"

"Yes."

"Oh my god. No wonder Fletcher wants to kill you. Where is it now?"

"In many places around the world."

"You must consider me an old fool. Now I know why you want my help. If you can blunt Fletcher's plan to kill you, you can keep your fortune. He's asked you for it, hasn't he? You're clever Pennington. I should have guessed it. You never change."

"All that's irrelevant. Yes, they want my money but once they have it, they're still going to kill me and then you. If this works, I'll pay you $1 billion. Then you won't have to go on the speaking circuit or write your memoirs."

"I'm not interested in your money. It doesn't belong to you or Fletcher or Lowery. It belongs to all the investors that you cheated. I have no use for it."

"Suit yourself, Alan. You've always been a high-minded asshole. You can have your principals and morality but you still fucked someone behind your wife's back."

"I've suffered for that mistake, Pennington, because I have a conscience. Your value system is monolithic. You were the perfect choice to run Treasury."

"Since you don't want any reward, just remember that you're doing this for your dear wife, Miriam. I'm sure she wants you alive despite your transgression."

The limousine pulled up to the White House security gate and the car was passed through. Chuck Lowery was waiting for Alan Solomon in the Oval Office. Bob Fletcher had flown down to Washington, D.C. and was waiting in the pantry off the President's office. In five minutes the men were ushered in to their meeting.

"Good afternoon Alan. How nice to see you again, it's been a few weeks, hasn't it? Hello Pennington, I didn't realize you were coming over with Alan. You must have something important on your minds to come together. The economy isn't slowing down that fast is it?"

Ludlow didn't wait for Solomon to respond.

"Chuck, I think you probably know why we are here. You certainly know why I came. Harrison Teasedale's death is all over the news and Bob Fletcher is certainly going to kill me next and probably Alan soon after. Alan and I have come here to convince you to change that decision. I've told Alan everything about my trading scheme with Harrison Teasedale. So now if you want to kill me, you will have to kill him."

Alan Solomon turned and looked at Ludlow with contempt.

"Pennington, I think your imagination is running away with you. Fletcher and I don't talk about all the things that you think we do."

"Look Chuck, you can play this charade any way you want to, but here's the fact that you and Fletcher and his private army should consider. Alan and I are standing together. He knows what happened to Harrison Teasedale and why. We all know about and helped execute your splendid plan to bring the US back to its prominent position in the world. That was noble but your latest tactics are not. You cannot kill the Secretary of the Treasury and the Chairman of the Federal Reserve. Even you know that is a risk that's not worth taking. We need to call a truce. We are in this together and we have to stay alive to protect our separate and mutual interests. If either of us dies, the whole scheme will be disclosed. We've taken care of that."

"Pennington, we set about to save this great country. Your motives were less noble. You and Teasedale were thieves. I cannot let that stand. You think that I don't know how to calculate risk? I faced death many times. I suggest you follow Bob Fletcher's instructions, whatever they are. If you don't, I think you will be taking a risk that you'll regret."

"Is it just about the money Lowery?"

"No, it's not just about the money. But you decided to follow a rogue agenda and committed treason. You were caught and now you will pay. There is some time to consider the long term consequences but if you don't comply with Fletcher's request, your long term won't last very long. It's unfortunate that you brought the Fed Chairman into your web since he has committed no crime. Regrettably, you have compromised him. I think this meeting is over gentlemen; I have some important national business to attend to. My advice to you is to follow Fletcher's instructions. I hope to see you both again…but I guess you will determine that."

Lowery pressed a button on his desk and the Marine stationed outside his office door opened it to signal that the meeting was over.

When Ludlow and Solomon left, Fletcher stepped out from the pantry. "That was good Chuck. Now I know why you're the President."

"I think that will shut Ludlow down. I would be amazed if you don't have what you need by 5:00 P.M."

"Alan Solomon is a schmuck. Why would he let Ludlow abuse him? If Ludlow doesn't come up with the account information should I take him out? That may require some additional planning. It will certainly embarrass our administration by having him be the leak for Teasedale."

"Maybe we can consider a truce for the time being and take Ludlow out later. It does mean that Solomon will have to go at some point as well. I didn't want this mess. I really didn't but Pennington Ludlow fucked this up to a fair-thee-well."

"I don't think anything has changed, Chuck. Accepting Ludlow's truce will just make it longer to resolve. Desmond has been trading all day and the executions have been better with Morgan Greenville out of the market. We've made a lot of money. We don't need Ludlow's entire pile but we should take what we already have. He is a traitor and he will have to die for that, sooner or later. It shouldn't take long for the Morgan Greenville connection to leak into the press. The FBI office has been brought in. I'm sure once they go over the evidence left behind at the house, they'll pay a visit on Morgan Greenville. Given how Teasedale must have traded, it isn't going to take very long to begin to put two and two together."

"I'm sure you've set up a mechanism to move that leak along."

"I have and the news should hit fast and furious starting tomorrow morning. One of Desmond's men is working that process. Teasedale's suicide and the mystery around it are going to shine a big light on Wall Street and his old firm. Questions about how they made all that money over the years are going to lead right back to Teasedale and his poor, sexy Mexican accomplice who happened to be the Treasury Secretary's mistress. Ludlow may have his truce but he'll be unemployed by the time the market closes tomorrow."

Tally Morgan, the Southampton Press reporter was making excellent progress on his story for the *NY Post*. His small town relationships with a dozen people working on the investigation gave him a great advantage over other reporters who were scrambling to come up with facts and angles. Besides his police contacts, he was friendly with the coroner; with the EMS teams; and even with the funeral home director who was given the bodies for safe keeping before autopsies were performed. Every one of his sources gave him something that allowed him to piece the story together. He had even learned that the FBI had been brought in to help analyze evidence that had been found in the house that had no direct linkage to the murder scene. Apparently the evidence had a financial characteristic that was beyond the Southampton police department's capability or expertise. One of Tally's sources told him that maybe Teasedale was involved in some sort of international financial ring. The front page editor at the *Post* was working on four inch headlines—"SEX SLAVE MURDER AND SUICIDE IN THE HAMPTONS." Rupert Murdoch was going to sell a lot of newspapers on Wednesday morning.

CHAPTER 33

New York City
Tuesday, May 29, 2007

John Aichenhead didn't have time to travel out to Southampton. The news of Teasedale's death was already hitting the financial news networks. The internet was conducting its own sensational probe. Aichenhead asked for and quickly received five other agents and a support team to help him accelerate his investigation. He dispatched two of his agents to Southampton to conduct field operations. From the preliminary information he received from the Southampton detectives in charge of the crime scene, the murder and suicide seemed pretty straightforward—particularly since it had been recorded on tape. Aichenhead had seen a lot of strange things in his life, but this story was particularly odd—one of the richest guys on Wall Street kills himself after murdering some Asian prostitute in his multimillion dollar home.

Aichenhead had googled Teasedale and didn't need to read too far to see that he was severely socially connected and had plenty of powerful allies in Washington, D.C. Aichenhead guessed that everyone had some secret—something dark that they hid from the

rest of the world. Teasedale's secret was that he was a homosexual
or some type of sexual deviant. One of Aichenhead's agents would
follow both paths to determine which one of them applied. Since
he had to establish a working theory of the crime, Aichenhead
thought that Teasedale probably killed the victim by mistake and
panicked. He killed himself rather than risk his own exposure and
a life sentence for murder. Once his men arrived in Southampton
and reviewed the tape, he might be able to confirm that theory. It
seemed pretty extreme but there didn't seem to be anything else
to hang his hat on.

   Still, Aichenhead knew that suicide was a radical act. It typically was not a decision made hastily, although men's suicides were
usually more violent than women's. Women preferred to die via a
cocktail of prescription drugs, hoping that they would never wake
up. Men liked to blow their brains out and make a big mess—a final
act of masculine irresponsibility. Aichenhead wondered why people
who had everything took so many stupid risks. Teasedale had no
good reason to die. He doubted the man suffered from depression
or some other mental disease, but another one of his agents would
check his medical history. Aichenhead knew that more of the story
would become clear once the autopsy was performed. He needed to
dig into the evidence that had been found in the house that did not
relate to the murder/suicide. The Southampton detectives had collected and categorized the papers discovered on Teasedale's breakfast room table. The police photographers had shot the breakfast
room from a variety of angles and had pictures of the table top that
they had obtained by using a ladder to produce those shots. Since
the pages were not numbered or part of a report, the Southampton
police numbered them and named them for their own evidence
purposes. They were scanned into the detectives' computers and
emailed to Aichenhead. He printed them out along with other notes
from the detectives and took them to a conference room that he

was using as a coordinating point for the investigation. Aichenhead laid the papers out on the table. They looked like reference notes. There were pages of numerical sequences that seemed to represent account numbers. Some of the sequences were grouped and some were listed individually.

The Southampton detectives had also emailed Aichenhead a copy of the statement that they had received from the Morgan Greenville employee who had discovered Teasedale's body. Aichenhead did not immediately notice that the statement was from Kirby Haines, the man he had interviewed for National Security clearance in early February. Aichenhead read the statement's section that dealt with the breakfast room table documents. The account numbers did not belong to Morgan Greenville. If the number sequences did not belong to Morgan Greenville, then who did they belong to? Aichenhead looked at the papers again that were setting on the table. What was Teasedale doing before his terminal sexcapade? Everything in front of him looked like reference documentation, but for what? They weren't related to Morgan Greenville activity. Aichenhead had two priorities: figure out what the account numbers represented and interview Tom Lynch, the CEO of Morgan Greenville. Aichenhead placed the Kirby Haines' statement on the table alongside the other printed documents, and noticed his name for the first time. Kirby Haines—the banker from New Jersey. His Saturday night date with Haines' assistant, Joanne Fruilli, had turned out better than he had expected. He added a third item to his priority list. He needed to visit Kirby Haines again and find out everything he could about Harrison Teasedale. Since Haines was working with Teasedale at the time of his death, he might know something that could help Aichenhead rationalize the case and understand the financial information he was trying to decipher.

Aichenhead was able to reach Tom Lynch quickly. He set up an appointment to see him at 5:00 P.M. that afternoon. Lynch had asked him about the rumors he was hearing regarding the circumstances surrounding Teasedale's death. Aichenhead told Lynch that he would fill him in on all the details he had when they met later. Aichenhead had less luck trying to reach Kirby Haines. He had not returned to the office and when Joanne Fruilli gave Aichenhead Kirby's home number and cell phone, Aichenhead's attempts to reach him were unsuccessful. Aichenhead figured that Haines probably went home and disconnected himself from the world at large. That was a smart move. Aichenhead would trek uptown after his meeting with Tom Lynch to pay a visit on Kirby Haines at home. The Teasedale murder/suicide investigation was going to severely screw-up his schedule. He'd be spending a lot less time on his favorite Village barstools until this case was over.

If his memory served him, Tom Lynch's office was a whole lot more opulent than Kirby Haines'. The space was big enough to throw a good sized party. "Mr. Lynch, I'm Special Agent John Aichenhead from the FBI. Thank you for agreeing to see me on such short notice."

"That's not a problem Special Agent. Aichenhead. That's an unusual name. Is it German?"

"That's what I've been told, sir. Plenty of jokes usually go along with it."

"I'm sure of that. Anyway Special Agent, what can you tell me about Harrison's death?"

"I'll tell you as much as I can Mr. Lynch, but my purpose here is to enlist your help in figuring out what Mr. Teasedale was preoccupied with before the time of his death. We believe we have the circumstances of his death pretty well pinned down but we're having a problem deciphering some evidence that was found at his home."

"I would be happy to help you Special Agent to the extent I can. Please tell me what you know. There are some vicious rumors circulating around. They could damage our firm. Harrison was a very senior partner here. I'm being pestered by reporters who are writing stories for tomorrow's newspapers that are going to be quite unsavory. We are operating a bit in the dark. Our one employee who flew out to discover the body was quite disoriented and couldn't really understand what he saw. I sent him home to deal with his shock."

"That was Kirby Haines?"

"Yes, it was."

"I've read the statement he gave to the Southampton police. Harrison Teasedale killed himself with a handgun after murdering his companion. Both bodies were found in Teasedale's basement gym. The victim was an Asian, probably eighteen or twenty years old. We believe he was a male prostitute. Teasedale videotaped their session in the gym. We have that tape and it includes both the murder and suicide. It also includes their sexual encounter in its entirety. The tape is explicit, lurid and quite brutal. We are protecting it so that it does not see the light of day. The men were engaged in deviant sexual activity that included sadistic and masochistic behavior. Mr. Lynch, were you aware of Mr. Teasedale's sexual preferences?"

"Absolutely not. Harrison was a gentleman and great philanthropist. I never saw him in a compromising social situation ever."

"He wasn't married?"

"No."

"Divorced?"

"No."

"Do you have many bachelors working here that are his age?"

"Well, frankly no. But Teasedale's private life was his own business. He was here to make money Special Agent."

"I see. I'm just trying to understand his motivations. Suicide is an important final statement."

"Teasedale had a clean personnel file. I will put you in direct contact with our Director of Human Resources when we're done. I can't believe what you're telling me."

"Mr. Lynch, what exactly was Mr. Teasedale's responsibility at Morgan Greenville?"

"He had numerous responsibilities but his most important job was running our proprietary trading desk."

"In that function, he traded the firm's capital like a giant hedge fund?"

"That's about right Special Agent. You seem to know a bit about our business."

"I read a lot Mr. Lynch. In his job, as head of proprietary trading, I assume he was successful?"

"Why yes. Under Harrison's guidance the firm's profits have grown exponentially. He is—was an expert risk trader. For the last six years, we have recorded record profits every year."

"Who did he report to? Where did he go to get approval for his trading decisions?"

"I am the CEO, but the firm is run by a management committee. Harrison was a member of that committee. Every member of that committee is responsible for their own business. Harrison did not need to ask our permission to run his business. He was his own CEO."

"That seems like an odd management structure. How could you control what he did?"

"If he made money, he was paid well and given more capital. If he didn't, we would have found someone else to take his place. Investment banking is a meritocracy."

"I gather that Mr. Lynch, but one that's driven by anticipated compensation. You only can make decisions by looking in the rear view mirror?"

"We don't really think of it that way Special Agent but I could see why you might be confused."

John Aichenhead was not confused at all. Tom Lynch was a figure-head. Morgan Greenville was like a collection of individual fiefdoms. There wasn't much oversight until something went wrong. Teasedale's death fit into that category. "Mr. Lynch, I need your help with some documents that we discovered at Mr. Teasedale's home. Did you see Mr. Teasedale over the weekend?"

"Yes, I did see him on Saturday night. He threw a magnificent cocktail party. Everyone was there."

"Did you talk to him after that?"

"No, I did not."

"He was supposed to fly back to Manhattan with you Tuesday morning?"

"Yes, he was but he didn't show up."

"Did you try to call him that morning?"

"Yes I did."

"But not the night before to confirm your departure the next day?"

"No, we had pre-arranged everything for our flight back to the city. We didn't need to speak."

"Are you aware if Mr. Teasedale was working on anything over the weekend?"

"No, not in particular. Harrison was a workaholic so I wouldn't be surprised if he was busy on something. He was in the middle of repositioning the firm's risk capital and had been very busy for the last couple of weeks."

"Is that so?"

"Yes. Harrison had been one of the great bulls on Wall Street for the last several years. But recently he decided that the run was over. He and his team had been very busy building new portfolio positions and unwinding old ones."

"Mr. Lynch. I have some pages with me that are copies of pages that were found on Mr. Teasedale's breakfast room table. Could you look at them and tell me if you recognize them?"

"Certainly."

Aichenhead removed a set of pages from his brief case and handed them to Tom Lynch. He put on his reading glasses and surveyed the sheets in a deliberate manner. When he was done, he looked up at Teasedale and handed him back the pages.

"Special Agent. I have no idea what's on those pages."

"We believe those sequences represent account numbers. Are you telling me that those are not Morgan Greenville related accounts?"

"They certainly have nothing to do with Morgan Greenville."

"If they have nothing to do with Morgan Greenville, can you tell me what Mr. Teasedale might have been doing with them. That is Mr. Teasedale's handwriting, is it not?"

"Yes, that looks like Harrison's writing, but I have no idea what those account numbers represent."

"Do you have internal policies that prevent your employees from having accounts at other firms?"

"Yes of course. We spend a great deal of money on regulatory compliance."

Aichenhead wondered whether Morgan Greenville's compliance organization was as well tuned as its approach to management oversight. "Mr. Lynch, those account numbers do not belong to Morgan Greenville's system and were found in Mr. Teasedale's possession. I am going to need to track those accounts down."

The next papers that Aichenhead pushed in front of Tom Lynch listed dollar amounts in long, continuous columns.

"Mr. Lynch, how much money do you think that Mr. Teasedale was worth?"

"I have no precise idea Special Agent. Maybe $500 -800 million. I just don't know."

"As you can see, the sum of the figures listed on these pages comes to over $9 billion. Is it possible that Mr. Teasedale kept accounts separate from the firm and had amassed a significant personal fortune?"

"Special Agent, that's preposterous. That is an enormous amount of money. As I indicated, Harrison was a very rich man."

"Mr. Lynch, I'm trying to figure out just how rich. I'm not sure how or if this relates to his suicide, but I need to get to the bottom of it. I'm going to ask your assistance on something else. We need to look into all the trading activity that Mr. Teasedale conducted in the month leading up to his death. I know this is unusual but I need your cooperation. If Mr. Teasedale violated your internal trading policies, the SEC is going to breathing down your neck. If we can get to the bottom of this account mystery, perhaps we can save you from a big headache."

Aichenhead was pushing Lynch. He needed to move the investigation along and if Morgan Greenville decided to stonewall, it would create a big delay.

"If you don't mind, I would like to talk to my General Counsel before agreeing to your request. I want to cooperate but I also want to make sure that we are protected. I'm sure you understand."

"I certainly understand. I would do the same thing if I were you. Given the possibility that Teasedale did not comply with your trading policies and operated with little or no oversight, I would want to speak to my lawyer also. Thank you for your time Mr. Lynch. I'll be back in touch soon." Aichenhead got up and left Lynch alone in his large office. Lynch had a major problem on his hands, he just didn't realize how big it was about to become.

The East Side Drive was always a pain in the ass at 6:00 P.M. in the evening. Aichenhead had the radio on as he moved slowly with the traffic. Teasedale's murder was the lead story on the all-news channels. Even though no official statement had been released by the Southampton police, everyone reporting on the deaths seemed to have excellent sources. Aichenhead knew he had to work fast. On the way up to Kirby Haines' apartment he called Nick Bowa to find out how his day went and whether he had been able to dig up any more information on the BLS employee information. Bowa answered his own phone—it was after 6:00 P.M. Aichenhead was impressed that Bowa was still slaving away.

"Hey Nick, it's John. What's up?"

"Not a whole lot but I have made some progress on the fifteen employees' previous work experience. I don't know whether this is a coincidence or whether former Special Ops and Seals typically go into similar professions after their duty is done."

"Tell me what you found."

"It seems like every one of the subjects that I have reviewed so far went to work with one of two private security firms or with a certain international consulting firm. I haven't tracked them all down yet but among the twelve that I did research, all of them went to work for one of those three firms."

"Do you have the names of the firms?"

"Yeah, but I never heard of them. Seems like everything is named after some underworld Greek or Roman god or mythological animal."

"That's pretty predictable. Anything common about those companies?"

"Yeah, in fact that's the oddest thing. All of them are headquartered outside the US and all of them list the senior executive or major shareholder as Robert or Bob Fletcher."

"Bob Fletcher as in President Lowery's Bob Fletcher?"

"I didn't know that President Lowery had a Bob Fletcher."

Aichenhead remembered that Bowa was a newbie. "Bob Fletcher is a very wealthy confidante and advisor to President Lowery. Most people don't know a lot about him. He keeps a low profile. He does a lot of international business as a contractor for the US government."

"I see. Well anyway, I'm still digging but all twelve employees that I've been able to track have Bob Fletcher in common. I just can't tell if that's a coincidence."

"Good work Nick. I'll be back to you. Keep plugging."

Aichenhead's mind was working. He needed to find out as much as he could about Harrison Teasedale from Kirby Haines. The information that Nick Bowa had uncovered was interesting. Aichenhead really didn't know that much about Bob Fletcher—just the normal rumors about a powerful guy. Why would at least twelve people in his employment leave their jobs to join the BLS during a twelve month period six years ago? Something was there but Aichenhead couldn't put it together. He needed a lot more help. He didn't have time to call Bert Washington. He would try to do that later. Aichenhead made a right on Park Avenue and headed north toward Haines' building. He found a spot by a fire hydrant and got out. He was greeted at the building's entrance by a uniformed doorman. Oh yes, the Upper East Side—a place where John Aichenhead felt completely out of place.

Aichenhead presented his FBI credentials to the doorman and told him that he needed to see Kirby Haines. The doorman called Haines' apartment using the building's intercom system. Aichenhead was shown to the elevator and taken up to the eighth floor where Haines was standing in his open door. He looked bad.

"Kirby, I'm sorry we have to meet again under these circumstances. May I come in?"

"Of course, Special Agent. How did you get involved in this?"

"Just a random assignment. My number came up and my boss remembered that I had a prior experience with Morgan Greenville. I didn't realize you were involved until I read the statement you gave the Southampton police. Are you alright? It was a gruesome crime scene."

"I don't really know. I can't get the picture out of my mind. I've known Teasedale from the first day I started at Morgan Greenville. He was the star—really the key guy. I can't believe he's dead. I can't believe he killed himself."

"Why Kirby?"

"Because he was so alive. He was in control of everything. We were completely engaged at work. He threw an incredible party on Saturday night. Now he's dead. It doesn't make any sense."

"Everything is on the video tape that the detectives recovered from the camera in the gym. The footage includes the murder and then Teasedale shooting himself."

"He must have been drugged or something. I'm telling you. Harrison Teasedale was not a guy who was going to kill himself."

"Did you know that he was a homosexual or had relationships with male prostitutes?"

"Everybody whispered that Teasedale was gay. So what? Being gay doesn't mean you go out and kill yourself?"

"Even if coming out of the closet would jeopardize his career?"

"Teasedale was worth hundreds of millions of dollars. He was the greatest trader on Wall Street. Do you think that anyone would care if he was gay or not. He paid a lot of people's bonuses."

"Suicide is the most difficult violent act to explain. He didn't leave a note. It seems like he just snapped after he realized that he had killed the other man. Did you know about Teasedale's private life?"

"No, I didn't know much. He was a workaholic who came to the office early and left late. He lived in a mansion not far from here and didn't entertain to the best of my knowledge. He was involved in certain charities and was socially active at their related events. Teasedale was a loner maybe even eccentric, but he didn't strike me as some radical pervert. You guys should be able to confirm that. If he was part of some underground deviant sex group, you'd find that out, right? My guess is that you won't find anything. All the guy did was work. You can't burn that candle at both ends."

"Kirby, tell me about your working relationship with Teasedale."

"Okay. About two weeks ago, Teasedale asked me to be join him on the proprietary trading desk. He said it would be a great opportunity to advance within the firm. I had just made Partner so I was very happy that he had chosen me."

"What exactly were you doing for Teasedale?"

"We were trading the firm's account. Recently, we were selling everything. Not literally, but Harrison had decided that the economy was about to take a turn for the worse and wanted to trade out of most of our long and less liquid holdings around the world. I was handling that element of the strategy."

"Did he explain why he had this view of the economy?"

"No and Harrison was not a guy who had much patience explaining why he did things. He thought the good times were coming to an end and he wanted Morgan Greenville to get out of the way while the rest of the Street got caught by surprise. We had been raising cash and trading around the clock for the last two weeks. That's another reason why I can't believe he killed himself. We wanted to finish things up this week and Teasedale was leading the charge. If he wanted to kill himself, he would have waited until the job was done."

"But his decision to kill his companion changed his timing."

"I guess you're right. Teasedale was a very classy guy. I just can't see him with a male prostitute."

"Everyone has their secrets, Kirby. Maybe you can help me with something else. In your statement, you were asked about the paper work that Teasedale left in his breakfast room."

"Yeah, I remember."

"You said that the numbers looked like account numbers but didn't correspond to anything at Morgan Greenville."

"That's right."

"Speculate for me Kirby. What do those numbers represent and why were those lists left on the table."

"I don't know. Maybe those account numbers belong to someone else. Maybe Teasedale was trying to help someone and was reviewing those accounts. I can't really explain it. Do you think they have anything to do with his death?"

"Not sure but I'm not a big believer in coincidences. It's a little confusing for me to think that Teasedale worked on something in the breakfast room but didn't pack it up in his brief case before deciding to pick up some prostitute for a night of fun. His overnight bag was packed in his bedroom, but his work papers were all over the table in the breakfast room. To me, it looked like he was working on some project and the papers were notes or lists that he needed for the work he was doing. The problem is that there isn't any other work product in his brief case or in the house. Just the notes on the table."

"I wish I could help you, but I really have no idea what those numbers represent."

"That's okay, Kirby. I have an analyst at our headquarters trying to track them down. It may take days or weeks or even months but hopefully we'll figure it out. What are your plans?"

"You mean for the rest of the day?"

"No, really tomorrow and Thursday. I need to know where you are going to be in case I have any follow-up."

"I'll be here or at work. Tom Lynch, my CEO, told me to take as much time as I need. I still feel pretty shaky. I may sleep in and go to work tomorrow afternoon. My girl friend may fly up to stay with me tomorrow."

"Where is she coming from?"

"Washington, D.C. She's the chief of staff for Treasury Secretary Ludlow."

"Sounds like a smart lady. Okay Kirby. I'm done for the time being. He's my card again. Call me if anything comes to your mind. I'll be in touch."

Aichenhead left Haines' apartment and headed back downtown in his car. He had a text message from Bowa. It simply read: "15 for 15—they all worked for companies controlled by Fletcher." Aichenhead headed south on the East Side Drive. He didn't believe in coincidences.

CHAPTER 34

New York City
Washington, D.C.
Wednesday, May 30, 2007

Wednesday's newspaper headlines were sensational and they quickly
fed the local television news desks with outrageous copy for the
early morning news shows. Tally Warner's article for the *New York
Post* provided the most detailed version of the events that led up to
the suicide of Harrison Teasedale. The spread in the *Post* included
pictures of Teasedale's Southampton estate and townhouse in
Manhattan. It also featured pictures of Harrison Teasedale and
Morgan Greenville's nameplate on their downtown headquarters.
Warner's three page article detailed Teasedale's Saturday night party
with George Michael's performance and his final sexual tryst with
the Asian prostitute, whose identity was still unknown. Warner
had even been able to obtain descriptions of what the victims were
wearing at the time of their deaths. Warner's article was so precise
that John Aichenhead was stunned by its accuracy. Many of the
facts that Warner reported were only known to the investigators
who were keeping everything under close wraps.

The most sensational element in his story was an allusion to
Teasedale's trading responsibility at Morgan Greenville. Warner
suggested that the authorities were looking into Teasedale's and
Morgan Greenville's trading activities in the weeks leading up to
Teasdale's suicide. He reported that evidence found in Teasedale's
home hinted of unauthorized trading activity. Aichenhead was
dumfounded. How had the reporter known about that evidence?
Aichenhead himself was waiting to figure out what the account
information represented. This two-bit reporter had already offered
a theory.

Tally Warner had spoken to many people to piece his article
together and his two co-authors had canvassed all their considerable sources to find out what they could. By no coincidence,
one of their unnamed sources was Monroe Desmond's senior
trader in Dublin. He suggested that there were rumors circulating about Morgan Greenville's trading—they were on the right
side of the market all the time. How could any firm be that good?
Harrison Teasedale was a connected guy: put two and two together.
Desmond's man was a valuable channel of information for the
Post reporters. His information would insure that the story would
have long legs.

Aichenhead had picked up his copy of the *Post* when he decided to
get a real cup of coffee Wednesday morning. He needed something
better than the mediocre brew he had made the prior day. As he
got ready for work, he reread Warner's article and circled several
sections that required his attention when he got to the office. His
team was working on the account number information, trying to
find the institutions that corresponded to the sequences. He knew
not to bother with US based companies. He told his people to start
with institutions in the best known foreign tax havens like The
Bahamas, Cayman Islands, and Barbados. They were also looking in
Europe, particularly eastern Europe and Southeast Asia. Aichenhead

jotted down a list of calls he had to make when he got to the office. Given the article, he had to contact the SEC and check whether they were in fact looking at Morgan Greenville's trading activity over the last several weeks. He also needed to follow-up with Nick Bowa and Bert Washington.

When he finished with his interview with Kirby Haines Tuesday night, Aichenhead had returned to his apartment around 8:15 P.M. All he had wanted to do was to get something to eat and drink, which he accomplished at The Spain. After he got home, he searched through his haphazard library looking for a psychology book on suicide. He found one and had fallen asleep reading it. He couldn't understand why Teasedale killed himself, and the book did not offer any credible insights that might have matched Teasedale's personality or profile. He was a very smart man who could have devised a strategy to save his life or create a defense to explain the murder. Kirby Haines had been adamant about his doubts. No one had given Aichenhead a good reason for Teasedale's suicide other than the obvious one. He wasn't satisfied.

After reading the *Post* article, Aichenhead needed to pay another call on Tom Lynch. He wanted Teasedale's trading information and he wasn't prepared to wait for Morgan Greenville's General Counsel to delay him further. The shit show had begun. Martha Torres would start to slowly apply the pressure on him. He didn't like the feeling that he was getting. There were a bunch of loose ends but theories and rumors were surfacing faster than his own investigation; that was not good.

When Kirby Haines awoke on Wednesday morning, he turned on the TV in his bedroom. At 6:00 A.M., the Teasedale suicide was the feature story. The news anchor relied on the *New York Post*

article. He even mentioned Morgan Greenville and possible trading irregularities. Haines couldn't believe what he was hearing. He checked his Blackberry. There were two unread messages. The first was from Hillary. The second was from Tom Lynch. He decided to call Lynch and dialed his cell phone number.

"Hello Tom. It's Kirby Haines."

"Good morning Kirby. Have you seen the New York Post this morning?"

"Not yet but I've been watching the news."

"Well when you do you will read something that's very troubling. The reporter suggests that Harrison could have been trading in some unauthorized manner. If that were true, it would be a major problem for the firm. I have to ask you a very simple question: are you aware of anything that Harrison might have been doing on an unauthorized basis?"

Tom Lynch was serious and Kirby Haines knew his answer to that question could have a big impact on his standing at Morgan Greenville. A month ago he had been made a prince. Right now he felt like his character was being impugned by a reporter's innuendo.

"Tom, I know nothing about anything that Harrison was doing that could have been unauthorized. We booked every trade. There were a lot of people involved. Harrison made the calls but everything was documented. I think the reporter is full of shit. It's a pile-on. People hate our success and they hated Harrison's power. Now that he's dead, they want to trample him into his grave. I've been on the desk for less than a month but I've never seen anything going on that was not above board and completely conforming to our rules."

"All right Kirby. I was hoping that would be your answer. The paper's allegation is going to create a firestorm. I'm expecting to get requests or subpoenas from a variety of agencies. I think it's better if you take today off. I know that you probably want to come in, but I think it's better if you stay away. I'm going to have Mary set a call up for you with someone on our legal staff. Otherwise, please don't speak to anyone about the case."

"Tom, I'm going to go crazy sitting around here doing nothing."

"I understand, but we have to keep a lid on this the best we can. I want you to go back over the last weeks and create a history of your trading activity and instructions from Harrison. I know our lawyers are going to want that done anyway. You might as well get a head start. That will keep you busy. If you get contacted by anyone, I want you to call me."

"I'll do that. You should know that an FBI agent visited me last night. He came here after seeing you. It was the same agent who cleared me for my Board seat on the Comsdef investment. He wanted to go over the statement I made to the police, which I did."

"Did he ask you about anything else?"

"Yes he wanted to know if I believed that Harrison could have been suicidal. I told him that I couldn't understand why someone like Harrison would take his own life. He also asked me about the account information evidence found in the house. I told him that I didn't recognize it and that it had nothing to do with Morgan Greenville."

"Okay. I'm sure I'm going to be seeing Agent Aichenhead again given the newspaper stories. Make sure you call me if he contacts you again. Our lawyers may want you to only answer questions with them present. I'll make sure someone calls you immediately."

"That's fine Tom. I'll stay here and wait for the call."

After Tom Lynch hung up, Kirby dialed Hillary in Washington, D.C. He reached her as she was getting ready to leave for work.

"Hey baby, it's me."

"Oh my god, Kirby. I can't believe the news this morning. This thing is breaking like the OJ case. What's happening?"

"I wish I knew. I just spoke to Tom Lynch. He wants me to stay put and speak to our lawyers this morning. He's fritzed about the insinuation that Morgan Greenville and Teasedale were somehow involved in some type of unauthorized trading. It's crazy. I told him that everything we were doing was documented and clean. I swear I don't know what's going on."

"Do you think it's possible that Teasedale was doing things that you couldn't know about?"

"I don't know, but I don't think so. I just can't believe that he killed himself. Something must have snapped. Trying to connect it to the firm's trading activity seems crazy."

"I'm going to try to talk to Pennington today about giving me a day or two off so I can come up and stay with you. He wasn't available at all yesterday. I guess after the weekend he had things to do, but he didn't tell me."

"Don't worry. I'm okay. I'm just going to hang out and wait for the lawyers to call. We can catch up later when you know something."

"I love you baby and want to be with you."

"I love you too. I'll be fine. Let's talk later."

When they hung up, Kirby switched the channel over to Squawk Box. Everyone was talking about Harrison Teasedale and Morgan Greenville. Kirby was getting more depressed but he couldn't stop watching the coverage.

John Aichenhead had a lot to do. If he didn't call Bert Washington early, he knew the day would slip away from him. Washington's project was secondary but he had made a commitment to him and he still had Nick Bowa bird dogging the Bob Fletcher connection to Washington's employees at the BLS. Maybe he could catch Washington on his way into the office. He dialed Washington's cell number.

"Hello, Bert Washington here." Washington was driving and answered his phone using his Bluetooth connection.

"Hi Bert, it's John Aichenhead."

"Hey there, I was wondering what happened to you."

"I got assigned to the Harrison Teasedale case and things got fast and furious in a hurry."

"I should say. What a story. Sounds like he was a major player with some very kinky habits."

"Apparently so. I'm heading up the investigation on our end but still trying to help you as best I can."

"I appreciate that. From the sound of the story, you may even have some unauthorized trading to deal with."

"I really can't comment, but frankly we just don't know. The story is actually a bit ahead of our investigation. We have a lot to do and the press is pushing the agenda which is something I could do without. Let's spend a minute catching up on your project."

"Sure thing. I looked at the list you sent me yesterday and checked their personnel files. Really nothing popped out. They all have impeccable reviews and have done great jobs. I know almost all of them personally or enough to say hello and have a cup of coffee."

"We've been able to do some additional work on their prior employment experience. It seems that all of them worked for one of three companies before joining the BLS. Those companies were foreign based and all of them were owned by Bob Fletcher. Have you heard of him?"

"I think so. He's one of the President's closest friends and confidantes. Isn't that the same guy?"

"Yep, you got him. Let me ask you a question: do you typically observe your people at work?"

"Yeah, I hate to sit in my office with the door closed. We have a lot of meetings and even sessions where I bring folks together to talk about how we can improve processes, the culture—you know the drill."

"I wish I did, but we don't have a lot of that fuzzy stuff at the Agency. If you think back over the last year or longer, would you have known if any of these individuals had prior relationships with each other?"

"That's an interesting question. Let's see. I guess I really don't think so. Everyone in the Washington office is very professional. We're more focused than chummy. I want to think about this group in that regard, but I have to say that I wouldn't have thought that any of them could have worked together before."

"Maybe they didn't. The companies where they worked might have been large or they might have been assigned to different offices in different countries. I honestly don't know at this point. I just thought I'd ask if you recognized any closeness among any of them."

"I really haven't John."

"We may want to pursue that further. You're the conspiracy theory guy. I guess my question to you is could this group, acting in concert, mess with your numbers? If the answer to that question is yes, my next question is why would they?"

"The answer to your first question is yes, John. And now that you've told me that they all worked for Fletcher and Fletcher is the President's best buddy, maybe Mr. Fletcher wanted the President's performance to look good. I think that's a pretty good answer to you second question"

"Bert, at least you're consistent. But we're about to travel into dangerous territory. I think you should noodle on those two questions some more while I try to get to the bottom of my murder/suicide case."

"You're job is a lot more exciting than mine, John."

"At this stage of my career, that's not a positive. I'll check in with you later."

When John Aichenhead reached his desk, he had a host of messages. On the top of his list was a call from Brian Doherty at the SEC. It hadn't taken them long to react to newspaper and TV reports. Aichenhead didn't know Doherty but called him back immediately.

"Hello, Brian Doherty? This is John Aichenhead at the FBI returning your call."

"Thanks for getting back to me so fast. That your real name?"

"Yes it is—forty years and counting."

"Better you than me. I wanted to talk to you about the Teasedale murder case. You're heading up the investigation?"

"Yes, that's right."

"I wanted to share with you some information that may or may not be helpful. We also may be a resource for your investigation."

"I appreciate that. What do you have?"

"Over the last several weeks, we've gotten some complaints from other firms about Morgan Greenville's trading activity."

"Is that abnormal?"

"Sometimes yes and sometimes no. Lots of folks complain but they are usually grousing about a single transaction where one party screwed another. The noise here came from several different market makers. All of them were complaining about Morgan Greenville's selling activity. A very large volume of trades were executed at prices well outside the indicated bid/ask spread in the marketplace."

"If the complainers weren't sellers, why did they care?"

"Some of them might have wanted to be sellers, but at the prevailing market price. If Morgan Greenville was arbitrarily taking the market down, that would impact all the other sellers and also impact how those other firms valued the same securities on their books."

"So what did you do about the complaints?"

"We have had initial conversations with the Chief Compliance Officer at Morgan Greenville but haven't really progressed our discussion. Given the newspaper reports this morning, I'm beginning to think we should get a closer look at what was going on. Harrison Teasedale ran the firm's trading business and any rumor about unauthorized trading would give us reason to kick the tires harder."

"Brian, let me tell you where we are. What I'm about to tell you is confidential but given your involvement it's probably appropriate to share it with you. The newspapers acquired information about our investigation that we were keeping a tight lid on. We found evidence at Teasedale's home that we have not been able to understand up to this point. There was an extensive list of account numbers that was found at the scene. There was also a dollar aggregation that may or may not have had anything to do with the account numbers that totaled about $9 billion. I have spoken with Tom Lynch and with Kirby Haines, who was Teasedale's trading partner at the firm, and neither of them recognized the account numbers or knew anything about Teasedale executing any trades on an unauthorized basis. I have members of my team trying to discover what institutions could be the home of those accounts. We've drilled a dry hole at this point."

"That's not surprising. That could be like looking for a needle in a haystack."

"That's what I'm afraid of but I do think we will ultimately find some homes for those accounts even if it takes months."

"We might be able to help you in that regard."

"I would appreciate that very much. What are you going to do about Morgan Greenville?"

"We're going to dig deeper. We had just been focusing on their selling activity over the last two weeks. Now with the questions swirling around the firm and Teasedale's death, I think we have to look much further. I'm going to call over to their General Counsel today and ask for their cooperation. I want to know what Harrison Teasedale was up to over the last year. I'm going to want to take a closer look at everything."

"I also intend to pay another call on Tom Lynch today. Do you have any problem if I tell him that we've spoken and are cooperating on this matter?"

"Absolutely not. I think cranking up the heat may get them a bit more serious a lot faster."

"Brian, thanks for your call and help. I'm going to send the account information that we discussed over to you office and I will call you sometime before the end of the day to compare notes."

"Sounds fine, John. I look forward to working on this together."

Aichenhead was happy to get the SEC's help. It was interesting that various parties had been complaining about Morgan Greenville's trading over the last couple of weeks. It certainly seemed out of the ordinary. Lynch and Haines had told him that Teasedale had become a big seller, but it seemed like he had conducted a fire sale. Why would Teasedale be such a rabid seller? Aichenhead thought about Bert Washington's hunch about the economy and his concern that his own numbers weren't right. How could Harrison Teasedale act with such conviction based on a hunch? Aichenhead understood the concept of hedging one's bets. Harrison Teasedale wasn't hedging. He was selling everything and bringing market prices down with him. It was time to rattle Tom Lynch's cage again.

CHAPTER 35

New York City
Washington, D.C.
Wednesday, May 30, 2007

John Aichenhead spoke to Tom Lynch on the phone and told him that the FBI and SEC were going to take a much closer look at Morgan Greenville's trading history over the last year. Aichenhead advised him to cooperate or subpoenas would be issued for the information in two hours time. Lynch reluctantly agreed to open the firm's trading book to speed along the investigation. At the same time, he adamantly denied that Morgan Greenville had participated in any unauthorized or illegal trading activity. He chose his words carefully since his General Counsel's office was beginning its own internal investigation. A team of SEC and FBI investigators showed up at Morgan Greenville's office before lunch. They knew what they were looking for if they could find it. The haystack at Morgan Greenville was quite large indeed.

Pennington Ludlow and Alan Solomon did not speak again after their Tuesday afternoon meeting with Chuck Lowery. Fletcher had not spoken to Ludlow since Tuesday morning, and Ludlow figured that his strategy of bringing Solomon into the equation must have had its desired effect. Ludlow had no delusions that he was completely out of the woods. He was sitting on top of a massive pile of profits. He knew that Fletcher would be back in touch soon. Chuck Lowery had warned him to follow Fletcher's instructions. Ludlow wasn't foolish enough to believe that he could walk away with a complete victory. Harrison Teasedale was dead and Bob Fletcher had a Wild West sense of justice. Ludlow could deal with Chuck Lowery. He just hoped that Lowery could control Fletcher. Ludlow's intercom sounded. Bob Fletcher was on the phone. That did not take long.

"Ludlow, I want you to listen to me very carefully. I have been waiting for the rest of the account information that you failed to deliver to me by our agreed-upon deadline yesterday evening. I am aware that you have brought another outsider into our discussion. That was very foolish on your part. You have this propensity and arrogance to believe that you can control the course of events. But you are sadly mistaken. If you don't give me the rest of the information by the end of the day, you will only have yourself to blame for the consequences."

"Listen Bob, I have already given you enough information to increase even your net worth substantially. Harrison Teasedale's share of the trading profits is going to languish in his accounts until it is claimed, and he obviously did not set up any beneficiaries given his lifestyle. Why don't you just take his share and we can call it a day. You seem to be bent on my total destruction and I want to find a compromise."

"Washington, D.C. seems to have the same effect on everyone who lives there. Everything is about compromise—you've lost your sense of right and wrong. I took out Teasedale without regard to his money. He was an outsider who threatened the economic order that we had established over the last six years. Lowery wants to spare your life for some reason. He's a risk manager. I'm a risk taker. If it were up to me, we wouldn't be talking right now. You have until 5:00 P.M. to satisfy my demands. If you fail to do so, good luck."

"I've offered you Teasedale's billions. I want to keep what you haven't taken already. It's a small pittance compared to what I'm giving you."

"Pennington, you think that you're negotiating a deal. I don't negotiate." Fletcher slammed the headset into its holder on the desk where he was seated. He wanted to kill Pennington Ludlow now more than ever.

When the call ended, Ludlow felt more confident. Fletcher had admitted that Lowery did not want him killed. His instinct was right. He had made a fair offer to Fletcher. If Fletcher wasn't satisfied with the billions he had been offered, that was his problem. The Alan Solomon tactic had worked. He called Solomon next. Solomon picked up his line after a few moments.

"Hello Pennington. The newspaper accounts of Teasedale's death are truly horrific. It sounds like Teasedale wasn't very careful with some of the financial information that you two were using. They found evidence of unauthorized trading in his house?"

"I have my doubts, Alan. The newspapers are speculating. Everything we did was coded. We took no chances. For all I know, Fletcher planted the rumors to try to put more pressure on me to give him all our profits."

"This is all so sordid."

"I'm calling to let you know that my tactic to bring you into the battle has worked. Fletcher called me just now and threatened me again but he let it slip that Lowery has no intention of killing me."

"Congratulations."

"No, you don't understand Alan. That means he has no intention of killing you either. The standoff has worked. I really believe we are both safe."

"Safe is a very relative term, Pennington. We may be alive but we don't know what their next move is. You may have won a battle, but my guess is the war is far from over."

"I'm giving you the half-full argument. I thought you would be relieved given your concerns about Miriam. You should be able to rest easier now."

"You're such a hypocrite Ludlow. This has nothing to do with Miriam—it's always about you. Thanks for the call."

Solomon hung up on Ludlow and went back to work. Ludlow was surprised at Solomon's reaction. He expected relief or an ounce of gratitude. Ludlow had come up with an idea that had probably saved Solomon's life. He had even given him back the only copy of the sex tape that had tortured Solomon's life for the last ten years. To Pennington Ludlow, Solomon was an ungrateful cur.

John Aichenhead's various teams were not making speedy progress. The team trying to decipher the account number information had nothing to show for their efforts. They were exerting significant pressure on various nations who supported evasive taxation practices but no matches were found. The same was true with their first passes in Europe and Asia. Almost all of the banks they interviewed had ten or twelve digit account numbers. Every account sequence in Teasedale's notes had nine digits or less. The team was determined to keep looking but was suffering from initial frustration. Aichenhead's other team that was investigating Teasedale's state of mind, medical history, and the recent activities leading up to his death were also empty handed. Teasedale had never undergone therapy and his medical record was completely clean. Given the

sexual perversion surrounding his death, the team had expected
to discover some record of sexually transmitted disease but found
nothing. Aichenhead had speculated that perhaps Teasedale had
a hidden illness that could have affected his state of mind. But his
medical history was completely normal and he was in good health.
The last month of his life did not reveal anything unusual either.
He had not traveled outside the country or anywhere else other
than Southampton. He had burned the midnight oil at work and
his social calendar was empty other than the safari party that he
threw two nights before his death. Nothing that the team found
pointed to a likely suicide profile. They were still trying to pursue
Teasedale's closeted life in the New York underground but so far he
was a complete unknown. Given the New York Post coverage and the
press frenzy, Aichenhead's team believed that Teasedale's involvement with other prostitutes or partners would quickly come to the
surface. But nothing had come up.

After lunch, Aichenhead received the findings of the preliminary
autopsy report. Teasedale had died of a gunshot wound to the head.
The video of his suicide informed the coroner that the gunshot was
self-inflicted. There was no evidence of alcohol in Teasedale's system
and his stomach was empty. A toxicology report that would indicate
the presence of other drugs or chemicals would take at least another
week to process. Aichenhead had learned nothing new. Everything
appeared to be just as the Southampton police originally described,
but Aichenhead was disturbed that he was missing a number of the
pieces. He was even more disturbed that the newspapers seemed
to be a step ahead of his own investigation. Someone knew more
than he did and he didn't know what or who it was.

Near the end of the day, John Aichenhead received a message
from Bert Washington that he wanted to speak if John had any
time after work. Bert Washington was dogged, if anything. All
Aichenhead wanted was a break from his frustration. He really

wanted some alone time with his books or at least a drink at The Spain. He'd call Bert when he got home. Before he left work, he checked in with Nick Bowa. Bowa had decided to follow the Bob Fletcher path and his employer relationship with the BLS subjects a little further. John pulled Nick into a conference room and closed the door. It was almost 5:00 P.M.

"Have you had any more luck with our class of fifteen?"

"Not a whole lot. I made direct calls to the three companies where the folks worked before the BLS and got an icy reception. I told them that I was calling on behalf of a headhunter who was trying to do some reference checks on the individuals. I was completely rebuffed by the HR officers I talked to. They said they couldn't release any information on any prior employees. When I suggested that was highly unusual since there was no continuing relationship, I was told that that was company policy. All three company representatives said exactly the same thing. It made me think that their common ownership might explain the similarity in policy."

"Bob Fletcher's policy."

"That's kind of what I was thinking."

"What else?"

"Since they worked outside the country as Americans, I was able to get some information from the IRS. Every one of them worked for these companies for several years before their decision to join the BLS and I can deduce that none of them were searching for jobs very long after they left."

"That's interesting."

"Yeah, it seems like they worked almost right up to the point when they were hired by the BLS. My guess is that they didn't spend months considering a host of offers."

"Thanks Nick. You're doing a great job. Keep up this kind of work and you're going to go far."

Some asshole had said the same thing to Aichenhead years ago.

He felt bad perpetuating the myth. At 5:45 P.M., Aichenhead left
the office. He had his full detail working on the Teasedale case. He
laughed to himself that Nick Bowa was making considerably more
headway on Bert Washington's theory than the FBI and SEC were
making on Teasedale and Morgan Greenville's trading rumors. But
the big questions in both projects still remained: why would someone want to deliberately manipulate the economic pronouncements
of the BLS and why would Harrison Teasedale kill himself?

Aichenhead was through his apartment's front door in about
fifteen minutes and had popped open a beer and settled on his
couch to call Bert Washington. Washington picked up his own
phone—his assistant had left precisely at 5:00 P.M. Civil service
has its benefits.

"Bert Washington here."

"Hi Bert. It's John Aichenhead. I thought I would check in
with you at the end of the day. I got your message earlier but this
Teasedale case has me pretty preoccupied."

"I've been thinking all day about the two questions you wanted me
to consider. And I've been thinking about Bob Fletcher as well."

"Sounds like you've been thinking a lot."

"Well that's right John. I can make a plausible case that because
of their positions it would be possible for those fifteen employees
to manipulate the data that we collect for reports like our jobs
measurement. When we conducted our internal audit we focused
on two Fed regions: Philadelphia and San Francisco. Two of the
fifteen actually head up our offices in those regions. Four others
have principal responsibility within those regions for data collection and oversight. The others in Washington, D.C. are very
senior economists and IT specialists. They all touch the data

before it gets aggregated into the reports every week and month. I'm telling you John, if they were working together they could pull it off."

"Okay Bert, I hear you. Tell me why they'd do it."

"Because they're all Republicans. You said they worked for Bob Fletcher before coming to the BLS. He's the biggest Republican fund raiser of them all, isn't he? Lowery's 'Economic Revolution' had to work. They were helping it along."

"Bert, I still need to deal with facts. Just because they're Republicans, worked for Fletcher and believe in Chuck Lowery's 'Economic Revolution' doesn't mean that they committed any crime. You told me that when you conducted the second phase of your audit that the numbers passed through untouched, right?"

"That's right."

"So why didn't the group manipulate them? How did they know to stand down?"

"I don't know. Someone must have told them."

"Who Bert? Who told them?"

"The only people that knew about that plan initially were Rosemary Guillson, Secretary Ludlow, and Hillary Thomas."

"You said Hillary Thomas?"

"Yes. She's Secretary Ludlow's Chief of Staff."

Aichenhead thought to himself that it was a small world. He recognized Hillary's name because Kirby Haines had identified her as his girl friend when he interviewed him Tuesday night. "But once you started the audit test, others must have known about it. Who else knew?"

"Let's see. One of my associate commissioners, Beverly Bittner, worked with Rosemary Guillson looking at the BEA and Rosemary's right hand, Ken Shue, oversaw the BLS work."

"Well Beverly Bittner was not in Special Ops or a Navy Seal. For your theory to hold water someone must have told your infiltrators to let the numbers pass through untouched. That leaves you, the Secretary of the Treasury, Rosemary Guillson and Hillary Thomas. My guess is that none of them has a Bob Fletcher connection."

"Okay. I see where you're going. If there is no connection to Bob Fletcher, there is no conspiracy theory. What about Ken Shue? You didn't screen him."

"You're right. We didn't look at BEA employees. I'll have my man check out Shue next."

"That's a good idea, John. I know you think all of this is circumstantial but I know there's something here. When the jobs report is announced on Friday, the markets are going to tank. If we hadn't conducted our audit process, I bet the numbers would be a lot better. An insider knew what we were doing and shut the operation down. It's either Hillary Thomas, Pennington Ludlow or Ken Shue."

"What happened to Rosemary Guillson?"

"She's a life-long Democratic from Boston. She's never believed in Lowery's economic bullshit. She's about as pure as you get in Washington."

"And what about you Bert? You were promoted with Lowery's blessing to become the first African American commissioner of the BLS. Maybe you've be cooperating with Lowery to help his performance. Isn't payback the predictable motive?"

"John, you must really believe that I am some kind of genius. Why would I even conduct an audit or contact you if I was complicit."

"Alright, I agree. You know, I don't believe in coincidences. I'm getting more and more uncomfortable with this because I didn't want to believe your conspiracy theory. There is some logic here but we are handling dynamite. Let's continue carefully and keep digging. I've got my hands full with the Teasedale case. It's on my front burner and moving faster than I can control. I'll call you tomorrow when we know more about Ken Shue and Hillary Thomas' background. I'm not going near the Treasury Secretary at this point."

"Okay, we'll talk tomorrow. And thanks for at least beginning to believe, John. We're going to prove something. I just know it."

CHAPTER 36

New York City
Washington, D.C.
Thursday, May 31, 2007

Bob Fletcher's Wednesday 5:00 P.M. deadline for Pennington Ludlow came and went. Fletcher wasn't that surprised. Ludlow had determined that he had secured a lifeline by bringing Alan Solomon into the equation. He wanted to strike a deal with Fletcher to guarantee that lifeline, but Fletcher wasn't going to cut a deal with Ludlow. Fletcher had been clear with Ludlow about his need to comply with his demands. President Lowery had told Ludlow the same thing on Tuesday afternoon. Ludlow's failure to meet their demands would trigger a series of actions that would spin Ludlow's once perfect life into a living hell. Ludlow thought he had won a truce, but he had underestimated Bob Fletcher's will to win at any cost. Now Ludlow would learn the true cost of his disloyalty to Lowery and Fletcher.

Monroe Desmond's senior trader spent nearly an hour on the phone feeding Tally Warner's co-author at the *New York Post* juicy details about Harrison Teasedale and Carmen Gomes on Wednesday night. The most lurid of the revelations had to do with Ms. Gomes longtime affair with Treasury Secretary Pennington Ludlow. The essence of the largest insider trading endeavor was delivered in a tidy package to the reporter. The *New York Post* had everything it needed to blow Harrison Teasedale's murder/suicide story into an epic Wall Street scandal. At the same time, Bob Fletcher had decided that he couldn't eliminate Carmen Gomes from his life. She was after all the greatest lay on the planet. Fletcher flew her out of the country to his home on Sardinia. He would explain everything to her afterwards. She would be grateful to be kept alive and he would accept her gratitude on every occasion that brought them together. She was his property again. He liked the idea of having her all to himself.

The *Post* headline on Thursday morning was a blockbuster, "TREASURY SECRETARY MISTRESS LINKED TO SEX SLAVE MURDER." The article in the *Post* told a shocking story. No one saw it coming—not Ludlow, not Morgan Greenville, and certainly not John Aichenhead. When Aichenhead wandered out of his apartment at 7:00 A.M. to pick up his coffee and the newspapers he couldn't believe the *Post's* banner. He sprinted back to his building to read the article, spilling a quarter of his coffee as he hustled home. The article cited sources close to the investigation but named no names.

The storyline read like a made-for-TV movie. Treasury Secretary Pennington Ludlow had been carrying on a ten year affair with a Mexican former beauty queen named Carmen Gomes. Many people knew about their relationship but kept silent because of Ludlow's senior position in the Administration. According to the sources, Gomes took information that Ludlow received as

Treasury Secretary and passed it on to Harrison Teasedale, the
trading genius at Morgan Greenville. Gomes got to know Teasedale
because Morgan Greenville handled Ludlow's blind trust and she
accompanied Ludlow to events where Teasedale was present. In
return for the inside information she relayed, including advanced
data on economic announcements like employment, CPI, and GDP,
Teasedale wired Gomes money which was deposited quarterly in
an account at a Mexican bank. According to the sources, she could
have received as much as $1 million dollars for her role in the plot.
Teasedale apparently used the information he received to build
Morgan Greenville into a trading powerhouse as well as for his
own personal trading benefit.

The article claimed that the SEC and FBI were closing in on
Morgan Greenville but were not yet in a position to bring charges.
Carmen Gomes was seen at Harrison Teasedale's extravagant
cocktail party on the Saturday before his suicide. Secretary Ludlow
attended the party as well, although they arrived separately, as was
their apparent habit. Because of Teasedale's homosexuality, the
relationship between Gomes and Teasedale was strictly financial.
The story indicated that the FBI was looking for Carmen Gomes but
feared that she might have already left the country. The *Post* article
featured numerous pictures including photos of Pennington and
Anne Ludlow, Carmen Gomes in a pageant bathing suit, and Tom
Lynch from Morgan Greenville. Aichenhead dropped the paper on
the floor and reached for his phone. It was only 7:35 A.M. He had to
talk to Brian Doherty before Martha Torres cornered him. Luckily,
he had Doherty's cell phone number. Doherty's phone rang three
times before he answered it.

"Yeah, Doherty here."

"Brian, it's John Aichenhead."

"I thought you'd be calling."

"Brian, what the hell is going on?"

"Honestly, I have no idea. I was hoping you were going to tell me."

"I know as much as you do. Everything in the *Post* is new information. I've never heard of Carmen Gomes and we have no evidence of her relationship with Harrison Teasedale. The allegations are obviously serious. It's like someone delivered us a treasure map. This is beyond strange."

"Isn't that the truth. We just started with Morgan Greenville yesterday. But with this article their haystack just got a lot more manageable. My guess is that Tom Lynch is going to be calling you or me before we have the chance to get to him. He must be shitting a brick. Have you been watching the TV?"

"No, I just got the *Post*."

"Well, the news is breaking everywhere. It's a repeat of yesterday, only a lot more salacious with gigantic implications. Morgan Greenville's stock is bid down 15% in the pre-market."

"We're going to have a hell of day. Maybe we should both meet at Morgan Greenville's headquarters at 9:00 A.M. I've got to speak to my office chief first. I'm sure she is pissed. Since the moment this case broke, we've been two steps behind everything. It's like the press knows the whole deal and is leading us along."

"I know what you mean. I'll meet you at 275 Vesey at 9:00 A.M."

"Alright. See you there."

The Fed Ex package that Harrison Teasedale sent to Kirby Haines sat under a two day old pile of mail. In fact, Kirby Haines had received so much mail that Joanne Fruilli had decided to put everything in a cardboard container and store it behind her desk. She wasn't sure whether Kirby was going to come in or not that

Thursday. She felt terrible for him but she understood the trauma
that he was experiencing from the shock of finding Teasedale and
his companion dead. She knew that Thursday morning was going
to be awful. Even Joanne Fruilli could sense that. On the ferry ride
over from Staten Island everyone was reading the *Post*. Morgan
Greenville was in big trouble. Teasedale had allegedly used inside
information to make the firm successful and him rich. This was
bad—very bad.

Monroe Desmond's men finally got the answer they were looking
for from Federal Express late Wednesday night before midnight.
One of the packages that had been picked up at the Fed Ex drop
box in Southampton had indeed been sent by Harrison Teasedale.
The recipient of the package was Kirby Haines. Desmond's men
did their work quickly and realized that Haines was Teasedale's
partner on Morgan Greenville's proprietary trading desk. He was
also the individual who flew out to Southampton and discovered
the bodies in Teasdale's house on Tuesday morning. His name had
appeared in all the articles written about the murder/suicide. Upon
getting this information, Desmond called Bob Fletcher who was
still in Washington, D.C. and told him the news.

"Okay, if Haines received the package, why haven't we heard
about it?"

"I have no idea."

"Well how about an educated fucking guess, Monroe?"

"Maybe he hasn't received it yet. Or maybe he's scared to
death."

"I'll accept those as two possible answers. Why don't you figure
out which one is correct."

"Yes, sir. I'll get on it right away." Two of Desmond's men were set up on Park Avenue by 6:00 A.M. to begin surveillance of Kirby Haines and intercept him if he left his building.

Fletcher accepted the obvious. Teasedale had told him the truth. It wasn't a desperate bluff. He had penned his confession and sent it to Kirby Haines to protect his own life. In a way, Fletcher admired Teasedale. He had taken a step to protect his life—on his own. Obviously Teasedale did not trust Ludlow. He was bent on his own self-preservation. But he was dead anyway. There could not have been another outcome. Fletcher's mind moved on to Kirby Haines. What did Haines know? Could Teasedale have brought him into his and Ludlow's scheme? Was he another outsider who would have to be dealt with? Maybe he was just the wrong guy in the wrong place. Fletcher didn't care. He needed to find out what Haines knew and he needed that information as quickly as possible. Haines had already spoken to the Southampton police and Fletcher surmised to the FBI as well. Given the story in the newspaper that morning, Fletcher figured that Haines might well be under the gun as Morgan Greenville was investigated for Harrison Teasedale's trading. Desmond's leaking partner had insured that, but none of them knew that Kirby Haines had been the object of Harrison Teasedale's lifeline attempt when they fed their story to the newspaper reporter a number of hours earlier. Fletcher needed to know what Haines knew but he had to move carefully. If he killed Haines, it would have to be a last resort. Things were already messy enough but working. Fletcher had crucified Ludlow with the story in the *Post*. He was effectively neutered. But Ludlow would understand that his outcome could have been worse—and fatal. He would be investigated but the lasting damage would be to his reputation. Not many captains of industry would be accepting Pennington Ludlow's invitations to DeSaussure Hall in the future even if Anne Eckhouse remained his wife after the lurid revelations of his decade long affair.

The press and their remote broadcasting vans hurried out to Chevy Chase where Pennington Ludlow and Anne Eckhouse lived when they were in residence in Washington, D.C. There hadn't been a really good Washington scandal since the Clinton/Lewinsky sensation. Pennington Ludlow was a chief architect of longest economic rally in modern US history. Now he was implicated not only in a decade long affair but in being the dupe in the largest insider trading undertaking ever uncovered. Ludlow was a prisoner in his own house and he was furious. Fletcher had turned the tables on him once more. Fletcher didn't want or need Ludlow's money. He had killed Teasedale and now effectively shot Ludlow in both knee caps. Ludlow was thinking quickly. He called Alan Solomon's home number. It was only 7:30 A.M. but Solomon picked up the phone.

"Alan, have you seen what they've done to me? You've got to help me. We made an agreement and you have stand up for me"

"Pennington? Is that you, Pennington?"

"Of course it's me you old fool. They're trying to destroy me, my marriage, and my reputation. You have to help me. There are a dozen reporters camped on my front lawn. What am I going to do?"

"Pennington, I'm sorry but I can't help you."

"Can't help me? You owe me. You've got to call President Lowery and tell him to fix this or we'll tell the press everything."

"You didn't hear me. I won't help you. You should focus on the fact that Fletcher could have killed you if he wanted, but he decided to let you off with a life sentence. You did the same to me ten years ago. You've got no story to tell the press Ludlow. You're in quicksand—open your mouth and you'll just sink lower. They are controlling the game and you can't win. No, I intend to live. You are alone Ludlow and you are going to pay the price for crossing them. If you have a brain, you should use it at this point."

"Fuck you, Alan! Fuck you!"

"What goes around comes around. How's Anne taking all this?"

Ludlow threw the cordless phone against the wall. He was alone. He sat down in his library and tried to anticipate his next set of moves. He needed to speak with his attorney first. The early reports had suggested that he was not suspected of any criminal wrongdoing. He had only been portrayed as a cheating husband who had been taken in by his Mexican mistress. Ludlow knew that Fletcher was prepared to drop the other shoe if he tried to defend himself. Ludlow's housekeeper appeared at the library's entrance.

"Mr. Ludlow, the White House is on the phone."

Ludlow picked up the phone that was sitting on his desk.

"Hello, Secretary Ludlow? It's Horace Grant. Please hold for the President."

In about thirty seconds, Chuck Lowery got on the line.

"Good morning, Pennington. That was quite shocking and disturbing news in the papers today. I feel terrible for Anne. How is she doing?"

"Listen Lowery, you can drop the bull shit. What do you want?"

"I'm very concerned that you've compromised the trust I placed in you Pennington. If the news stories are correct, I don't think you can continue in your position as Treasury Secretary. I'm asking you for your resignation."

"Drop dead, Lowery. You and Fletcher have absolutely fucked me. I'm not resigning from anything. Maybe Alan and I should just go to the *Post* and really set the record straight."

"You know that would be a foolish thing to do, and I never considered you a fool. I spoke with the Fed Chairman before I called you. I think you understand that you are alone on this one, Ludlow. No one is going to believe you. You'll just look desperate and unstable. I've given you a choice, Pennington, and it's really not the worst outcome. You should think about that. I intend to announce your resignation before the end of the day. Please tell Anne that I asked for her. Good-bye."

Ludlow was done. Lowery and Fletcher had outgunned him. Ludlow called his lawyer who agreed to come out to Chevy Chase to plan his next steps. Anne Eckhouse had left through the servant's entrance and was headed to the airport to fly down to DeSaussure Hall. It was hot down there, but nothing like it was in Washington, D.C. that morning.

John Aichenhead finished getting ready for work and was preparing to leave his Minetta Street walk-up when his cell phone rang. It was Martha Torres. Her call was expected.

"John, it's Martha. What the hell is going on in the Teasedale case? Did something happen last night after we spoke that you decided not to tell me?"

"Of course not. The press coverage today is all news to me. I spoke with Brian Doherty a few minutes ago and he confirmed that his team at Morgan Greenville hadn't come up with anything yet. I'm meeting him over at their headquarters at 9:00 A.M."

"At this point, we're all looking a little stupid. Do you know anything about this Mexican woman?"

"Never heard of her."

"Anything in the Teasedale evidence about their relationship or his insider trading?"

"Absolutely nothing."

"John, where is all this stuff coming from?"

"At this point, I have no idea, but I plan to find out. When I'm done with Tom Lynch, I'm going to pay a visit to the writers over at the *New York Post*. They seem to know everything."

"We need to get control of this investigation. I know I'm going to be hearing from the US Attorney at some point this morning. It would be nice to have some answers to the questions I expect him to be asking. Some evidence of criminal wrongdoing might be helpful as well."

Aichenhead ignored her sarcasm. He was frustrated just like her. "I'll call you around lunch and let you know where we are. I'm going to put two agents on the Carmen Gomes angle. Everyone else is chasing down the other leads."

Aichenhead wondered whether he should tell Torres about the work he had been doing for Bert Washington. There was no direct connection but Washington was convincing Aichenhead that there could be a conspiracy to disseminate inaccurate information to shore up President Lowery's "Economic Revolution." Torres' last sarcastic remark convinced Aichenhead that maybe he should keep his freelance project to himself for a while longer.

When Aichenhead was finished with Martha Torres, he called Tom Lynch's direct line at Morgan Greenville. One of his three administrative assistants answered the phone. It was still only 8:00 A.M. Aichenhead told them that he and Brian Doherty would be down to speak to Lynch at 9:00 A.M. and Lynch should clear his calendar for the rest of the morning. Lynch had gotten to work very early having been tipped off about the *Post*'s article. At 8:00 A.M. Lynch was already on a telephonic conference call with his Board of Directors. Morgan Greenville's outside counsel was participating in the meeting as well, along with its team of litigators. Lynch was preparing for the worst. In pre-market trading, Morgan Greenville was being hammered. When Lynch's assistant passed him a note alerting him of Aichenhead and Doherty's planned visit, he had her call Kirby Haines and tell him to get down to work as soon as possible.

On the one hand, Haines was glad to get out of his apartment and get back to his office downtown. On the other hand, he knew that he was in for a grilling. He was the closest partner to Harrison Teasedale and his recent trading activity. That being said, Haines really didn't know what Teasedale did moment to moment on the trading floor. Teasedale gave Haines his orders and he executed them. Teasedale was selling and buying on this own even though he was never more than 50 feet away from Haines. He had told Special Agent Aichenhead and the Southampton police all he knew. He never saw Teasedale do anything illegal or break any internal policy. The *New York Post* apparently had a lot of contrary evidence. Before leaving the apartment, Haines called Hillary Thomas to confirm the flight she would be taking to travel up to New York.

"Just tell them what you know Kirby. That's all you can do. If Teasedale was crooked, they'll find all the evidence. You're not guilty just because you sat in the same department."

"I know. I know, but if the story is true, Morgan Greenville is out of business. I remember what happened to Drexel Burnham. The government could shut us down tomorrow."

"Don't get ahead of yourself. You don't know what's going to happen. Look at me. My boss is toast too. He's conducted a ten year affair with some Mexican bimbo and she used him to make a million bucks. If that story is true, Pennington Ludlow has a half-life of about 48 hours. I'll be in the unemployment line before you! We're the perfect couple leading parallel lives, Kirby. What great fucking luck."

"You can say that again. When can you get up here or do you have to stay in Washington because of Ludlow?"

"I'm not sure. My guess is that he's huddled with lawyers trying to figure out how to defend himself. I may not hear from him at all. Even if I have to wait until the end of the day, I'll be up there by dinner."

"That sounds good to me. At least we'll be together. We can toast to our careers going straight down the toilet."

"Let's hope you're wrong. I'll see you later. Love you."

"Love you too."

Kirby called a radio car and finished getting ready to leave. His doorman called up ten minutes later to tell him that his car was downstairs waiting. Kirby grabbed his brief case and rode down with the elevator operator. He rushed through the lobby and into the warm air. The doorman was holding the door of a black town car open for him and Kirby jumped into the back. It took him a split second to realize that there were two men in the front seat. The driver locked all the doors and pulled away from the apartment building. Kirby tried the door handle. The man in the front passenger seat, Tim Rivers, turned around and pointed a gun at Kirby's forehead.

"Mr. Haines, I suggest you sit back, shut up, and listen to what I am about to tell you."

Kirby looked into the black barrel of the gun that was staring him in the face. He realized he wasn't dealing with some random kidnapping. These men knew who he was and they seemed deadly serious.

"Okay, don't shoot me. Who are you?"

"I'll ask the questions Mr. Haines. Have you reported to work since you discovered Harrison Teasdale's body?" Haines' hands were shaking like an old man's.

"No. I was told to stay at home."

"Has your secretary sent you your mail while you've been home?"

"No as a matter of fact. I hadn't even thought of that. No everything must be waiting for me there. Why?"

"I said I'd ask the questions. We are investigating elements of Harrison Teasedale's death and his potential violations of The

Patriot Act. We have learned that he sent you a package before he killed himself. The package was sent via Federal Express to your office. We believe the contents are incriminating and we need to confiscate that package from you as soon as possible. That's why we picked you up and why we are taking you downtown. Is that clear?"

"I guess so. You said violations of The Patriot Act?"

"Yes. Mr. Teasedale maintained banking accounts in countries that are hostile to the US or where we have limited diplomatic relations. He did not report those accounts to the government which is required by regulation."

"Why would Harrison send me anything before he killed himself?"

"We cannot answer that question Mr. Haines but we have our suspicions."

"What do you want me to do?"

"We need that package. You and I are going to go up to your office and find it."

"If you know it is there, why didn't you just go up and get it yourself?"

"We work for an agency that operates outside the jurisdiction of normal law enforcement channels. We just discovered the package's existence. As you can see, we have our own methods and I expect you to do exactly what we tell you. If you don't there will be consequences. You were Teasedale's partner and he violated sensitive government laws and regulations. We can simply arrest you now and detain you for as long as we like. Would you prefer that option Mr. Haines?"

Haines was rattled. He wasn't sure who he was dealing with but they weren't kidding around. He'd watched enough TV to know that there were all kind of secret organizations within the government. He was dealing with one of them.

"No, I wouldn't prefer that option. But I have no idea whether Harrison Teasedale sent me a package or not. Even if he did, I have no idea whether it's sitting on my desk or was lost somewhere between here and Memphis. I'm happy to take you upstairs and see if it's there. But I would like it if you stopped pointing that gun at me."

"We know the package was delivered. Federal Express confirmed its arrival."

"They didn't tell you about our mailroom did they?" Kirby's ill-timed attempt at humor was not received well by Rivers.

"The nation's security is no joking matter, Mr. Haines. You were Mr. Teasedale's partner and may be an accessory to his crimes. Your complete cooperation is required. You should think about that."

"Look, I told the FBI that I've done nothing wrong. I just hope that the package is really there. I wasn't kidding about the mailroom."

The black radio car left Haines and Rivers off at 275 Vesey Street and then circled and pulled up behind four other radio cars that were already waiting to take Morgan Greenville employees to meetings outside the office or to the airport. The men entered the building. Haines flashed his ID card to the security scanner and escorted Rivers past the on-duty guards as an "accompanied guest." They walked through the lobby and stepped into the elevator. It was 8:45 A.M. As the door of the elevator began to shut a hand reached in to stop the doors from closing. Haines was nervous and in a hurry and pissed at the delay since there were five other elevators in the bank that were going to the same twelve floors. Rivers was standing next to him with his hand on the middle of Haines' back. As the doors reopened, John Aichenhead stepped in. His eyes met Haines' immediately.

"Kirby, I'm on my way up to see Tom Lynch. I didn't expect you'd be coming back to the office today."

Haines was flustered and felt Rivers' index finger pushing into his back. "Lynch called me and told me to get my ass down here. Given the newspaper reports, he wants me around to answer any questions that may come up."

"We've got a lot of ground to cover. Are you going directly to Lynch's office?"

"No, I've got to do something first."

Kirby was thinking fast about whether he should tell Aichenhead about the man standing next to him who had come up to get Teasedale's package.

"Maybe I'll get off with you. I have a couple things I need to ask you before I go to Lynch. You okay with that?"

"Ah, well sure I guess."

"You don't sound sure. What's up?"

The elevator doors opened on the 20th floor for a young banker who had picked up some breakfast at Morgan Greenville's cafeteria. Rivers suddenly pushed his way past the other passengers, escaping just as the doors closed behind him. A simple twist of timing had thwarted his opportunity to intercept Teasedale's confession. It took Haines a few seconds to understand that his undercover agent had just left him and Aichenhead on the elevator.

"We've got to get to my office fast."

On the 28th floor the two men got off the elevator, Kirby rushing down the corridor to his office with Aichenhead close behind. Aichenhead remembered following Joanne Fruilli's tight body through the same maze a few months ago. When they reached Haines' office, Joanne was not at her desk. She was probably on an errand or in the ladies' room. Haines waited for Aichenhead to follow him in and closed the door behind them.

"So what's up that you couldn't tell me in the elevator?"

"Two guys from some secret government agency picked me up at my apartment this morning and brought me down here. The man

standing next to me in the elevator who rushed out onto the 20th
floor was one of them. He told me that they knew that Harrison
Teasedale had sent me a package the night of his death. He wanted
to know if I had received the package and opened it. I told him
that I hadn't been to work and never got my mail. I know nothing
about any package. He said it had something to do with The Patriot
Act and national security. He was coming up with me to get it. The
other guy is waiting downstairs in the car. Do you know anything
about this?"

"I know absolutely nothing about this. Did they show you their
identification?"

"No. They said they operated outside the jurisdiction of normal
law enforcement. It seemed like stuff I've seen on TV."

"Listen Kirby, that's total bullshit. Those two guys do not work
for the government, believe me. I don't know who they are and I
don't know how they could know anything about some package
from Harrison Teasedale. Maybe it has something to do with all
that paperwork that was on Teasedale's table in the breakfast room.
You said the car that brought you here is waiting downstairs?"

"Yes. And the guy who came up with me in the elevator had a
gun and he wasn't shy about pointing it at me."

"Those guys are not government agents." Aichenhead quickly
dialed in the information and description of Rivers that Kirby gave
him. With any luck, the police might find the two "agents" before
they had time to make their escape.

Joanne Fruilli had walked back to her desk and flashed a big
smile through Haines' glass office wall when she saw Kirby back in
his office and John Aichenhead with him. She and John had gotten
into a little sexual mischief on Saturday night. She opened the door
and stuck her head in for a moment.

"Hi Kirby, I'm so glad you're back. Hi John, it's so nice to see
you again."

The men nodded but were oblivious to her presence. She knew something was wrong.

"Hey Joanne, did I get any Federal Express packages while I was out?"

"Let me see. I put everything in a carton by my desk. You got a lot of mail." Joanne bent over behind her desk and searched through the container where she had stored Kirby's mail.

"Yes, there is a small box here from Federal Express. Oh my god, it's from Harrison Teasedale."

Haines went out to retrieve the package and brought it back into his office. "Well, they were right. Now I'm really scared. What are we going to do?"

"We're going to open Teasedale's package and see what this is all about."

John Aichenhead asked Joanne to call up to Tom Lynch's office and let him know that he was going to be delayed for about an hour. It would have been a smart idea for Haines to call his General Counsel before sitting down with Aichenhead to open Teasedale's package, but he wasn't thinking clearly. His ride to work with Rivers, his running into Aichenhead, and now the package from Teasedale had knocked him off balance. Behind Haines' closed doors, Aichenhead opened up the Federal Express package and took out the envelope that was addressed to Kirby Haines. Aichenhead passed the envelope to Kirby. "Why don't you open it? It likely contains evidence that is relevant to my investigation but it is addressed to you."

Haines opened the large manila envelope and pulled out another sealed envelope and a letter with the instructions that Teasedale had included for Haines to follow. Haines read the letter's instructions out loud: "Do not open the attached envelope without my personal okay. Store the envelope in a safe deposit box to keep it secure. In the event that something happens to me, deliver to the FBI." Haines looked at Aichenhead and silently pushed the sealed envelope across the table to him. Aichenhead picked up the envelope and opened it. It took Aichenhead about five minutes to scan Teasedale's fifteen page confession.

Teasdale's letter was sensational. Aichenhead had to read it again carefully after he was done the first time. Ludlow had approached Teasedale at the beginning of 2001 with his scheme. Ludlow passed along sensitive economic information using codes from that time forward. Teasedale opened and maintained trading accounts around the world for his and Ludlow's benefit. He also used the information he obtained to trade for the benefit of Morgan Greenville. The dollars involved were staggering. For more than five years, Teasedale had traded using the inside information and had made total profits for himself and the firm of almost $80 billion pre-tax. Teasedale didn't mention Carmen Gomes at all in his letter. Aichenhead made a mental note of that. But Teasedale devoted the end of his letter to the most devastating aspect of this incredible scheme: in mid-May, Ludlow had revealed to Teasedale that the information that they had used to amass their fortune was inaccurate data manufactured and disseminated with the support of Pennington Ludlow and other higher-ups, to sustain the country's economic revival. Teasedale had been told by Ludlow that the economy was about to hit the wall. For the two weeks leading up to Memorial Day he had been liquidating a massive number of long bets on behalf of Morgan Greenville, Ludlow and himself. Bob Fletcher, President Lowery's close friend and advisor, had learned of Ludlow and Teasedale's scheme and travelled to Long Island to deal with their transgression and Ludlow's disloyalty. Teasedale was afraid for his life and wrote his fifteen page missive in an attempt to save himself and barter a trade with Fletcher if needed. Aichenhead put the letter down. Teasedale had obviously run out of time.

Aichenhead ignored Haines for a few moments while he thought.

What did he have? He had some facts and some allegations from a dead man. Aichenhead was still confused. Teasedale murdered his companion and shot himself the night that he mailed the package to Kirby Haines. He had the video tape proof of those facts. Before he died, he spent considerable time penning his only hope to save himself—a diary that would only be read in the event of his death. And he wrote that diary because he was frightened that Bob Fletcher would kill him. But Teasedale killed himself first after a sadomasochistic romp with an Asian prostitute.

The *New York Post* had a source who was feeding it a pretty good story, but one that contained some apparently erroneous information and omitted some other big news which Teasedale's confession contained. One thing was for sure: Teasedale and Ludlow together had concocted and executed a criminal scheme that constituted the biggest insider trading scandal in the history of Wall Street. Another thing was for sure: Morgan Greenville was going out of business by the time all the dust was settled.

Aichenhead mused to himself. Bert Washington was right all along. Son of a bitch. The numbers were wrong—at least according to Harrison Teasedale. Aichenhead's investigation had taken a giant step forward. An hour ago Martha Torres was ready to remove his head. Teasedale's package had changed everything. Kirby Haines interrupted Aichenhead's thoughts.

"I know you can't tell me everything in the letter but how bad is it?"

"It's real bad for Morgan Greenville. When we go up to see Lynch, I'll explain everything. Teasedale does not mention you in his letter at all. You've said you were only following orders and I believe you. Teasedale doesn't implicate anyone else at your firm, but his confession is damning for Morgan Greenville and for some others."

"Oh my god. I just made Partner. What's going to happen to us?"

"I think it's premature to worry about that."

"Okay, but how about those guys who abducted me this morning? They know where I live. Who's going to protect me? And Hillary's coming up from Washington later today. We can't stay at our apartment."

"I'll take care of that Kirby. With any luck, those men who brought you down here might already be in custody. But you are going to have to stay here for the time being. You're not to leave the office. We'll call your girl friend together later and make the right arrangements."

"Okay then. What's next?"

"Let's go up and see Tom Lynch. Brian Doherty from the SEC is here. I'll have to speak to Brian first. I'm sorry Kirby. This isn't going to be pleasant."

Aichenhead and Haines left his office. They passed Joanne who offered a smile but Kirby wasn't smiling. They took the elevator up to the executive floor and Haines was put in a conference room. Aichenhead saw Brian Doherty sitting in the reception area outside Tom Lynch's office.

"Brian, I'll be with you in a couple minutes. I have to call into the office."

"No problem. Lynch is still tied up on a Board call. He isn't going anywhere soon."

As Aichenhead pulled out his cell phone to call Martha Torres, it rang in his hand. His caller ID showed Nick Bowa's name on his screen. "Good morning Nick. What's up?"

"I just thought you should know. Ken Shue at BEA—he worked for one of Bob Fletcher's companies before signing on board. Now we're up to sixteen correlations. I bet there are probably more."

"Thanks Nick. I'll explain later, but that's important news. Really good job."

Aichenhead knew that Ken Shue was no coincidence. Bert

Washington's gut had led him to the biggest fix in Washington, D.C.'s long history of sordid affairs. Fletcher's former employees must have been involved in the generation of the inaccurate information, probably under the specific direction of Fletcher or maybe even President Lowery. Ludlow passed the information on to Teasedale who used it to beat the markets. The only irony was that Teasedale didn't know that the numbers were inaccurate until Ludlow told him weeks before his death. The pieces fit together but it would be extremely difficult to prove unless someone confessed and he doubted that Fletcher or Ludlow or President Lowery was ever going to admit to any of this. Teasedale's confession from the grave was important but he was also now the biggest criminal in Wall Street history.

CHAPTER 37

New York City
Washington, D.C.
Thursday, May 31, 2007

Tim Rivers had made his way downstairs and out of 275 Vesey Street as fast as he could. He couldn't believe his bad luck. He was within minutes of getting his hands on Teasedale's Fed Ex package and now he had nothing. He jumped into the black sedan, idling in the radio car waiting lane, and the men hightailed it as they heard the approaching sirens from multiple police cars converging on their location. While they made their escape using the maze of streets surrounding the World Financial Center, Rivers phoned Desmond who was waiting for his call.

"Something happened. I had Haines in my possession and we were about to ride up to his office when someone got in the same elevator who knew him. My guess is that he was FBI or a New York City detective. I had no choice but to escape. They must have alerted the police and we had to scramble. We're going to ditch this car since Haines probably gave them a description."

"Godfuckingdammit. If Haines got the package, the FBI will

have it next. Okay, get out of there as quickly as you can. Split up and make your way back to Washington, D.C. That's where the boss is. I've got to call him right away."

Desmond hung up and called Fletcher. Fletcher was apoplectic when he heard the details of Rivers' botched mission. He was thinking fast. He didn't know what Teasedale wrote in his narrative but he knew that Ludlow was probably the main character and he played some supporting role. He could speculate on President Lowery's inclusion but Fletcher would never know that for sure. Everything was suddenly collapsing around him and time was compressing. Moments after Fletcher finished with Desmond, he called his pilots. He had to get out of Washington, D.C. immediately. His stateside residences would not be safe. The nearest point he could safely travel to quickly was Dublin. He told his pilots to prepare a flight plan and fuel up his Citation. He wanted to be wheels up in an hour and he would call Chuck Lowery on his way to Reagan National.

Fletcher packed up a few essentials from his suite at the Mayflower and rushed down to the Cadillac Escalade that was waiting to speed him out to the FBO. He dialed Lowery's personal line and Horace Grant answered the phone.

"This is Horace Grant speaking."

"It's Fletcher calling. Get the President immediately."

Lowery and Fletcher spoke for only five minutes. They had to try to stop what seemed inevitable while Fletcher beat a full retreat. Lowery, the cooler head, enumerated their risks. Harrison Teasedale was a dead witness who was culpable for the biggest insider trading scandal in US history. Although they didn't know precisely what Teasedale had written, they had to assume that he told the complete story of his and Ludlow's trading scheme. All of Teasedale and Ludlow's account information would be in the hands of the FBI. Desmond's crew wouldn't be able to loot them now. In fact, Desmond would need to destroy the electronic traces of the few wire transfers they had completed during the week. Teasedale had likely implicated Fletcher and the veiled threats he had made to Teasedale over Memorial Day Weekend. How far had Teasedale gone? Lowery had to assume that Teasedale described the scam that was Lowery's "Economic Revolution." But even if Teasedale had divulged everything, what could actually be proven? Teasedale would only have been repeating something that Ludlow had told him. No one knew about Fletcher and Lowery's own trading scheme. At best, Ludlow would go from being a dupe in a sex-induced passion play to being Teasedale's co-conspirator. Lowery and Fletcher's biggest threat was now Pennington Ludlow. With Teasedale's narrative, the FBI would move on Ludlow and take him into custody. And he would fold like a house of cards. Both men agreed that Ludlow had to be killed. With Ludlow dead, they'd have a shot at keeping their fortunes and their freedom. Fletcher had two excellent operatives with him in Washington, D.C. and Rivers and his partner were on their way there as well. They would have to clean up the final loose end. Lowery could not be implicated and Fletcher would be on his way to Dublin. They would only have one chance. Fletcher and Lowery hung up but not before saying the same thing they said before every mission they ever flew—"Not self but country." The old Navy motto had managed to keep them alive for many years.

After John Aichenhead hung up with Nick Bowa, he called Martha Torres. He had to tell her about Teasedale's confession and Kirby Haines' near death encounter. He'd also have to tell her about his moonlighting project with Bert Washington. Now it was vitally relevant. He called into the office and got switched over to Torres' line.

"Martha, it's John. We hit the mother lode." Aichenhead took her

through Teasedale's fifteen page tell-all. He also described Kirby
Haines' near miss that morning with his would be kidnappers. He
didn't know who they were but they knew about the package that
Teasedale had sent to Haines and would have gotten it if luck hadn't
intervened. Aichenhead described Secretary Ludlow's principal
role in the insider trading scheme and the $80 billion windfall
that Teasedale attributed to their six year trading spree. When he
paused to take a breath, there was only silence on the other end
of the phone.

"Holy shit, John. This is even worse that I could have imagined.
Pennington Ludlow is behind everything. He must be the key to
this entire plot. He could be the hand behind Teasedale's death and
Kirby Haines' abduction. The *Post* articles must be part of his cover
up. I've got to speak to the US attorney."

"Martha, there's something else I have to tell you. Please listen
and don't go ballistic, but I think it's relevant."

"Go ahead."

"An old acquaintance of mine is the Commissioner of the
BLS."

"I'm no good at Jeopardy, John. What's the BLS?"

"It's the Bureau of Labor Statistics. They calculate and publish a
lot of the economic data that Teasedale was getting advanced notice
of and using for his insider trading."

"Okay, go on."

"The Commissioner's name is Bert Washington. He called me
over Memorial Day weekend to get some advice and a little help.
He had this theory that the numbers they were releasing at the BLS
weren't accurate. A few months ago he conducted an audit of their
procedures and everything went perfectly."

"I'm not sure where you're going with this, John."

"Hold on. I'm getting there. Washington only became more
concerned when the audit showed no problems—nothing. You

and I both know that nothing involving the government works perfectly—and that was Bert's common sense conclusion. Anyway, he decided to conduct a second stage test. He passed false data into his systems and it came out the other end unadulterated."

"So that was good news as well."

"Not exactly. The false data passed through his systems but everything else turned negative. His test showed that even the numbers they released for the April jobs report were directionally wrong. Tomorrow they are going to release May's numbers and April's revision, and they are going to show an economy that has hit a wall. Nobody is going to see this coming."

"I'm still confused, John. Pull it together for me. What does this have to do with Teasedale's confession and Ludlow's possible involvement?"

"Teasedale's confession states that Ludlow told him in mid-May that the information they had used for their trading scheme was inaccurate and manipulated. Bert Washington had his own suspicions and asked me to help scan through his employee files to see if I could find anything unusual."

"You checked out personnel files for Washington's employees? Are you nuts?"

"Martha, hold on. I know it wasn't right but what I found out is important. At least fifteen employees at the BLS used to work for companies owned by Bob Fletcher."

"President Lowery's Bob Fletcher?"

"Yes, and the same Bob Fletcher mentioned at the end of Teasedale's confession. Ludlow told Teasedale that Fletcher and the President knew about their insider trading. One or two other facts: Pennington Ludlow was the only Cabinet level Secretary that knew about Bert Washington's false data test. And one of Bob Fletcher's former employees was the project manager for the last phase of his audit."

"So what you're suggesting is that Bob Fletcher and Pennington Ludlow orchestrated this bogus dissemination of economic data and Ludlow and Teasedale used it to trade illegally."

"Yeah, that's it in a nutshell."

"I know you're holding something back. Why did they need false data? Ludlow had the access to information in advance to make money. The plain facts, whatever they were, were good enough to make that scheme work."

"I think the insider trading part of this story may actually be just a footnote. I think they were manipulating the data to keep President Lowery's 'Economic Revolution' chugging along."

"Holy shit, John. Now you're really playing with dynamite."

"I know Martha but it all fits together. Teasedale's confession is that map that connects all the points. Bert Washington's hunch was right. There's a lot more at stake here than just the biggest trading scam in history. This thing has global ramifications."

"If you're right, John, this is way beyond our scope of enforcement. We've got to move this up the chain of command."

"I get that, but we also have to think about who we can trust."

"What do you think we should do?"

"We have to get to Pennington Ludlow before Bob Fletcher does."

"Do you really think he'd kill the Treasury Secretary?"

"Ludlow is the only one who can corroborate Teasedale's confession."

"My God, John, we don't have much time."

"And we're acting without a complete set of intelligence. I'm going to put Haines in protective custody. His close call this morning will guarantee another visit from whoever wanted Teasedale's package. They'd probably prefer Haines dead now. Teasedale's confession changes everything. We have to consider multiple scenarios and potential outcomes. Whoever really is responsible is going to move to erase all the evidence as quickly as possible. Haines could be a target. Ludlow could be a co-conspirator with Fletcher or he could be the next target. President Lowery could be involved. Haines' girl friend is Ludlow's chief of staff. We got to get her out of sight as well. She may know something about Ludlow's involvement."

Aichenhead and Torres were realizing that they were in a race against time. Whoever got to Pennington Ludlow first controlled all outcomes.

"You said that Teasedale mentioned $80 billion of profits from his and Ludlow's adventure?"

"Yep."

"There's more to this story, John. I'd bet my badge on it."

Aichenhead and Torres quickly understood that they were deal-ing with the world standing and credibility of the US government itself. They were in over their heads, but they didn't know who they could trust and they only had hours to execute a plan that they hadn't begun to concoct.

"John, we've got to get to Washington, D.C. as fast as we can and meet with the Director."

"You're probably right. I just hope we can trust him. And I've got to get to Bert Washington. If Ludlow is the brains behind this and knew about Bert Washington's suspicions, Washington is at risk himself. We'll take Kirby Haines down with us. We really don't have much time. This thing could blow up in our faces. We need everyone in the same room before 4:00 P.M."

"Who's working on this from the SEC?"

"A guy named Brian Doherty."

"Okay. We have to keep him out of this loop for the time being. Tell him to deal with the Morgan Greenville piece and not a hint about Teasedale's confession. No one else can know what we know at this point. I'll arrange for a plane to leave out of Teterboro. Be there by 2:00 P.M."

"Okay. I take care of everything on my end and see you there at 2:00 P.M."

CHAPTER 38

Washington, D.C.
Thursday, May 31, 2007

Bob Fletcher had about 20 minutes to plan and effect the elimination of Pennington Ludlow. Chuck Lowery had demanded his
resignation by the end of the day, and Ludlow was huddling with his
lawyers to consider his options. Fletcher's two assassins would have
to confirm his exact whereabouts. Ideally, Ludlow's death would be
best staged as a suicide caused by the impending revelation of his
central role in Harrison Teasedale's insider trading scandal. But a
heart attack would be equally effective. Fletcher had to make sure
that Ludlow didn't talk. With only Teasedale's confession, the finger
would point squarely at Ludlow. His suicide or panic driven heart
attack would make sense when the FBI disclosed Teasedale's confession. Teasedale's allegation that Ludlow promoted the release of
inaccurate economic pronouncements to spur on President Lowery's
agenda would be hard to prove. Fletcher might catch some heat
because of his inclusion in Teasedale's narrative, but the two main
characters' voices would be silenced forever. When the shit hit the
fan, Fletcher would be out of the country and ultimately protected
by Lowery. Fletcher told his driver to step on it.

President Lowery was going to have to lure Ludlow to the White House—perhaps under the guise of reconsidering his decision demanding Ludlow's resignation. Fletcher's men would have one chance to intercept him en route. The plan was extremely high risk but there wasn't time to consider another alternative. Ludlow would be kidnapped and poisoned. Fletcher remembered Ludlow's description of how he killed his former chief of staff, Matthew Perry. He said he had use aconite to cause his apparent heart attack. By the time Fletcher was taxiing toward an active runway for take-off, the team he left behind in Washington, D.C. had their complete instructions. Fletcher phoned Lowery one final time and simply told him to summon Ludlow to the Oval Office. Lowery understood. They had reached a point of no return. They knew that conversation might be their last one for a long time.

Horace Grant called Pennington Ludlow's residence and asked him if could meet with the President at 2:30 P.M. When Ludlow tried to resist the invitation, Grant told him that the President wanted to have a private conversation with the Secretary to see if there were any possible alternatives to the preliminary decision he had reached earlier that morning. Hearing that news, Ludlow changed his mind, believing that a private, in-person conversation might give him the chance to exit his Cabinet post on his own terms. Ludlow agreed to Grant's invitation. He'd need to leave his residence in Chevy Chase around 2:00 P.M. to get to the White House on time. Ludlow alerted Kurt Denton of his itinerary. His biggest problem getting to the White House would be his driver's fight to break through the barricade of reporters who were encamped at the end of his driveway.

John Aichenhead informed Brian Doherty that he would need to

JAMIE SINGLETON

proceed with Tom Lynch on his own. He told Doherty that Martha Torres had summoned him back to her office for a meeting with the US Attorney for the Southern District of Manhattan. He would be back in touch with Doherty later on when he was finished. He felt bad about deceiving Doherty but he had no choice. The SEC was an oversight body. The FBI was enforcement and they needed to consolidate their witnesses and sources and secure Pennington Ludlow. The knowledge of the existence of Teasedale's confession was highly sensitive. No one knew about it other than Kirby Haines, the men who had tried to obtain it from him, and their boss. Aichenhead couldn't be sure whether Pennington Ludlow was the mastermind behind this incredible plot or know with certainty the extent of Bob Fletcher or President Lowery's actual involvement. But he understood that he had to make a move on Ludlow. His gut told him that if he waited until they landed in Washington, D.C. and spoke to the Director, that it would be too late. Aichenhead's encyclopedic mind was racing.

After he explained his situation to Brian Doherty, Aichenhead went to the conference room where he had left Kirby Haines and told him they were leaving. Haines was still confused but got up and the two men proceeded to the elevator bank and rode downstairs to the lobby and walked out to Aichenhead's car. Haines didn't even have time to get his suit jacket or tell Joanne he was leaving. When they were in the car, Aichenhead explained what was going on.

"We're going to my apartment for a short time. You should be safe there until we head out to Teterboro. I'm taking you down to Washington, D.C. at 2:00 P.M. and we have a meeting at FBI Headquarters with the Director at 5:00 P.M."

"What's the deal John? You're not telling me much."

"No I'm not. This case is breaking fast and you are a material witness. You're the only person who has had a close encounter with someone who knew about Teasedale's package and maybe the circumstances surrounding his suicide. Since you can ID him, he may decide that you're expendable. That's why you're sticking with me and we're going to my apartment for the next couple of hours. We need to call your girl friend. I need to speak to her."

"What does Hillary have to do with this?"

"She's Pennington Ludlow's Chief of Staff and he's a person of interest that we need to interview. She could know something that would be valuable to our investigation."

"Hillary's completely clean."

"I have no reason to doubt you Kirby, but I think you would feel better if she was out of harm's way."

"You think she's in danger?"

"I can't be sure, but I'm not going to take any chances."

Aichenhead was going to have to take some risks if he was going to get to Pennington Ludlow first. Perhaps Hillary Thomas represented an option in a plan he was only just beginning to form.

When Aichenhead and Haines got to Aichenhead's apartment, John placed a call to Bert Washington. After a short wait Bert Washington picked up his extension.

"Hey John, I wasn't sure you'd be able to talk today. This Ludlow revelation is unbelievable."

"There's a lot more to this story than what you've read today. You were right about everything Bert—everything. I can't explain it all over the phone. We have to be careful. By the way, Ken Shue also worked for Bob Fletcher before moving over to the BEA. I would guess that the list doesn't stop there. Listen to me. I need you to stay in your office. Do not go out and run any errands. Order your lunch in today. Cancel any meetings outside the office. Is that clear?"

"It's clear but I don't really understand why you're so concerned."

"You'll have to trust me on this one. I'm flying down to DC at 2:00 P.M. and I'm going arrange to have you picked up and brought over to FBI Headquarters for a meeting with the Director at the end of the day. This case is breaking fast and you are a pivotal witness. Given the infiltration at the BLS, I want to make sure you make it to that meeting. I'm going to send an agent over to your office now to keep you company until an FBI escort picks you both up later on. You okay with that."

"Well I guess so, John. But you've got me a little worried."

"Don't worry. All the pieces are falling in place and I will explain everything in person before we meet with the Director."

"Okay man. I'm in your hands."

Aichenhead hung up and caught Haines checking out his apartment. John was a little embarrassed. His apartment was his sanctuary. The only living creatures who dealt with its condition were his cats.

"Sorry about the mess. This isn't exactly Park Avenue."

"Jesus, you have a lot of books. Have you read most of them?"

"Read them all."

"That is wild. How come?"

"I don't know exactly. I suppose I understand books better than I understand people. It's all there in black and white. My job isn't straightforward. Words in books are ultimately translated into logic. I guess I just find order when I read them."

"I wish I had time to read. I used to but the job got in the way. There's not a lot of time to contemplate."

"That's too bad. It would probably make your life easier if you had time to think."

Aichenhead instructed Haines to call Thomas and explain that he needed to speak to her.

"Hillary? My name is Agent John Aichenhead with the FBI. I need you to listen to me very carefully and do exactly what I tell you. Do you think you can handle that?"

Aichenhead laid out his hastily hatched plan. He had to trust

Hillary—there wasn't another choice. She was going to speak to her boss urgently. She had to warn him of his imminent abduction or possible assassination. He had to get out of his house as quickly as he could reasonably arrange it and create whatever diversion was possible. Aichenhead didn't have all the pieces. He only knew that Ludlow should react based on his instinct for self-preservation. If he was a target and not a co-conspirator, he would heed Hillary Thomas' advice and get to some safe house. If he was a co-conspirator, he was going to run anyway.

"Hillary, do you think you can pull this off."

"I think so. I'm just a little freaked out. What if he's innocent?"

"Listen to me Hillary. The one thing we know is that Pennington Ludlow is not innocent. He is a lot of things, maybe even a murderer, but he certainly is not innocent."

"Okay, I'll make the call. I'll let you know when it's done."

At 1:00 P.M. Aichenhead and Haines left the apartment and got on the road. From downtown they'd have to travel up the West Side Drive. Aichenhead turned on the radio to determine whether his best option for leaving the city was the Lincoln Tunnel or George Washington Bridge. With no delays he decided to take the bridge. Forty-five minutes later, they passed through the security gate at the entrance of the Signature FBO at Teterboro Airport. Martha Torres was already there waiting for them. Aichenhead introduced her to Haines and they walked out and boarded the government jet. At precisely 2:10 P.M. they were wheels up and heading to Washington, D.C. for the biggest meeting in any of their lives.

At 1:15 P.M. Hillary Thomas called Pennington Ludlow on his secure cell phone. She told him exactly what John Aichenhead had told her to say. Ludlow seemed to gasp knowingly on the other end of the line but said nothing but 'thanks' and hung up. Hillary called back Aichenhead and told him it was done. Aichenhead told her to get over to FBI headquarters as quickly as she possibly could.

Kurt Denton got into the backseat of Ludlow's black Chevy Suburban and his driver pulled out of the property at 1:50 P.M. The reporters scrambled, some of them trying to chase the car on foot as it rolled down the quiet street. Fletcher's men were waiting nearby and put their plan in motion. They pulled out of a driveway up the street and began their pursuit. Kurt Denton was going to the White House to meet President Lowery, but Pennington Ludlow was not. About ten minutes later a second car left the Ludlow residence. Fletcher's men were long gone and were closing in behind Kurt Denton's darkened Suburban—they had full authority to improvise. But Pennington Ludlow had to die, whatever the cause.

Aichenhead and Torres touched down at Reagan National at 2:45 P.M. They had wanted to land at Andrews Air Force Base but were diverted because of higher priority flights. Once on the ground, the three passengers hustled out of the plane's hatch and into a waiting vehicle. Torres had hoped that they could get into the city quickly, particularly since they were traveling at a time when almost everyone else was working. As they approached the Theodore Roosevelt Memorial Bridge they hit a wall of traffic. Their driver radioed ahead and got word that there had been a major accident on the south bound side of the highway that involved one or two fatalities. By the time they made it to the bridge and crossed over it, they were running about twenty-five minutes late.

Bert Washington had been escorted over to the FBI building and was waiting in a conference room when Aichenhead, Torres and Haines showed up. Another agent brought Hillary Thomas in from a separate room. Kirby and Hillary held each other for few moments while Washington and Aichenhead shook hands and nodded incredulously at the extraordinary conclusion of their unauthorized investigation. On the flight down, Aichenhead had told Torres about his decision to "save" Ludlow's life by preventing his assassination. Torres was upset that Aichenhead had not sought her approval of his plan but ultimately understood that Hillary Thomas was their only available option. The unwelcome consequence was that they had no idea where Pennington Ludlow would hide himself. Had he listened to Thomas? Was he actually a co-conspirator and running to save his life? They didn't have that answer, but they had to get ready to debrief the Director in short order. He wouldn't be happy with any of this; who could be? They had uncovered the financial crime of the century and perhaps the biggest political scandal in the country's history, but they wouldn't be able to tell the Director the whereabouts of their lynch-pin witness. Torres put out an APB for Pennington Ludlow, and then they got down to work to prepare for their meeting with the Director.

The accident on the south bound Washington Memorial Parkway snarled traffic for hours because of the two fatalities and the need to perform a careful investigation. When the participants in the meeting at FBI headquarters broke at 4:30 P.M. to get coffee and use the facilities, the headlines were streaming across the TV monitors located throughout the public areas of the building. Secretary Pennington Ludlow had been killed in a car accident on his way into the Capitol to visit the President. He was pronounced dead at the scene.

CHAPTER 39

Washington, D.C.
September 15, 2007

The Senate Judiciary Committee hearings started in earnest after
Congress returned from their summer recess. It was an extraordinary circus that made the Watergate debacle look like a mere
daytime drama. The Committee painstakingly went through
witness after witness trying to prove the incredible allegations in
Harrison Teasedale's confession. There was no dispute when it
came to the financial crimes committed by Teasedale, Ludlow and
Morgan Greenville. The two infamous insider-traders were dead
and Morgan Greenville was effectively being liquidated by the
government. The Democrat Senators on the Committee weren't
worrying about that. They were on a crusade to debunk President
Chuck Lowery's "Economic Revolution" and establish it as the
greatest work of fiction in the modern era.

After three months of intensive investigation using sweeping
subpoena power that worked everywhere except the Oval Office,
the Independent Counsel had produced a case that didn't go very
far beyond Teasedale's explosive confession. A slew of indictments

had been filed that decimated Monroe Desmond's small army of infiltrators at the BLS and BEA. But Ken Shue and all the others denied any connection to Bob Fletcher or President Lowery. Fletcher himself had still not returned to the United States. And every deal to offer him immunity in return for his testimony had been rebuffed by his legal representatives. No one knew for sure where Bob Fletcher was, except of course for Monroe Desmond who had still avoided any detection by the SEC. Fletcher and Lowery's fortunes had been secured. Lowery's reputation had been besmirched but he was a very rich man. When the time was right, Lowery and Fletcher would reunite and they would share with each other just as they always had for the last forty years. Carmen Gomes still had plenty of beautiful young friends and Fletcher's inventory of cheese had not been diminished.

Bert Washington became a household name after testifying before the Senate Committee for most of a week. Cathy and the kids watched CSPAN everyday once the hearings got under way. When Cathy had a court appearance, she made sure to TIVO the broadcast. Bert Washington became a hero of the resurgent Democratic Party. Having been idled during Chuck Lowery's first seven years in office, the Democrats were in full attack, ruefully assailing a corrupt administration and a failing economy. Bert Washington was the man who uncovered the entire debacle. The next step he was going to take was going to be his biggest one yet. All the hopeful Democratic Presidential candidates were considering him for a Cabinet level position—either at the Department of Labor or Commerce. He was an African-American, a hero, and now a media darling. Cathy was keeping him tethered at home to ensure that his ego didn't float him right out of Bowie, Maryland and down to the Chesapeake Bay. But she was so proud of him. Bert Washington's long trip from East Orange, New Jersey was nearing a triumphant last leg.

Alan Solomon announced his resignation as Fed Chairman shortly after Pennington Ludlow's death. He and Miriam quietly sold their house in Georgetown and moved up to New Hampshire where he decided he would write his memoir. Although he never knew the precise circumstances surrounding Ludlow's death he had an intuitive understanding of the event and never asked a question. Before Solomon was called to testify before the Senate Committee, President Lowery had called him. He reminded Solomon that Ludlow had stood alone and his actions had damaged the country greatly.

"The nation is taking a beating because of Ludlow's greed, Alan. You can help America one last time. I truly appreciate your service to the Country. You are one of the good guys. I know I can count on you to help preserve the nation."

Lowery's words stuck in Solomon's mind. Alan Solomon didn't have the guts to tell the world what he actually knew. He had never wanted to play a role in Lowery and Fletcher's scheme, but Ludlow had forced him to and Solomon couldn't risk the only life he knew to stand up for the truth. He had marginalized his principles and stood on the sidelines while men were murdered and the guilty avoided prosecution. He just wanted to live out the rest of his life with Miriam on the shore of Lake Sunapee and get out of the game that had contorted his sense of values for the last seven years. Alan Solomon's testimony led nowhere. As Fed Chairman he was independent of the Executive Branch and he wasn't going to volunteer what he knew. He turned out to be the eunuch at the orgy.

John Aichenhead watched the early Senate hearings whenever he could. He had never replaced his broken old television whose main purpose was to hold books in its metal stand. So he caught bits and pieces of the spectacle at work or when he could convince one of his bartender friends to switch on the CSPAN loops after work and before other patrons screamed for ESPN. He had spent

his own time before the Senate Committee and his bar-stool buddies razzed him about his unflattering suit and annoying inability
to hear the Senators' questions when asked the first time. But they
had a new, higher regard for John Aichenhead. He was the man in
the center of this political tempest. And he was the magician who
pulled the proverbial rabbit out of his hat.

CHAPTER 40

Washington, D.C.
October 1, 2007

On October 1st, the day that should have marked the conclusion of the Senate Committee hearing, Pennington Ludlow walked through the rear door of the Senate hearing room escorted by John Aichenhead and Martha Torres, gliding indifferently through the stunned and silent room. It was certainly the most dramatic moment in television political history. Ludlow had been buried almost four months ago at DeSaussure Hall over the objections of his wife who ultimately decided not to contest his last request. Anne Eckhouse would have divorced Pennington Ludlow over his affair with Carmen Gomes, if she had been given the chance. She was not the type to stand by her man. But Anne wasn't given the chance to exercise that option. In his will, Ludlow had requested that he be buried down at DeSaussure Hall on a hill where he used to love to survey the horizon that stretched beyond the marsh. Despite her anger, Anne Eckhouse had acceded to his request. Some of the men, supervised by Muddy Simmons had dug the hole for Ludlow's casket. There was no rite when he was interred—it was just a hole that had to be dug and filled back up again.

Senator Marvin Abler banged his gavel repeatedly. The noise, confusion and flash from hundreds of cameras were dizzying. Except for Senator Abler, no one else on the Committee knew about the surprise witness. Minutes after the fiery accident that killed Kurt Denton was reported by the news services, a panicked Pennington Ludlow had called Hillary Thomas to help him negotiate his surrender into protective custody. John Aichenhead had moved swiftly. Denton's remains were secreted away and the autopsy results were rigged. To the world, and more importantly to Chuck Lowery and Bob Fletcher, Pennington Ludlow had been burned beyond recognition in the fiery crash. President Lowery's public relations machine had issued a release that confirmed that Ludlow had been on his way the President's office to tender his resignation and take full responsibility for the insider trading scandal. Ludlow was vilified in his death. His official funeral was a very small affair. Chuck Lowery and Bob Fletcher knew that they would not escape unscathed, but their principal conspirator was dead, along with his Wall Street accomplice and Alan Solomon would not say a word. Lowery figured he was safe except for the predictable partisan war that would break out over his failing fiscal policies and the dismal economy. There were no witnesses to testify against him.

"Ladies and gentlemen. Order please. Order please!"

The Senate hearing room slowly began to quiet down.

"Could you please state your name and raise your right hand to be sworn in."

"My name is Pennington Ludlow."

Ludlow spent ten days testifying before the Senate Judiciary Committee. The story he told was surreal. He named names and detailed the entire sham that was Lowery's "Economic Revolution," mortally wounding the Presidency. The media ate at the trough like insatiable animals. Three weeks after Ludlow's improbably resurrection, Lowery announced his resignation during a prime time address to the nation. While he admitted nothing, he talked about the Herculean work his administration had done to restore America back to a position of respect in the world. If he was going down, he was going down like a Navy fighter pilot. He really only knew one way to be. He still looked like he stepped out of central casting: his blue eyes trying to touch the shrinking set of empathetic supporters watching his vainglorious final act. The articles of impeachment being drawn up by Congress never made it to the Senate floor. But the Justice Department was readying a full assault on the once unbeatable hero.

CHAPTER 41

Washington, D.C.
New York City
Beaufort, South Carolina
November 28, 2007

The period following the conclusion of the Senate Judiciary Committee hearings and the indictment of former President Chuck Lowery and Bob Fletcher by the Justice Department had all the malaise and depressed emotion of a natural disaster.

Morgan Greenville had been seized by the SEC and Treasury Department. It was one of those institutions that was considered too big to fail, but fail it did. The firm filed for protection under Chapter 11 of the bankruptcy code, but Morgan Greenville's outcome was an orderly liquidation of its assets and businesses. All of the Partners' equity in the firm was wiped out. Some Partners like Tom Lynch lost almost $800 million while new Partners like Peter Bolger and Kirby Haines only lost a dream. For everyone it was a sad time. All the hard work and personal sacrifice that had been directed at building their careers and the fortune of their firm had been wiped out by the actions of Harrison Teasedale—and he wasn't even alive to take the blame.

After the government moved to seize the investment bank, the employees slowly returned to their offices to remove their personal possessions and the mementos that commemorated all the transactions they had worked on during their careers there. The news media loved it. How grand to watch the fall of Wall Street's biggest winner. Television vans were lined up the length of Vesey Street in front of Morgan Greenville's headquarters to capture the human suffering of the firm's demise. It made for great theater and was all rather pathetic.

Kirby Haines drifted in and out of a daze during the six months after his emergency trip to Washington, D.C. and FBI's headquarters. Through it all, Hillary Thomas kept by his side. They were the unknowing witnesses to the biggest financial scandal in US history. No one worked closer with Teasedale and Ludlow than Kirby and Hillary did. Both were forced to testify before the Senate Committee and spent months with the Independent Counsel's office helping it put together the pieces. Their lives had been placed on permanent hold. Haines had a hard time coming to grips with the irony of it all. He had never felt more alive than when he was promoted and working with Harrison Teasedale. His dreams had become his reality and in a matter of several weeks time, everything had died. From a monetary point of view, he had not lost as much as most of the Partners, but a significant percentage of his bonus had been paid in stock over the last three years. All in all, he figured that Morgan Greenville's bankruptcy flushed about $20 million dollars of his net worth. For a barely middle-class kid from Maplewood, New Jersey, that was a fortune.

Haines had no choice except to start over. Peter Bolger had already found a new gig with a smaller investment banking boutique that hired him as a Managing Director. Haines' close involvement with the overall investigation had completely limited his ability to look for anything. He hoped there would be lots of private equity shops who would consider him a valuable contributor to their franchise but he didn't know what the world had in store for him. He had come to realize just how fickle life could be.

Thomas' situation wasn't that dissimilar. Her political party was out of favor and would certainly lose the White House when the elections were held next November. It was premature for her to consider a run for the House of Representatives at this point. She had been Pennington Ludlow's Chief of Staff. That was a handle that would be as hard to lose as Special Agent Aichenhead's surname. Other than Kirby, the two people who kept her spirits up were Bert Washington and Rosemary Guillson. They genuinely liked Hillary and knew that she had been dealt a very bad hand. Bert understood her dilemma the best. He was a person who would give her the second chance. He was that type of guy.

Martha Torres had won a great deal of praise for the work of the New York Office in uncovering the entire case and all of its intricacies. She got the promotion she was hoping for which moved her back to Washington, D.C. Only one woman stood ahead of her on the FBI organizational chart and Torres knew that her career was in fail-safe mode. She made sure that Aichenhead received the appropriate commendation for his work on the Teasedale murder, Morgan Greenville insider trading and the fraud case at the BLS and BEA. But John Aichenhead was not going to Washington, D.C. with Martha Torres. He was getting a new boss like every other agent assigned to the New York office.

Aichenhead's work over the last nine months had resulted in one positive development: his relationship with Joanne Fruilli. He still had time for drinks at Floyd's or The Spain but his propensity to read two or three books each week was being challenged. He didn't mind it in the least. He was beginning to remember the benefits of companionship. Aichenhead was taking his time but was open to considering more risk. He knew that his work with

Bert Washington had broken the case. He had taken a big risk with someone he barely remembered. Every rational bone in his body had told him not to get involved, but for some reason he hadn't listened. That had made all the difference. Maybe Joanne Fruilli was his next test. The benefits of taking a risk with her were confirmed every morning when they woke up in each other's arms and made love before tackling another day.

Pennington Ludlow pled guilty to charges that would have put him away for 350 years. His cooperation with the government's investigation offered him the potential for parole in 25 years. Chuck Lowery's trial would not even begin for another year. Ludlow gave the government as much detail as he could about Lowery and Fletcher's dealings but he didn't know about their vast hidden fortune. It wouldn't do Lowery much good in prison where he was going to trade one set of pinstripes for another.

Muddy Simmons was dumbstruck when he heard that his boss was still alive. He had felt a confusing sense of loss when he tossed the last bit of dirt on the coffin that he thought held the body of Pennington Ludlow. He and his sons said a quiet prayer that day and wondered what the future would hold for them. He didn't much like the idea of digging up the dead body, but Anne Eckhouse had ordered it done and she had no intention of letting Kurt Denton rest in peace on her property. Muddy thought bad luck would come his way, but he guessed it already had.

Whether Pennington Ludlow was dead or alive, it did not really make much difference in the end. When the men from the funeral home loaded the dirty coffin into their hearse, Muddy stared into the empty hole on the hill that overlooked the marsh in the distance.

What would become of DeSaussure Hall now? Everything was going to change. Ms. Eckhouse was a good owner but she had no husband. Muddy wasn't so much worried about himself, but more about his sons. They all belonged to this place. It was everything that they ever had. From the stories that he heard, Mr. Ludlow had done some bad things and his actions had hurt many people. That person seemed different from the man that Muddy Simmons had admired. Along the way something must have happened to Mr. Ludlow. He had strayed. Muddy didn't understand why. In his world, there were the good guys and everyone else.

Muddy took a drag on his Chesterfield and blew out the smoke. He had thought that Mr. Ludlow was a good guy but he had been wrong. Everything that had become standard in Muddy's life was now subject to change. And it had all happened so fast. Muddy looked out at the Goose Creek. Its water flowed back and forth according to the tides twice a day. The Creek had meandered over hundreds of years and its sharp backward turns made for some good fishing spots where the fish liked to feed. Muddy observed those deviations of the Creeks' path as a normal result of nature's influence on the small river. He considered that maybe his life had never really been that standard after all. He figured that whatever was going to happen to DeSaussure Hall next and his life there would just be another turn in the natural order of things.

ENDNOTE

The US Federal Government has the responsibility for aggregating, analyzing and publishing all of the economic measurements and calculations of critical data used by capital markets investors, economists and corporate executives to craft investment strategies and make capital decisions. The Federal Reserve relies on this information to formulate its interest rate policy for the United States. Within the US government, the Department of Labor and Department of Commerce are separately responsible for determining specific indicators of economic activity. Inside the Department of Labor, the Bureau of Labor Statistics ("BLS") employs approximately 2200 employees, principally located in the major metropolitan economic cities across the country, and operates with an annual budget of approximately $550 million. The Bureau of Labor Statistics reports a variety of critical economic measurements including employment figures, jobless claims, the Producer Price Index and the Consumer Price Index. It is the largest of the government agencies responsible for calculating critical financial information.

The Department of Commerce also publishes a substantial volume of economic information. Inside the Department of Commerce, the Economics and Statistical Administration ("ESA") and its affiliate sub-department, the Bureau of Economic Analysis ("BEA") separately release economic measurements. The ESA publishes reports on Durable Goods, Manufacturers Shipments, Inventories and Orders, and Residential Construction and employs approximately 50 economists and administrators, headed by an Under Secretary of Economic Affairs and Chief Economist who also oversee the functions of the BEA and the Bureau of the Census. The BEA is responsible for calculating such critical indicators as Gross Domestic Product, Personal Income, and the Balance of Payments. The BEA employs approximately 550 individuals. The total budget for the ESA and its sub-departments, including the BEA and the Bureau of the Census is roughly $80 million—a tiny figure for an enterprise responsible for getting so much right.

A great deal of responsibility rests with the analysts and economists who work for the BLS, ESA and BEA. These organizations comprise less than 3000 employees who are spread out across the country gathering an enormous amount of fundamental economic information generated by 300 million American consumers and business operators every month. Their reports are eagerly awaited by a global investment community who invest trillions of dollars based on what that information tells them. While these agencies have mission statements that pronounce their allegiance to the pursuit of accuracy without failure, interestingly, there is no internal audit staff that functions in a manner similar to public corporations, but in their case, reporting directly to the US taxpayer. In the private sector, a system of individual accountability based on carrot and stick incentives is used to drive excellence in the workforce. In addition, the government, using legislation like Sarbanes-Oxley, brandishes the threat of criminal recourse to insure that the financial accounting that underpins those incentives is accurate. This approach to accountability does not exist in the civil servants' work place and transparency is a concept that will never be pursued. What if some of those analysts and economists working at the BLS, ESA or BEA miss a little data, or fail to include information from certain geographies, or simply just don't care? Perhaps worse, what if some of them do care about the figures that they produce for public consumption? What if they care too much?